UNRAVELED TIES

DAWN TAYLOR

ISBN: 978-0-9996154-2-3 Print
ISBN: 978-0-9996154-3-0 eBook

Editor: Brian Paone
Copyeditor: Nina Johnson
Cover Designer: Sydney Blackburn
Author Photographer: Mark Lingl Photography

For more information, please visit my website: dawnmtaylor.com

This book is dedicated to Toby,
my faithful feline companion of fifteen years.
RIP
You were one special cat.

TABLE OF CONTENTS

CHAPTER 1

Thanksgiving Day, 1975

The incessant pounding on the apartment door jarred Janet Harding from her indulgent slumber. She squinted into the darkness until her eyes focused on the alarm clock's hands pointing to 6:18 a.m.

Way too early to rise on a non-school day. Better not be those pesky kids pulling a prank again.

The children in the complex targeted Janet because she was a teacher at Franklin Elementary *and* the only teacher residing at Cambridge Apartments. Janet suffered the repercussions each time another teacher assigned extra homework, or worse—detention. The immature reasoning of the mischief makers justified the taunting of *any* teacher.

"Coming!" Janet shouted and pulled on her robe.

The rapid knocking continued in loud and steady thumps, alerting her to an urgency beyond a childish practical joke.

She paused to sniff the air. When she detected no smoke odor, she was satisfied she had not been roused to escape a fire. She slid into her slippers and swung open the door.

"Janet. Janet, did you see this?"

A stout Mrs. Parker stood before her, best known as the apartment complex busybody and caretaker's wife.

"Just woke up. What?"

Mrs. Parker thrust a folded holiday edition of the *Mason County Press* at Janet. "This. I'm so sick. Sick!"

Janet skimmed the print, searching for the news riling Mrs. Parker. The front page contained a photo of President Ford pardoning a turkey at the White House, a grand opening announcement of Herman's Furniture Barn, and the local weather forecast for holiday travelers. Janet continued to scan the newspaper. When nothing of importance caught her eye, she wondered if the students had enlisted Mrs. Parker to execute their latest prank.

"Look in the lower corner," Mrs. Parker directed.

Janet gasped.

She read the headline for a second time: *Endover Girl, 7, Dies at Foster Home*

"Don't you teach those second graders, Janet?"

Janet ignored her neighbor and read the short article.

> *Mason County Sheriff's Department responded to a medical emergency at the home of Marvin and Ethel Fletcher. The child identified as a seven-year-old female was found unresponsive and transported by ambulance to Mercy Hospital in Bancor. She was pronounced dead on arrival. Charges are pending autopsy results. Mason County Social Services has relocated the remaining wards with licensed foster families in the county.*

Mrs. Parker tapped her foot and wrung her bathrobe belt waiting for Janet to digest the horrific news. She observed Janet's pallor and remarked, "She *is* your student, just as I thought."

Janet did not bother salvaging the sheets when the newspaper slipped from her hand. She returned to her silent apartment and closed the door, leaving Mrs. Parker speechless for the first time in her life.

Janet flung herself on her bed and threw the blanket over her head. She gulped three quick breaths. The sensation of drowning prevented her from releasing the air burning her lungs. Her throat muscles constricted until the passageway narrowed into tight, unforgiving bands. She clenched her jaw until a single earsplitting wail spiraled from the depths of raw despair. The howl's force did not nullify the weight of her regret and worthlessness.

Janet exhaled in rapid puffs. She could breathe again.

A deluge of tears streaming down her cheeks dripped unto her lips. Salt. An ocean of tears. She deserved to drown; she had failed Lucy Campbell. Failed her. There was no redemption. No second chances. Lucy was dead. *Dead?*

The little girl's life had been as unremarkable as the paltry notice announcing her death. Janet *had* tried. She had pushed hard for someone—anyone—to help Lucy. No one had listened; the horrible truth was nobody cared. And Janet? Despite her concerns, she had given up too.

Janet recalled everyone she had reached out to—parents, the principal, the social worker, and even a physician—yet nobody bothered to take a deeper look at Lucy's deteriorating behavior. The acceptable solution had been to shuffle Lucy to a foster home.

"I hate this godforsaken town!"

Later that afternoon, Mrs. Parker returned to Janet's door and gently knocked. When her rapping went unanswered, she placed a tray containing a pumpkin-pie slice to the side of Janet's entryway. The following morning, Mrs. Parker was shocked when she retrieved the tray. A key and a note accompanied the untouched pie.

Janet had packed her meager belongings—mostly clothing and books—into her car and had driven to her childhood home. She treated her mother to Thanksgiving dinner, knowing it would be their last shared meal due to Gladys's advanced age, or more likely, Janet's vow never to return. Her days of living in Greenville were over, and she planned to drive west to San Diego. Her early retirement would officially begin with a Monday morning call to Franklin Elementary.

She wasted no time analyzing that losing Lucy had been the catalyst to push her retirement into action two years earlier than she had planned. The despairing community of Greenville, filled with lively gossips and dying cornfields, had sucked the life out of her for fifty-three years. If she did not escape now, she would die too.

Janet drove to Mercy Hospital in Bancor. She parked and stared at the ominous brick building guarding the sick. The upper windows beamed with light, reassuring families that doctors and nurses tended to patients around the clock in their determination to save lives. The darkened basement panes concealed death. The mortalities—rarely more than one at a time—occupied the morgue. Somewhere, past the antiseptic-scented hallways leading to the cold chamber, Lucy lay motionless under a white sheet, a numbered tag replacing her name.

Tears trickled down Janet's face. She resisted the urge to remove the tissue from her pocket. Her discomfort was minimal compared to the pain Lucy had suffered during her seven years. Janet stared at the window, with her fingers pressed against her lips. This was their private moment; she whispered a goodbye to the little one she would never forget.

Perhaps we both can find peace.

She formed the sign of the cross, kissed her rosary, and whispered a prayer to St. Nicholas, the holy guardian of children. She flung the rosary onto the open map laying on the passenger seat and drove in a committed determination toward the Pacific Ocean, the waves beckoning her with the promise of solace.

The first leg of her journey passed quickly, but now Janet maneuvered through the slowing holiday traffic. Rain that began a half hour ago transformed into sleet and coated the windshield with a thin barrier of ice. Although the fan's loud hum annoyed her, she flipped the defroster setting on High. Some inexperienced drivers, likely travelers from the southern regions unaccustomed to the rapid shift of Midwestern weather conditions, pulled onto the highway shoulders in their vain attempts to wait out the storm.

Hours of driving tired Janet, and she realized she had not eaten since she shared the meal with her mother. Her weary eyes abandoned the focus of the road to read a billboard advertising bed-and-breakfast lodging available five short miles ahead.

Janet imagined the comfort of sleeping under a vintage bed's canopy after soaking in a clawfoot tub filled with deep, warm water scented with aromatic bath oil. Her previous stay at a charming Victorian included a welcome basket of assorted teas, fresh fruit, and decadent Belgium chocolates. She wondered if the innkeeper would serve a meal at this late hour.

"A hot meal and a warm bath sound good about now," she said above the fan's hum and the windshield wipers' rhythmic beating.

She returned her gaze to the road.

What the—

A van with Florida license plates pulled away from the highway shoulder and skidded as it entered the lane ahead of Janet's vehicle. Janet tightened her grip on the steering wheel. She struggled to avoid hitting the van while maintaining control of her car, but the slippery road surface was like a sheet of glass. Her car zigzagged behind the van as it continued its own wild path until its final spin grounded it sideways across both lanes. She glanced into her rearview mirror and screamed.

The impact of the approaching semi-trailer truck careened her compact car against the van into multiple folds, like a hellish version of an accordion.

Rushing from his truck to the twisted wreck, the anguished driver whispered an apology Janet would never hear.

Two days later, Mrs. Parker poured a cup of morning coffee and unfolded the local newspaper as she headed toward her breakfast nook. The boldness of the headline commanded her attention, and she felt her grip loosen on the cup handle.

Area School Teacher Perishes in Car Accident

"Oh, for the grace of God!" she exclaimed as her cup shattered on the tile floor.

CHAPTER 2

Present Time, 1995

Daisy stared into her closet while tapping her finger against her lips in frustration. She uncrossed her arms and tossed hangers draped with clothing into a heap on her bed, destroying the arrangement she had spent an hour creating. Originally, she had hung the clothing by style: blouses, skirts, and then slacks. Anger replaced her anxiety when the order had not pleased her. What had she been thinking? She seldom wore skirts, and now they filled the prominent space. During her second attempt, she hung the blouses in the center, but the varied patterns of stripes and plaids unsettled her. Only one real solution remained—to organize by color. Daisy glanced at her bookshelf for affirmation. The volumes' covers, arranged in bands of blue, green, and red— incidentally, the color names were also in alphabetical order— achieved a calming effect. In fact, once she had grouped the books, she hardly noticed them until she dusted the spines on Mondays and Wednesdays.

As she returned the clothing to the rod for the final time, her phone rang, and Daisy ignored it, as she had the previous times. The interruptions destroyed her concentration since she had torn apart her closet two hours ago. Daisy resisted the urge to shatter the phone against the wall. No use ruining her new Nokia just because the caller annoyed her.

She surveyed the clothing arrangement and closed the door in satisfaction. She now craved her relaxation technique she referred to as "herbal therapy," to quiet her mind and stop the miniature bolts of anxiety from attacking her insides.

Daisy opened her jewelry box. The ballerina, posed eternally with her hands clasped above her head, twirled faithfully to the mechanical music, as she had for the past nineteen years. Daisy's father, Dan, had presented her with the jewelry box on her sixth birthday. Even as a child, she understood her father's constant gifting habit was intended to lessen the grief from her sister Lucy's death, rather than commemorate special occasions.

Daisy reached for the joint hidden under her bracelets. She lit the marijuana and closed her eyes, savoring the pungent smoke drawn deep into her lungs. When she finally exhaled, she traced the ballerina's pink tutu with her finger as she remembered the one she had owned as a five-year-old.

She had lent her precious tutu—one of the few possessions she had cherished—to Lucy to complete her Halloween costume when Daisy was five and Lucy was seven. One month later, Lucy was dead. Killed. Murdered. Daisy sucked a long second drag and recalled the dreadful day.

Thanksgiving Day, 1975, and Daisy appreciated the two-day reprieve from kindergarten. There was plenty to be grateful for—her father had promised he would bring Lucy home. When Daisy woke, she was disappointed her daddy had not returned.

"Where's Daddy? And Lucy?" Daisy asked her mother.

"Goddamnit. Nothing good on TV today but those stupid-ass holiday parades. Christ, like they have to show the same thing on all three channels," Doreen complained.

Daisy stood on tiptoes and gripped the windowsill. "Daddy's not home. Him said him was bringing Lucy home."

"Don't know where in the hell he is. He ain't been home all damn night long. If he was bringing anyone home, his ass would be here by now."

Daisy clapped. "Me see his truck. Hooray!" Ignoring the mid-

morning chill of the crisp fall air, she rushed outdoors. "Daddy, where's her?"

Dan scooped his daughter into his arms. "Get inside, it's cold. What're you doin' out here barefoot and in your nightgown?"

Doreen rose from the couch as Dan entered the kitchen. "And where in the hell have you been all damn night?"

Dan hung his head as he released Daisy. "Never mind. You—"

Daisy rushed to the window a second time to see what had captured her father's attention. A deputy with a passenger in a squad car entered the Campbell's driveway.

"Honey, go to your room. Daddy's gotta talk to these men."

"Men?" Doreen asked. "What men?"

Dan opened the door before the officer knocked.

"I'm Deputy McGwin, Mr. Campbell. Remember me?"

"Sure, I remember. What's this all about?"

"Mind if Reverend Marshall and I come inside?"

Dan motioned them in and shrugged in response to Doreen's questioning eyes.

"What're you here for?" Doreen demanded and lit a cigarette. "Seems most people are spending the day with family. You work on Thanksgiving?"

Deputy McGwin removed his hat. "We're here on official business, Mrs. Campbell."

"I ain't no Mrs. Campbell. Think I told you that once before. What're you arresting Dan for?"

Reverend Marshall glanced sideways at the deputy. "If we could all sit and—"

Doreen pointed at the elderly pastor. "We ain't no church-goers, so I don't know why your ass is even standing in my house, to tell you the truth."

Dan shook his head and pulled his angry wife from the frail old man. "Doreen!"

When the arguing started, Daisy hid under the kitchen table. She remembered the man wearing the brown-and-tan uniform with the shiny boots. *He was the same man who had taken away Lucy. Now she trembled, wondering if he had returned to take her away too. Nothing could have prepared the five-year-old for the news the men shared.*

Deputy McGwin stepped between Doreen and the reverend. "I'm going to tell it to you straight. There is no arrest, but we are here on official business." *He blinked away his glare at Doreen and softened his tone to address Dan.* "I'm sorry. So sorry to be the one to tell you."

Just as Daisy braced herself for the deputy to drag her from the house, the man uttered the six words that changed her life forever.

"Your daughter, Lucy, has passed away."

Daisy heard her father moan as his knees bent. He collapsed on the floor at the opposite side of the table.

Doreen advanced toward Deputy McGwin. "What the fuck are you talking about? She's in that damn foster home you put her in, and now you're telling us she's . . . she's . . . "

Reverend Marshall knelt beside Dan. "I'm so sorry, Mr. Campbell. Allow me to help. Perhaps a prayer at this time is appropriate."

"We ain't no church-goers! Are you deaf? What is appropriate is for the likes of you two to get the fuck out of my house. You hear me? Out!"

The officer ignored Doreen's theatrics and reached for Dan's elbow to assist him to stand. "I'm so sorry, Mr. Campbell. Really, I am."

Dan stared at the officer and rubbed his temples. "How? Wha . . . what happened?"

"Not sure yet. She was sleeping and just didn't wake up."

Daisy gasped. Didn't wake up? Lucy always woke before she did.

Dan stuttered. "When . . . when did . . . "

Deputy McGwin glanced toward the floor. "I'm afraid late yesterday afternoon."

Doreen uncrossed her arms and shook her fist. "Yesterday? And you're just telling us now?"

"Ma'am, we tried—"

"Oh, bullshit you tried. How?"

Deputy McGwin held up his palm. "If you'll allow me to finish, please. I made two attempts last night to inform you." *He glanced at the reverend for silent confirmation and continued after the reverend nodded. "Apparently, nobody was home. At least nobody answered the door either time we knocked."*

Doreen rolled her eyes. *"I don't answer the door when I'm home alone at night. See, Dan? See what your damn out-all-night drinking did?"*

The officer disregarded Doreen's seething accusation and focused on Dan. "Give yourself some time today and come by the station tomorrow. We'll have more information for you then. Again, my condolences." He placed his campaign hat on his head and added, "We'll see ourselves out."

"Damn right you will!" Doreen shouted.

Daisy inhaled the final puff and crushed the marijuana roach into an ashtray. The ballerina's dance had never cured her sorrow. They had always been the Campbell Sisters: Lucy and Daisy. The loss of her sibling left an inconsolable heartache, no matter how many gifts, like the new Nokia, her father had purchased.

The phone's ringing snapped Daisy into the present.

"Hello?"

"Well, it's about time you answer!"

"Jeez, Tasha. You sound just like your mother."

"*Our* mother, and that's why I'm calling."

Daisy was relieved she was stoned. Any news concerning Doreen was bad news. Daisy lacked the interest and the energy to deal with the constant drama.

"Tasha, honey. You know I love you, but her? No."

"She's always complaining about heartburn and back aches. She won't even leave the couch to answer the phone. What if her diabetes is getting worse? I don't know."

Maybe she shouldn't exist on a steady diet of cigarettes and sugar-laced Pfizz soda, Daisy thought.

Daisy conceded. "If you want to come over, I'm here. Okay?"

Daisy heard her half-sister sigh before replying with a weak *okay.*

Daisy hung up and groaned. *What bullshit had Doreen filled the poor kid's head with this time?* She felt sorry for the seventeen-year-old stuck living with their mother. The six months Daisy had endured prior to the court awarding her father custody had been long enough to suffer Doreen's abuse, after being her pawn for the first five years of Daisy's life. Anxiety filled Daisy each time she thought of Tasha living in a rundown trailer at Westside Wheel Estates—the county's magnet for attracting criminals and junkies.

"Door's open!" Daisy yelled.

She rummaged through her always-bare kitchen cabinets for a snack. She craved something salty and crunchy after finishing a joint, but she settled on a cookie when she found no chips.

Better than nothing at all, she thought and allowed herself one bite.

Each time Tasha visited the small apartment, the tidiness amazed her. The open cabinet exposed plastic containers with attached lids, stacked in perfect rows. Daisy's neatness was a stark contrast compared to Doreen's clutter and chaos, but Tasha did her best to clean up after her mother.

Tasha sat on a kitchen chair. "Hey, sis."

"Hey, you. Now what's up?" Daisy asked, turning toward the stove. "Making some coffee, want some?"

"Sure . . . If you have milk or cream."

"I do, but you gotta start drinking it black. You know, like an adult."

Tasha stared ahead at the spice rack. Basil, cinnamon, dill, pepper, salt. The tins' alphabetical order did not surprise her.

"Gonna be eighteen next year, but I feel like I've been an adult my whole life, you know?"

Daisy poured water into the coffee maker. "Living with Doreen ages everybody. Ever notice how old our dads look?"

Tasha ignored her sister's chuckle.

"Oh, come on," Daisy said. "Not that I care, but what's she done now?"

Tasha looked at the floor. "She's sick. Complains constantly. I don't know what to think, really."

Daisy set two cups of coffee on the table and reached into the refrigerator for the milk. "She's *always* sick. It's just to get attention." Daisy raised her eyebrows in a faux-surprised expression. "Oh look, it's working! Somebody actually gives a shit about Doreen."

"That's not fair, Daisy. She's sick. She's got diabetes real bad. What *if* it's getting worse? It's so hard to tell when she complains so much. You can't just ignore that and ride her ass."

Daisy squinted in irritation that her high had ended. The haze that clouded her mind was preferable than listening to her half-sister harp for sympathy for their mother. "You weren't there."

Daisy's words hung in the air.

After a moment, Daisy sat and reached for her napkin holder. She shuffled the napkins until all their edges lined up perfectly and replaced them.

"I know, but—"

"No, you *don't* know. You don't."

Silence lingered between the sisters until Daisy spoke again.

"I know you had it rough growing up with her too. But your dad worked on the farm and was always around. My dad worked in Greenville, and we were stuck with her in Endover. Nobody was around to witness the horrible things she did to us."

"She was mean to me too when I was little."

"Mean?" Daisy scraped the chair against the floor and stood. "One time, she slammed my head into a kitchen cabinet and knocked me out. Bruised the whole side of my face and made me lie to my dad. Yeah, I fell off my bike, all right. And all that because she was out of cigarettes and having a nicotine fit. My offense? I said I was hungry."

Daisy rubbed her palms in a manic motion. Her animated expressions held Tasha spellbound as her sister rambled about her past hurts.

"But, my favorite," Daisy threw back her head and smoothed hair from her face. "Oh yeah, my *very* favorite Doreen-cigarette story was when she singed my hair before school. Told me she could light my whole head on fire if she wanted to. Don't remember what I did to deserve that." Daisy pointed her finger at her sister. "So, don't try to get me to feel sorry for her, because I don't, and I won't."

Tasha stood and swung her purse strap over her shoulder. "Got it."

Daisy returned the remaining cookies to the cabinet, careful to leave the one-inch space between the package and the canned goods.

"Good."

"Those steel wool pads and brush did the job," Dan said. "Come check out my clean grill, ready to fire up for the summer."

Jenny followed her husband to the deck to inspect the old, red Weber grill.

"Nobody uses charcoal much anymore. Don't know why we can't buy a gas one," Dan said.

"Because your credit card ain't paid off yet, remember?"

Dan frowned. "Well, Kevin's giving me Saturday off for a change; we should have a cookout."

Jenny bit the inside of her cheek. "This Saturday?"

Dan tightened the bolts on the grill's legs. "Yeah, I don't get very many off."

There goes my shopping trip in Bancor. Stay home and cook. Great! Jenny thought.

"I'll call the girls, then," Jenny replied.

"Girls?"

"Well, Daisy *and* Tasha."

"You know how I feel about having anything to do with Doreen, for Christ sakes."

"C'mon, Dan. It's not Tasha's fault that Doreen is her mother any more than it's Daisy's. I feel sorry for the kid. You remember what it was like to live with that woman."

Dan tossed his pliers. "Do what you want."

"Not if it's going to—"

Dan surrendered. "You're right. She's just a kid. Probably a mixed-up one, living with that spiteful bitch."

"I'll give them a call." Jenny turned to hide her grin. "Both of them."

As much as Daisy enjoyed returning home to visit her father and Jenny, she abhorred the memories of the homestead. The old concrete-block garage where her grandfather had repaired bicycles held nothing but tarnished remembrances of his cruelty. The marijuana and occasional pills sometimes blocked out the recollections of his abuse.

Daisy guessed, since Lucy had been two years older, her sister likely had suffered more abuse from their grandfather than she had. She remembered her father's nightly rescues as Lucy screamed and kicked away twisted sheets during her night terrors.

Daisy's nightmares persisted into her adulthood, with symptoms comparable to Lucy's. Daisy woke drenched in sweat after swatting away the old man's dirt-encrusted hands. She not only felt his sickening touch, she *smelled* his scent. The mixture of oily rags, burning cigarettes, and his foul body odor lingered in her bedroom long after she snapped awake. The man died a few months before Lucy, yet his malevolent soul invaded Daisy's dreams and transformed them into wicked reveries. Daisy rubbed her arms and eased the goosebumps erupting like miniature landmines on her skin after she had hung up the phone, accepting Jenny's invitation.

When the phone rang a second time, Daisy secretly wished Jenny had dialed again to cancel the dinner invitation.

"Are you still mad?" Tasha asked.

"No, are you?" Daisy replied.

"Well, I never was. Not really. Anyway, Jenny called. Are you going there Saturday? Because I'm not going if you aren't. It would be too weird, you know?"

"I'm going."

"Good," Tasha said. "Then swing by and pick me up on your way there. No sense in both of us driving."

Daisy huffed. "I'll pick you up, but you better be waiting at the entrance. I'm not driving—"

"Anywhere near my trailer. I know. I'll be ready at four."

"On the dot. Four," Daisy instructed.

When Saturday arrived, Daisy drove the highway from Greenville to Endover. She balked at Tasha's begging for a ride since she lived less than two miles from the Campbells, until she remembered her sister's insecurities spending time in Dan's presence. Daisy wished her father could overlook the girl's physical resemblance to their mother and treat Tasha in a decent manner.

Jenny answered the door with a grin. "Well, come on in, you two. So glad you could make it. Been awhile."

"Thanks. Where's Dad?" Daisy asked.

"In the backyard, tending to the charcoal grill. Been wanting him to buy a gas one, but you know your dad. Stubborn is his middle name."

"My dad sold his gas grill. Had to pay Mom child support," Tasha said.

"You've got a good dad," Daisy said. "We both do."

Jenny motioned for her guests to follow her to the deck. Dan had mastered the charcoal lighting and was relaxing in a lawn chair, nursing a Red's.

"Well, Daisy, glad you could make it," he said, focusing on his daughter while ignoring Tasha. "What'll you have? Beer?"

Tasha winked at Daisy and answered first. "Sure!"

Dan sneered. "I was asking Daisy."

Tasha hung her head and whispered, "Sorry."

"Well, she ain't old enough, but since I'm driving, one can't hurt," Daisy answered.

Dan snorted and leaned back in his chair. "I drank my first beer on a date with your mother. Never could quit after that." Dan laughed until Daisy's weak slap on his shoulder silenced his and Jenny's giggling.

Daisy handed Tasha a beer from the cooler. "*Ha-ha.* Funny, Dad."

"What'll you have, Daisy?" Dan asked.

"Ice water would be fine." She lifted her long braid from her nape. "It's humid for a spring day."

Dan scrutinized Tasha's monochrome wardrobe. "Makes you wonder why some people wear black clothes on such a hot day."

Daisy chuckled. "Says the guy who wears flannel shirts year around."

Jenny ignored both her husband and Daisy. "I like your outfit, Tasha. Wish I could look half as good as you. In a way, you remind me so much of your mother when she was younger," she said, not-so-subtly taking a jab at Dan for having to cancel her shopping spree to host his gathering. "By the way, how is Doreen?"

Tasha ignored the weight of Dan's stare and directed her attention to Jenny. "Okay, I guess. Sick a lot."

Dan's scowl produced the predicted reaction his wife sought.

"Well," Jenny said, slapping her thighs before standing, "let's all hope she gets better, honey. Now, who's ready for some taco dip?"

"Do you need some help?" Tasha offered.

Dan raised his palm. "We got it. Relax."

After the couple disappeared through the patio door, Tasha turned to Daisy. "I don't think your dad likes me. Maybe I shouldn't come over."

"*Naw,* he just . . . well, you know—"

"He hates Mom. I know that."

"Not saying he doesn't. He's not an ass, not really."

Jenny returned with a bowl of barbeque sauce and a brush while Dan tagged behind, carrying a platter of chicken.

"Put yourself to some use, Dan. Get that chicken sizzling." Jenny turned to Daisy. "Oh shucks, I forgot your ice water."

Daisy followed Jenny into the kitchen. "Let me help."

Jenny pulled two salad bowls and the taco dip from the refrigerator. "If you can carry one with your glass, that would be great, honey."

Dan tended the chicken while the women discussed their favorite television shows. The homemade barbeque sauce Jenny had prepared filled the backyard with a tantalizing aroma. By the time Jenny had set the table, Dan had filled the platter with steamy chicken.

"Dig in, girls. Nothing better than grilled chicken," Dan said.

Jenny removed the lids from the salad bowls and distributed plates and silverware. "Smells delicious."

Tasha surveyed the table brimming with food and did not hesitate to fill her plate. She gripped her fork in her fist and shoveled pasta salad into her mouth.

Daisy speared a chicken wing and scooped a tablespoon of potato salad onto her plate, flattening the mound with her fork—a trick that gave it the appearance of filling much more of her plate than it actually did. She calculated the calories—ice water: zero; chicken wing: eighty; salad: approximately fifty. She was under her goal of one hundred and fifty calories for her noon meal. The tightness in her throat relaxed enough to consume the first bite.

"Christ sakes, Daisy," Dan scolded. "There's plenty here. Take more than just a skinny ole wing."

Three sets of eyes focused on her plate.

"I'm fine."

"Well, you're just shrinkin' away into nothin'. By the looks of your plate, you don't care for my grillin'."

"I said, I'm fine, Dad. I ate a late breakfast."

"Dan, enough!" Jenny reprimanded. "How 'bout another beer?"

Dan's eyes remained glued to his daughter's plate. "Sure."

Daisy expected her father to scrutinize her plate, but his comments were counter-productive. Maybe he had forgotten the only real meals she had enjoyed as a child were the ones he served after she and Lucy had waited hours for his return from work while their mother shunned their hunger pangs.

Tasha distracted Dan's fixation on Daisy. "Your salads are really good, Jenny. Been a long time since I ate potato salad."

"Bet you don't get many meals like this at your house," Dan replied.

The tablecloth hid Jenny's kick to her husband's leg.

"I do most of the cooking. I don't mind," Tasha confessed.

"All girls should know how to cook. Next time, come over early. I bet you've got some recipes I'd love to try," Jenny said.

Dan swigged his beer. "The only effort Doreen ever made towards makin' a meal was ordering off a menu. Half the time, she was too damn lazy to even do that much."

Daisy ended her discomfort and the silence around the table by standing. "I'll clear the plates, if everyone's finished."

Dan patted his belly. "Time for another beer for me. It was all good, Jen."

Daisy gathered the plates and silverware. She had already filled the sink with sudsy water before Jenny and Tasha arrived in the kitchen, carrying the serving dishes.

"Honey, you don't need to restack the plates and sort the silverware. Just toss them into the sink. They're nothing special. No need to be careful with them."

Daisy ignored her instruction. "Just the way I like doing them."

She wished Jenny would stop hovering. She was capable of washing a few plates.

Daisy scrubbed the first plate in six rotations before rinsing it and placing it in the drainer rack. She reached for the second plate. She had completed four rotations of the sponge when Jenny interrupted her by reaching for a salad bowl lid from the stack. Daisy sighed. She started the silent counting from the beginning and continued the ritual until she had washed the remaining plates and platters. She fished into the suds for the butter knives first, then the forks, and finally the spoons. She rinsed the remaining soap from the sink's bottom and folded the dishtowel into even thirds before hanging it on the wall peg.

"Thanks. You're a big help," Jenny said, then slapped her forehead. "Oh, before you leave, here's some of your childhood things I found while cleaning the basement. I'm sure you'll want them."

Jenny offered Daisy a cardboard box.

Daisy scrutinized the box, not much bigger than a file folder. From the size of the carton, she knew it could have contained all her toys—there had been so few of them. Lucy's familiar scrawl labeled the side panel with one word: ART.

"It's kinda . . . dusty. Do you have a bag I can cover it with?"

"Well, like I said, it's been tucked away in the basement. Let me see if I have one."

Daisy cringed as Jenny set the filthy box on the table. After rummaging through a container stuffed with grocery bags, Jenny dug deeper and removed a large plastic bag.

"Here," she said and handed it to Daisy. "This one should work."

"Nashville?" Daisy questioned, reading the bag's decal. "When did you go to Nashville?"

Jenny cleared her throat when Dan entered the room.

"*Ah* . . . it was when you—"

Dan bumped Tasha to stand next to Daisy before he spoke. "You were away."

Daisy sucked her bottom lip.

Tasha held the box while Daisy slid the souvenir bag over it. "Ready to go, Daisy?"

Daisy nodded. "Bye, Dad. Thanks, Jenny."

During the short drive to Tasha's home, Daisy listened to her sister rave about the black nail polish she had purchased at a discounted price.

Throughout the past fifty years, the trailer park's name had changed from Haven Manor to Montgomery's Park, to Carriage Homes, and now it had been christened with the faux-classy name of Westside Wheel Estates. The litter tangled in the weeds between the decrepit trailers reminded Daisy of the muddled condition of her Grandfather Al's yard. Children wearing ragged clothing chased each other in make-believe games to escape the poverty surrounding them.

Doreen's life began in Haven Manor with her brother, Timmy, and alcoholic mother, Judy. Marrying Dan had granted her an escape from the trailer park. Marrying Roy Ferch had advanced her to a beautiful ranch home on eighty acres. Life had now come full circle. Two divorces later, the trailer park reclaimed Doreen.

"Don't suppose you'll drop me off at the trailer?" Tasha asked, knowing the answer.

"Suppose not. You know my rule. Besides, I have to review my notes for a photo shoot assignment. Better get my ass in gear, if I wanna get paid."

Tasha ran her tongue over her teeth. "Okay, then." She winked. "Thanks for the beer."

Daisy smiled. "*Shh!*"

Daisy hugged her sister, who reminded her of Lucy, even if she would not admit it.

"Can't you ever come in without slamming that goddamn door, Tasha?" Doreen growled. "Christ, I was finally resting."

Tasha dropped her gaze and concentrated on the cracked vinyl floor. After seventeen years of enduring her mother's wrath, she should have been more hardened. Doreen's words always sliced into her daughter, cutting new wounds over old scars.

"Sorry, Mom."

Doreen lit a Brandt. "Sorry my ass. I needed an insulin shot an hour ago. Suppose you could do that tiny favor for me? Now that you're home from God-knows-where."

Tasha prepared the injection. She swabbed Doreen's shoulder with a small alcohol pad. "Ready?"

"You fucking think so? Or would you rather I go comatose first? And just where in the hell were you?"

Tasha jabbed the needle into her mother's upper arm. She tossed the pen and pad into the heaping garbage mound threatening to spill from the trashcan. She secured the plastic bag, and as she headed out the door to the dumpster, she answered. "Out with friends."

When Tasha returned, Doreen was reclining on the couch and sipping a Pfizz.

"You know the doctor said to give up that soda, Mom."

"Don't give a shit what anyone says. Never have, never will. Why don't you worry about your friends instead? And just what *friends* were you out with? Better not be that black kid."

"Mom!"

"Don't care. That damn bunch of out-of-towners ain't nothing but trouble. Mom's a whore, probably a junkie too."

"Jermaine's not like that!"

"They're *all* like that. And what kind of fucked-up name is *Jermaine* anyway? God."

Tasha mimicked her mother's high-pitched voice. "Well, what kind of name is *Tasha*?"

Doreen blew smoke from her nostrils. "Well, after giving two daughters names that ended with a *Y*, I thought maybe I could get a decent kid by naming one with a different ending. Guess I was wrong."

Tasha's chin trembled as she fought impeding tears. She tossed the remote control to her mother before slamming her bedroom door hard enough to shake the trailer-house frame, but not strong enough to rattle her mother's senses. She cranked up the Rancid CD Jermaine had loaned her. The title, *And Out Comes the Wolves*, appropriately described her life with her mother.

Tasha maintained an *A* average in her high-school courses. She managed the household by cooking all the meals, washing laundry, and cleaning the crappy trailer to the best of her ability. Nothing she did was ever good enough for her mother.

Maybe Daisy was right. Soon nobody would care about their mother.

Nobody.

CHAPTER 3

Daisy hesitated before placing the dusty box on her sanitized table, but her curiosity compelled her to unsecure the overlapping flaps and peek. She smiled when a tuft of blue fur emerged from the folds.

"My bear! Gosh."

The lid's pressure had flattened his nose, but he was her bedtime companion all right.

Daisy had shared her childhood bed with Lucy and their kittens. She remembered Lucy's companion had been a yellow lion with a brown mane. When she had sought comfort after Lucy's death and searched for the lion, her father had told her Lucy had taken it to Heaven. The explanation held a hint of truth. Lucy's burial included the toy—a ceremony Daisy had been spared from attending.

She dug deeper into the box and pushed aside a few broken crayons to examine the stack of sketches. She smiled at the princess images she and Lucy had spent hours creating. The pictures they had drawn when they had been four and six, or maybe five and seven, preserved their positive outlook into the world of make-believe. Dozens of pages featuring princesses with flowing blonde locks and wearing sparkling ball gowns filled the box. Daisy chuckled at a scene of a princess holding a wand above a calico cat with LUCY AND MARGIE written across the top. She set it aside to frame in honor of her sister.

She sifted through the yellowed pages until she reached the last sketch. Daisy gasped and covered her mouth and nose in a prayer-like pose. The scene, drawn with a black crayon, contrasted with the vibrant colors of the other drawings. A building formed from rectangles—Grandfather Al's block garage?—consumed most of the page. A stick figure wearing a cap stood next to the building, but the image was barely visible under the circular scribbles meant to obliterate him. Above the figure, the letters G PA appeared in Lucy's handwriting.

Daisy folded the paper and tucked it under the cheerful princess sketches. She stuffed the box into the bag and slid it under her bed—into the darkness where all children's shameful secrets belonged.

The next morning Daisy brewed her coffee before rushing to shower. She had ninety minutes to get dressed and drive to Bancor for her photography interview. Drying and braiding her long hair took an entire half hour if she wanted to look presentable. She chose to wear her official meeting ensemble of black polyester slacks and striped blue blouse. Her appearance, in addition to nodding and agreeing to her client's whims, was important to land a new client.

Last night she had gathered her camera, portfolio, and business cards in anticipation of her appointment. If she could establish herself as a professional photographer, she could cease her existence of eating macaroni-and-cheese dinners and relying on her father's handouts.

When she successfully tamed her unruly hair and completed her outfit with rhinestone earrings, she loaded her gear and drove to the client's farm. Although Daisy had lived in Mason County her entire life, the multitudes of unmarked gravel roads always confused her. More than once her father had attempted to teach her to sense directions and to rely on landmarks to no avail. Dan had groaned each time Daisy exclaimed in frustration that every gravel road appeared identical to the preceding one.

During their telephone conversation, the kind woman had patiently explained the route to her house and paused between each direction to allow Daisy to write notes.

When you leave Bancor, turn right. Follow that blacktop until you see a curve. Follow that curve to the left. After about, oh, a mile or two, you'll see a gravel road to your right. There's a yellow house there. Turn right, and stay on the road for about five or six miles. My house is the first one you'll see. It's a big, ole white farmhouse with a porch and a barn. My name's on the mailbox. You can't miss it.

Daisy wondered why people always ended directions with *you can't miss it.* Of course you could, because she usually did. Since today was important and she needed to arrive on time to create a good impression, she paid extra attention to the directions. Daisy sighed with relief when she saw the yellow-house landmark. She was driving in the right direction for once.

She drove for a few miles but panicked when there was no sign of the white farmhouse. Had she already driven five or six miles? She should have reset her odometer, as her father had instructed in his last desperate attempt to teach her country driving.

Daisy drove past a pasture of cattle. The lady had not mentioned cows. Surely, she would have if it were important. Maybe she took the wrong turn after the yellow house. Just as perspiration dampened her blouse, a white house with a porch came into her view. She breathed deeply and calmed herself. The name on the mailbox confirmed her arrival at the proper address.

The muffler's roar alerted a German shepherd and Border collie to her presence, and they chased her Nissan the length of the long driveway. Daisy glanced into the rearview mirror and slowed to avoid hitting the dogs when they raced close to the tires. When she parked, the dogs trapped her inside as they circled her car and barked their announcement of an intruder.

"Shit!"

A woman with a stunning shade of short white hair appeared.

Her floral-print dress covered with a full apron and sensible black shoes indicated her advanced age. She hobbled from the porch, waving her cane and scolding the dogs.

"Kipper, Max. Quiet!"

The dogs ceased their barking, hung their heads in defeat, and trotted toward the barn.

"Sorry about the dogs. Forgot to warn you." The woman's scowl at the dogs melted into a smile. "I'm Mrs. Wendworth. It's safe to come out."

Daisy opened the door and handed Mrs. Wendworth her business card. The woman barely glanced at the logo of the intertwined *D* and *C* that comprised the business name, DC Studios.

"I'm Daisy."

"Glad to meet you, honey. Come on in. I'm anxious to start planning this wedding."

Daisy followed her into a sparely furnished but comfortable farmhouse. The massive kitchen was larger than Daisy's entire apartment. Daisy inhaled the aroma of freshly baked cinnamon rolls as she accepted the woman's gesture to sit.

Mrs. Wendworth poured coffee into dainty floral teacups with saucers, a stark contrast to the mugs Daisy owned with the Freedom Oil logo.

Daisy accepted the coffee with a meek *thank you* and reminded herself to act like a respected photographer and not a nervous, bumbling idiot. Her utility bill was past due; she needed this assignment. She opened her binder and referred to her notes.

"The bride's Amanda Sparks. Will she be joining us?"

Mrs. Wendworth sliced apart the cinnamon buns and set two on small plates on the table. She motioned for Daisy to enjoy the pastry as she slid a filled plate toward her guest.

"Afraid not; not today. Amanda's my granddaughter and lives in New York. Her mother—my daughter, Liz—insists Amanda's wedding take place here at the farm. Family tradition and all. Can I get you some cream? Sugar?"

"No, thank you. I'm fine. Your rolls smell delicious."

"Take a bite, sweetheart. Don't mean to get your papers messed up with sticky fingers though. Where's my manners? Getting old is terrible, you know it?"

Her host's antics amused Daisy. Since she had never experienced a grandmother's hovering, Daisy basked in the attention.

"So, the wedding's going to be here?" Daisy asked.

Mrs. Wendworth returned from the pantry with a stack of paper napkins she haphazardly tossed on the table.

After Daisy had placed one on her lap, she straightened the pile until all the edges lined up perfectly and returned them to the table center.

"The wedding's going to be held in my barn, much to Amanda's displeasure. Growing up in New York, she's always set her sights on a glitzy, upscale ceremony in some posh, highfalutin venue. Oh, the fights she and Liz have had, but I give Liz credit," she said as she drizzled vanilla icing onto the rolls. "She stuck to her guns, and Amanda will be the fourth-generation bride to exchange vows in that barn you see out the window."

"Wow," Daisy exclaimed. "And Amanda is okay with that?"

Mrs. Wendworth chucked. "She is, since Liz and I are footing the bill. We agreed to allow her to throw a second lavish reception in New York to wow her friends. So, that's that. Let's open your picture book. I'm anxious to see your work."

Daisy opened the portfolio and slid it across the table. "I'm going to be honest. I've only shot photos at two weddings. Most of those photos in my collection are baby portraits."

Mrs. Wendworth hummed and rubbed her crooked finger over the vinyl sheets as she inspected a series of wedding photographs.

"This one here," she said and pointed. "This the Baptist church in Greenville?"

Daisy nodded. "That second one was an outdoor wedding in Endover. The couple couldn't afford a fancy affair, but I think I captured their happiness on their special day."

"Yes, look at those grins."

Mrs. Wendworth flipped pages until she reached the section of baby photographs.

"Babies. Gotta love them. Not the easiest thing in the world to manage. Hard to get them to sit still for a picture, I imagine."

"They can be challenging," Daisy answered. "Sometimes, I shoot twenty frames just to capture one smile."

"Well, I tell you what. Probably going to take at least that many to pry one smile out of Amanda. You think you're up to that?"

"Sure. I'd like to look at the barn, see what kind of lighting is available, those sort of things, but, yes, I'd love to photograph your granddaughter's wedding."

Mrs. Wendworth grinned. "Good. It's settled. Let me grab my checkbook from my desk while you finish that roll. More coffee?"

Daisy returned her smile. "Yes, please. And thank you. Thank you so much."

Mrs. Wendworth filled Daisy's cup and left the room to write the check. Daisy pulled the bun into pieces until she was satisfied it appeared she had consumed half of it. When Mrs. Wendworth returned, she handed Daisy a check written in the amount of two-hundred-fifty dollars.

"That enough to hold the date? I must be losing my mind, sweetheart. Haven't even mentioned it. The wedding's set for May twenty-seventh, the Saturday of Memorial Day weekend. That work for you?"

Daisy slid the check into her binder. "It sure does."

"Well, that's still a ways off. We'll have time to discuss the details later. Finish your coffee before it gets cold."

Daisy drank the last swallow of coffee and began stacking the plates and cups.

"Leave that, Missy. Let me walk you to your car. Make sure those mangy mutts don't come after you."

Daisy waved goodbye to the kindhearted woman. On the drive home, her mood remained giddy as she anticipated presenting the check to her father. She had snagged a wealthy client whom offered a hefty deposit before Daisy had the chance to requested one.

When Daisy arrived home, she checked her calendar. Since Tuesday was her designated laundry day, she decided to head to the laundromat to wash her linens while she waited for her father to return home from work. Daisy abhorred using the public facility, but she had no choice, since her small apartment could not accommodate appliances. After she sanitized the wash load with a healthy cup of bleach, she inspected the dryer's interior for gum wads placed by pranksters. She wiped the dryer's interior with a dampened paper towel before plunking her remaining quarters in the slot. The towels tumbled for what seemed like hours before the dryer drum completed its last rotation. Anxious to leave, she scooped the dried laundry into a basket and drove home.

She folded the washcloths into squares and stacked them on the right side of the shelf, sliding them all the way back to touch the cabinet rear wall. She methodically folded the towels in half and rolled the terrycloth into thirds before storing them an even inch from the washcloths.

Daisy returned her laundry supplies to the bottom shelf. The detergent bottle, bleach, and fabric softener bottles faced outward with their labels visible. Satisfied she had completed her laundry, she tucked the check in her pocket and drove to her father's house.

Her grin had not dissolved since she left the farmhouse.

"Twice in one week? My girl must be needing money again." Dan smiled and swatted Daisy's arm.

Daisy unfolded the check and presented it to her father. "Money? Won't be needing a loan, not any time soon anyways."

Her father's grin vanished. Without a word, he slapped the check on the kitchen table and opened the refrigerator. "I need a beer. Want one? 'Cause you're gonna need one."

"Did you see that amount? Two-hundred and fifty dollars!" Daisy gushed. "And that's just the deposit."

Dan chugged his Red's before answering. "Saw that, yeah."

"Well, what? What?"

"Daisy, did *you* look close at that check?"

Daisy blew an exuberated sigh. "Sure did. It's made out to DC Studios. My company. Why?"

Dan slammed his beer on the counter and ignored the erupting foam cascading over the aluminum rim. He closed his eyes and massaged his neck.

"What's wrong with the check, Dad?"

"The woman's name."

Daisy studied the signature. "Yes, Mrs. Wendworth, the grandmother who hired me."

Dan opened his eyes. "Abigail Wendworth, Daisy."

Daisy shrugged.

"You went to her place today? A big white farmhouse past Bancor?"

"Yes," Daisy said. She crossed her arms and did not attempt to hide the defiance in her voice. "Found it all by myself too!"

Dan rubbed his forehead. "You're still not getting it."

"What? What am I supposed to get?"

Dan tossed his empty can into the sink and opened a second beer. "She's the one."

"She's the one . . . what? What, Dad?"

Dan looked away. "It was her farmhouse where . . . " He took another swig. "She's the one. The sister of . . . "

Daisy tucked the check into her pocket and headed toward the door. "I don't know what you're talking about!"

"Damn it, Daisy. Listen!"

The urgency in his tone prevented her from taking another step. She turned and faced her father.

"She's the one who was there when they killed Lucy. Her house. Her sister."

CHAPTER 4

Daisy rushed to her car. The tears stinging her eyes reminded her she could not escape the shadow of her sister's death. Lucy had been dead longer than she had lived, yet her essence—her constant presence—had once again tarnished Daisy's life. Since her childhood, Daisy had endured the stigma of Lucy's murder, from the hushed tones of strangers pointing at her in stores, to the cruel remarks uttered by her classmates.

Daisy tossed the check on her dresser and opened her jewelry box, alerting the ballerina to spin her dance. She fetched her last rolled joint and lighter and lay on her bed, smoking. Why did everyone expect her to know the details of Lucy's death when she had only been a kindergartener when it happened? As she had aged, she longed to understand the circumstances and wanted to ask questions, but the adults with the first-hand knowledge had silenced her. Her father expected her to know Mrs. Wendworth; but, how could she? Her triumph of locating the farm and securing the contract enhanced her self-esteem. Her life was finally on the right track, but now her ambitions had been derailed.

After the marijuana dulled her senses, she decided to meet Mrs. Wendworth the next day and return the deposit. She could not betray her father, nor Lucy, by accepting the check. She convinced herself that future opportunities would come her way, fully aware that few clients called her phony studio, which, in reality, only consisted of her camera and binder.

The next morning, she wore her black polyester dress slacks accented with a red blouse to meet Mrs. Wendworth and cancel the shoot. She knew she should have called first, since it was unprofessional to meet a client without an appointment. Her action held no consequence; after today, she would no longer have a contract.

She referred to the directions and easily found the farm again. Maybe her father was right; she just needed to focus. The two dogs sprang from the porch and barked in tandem in a frantic pace until Mrs. Wendworth silenced them with a wave from her cane. When the dogs retreated, Daisy exited the safety of her car and approached her client.

"Well, what a surprise. Wasn't expecting you, or was I? My mind's half gone these days."

"Sorry, I should have called. Is this a bad time?"

"Missy, when I spend my days out here alone in this big ole house, any time is a good time for company. You just come right on in, honey."

Daisy followed her into the kitchen. Peanut butter and sugar cookies cooling on wax paper covered the counters. Daisy inhaled the sweet aroma of vanilla and remembered her childhood neighbor, Margaret Kahler, who spent her spare time baking delicious cookies.

"Sit. Just baking for the church supper tomorrow. Seems like they never refuse the sweets." Mrs. Wendworth poured coffee into her fragile teacups and placed them on matching saucers. She filled a small plate with cookies before sitting down. "What brings you back, honey?"

Daisy studied the tablecloth's floral pattern. "I need to return your check. I can't—"

"Oh, don't tell me the date won't work. Shucks. I was looking forward to you being here. Since you're about the same age as Amanda, I was hoping you'd get her to smile. Did I mention she's wearing a vintage wedding dress?"

Daisy inhaled a deep breath and held it.

"Something's troubling you, dear."

Daisy jutted her bottom lip.

"Well, most things can be resolved with a good chat, at least that's what my mother used to say."

Daisy considered the elderly woman's gentle expression. Maybe her father was wrong. How could kindhearted Mrs. Wendworth allowed anyone to hurt Lucy?

"My dad says he knows you."

"Well, I'm sure he does. I've lived on this farm my entire life. Sold eggs to plenty of people. What's your daddy's name?"

"Dan. Dan Campbell."

"The Campbells in Endover?"

Daisy nodded and fought the impeding tears.

"Oh my goodness gracious. I had no, no idea."

The purple-and-green floral motifs on the tablecloth commanded Daisy's attention as she centered her cup and saucer upon a flower's center. "Have to give you the check back. Because . . . "

Daisy leaned backward when the woman's wrinkled hands covered hers.

"You don't have to give back anything. Not unless you want to hear my side of things and then decide." The woman whispered the next sentence. "Don't know what you heard."

Since Daisy remained seated, Abigail acknowledged her guest's acceptance and continued. "I took care of your sister that day. She was in a foster home of my sister's. Ethel and her husband asked if I would look after her, since they had to go to court. The hearing was about custody, if your sister would return home or stay with Ethel. Well, if I'm going to be telling the truth, I'm going to be telling all of it."

"Lucy," Daisy murmured.

"Yes, that was her name all right. Never forgot it. A beautiful name for a beautiful child. And like I said, truth be told, I prayed all morning long that Lucy would be returned to her family—*your* family. She was just a tiny, little thing. If I remember right, she was about seven but not much bigger than a five-year-old. Anyhows, she was no match for Ethel. God bless her, and she was my sister, but Ethel was a mean, spiteful person. Hated kids but took them for the county money. Wanted me to take some in too, but I said no. If I couldn't love a child like my own, it wouldn't be right. You follow me?"

Abigail did not wait for a response before continuing her account.

"So, like I said, Ethel and Marvin dropped her off." Abigail smiled at a memory she was about to recount. "I took that little girl outside and she got all excited when she saw a cat."

Daisy grinned, imagining her sister's excitement.

"I figure the girl's a country kid, don't know why she got all excited about a farm cat, but I led her into the barn. Tell her there's all kinds of them for her to play with. I sprinkled some food for the tame ones to appear and left her alone to enjoy them."

"Lucy loved cats."

"Well, I guess so. She spent all morning in that barn."

"So, how . . . ?"

"I'm getting to that part, honey. Let me heat up your coffee." Abigail hobbled to the stove and returned with the coffee pot and filled both cups. "It's probably nothing like what you've been told, you know that?"

"Haven't been told anything. I never knew about you until my dad insisted I return the check."

"Seems folks think children are too young to understand things, it's just their way. Was Ethel's way too. We all sat down to eat lunch at this very table, honey. I sent Lucy to wash her hands, and Ethel starts recounting the court happenings. Bragging how she was going to keep the child since the mother didn't show up in court and all the money she was making off those poor foster kids. Made me sick to my stomach, to be honest with you, but she's family." Abigail clicked her tongue in disgust. "I just wanted them to finish their meal and go home."

Abigail sipped her coffee and sadness replaced her sickened expression.

"That's when it all started, because of Ethel's bragging. Poor little Lucy heard all of it. All of it! She pitched a fit. I mean, what kid wouldn't have?"

She wrapped her hands around the warmth of her cup. "That's when Ethel—"

The cuckoo clock in the living room interrupted Abigail. After ten long chortles ended, Abigail collected her thoughts and spoke.

"That's when Ethel lost her temper, not that she ever had any patience to begin with. She shoved, oh, I don't know how many pills, into that baby's mouth. Almost choked her to death right then and there. I pulled Lucy unto my lap and rocked her to sleep. Marv carried her to the car, and it was the last I saw of her. The last . . . "

Daisy comforted Mrs. Wendworth. "So, it's not your fault."

"Maybe not, but I should have done more for that child. Should have told Ethel to knock it off, quit treating kids that way, but I didn't. I didn't, and I've regretted it every day since."

"Nobody's ever told me this before. So, that's how it happened?"

"Your father has a right to hate me. Can't say I blame him, or anyone for that matter."

"What happened to Ethel? She doesn't still live around here, does she?"

"No, baby. She got arrested for manslaughter. I had to testify against her. My own flesh and blood, but like I said, the truth is the truth. She got put away for something like fifteen years, but it didn't matter. She died after two years in confinement. Bad heart, which was just as good of a sentence as any."

"I'm sorry."

"Well, I'm the one who should be saying sorry to you. If you think about it, we both lost a sister that day."

Daisy pondered Abigail's statement. "We did. I guess we both did."

"If you don't want to take those wedding pictures, I understand. Just thought you should know the facts of what happened here. Your sister was a beautiful child." Abigail hummed and nodded. "Most beautiful child I ever saw, and I include my own in saying that."

Daisy brushed away a tear in response to Abigail's watering eyes. "May twenty-seventh?"

Abigail rose and hugged Daisy. "Yes, May. Thank you, honey."

CHAPTER 5

Doreen rose from bed and slipped into her wrinkled robe. Her feet were cold, and she searched for her slippers. Her cast-off clothing formed lumpy mounds on the floor. She remembered kicking off her slippers before bed, but now she could not locate them.

Doreen banged on the door of her daughter's bedroom. "Tasha! Find my slippers."

"Mom, I'm out here in the kitchen."

"Well, wherever the fuck you are, get my damn slippers, will you?"

Doreen hunkered down on the couch and wrapped herself with a blanket. She lit a Brandt and enjoyed the first drag of the day.

"Socks? I said slippers for Christ's sakes."

Doreen snatched the socks from her daughter's hand and threw them on the floor.

"Going to be late for school. I'll look later. At least the socks will keep your feet warm. Coffee's ready," Tasha said and placed a steamy mug on the end table.

"Better get your ass home right after school. You hear me? You have to clean my room. And put shit where I can find it! And I need a ride to the store."

Tasha swung her backpack over her shoulder. "Yep."

Doreen grumbled at the closed door. "Goddamn daughters. Should've had boys, at least they take care of their mothers when they're old and sick."

Doreen tuned the television to soap operas and talk shows, but none held her interest. Her aching back made it impossible to relax. She blamed her chronic pain from waitressing the large trays of drinks at Jake's Keg years ago; although, her employment had only spanned three months. One summer season had been long enough to snare Roy, but she had been unable to keep her cash cow.

The paltry alimony and child support payments arrived on time but barely covered the rent or prevented disconnection warnings from the utility company. Doreen conceded to disclosing her financial records to Mason County Social Services in exchange for medical assistance coverage and the fancy EBT card that she referenced by the common name of food stamps. Since her birth, Doreen's daily existence had been a battle. *Better than nothing at all* was the adage of her life. She considered having the phrase tattooed around her arm like a warrior's bracelet, but tattoos required money.

Roy. How had she ever messed up that one? He'd been so gullible; he actually believed she loved him. She loved him all right: his ranch, his sprawling house, his money. His long history of bachelorhood had been problematic. He was too rigid. His constant complaining about things out of place and his demands that Doreen cook and clean were all too much for her to handle. She concluded the man had not sought a wife, he wanted a live-in maid. She did her share by managing his farm accounts and received the blame when he lost his dairy business.

Doreen lit another cigarette and focused on the television to drown out the arguing from the next trailer.

"Just another fucking day in paradise."

Tasha hopped in her car and ignored the woman holding an infant while screaming at the guy who sometimes lived in the next trailer. She drove down the lane to Jermaine's. After three long horn blasts, he lazily strolled to her Chevy.

"Good morning, sunshine," Tasha greeted him and shifted into Drive.

Jermaine grunted and pulled on his stocking cap. "Stop at Delores's Diner. Wanna grab a sausage biscuit."

"Can't. We'll be late for school."

"Well, maybe we won't go today."

"It'd be a good idea if I didn't have a chemistry exam today."

Jermaine scoffed. "You plan on becoming a scientist? Really?"

"No, *jeez.*"

"Then what the fuck does it matter? Christ, it's going to be too nice of a day to be stuck inside. Let's ditch."

Tasha considered his offer. "Chemistry is my third-hour class. I'll take the test and meet you at the car." She grinned and added, "Then we ditch."

Jermaine smiled. "Now you sound like the girl I love."

Jermaine leaned against Tasha's car and watched students scurry for a quick break outside the school's prison-like walls before heading to the next scheduled class. He smiled when Tasha approached him.

"The good girl ditched, can't believe it."

Tasha unlocked her car and tossed her books on the back seat. "Don't you even think it's going to be a habit for me. Doing it just this once. Where are we going?"

"Drive to the park. There's something hidden on the back road I wanna show you."

Tasha drove across town and entered the city park. She stopped at the far end until Jermaine instructed her to continue driving down a single lane, which wasn't a true road since grass grew between the ruts.

"What's behind here?"

"Keep going," Jermaine said. "You'll see."

Tasha drove a short distance. The tires bounced as she maneuvered the ruts.

"We're gonna get stuck."

"*Naw.* Stop now."

Tasha scanned the area. The grove of trees bordered the city park and formed a small clearing. She stepped from the car. "What're we doing back here?"

"Just follow me, Tash."

Jermaine approached the edge of the clearing and stopped when he pointed to a widespread stack of bricks covered with soot and ashes. "Found this a couple of days ago. Looks like an altar or something."

Tasha hugged herself. "Creepy."

"Thought you were into this dark shit. Somebody's been back here, sacrificing something . . . or somebody."

"Knock it off, Jer."

He laughed. "So, the girl who watches horror movies is freaked out? I love it." He rubbed the ashes from the abandoned barbeque pit and sniffed his fingers. "Wonder what they're burning back here?"

"Don't know. Don't care."

"Better quit wearing that goth get-up, Tash. You're not fooling anyone."

"Whatever." She sighed in a feigned attempt to sound bored. "I have a new book in my backpack. Hold on."

They returned to the car. Jermaine ran his hands over the cover. "O-U-T-R-E. Outer. What the fuck does that mean?"

Tasha chuckled. "It's not *outer*, dumbass. It's pronounced, *ooh-tray*. French word for bizarre, odd." She rolled her eyes and added, "Oh, the things I learn at school."

"*Huh.*" Jermaine thumbed through the pages. "Chapter Five: Hexes and Spells. Maybe I could make my old lady disappear."

"Yours and mine both."

"You know what I hate the most about my mom?" Jermaine asked.

"No, what?"

"She spends the damn day with a needle in her arm and out all night, chasing the next score. Why in the hell did she even have me, Lakeisha, or Ty if she didn't want us?"

"Don't know."

Jermaine squinted. "We all have different dads. Because of her, none of them come around. How could they? She keeps moving us around. Nobody gives a shit."

"I know," Tasha said. "My mom's the same way. Was mean to my half-sister, Daisy, and her sister who died, then she had me. Mom treats me like shit all the time. Just like your mom; why keep having kids if you hate them?"

"Fuck if I know." Jermaine handed *Outre* to Tasha. "I don't believe in no magic spells. Revenge is the only thing that works."

"Revenge gets you in trouble."

"Sometimes it's worth it."

"Like what?" Tasha asked, leafing through the book.

Jermaine wiped sweat from his face and unto his shirt's hem. "You really want to know?"

"Sure."

"I'm not fooling, Tash. If I tell you shit, you gotta keep it quiet. I mean it. People only get caught 'cause they brag. I'm not bragging, so if I tell you . . . "

"Okay. Lips sealed."

She closed *Outre* with a snap.

"Well, this was back when we lived in Chicago, okay? My mom had this creepy boyfriend, Jerry. I never liked the way he looked at my sister, and he beat on Ty a few times." Jermaine crossed his arms. "So, one day, I figure I'll get rid of his ass. Piss him off so bad, he'll just pack up his shit and leave."

Tasha eyes widened. "What did you do?"

"I waited 'til the bastard passed out next to my old lady, and I stole his wallet. Besides his driver's license, he had a credit card and cash. I counted six hundred dollars on that fool. I took the cash and put the wallet back in his pants pocket. When he woke up the next morning, he finds out it's gone. He blamed my mom, but she swore she didn't know nothing about it. He called her a whore and a thief and beat the shit out of her right in front of us."

"You didn't do anything?"

Jermaine jutted his chin. "Nope. He split her lip and pounded her head. Damn near broke her jaw, I remember that. Knocked her down and stomped on her."

"But why didn't you help her? Give him the money back?"

"Because it was the only way to make him leave for good. I figured she deserved it. She let him beat on Ty and didn't do shit to help him. I didn't feel sorry for her. Didn't then, don't now."

"Wow." Tasha mulled over the story. "What did you do with the money?"

Jermaine chuckled. "Spent it like fucking Christmas shopping. Ty got a gaming console, figured he earned it. Lakeisha bought some new clothes, and I blew mine on partying. You gotta make people suffer when they deserve it. If they have it comin', well, so be it."

"Well, I don't know—"

"You don't know? Seriously? Do you like your mom screaming at you all the time? Calling you names? Making you do all the shit she's too lazy to do herself. That's okay?"

"No, but . . . "

"There is no *but*, only revenge. When you get sick and tired of it, you'll agree. You just ain't there yet."

Tasha glanced at her watch. "Shit, I gotta take my mom to the store. Can't believe it's this late."

Returning to the trailer court, Jermaine asked Tasha, "So, do you or don't you believe in all this voodoo shit?"

"*Jeez*, it's not voodoo. Don't you know anything? It's like being spiritual and the balance of darkness and light, good and evil, things like that."

"Well, I do my own balancing in life. Even out the bullshit a little bit at a time."

"It sounds so . . . "

"Violent? Yeah, sometimes that's what it takes."

Tasha parked the car. "Home sweet home. I gotta get my Mom to the store. Catch you later?"

"You know where to find me," Jermaine said.

He walked down the lane with his hands in his back pockets.

Doreen wasted no time yelling when Tasha walked through the front door. "Christ, we have to get going to the store. Told you this morning I was out of stuff. You ready?"

"Yeah, just dropped off Jermaine. Ready."

Doreen shoved her Brandts in her purse. "What'd I tell you about running with that boy? Better not be spreading your legs for him. No little darkies are gonna call me Grandma."

"Mom!"

"Get in the car. Let's go."

Jenny reached into the dairy cooler at the rear of Kemp's Grocery for milk. She paused when she heard two familiar voices bickering near the store's entrance.

"Grab a cart, not a basket. How many times I gotta tell you we need to stock up today?"

Jenny stepped back when she spotted Doreen, hunched in her perpetual bad posture, and Tasha enter the store. She was not in the mood for another one of Doreen's public confrontations. She usually timed her grocery shopping—actually, *all* of her shopping during the school hours, since she knew Doreen's outings depended on her daughter's chauffeuring. Today, Jenny's errand list had been longer than usual, and she had reserved the grocery shopping for last.

Jenny set the milk in her cart and approached the cleaning-supply aisle. Knowing Doreen's lack of housekeeping skills, Jenny assumed Aisle 4 should be safe. She would get the steel wool pads and exit the store without Doreen noticing her.

"Not that kind. Get the cheap shit off the bottom shelf. You too damn lazy to bend?" Doreen shouted to Tasha.

"But I have to use twice as much of that generic dish soap to get the dishes clean, so why can't we just buy the good stuff?"

Doreen pointed to the bottle. "If you have to use twice as much and it's cheaper, then it all works out the same. Jesus Christ, don't they teach math in school anymore?"

Doreen spotted her rival as Jenny rolled her cart into the aisle.

Jenny decided to forge ahead, grab the steel wool pads, and exit to the checkout.

"Well, lookey here! It's the whore who lives in my house."

Tasha blushed at her mother's mortifying remark. She lowered her head and studied the bottle's label.

Jenny greeted Tasha while ignoring Doreen. "Hi, Tasha."

Tasha's eyes darted from Jenny to Doreen and back to Jenny, as if she were watching a tennis match. Tasha mouthed a silent apology to Jenny when Doreen's grip on the cart prevented her daughter's escape.

"So, how's *my* house?" Doreen taunted.

An elderly nun, Sister Maria, shuffled between the two enemies unaware she had entered a battle zone.

Jenny ignored Doreen's goading and reached for the carton on the opposite side of the aisle.

"Bitch is deaf. I asked, how's my house?" Doreen quizzed.

Jenny spun around to witness Sister Maria's audible gasp, accompanied by a flash of horror flickering in the old woman's eyes.

Doreen stood straighter than she had in years, attempting to intimidate her former friend.

Jenny tossed the box into her cart. "How's *your* house? *Hmmm.* Been clean for nearly twenty years now. You surely wouldn't recognize it. Has a happy husband who lives there too. Thanks for asking."

Doreen scrunched her face and shook her fist. "Whore, you don't know shit!"

"Oh, my word," Sister Maria uttered and covered her ears as if the curse words had set her coif afire. She lifted her cane to quicken her pace and nearly collided with the storeowner, Bill Kemp, as he rounded the corner.

"Ladies, please! If you can't conduct yourselves properly, I'll ask you to leave. Customers can hear you two aisles away." He apologized to the frightened nun. "I'm sorry, Sister."

Tasha searched the aisle for her acquaintances and felt relieved none of them were there to witness this embarrassing scene. She imagined her classmates' snickers throughout Greenville High about her foul-mouthed mother tangling with Jenny in a big brawl at Kemp's. She had barely recovered from Doreen's horrific confrontation with a Dan a week ago at First Stop Hardware.

"Bill, I'm sorry for the commotion," Jenny replied. "I—"

Doreen interrupted. "Don't worry about me coming in here anymore. Your damn prices are sky high anyway."

She shoved the cart toward Bill Kemp.

"Please take your business elsewhere, ma'am. I'd appreciate it."

"Don't fucking worry about it." Doreen pointed at Jenny and added, "Just keep catering to the whores. Maybe that nun can pray for her."

Tasha trailed six steps behind Doreen as they vacated Kemp's. She scanned the parking lot for her friends. Maybe it was a good thing Doreen got them expelled from Kemp's; now she did not have to worry about Doreen's displays of spiteful behavior toward Jenny.

Doreen lit a Brandt and plopped in the car seat. "Fuck, we still need shit. Now we've got to drive all the way to Bancor."

"We need more gas to do that," Tasha answered.

"I won't have money until that piece-of-shit father of yours sends child support. Drive to Freedom Oil and get some cigs and Pfizz. Then go home. Just go the hell home."

Tasha parked the car at the convenience store. Doreen puffed two cigarettes waiting in the car while her daughter purchased the items. Tasha exited the store and met her friend, Kristi.

"Where were you after chemistry class?" Kristi asked.

Tasha tilted her head toward the car. "*Shh.* Talk later, okay?"

Doreen's voice exploded like a string of annoying firecrackers. "Will you hurry the fuck up?"

Jermaine's voice popped into Tasha's head. *I do the balancing in my life.*

When they returned home, Tasha slid the six-pack of Pfizz into the refrigerator.

Doreen paused on her way to the couch to answer the knock on the door. "What do *you* want?"

The young man stood on the makeshift steps, dressed in a white tee-shirt and ragged jeans. His baseball cap worn backward indicated his lack of intelligence to Doreen.

"Tasha home?"

"Tasha. Tasha! There's a darkie on the doorstep."

Jermaine glared at Doreen. He fought the urge to punch the thin, hunchedback hag. He sucked his lips to prevent blurting a retaliating insult.

"Hurry, little girl. I think this one's swallowing his lips. From the size of them, I didn't think that was even possible."

Jermaine backed down the steps. He smacked his fist into his palm while he waited for Tasha.

"Mom, can't you ever be nice? Ever?"

"My house, my rules. Got that? If I don't want black boys sniffing around, then they don't come around. What part of that don't you understand? Christ-o-mighty, I ain't no darkie lover. You ain't going to be one either."

Tasha sprinted to catch up with Jermaine as he headed toward his trailer.

"Sorry, Jer. I don't know why she acts like that."

"Don't make excuses for that cunt. Too bad she's your mother, but that's not your fault. Wanna come in? I need a beer."

Tasha silently followed him. The Porter's trailer was the identical size of the one she and Doreen leased—only the retirees could afford the doublewides. Screeching sounds emitting from a drag racing videogame bounced from the walls of a nearby bedroom. Tasha recognized Ty's shouts and those from several other boys and wondered how they all managed to fit into such a tiny room.

Jermaine swiped away empty syringes from the coffee table unto the floor. Overflowing ashtrays and empty pizza boxes dominated the opposite side of the table. While he retrieved two beers from the refrigerator, Tasha gasped at the flytraps—usually hung in cattle barns—suspended over the kitchen table in long, amber spirals of adhesive tape.

 The dead and twitching flies stuck to the glue induced a gagging reflex that only stopped when she realized the table's use was for storing junk, not dining. The assortment of empty beer and soda cans collected any fly that dropped next to the stack of the unpaid bills. Cardboard boxes covered with stained blankets served as storage and occupied the space intended for chairs.

Jermaine handed Tasha a beer. "Here."

"I really am sorry, Jer."

She followed him to the couch. Jermaine pointed the remote at the television that was always on regardless if anyone was viewing a program. After scanning the channel lineup, he settled on a sports channel.

"Makes no difference. Heard that shit all my life. Hell, I even hear that shit from my own mom. I'm black, she's white. Makes her better somehow. Like I said before. What the fuck, did I ask to be born?"

Tasha patted his arm, but he slid away. "Where's your mom now?"

"Who knows? Scoring drugs? Whoring around? Spreading her legs for a poor black man and wishing he was rich? Who gives a shit?"

Tasha sipped her beer.

Lakeisha entered the trailer with three of her friends.

"Get back outside. I'm watching TV. Ain't gonna listen to a bunch of gigglin' girl shit," Jermaine shouted.

Lakeisha scrunched her nose. Her one-finger salute to her bossy brother induced the predicted laughter from her friends. As Jermaine rose from the couch, his sister and her entourage scrambled outdoors.

Tasha turned to Jermaine. "In six months, I'll be eighteen. I'm gonna get as far away from this depressing town as I can."

Jermaine chuckled. "On what? Your good looks? You need money to get away. Lots of it. Why do you think so many ain't left?"

Tasha placed her empty beer can on the table. "I only know I'm leaving. One way or another."

CHAPTER 6

Daisy scrutinized her father while he worked on his truck engine. When she gathered no clues to his present mood, she plunged ahead. "I didn't return the check."

Dan wiped his greasy hands on a rag. "Why not? The old witch wasn't home?"

"She was home."

He slammed the hood. "Tell me you ripped it up in front of her and left."

Daisy looked away. "No, it's still in my purse. I'm keeping it." "Why?"

"Because she hired me and—"

"She gave you blood money!" Dan shouted. "Don't you get that?"

"It wasn't like that at all. She told me . . . She told me what happened."

Dan threw down the rag. "Filled you full of shit, that's what she did."

"Well, it was a hell of a lot more than you or anyone else ever told me!"

Dan smirked. "Really, Daisy? Was I supposed to sit you down at five years old and tell you that the Fletchers and that woman killed your sister?"

"Look at me, Dad. No, *look* at me. I'm not a little girl. Nobody's ever told me what really happened. Do you know I used to be afraid to sleep? Scared I'd never wake up like Lucy? That's all I knew until today."

Dan approached his daughter. "Here's all you need to know.

Those damn people killed my daughter, my Lucy. If you want to do business with them, then get the fuck out of here. I don't know you anymore!"

"But, Dad!"

"Fuck! After all you do for your kids . . . "

Jenny heard the loud voices and stepped outside. Dust trailed Daisy's Nissan as the tires spun gravel in her quick acceleration to the highway. Dan slapped his palms on his truck hood and kicked a tire.

"What's going on?" Jenny asked Dan.

"Just say I have no daughters any more. Leave it alone."

Jenny did not hesitate to follow Dan's demand. She returned to the kitchen and shook three extra-strength Aspirin from the bottle. Doreen's insane raving at Kemp's had induced her pounding headache. Dan's tantrum layered a blinding intensity to her brain's throbbing. She considered her pain and swallowed an additional capsule.

When the trio had been younger, she had escaped their craziness by abandoning them to argue during their frequent martial spats while she sought the solitude of her single life. Getting involved with Dan had changed all that and marrying him thrust her into the spotlight she had avoided.

Maybe she should have walked away when she had the chance.

No, she thought. *I should have run.*

CHAPTER 7

Roy Ferch sat on his usual bar stool at Jake's Keg. Months had passed since he had frequented the bar, and if he were honest with himself, he was lonely. Not lonely for female companionship but longing for the sound of people's voices to convince himself he was alive. He had holed up in his small apartment most of the winter, watching westerns and going stir crazy; not exactly the activities he had engaged in before he had married Doreen. Spring had arrived, and he vowed to get out and enjoy the fresh air and sunshine, even if it only meant savoring it during the short trek from his truck to the bar.

Before his marriage to Doreen, Roy had been a successful dairy farmer with a routine his friends could set their watches by. He would enter Jake's Keg on Friday nights, promptly at seven o'clock. He would order his usual Phillips whiskey with no ice and finish the second one by nine, before the loud music began. He had been a bachelor not by choice, but because his shyness, combined with his enormous nose, had labeled him as undesirable-husband material. Roy had been satisfied living a solitary life, milking his cows and saving his dollars rather than immersing himself as a target for the locals' gossip.

He had watched Doreen every Friday night for two months back in 1977. She had been stunning back then. Her long brunette hair and deep-set eyes contrasted sharply to the other waitress, Peggy, whose round figure prevented her ease of navigation around the crowded tables. Roy never joined in the discussions with the other men when they whispered about what a great ass

Dori had; although, if pressed for his opinion, he would have admitted to stealing a look or two.

The waitress named Dori never seemed to smile except when Roy tipped her a five-dollar bill for each round of his whiskey. Roy looked forward to her wink, but he could not muster the courage to speak to her. He did not understand much about women, but they all liked appreciation, that much he did know.

Doreen finished her shift early after she had lamented to Jake about her backache. While his customers appreciated Doreen's sweet rear, she was nothing but a pain in the ass to Jake. If he had not been so desperate for coverage during Wanda's maternity leave, he never would have hired Doreen. Rather than listen to her complain all night, he relented and allowed her to leave after he called Peggy, who agreed to pick up the shift for the additional wages and tips her broadness attracted.

Doreen pulled on her coat, lit a Brandt, and started the two-mile trek home. Headlights behind her illuminated the road. She lifted her hand to flip off the jerk forcing her to walk along the ditch when the truck stopped.

"Need a ride?"

She recognized the driver as the Friday-Night Farmer.

"Sure would. These shitty shoes are no good for walking."

The man leaned across and opened the passenger door.

Doreen climbed into the immaculate cab. Although the truck was an older model, it smelled brand new. She expected to see an air freshener dangle from the rearview mirror, but there was nothing. She doubted the locals' talk of this man being a rich dairy farmer when she could not detect any lingering scent of cattle manure.

"Where to?"

Doreen looked away. "Sunrise Motel."

"The motel . . . just up the road?"

He sensed the hesitation in his voice had made the waitress uncomfortable.

"Cheapest place I could find after my divorce. Don't worry, not trying to hustle you."

Roy's face reddened. "Well, it's not that."

Doreen opened her purse and shook a cigarette from the pack.

"*Ah*, no smoking in the truck, if you don't mind."

She pushed the cigarette behind her ear and pointed. "There it is."

Doreen swung open the door before the truck rested to a stop.

"I'm sorry. I didn't introduce myself. Roy. Roy Ferch."

The waitress slammed the door and reached for her fallen cigarette that had landed an inch from a mud puddle.

"For fuck's sake," she muttered.

Roy heard her say *thanks,* and he grinned as her firm ass sashayed under the neon MOTEL sign. The following weekend, Roy surprised Jake's crowd with his attendance on both Friday *and* Saturday night and staying long after the loud music began.

Roy's five-dollar tips not only attracted Doreen to the homely farmer, but also the observant eyes of Jake's crowd. Roy, clad in his flannel shirt and jeans, appeared similar to the other farmers; only his generous tips raised the eyebrows of the patrons on nearby bar stools. He longed for female companionship, but the only two available women were the desperate divorcee at the end of the bar or the pretty waitress who never smiled. Roy continued his subtle approach by offering Doreen rides to the Sunrise Motel when her shifts ended.

The bar patrons relished observing Roy's infatuation with Doreen. Gossip flowed between the stools at Jake's Keg when a few of the drinkers spotted Roy's truck parked at the motel. Since Roy's romance was more intriguing than sport scores or the current market price of corn, the regulars could not resist hurling barbs at the Friday-Night Farmer.

Chuck Barnett patted Roy's back and snickered. "Getting some of that sweet ass at the No-Tell Motel, Roy?"

"Don't know what you're talking about."

"Roy, for the last twenty years, we all thought you was queer. But now, seeing that old truck of yours parked at the Sunrise on weekends . . . Well, let's just say, good for you. If I wasn't married, I'd be dipping my wick in her too."

Chuck's bear-sized palm slapped Roy's back once more before he returned to his buddies at the far end of the bar. When Roy glanced in Chuck's direction, the men raised their beers in a silent toast that concluded in roaring laughter.

Doreen invited Roy to Room 3 that night.

Roy scanned the meager furnishings as Doreen tossed armloads of dirty laundry from the chair to heaps scattered on the floor. Crumpled bags from Delores's Diner concealed the scorched hotplate on the small counter. The greasy odor of garbage spilling over the tiny trashcan and the heavy fog of cigarette haze clinging to the walls repulsed Roy.

"Sorry. If I knew I was having company, I would've cleaned up this shithole."

She motioned for him to sit while she lay back on the bed. He removed his cap in respect but maintained it on his knee. Doreen lit her third cigarette since they had arrived fifteen minutes ago.

"Must be lonely living on a big-ass farm."

Roy squinted in puzzlement and before he could answer, Doreen continued.

"Sure as hell ain't lonely in this goddamn cracker box."

Her exploding laughter perplexed Roy, as everything about her did. She was a foul-mouthed chain smoker who had no qualms declaring her dissatisfaction with everything in life, yet he was attracted to her. She was an enigma. An enigma with a great ass.

Roy cleared his throat and forced the question from his lips before he lost his nerve. "Maybe we should go out sometime."

Doreen grinned. "I'd like that."

Her three-word reply had sealed Roy's fate. Doreen Farnsworth Campbell became Mrs. Ferch two months later, and she gave birth to Tasha eleven months after the wedding day. Rumors circulating about Roy's sexual preference had been squelched, but his reprieve soured as he spent more time in the dairy barn, listening to the cattle's bellowing instead of the constant complaining from his bride.

Seven years had passed since he had divorced Doreen, but he would never forget the memories of their torturous union. When she had refused to cook and clean, he had hired help. Roy would milk his cows three times a day, every day, rain or shine. To lessen the load of his responsibilities, he had put Doreen in charge of handling his farm's financial ledger and had entrusted her with the business checking account. He had instructed her to deposit checks and pay the operating expenses. He naively never questioned her ability to handle the responsibility.

When he noticed new furniture and television sets popping up in every room, he inquired if everything was paid, and Doreen always answered with a nod. Roy justified her increasingly expensive wardrobe selections and frequent visits to the beauty parlor by acknowledging her poverty-filled background had not permitted such indulgences. Since she spent as much money on their daughter's whims as her own, Roy remained mum and turned a blind eye when his wife transformed a guest room into storage for her shopping excesses. He was never sure what the purchases were, since most of the items remained in the store bags in which they had arrived. When Doreen was happy, the household ran smoothly, and that was sufficient for Roy. As long as she paid the bills, he could accept her frivolous shopping trips.

A simple task he performed one day plunged Roy's world into a downward spiral. While dumping office trash into the burning barrel, his belt buckle snagged and ripped open the plastic bag and exposed its contents. To Roy's horror and disbelief, unopened envelopes from the bank and the county assessor's office spilled from the bulk. When he read the notices, he discovered his farm was in foreclosure due to three years of unpaid county property taxes, and his checking account was overdrawn. His savings account was non-existent.

He had farmed his entire life, inheriting the dairy business from his father, and now he had lost it. Instead of using his fists against Doreen, he filed bankruptcy. The only thing in his life that mattered was his daughter, Tasha.

After his divorce, Roy resumed his Friday night ventures to Jake's Keg, but he never tipped another waitress. This Friday night was quiet, since it was early. Two men he knew only as Stubs and Hank sat in the center of the bar, trading barbs with Jake over the latest basketball victories as scores scrolled across the bottom of the television screen.

All four men glanced at the door as Dan Campbell entered. He acknowledged the men with a single *hello* before sitting on a stool near Roy.

"Get you a Red's?" Jake asked needlessly and placed a pilsner on a square cardboard coaster. He lifted Dan's ten-dollar bill from the counter and rang up the sale, slapping the change on the bar surface before resuming his sports conversation.

Roy greeted Dan by raising his whiskey-filled glass.

"Roy. How's it going?"

"Been better, been worse. You?"

Dan replaced the glass on the coaster after gulping three swallows. "'Bout the same. Nothin' ever changes, huh?"

"Nope. Not really." Roy checked the time on his watch. "Going to pick my daughter up in an hour."

"Good kid," Dan remarked. "She was over with Daisy last weekend."

Roy nodded. "Hard to believe we've both got good daughters . . . considering."

"Yeah, no shit," Dan agreed. "Considering. Got time for another? I'm buyin'."

Roy chuckled. "One more, then I'm the hell out of here before the loud music starts."

Roy brushed imaginary dust from his truck's dashboard. He straightened his cap, turned the ignition key, and pushed in the clutch. As he drove to Westside Wheel Estates to retrieve Tasha, his thoughts floated back to his failed marriage to Doreen.

He had rescued her from the rundown motel room and made her comfortable in his five-bedroom, three-bath ranch home. Marrying Doreen had been his chance for happiness, and his proudest day was when his daughter was born.

Doreen had named her, but he did insist her middle name honor his mother, Alice. He recalled Tasha wearing little bib overalls and pink rubber boots when she accompanied him in the dairy barns. He labeled her with the affectionate name Lil Dumplin'.

She turned ten in 1988—the year the county had foreclosed on his property. Without a source of income, Roy swallowed his pride and begged his cousin Johnny at First Stop Hardware for a position. When Johnny offered his basement den to Roy until he could piece his life together, Roy also accepted the room while realizing it was no place to raise his young daughter.

Desperate and with no funds to hire an attorney, he allowed Doreen to retain custody of Tasha. His friends advised him the court would likely award custody to the mother despite Roy's unchallenged parenting skills. Doreen accepted Roy's alimony and child support payments and rented the trailer. Although Roy maintained regular visitation, he could only imagine how living with Doreen in the trailer-park environment affected Tasha.

He parked in front of the shabby trailer. Thick weeds spouted around the foundation, making it hard to distinguish if metal skirting enclosed the trailer. The front steps consisted of nothing more than two broken pallets stacked upon one another. Nearby, a group of elementary school-aged children formed a circle and passed a cigarette. *This has been Tasha's life for the past seven years.*

Roy honked one long and two short blasts, signaling his arrival. He refused to approach the door since Doreen's public displays of rebuke not only demoralized him but also embarrassed even the hardened residents who witnessed her shameless antics.

Tasha swung her purse over her shoulder. "Dad's here!"

Doreen smirked while lighting her Brandt. "Well, let's hold a fucking parade. The clown's arrived."

"I'll be home in a few hours. We're going out to eat."

"Don't worry about me none. I'll just sit here and monitor my blood sugar. Gets all fucked up when nobody bothers to bring me food. But hey, *you* have fun."

Tasha sprinted toward the door and left without a word.

"Goodbye to you too, Daddy's Lil Dumplin'."

"Hi, honey. In the mood for Delores's Diner, Ricci's, or maybe swing up to Bancor for a real treat?"

"Hold on, Dad. There's Jermaine. We talked about hanging out tonight before I remembered you were coming. Could . . . Would you mind if I invited him? Please."

Roy identified with the young man's slouch as he strolled with his hands in his back pockets. He seemed to bear the world's weight on his shoulders.

"Not at all. A friend of yours is a friend of mine."

Roy shifted into Park as Tasha called out to Jermaine. "Hop in, Jer. My dad's taking me out to eat. We want you to come."

Jermaine leaned forward to inspect the driver. Although the man offered a smile beneath his thin mustache, Jermaine remained guarded.

He ignored the plea in Tasha's eyes while he answered. "*Naw,* I gotta check on Ty and his friends. My mom ain't home. Don't know when—"

"That's okay," Tasha interrupted to spare Jermaine from disclosing his familial situation. "Talk to you later?"

"Sure, I guess," Jermaine replied before walking away.

Roy headed to Ricci's. He glanced at his daughter and asked in a teasing manner, "That guy is just a friend, *huh* Tasha?"

Tasha playfully slapped her father's shoulder. "Oh, Dad, it's not like you think."

"How do you know what I think?"

"Sorry, I'm just used to Mom insulting him, that's all."

"Imagine that, Dori insulting someone. Let me guess. He's too tall? Not very bright?"

Tasha offered a clue. "You're overlooking the obvious."

Roy snapped his fingers. "Oh, I got it. He's a guy."

"She hates him because . . . because he's black."

Roy turned his eyes from the road and faced his daughter. "What? Are you kidding me?"

"Who kids about Mom?"

"Right, I guess nobody. Well, I sure as hell don't agree with that."

"Nobody agrees with Mom. Nobody likes her."

They rode the remainder of the trip in silence as Roy maintained his policy to refrain from speaking ill of Doreen to their daughter. He tried to think of at least three people who liked or even tolerated his ex-wife.

He could not name one.

CHAPTER 8

After depositing Mrs. Wendworth's check, Daisy calculated a balance of two hundred eighty-seven dollars and fifty-one cents in her checking account. After paying her rent, which was due in three days, she would have less than sixty-two dollars for other necessities. Daisy cursed her dependence on her father for her living expenses, but she had never been able to maintain employment longer than a few weeks.

Bill Kemp had hired her as a cashier. Between ringing up customers' purchases, her duty was to maintain pleasing presentations of the store's products—or "front and face," as Bill instructed her in the retail jargon. Daisy had immersed herself in the process of aligning the canned goods and disregarding impatient customers waiting at the checkout. After several incidents of customers' complaints, Bill had no choice but to fire her.

Shortly after her cashier termination, Daisy had been hired at First Stop Hardware to stock shelves and control inventory. The manager was infuriated when she spent the entire morning rearranging paintbrushes by sizes, mixing the brand names with no attention to the appropriate pricing. He ordered her to return the stock to the original peg locations. Daisy fled his yelling by rushing to the restroom and vomiting her anxiety. When she returned to the sales floor twenty minutes later, the manager ignored her tear-streaked face and handed her a final paycheck.

Dan rescued Daisy each time she lost a position. He wrote checks to cover her rent and supplied Daisy with cash to cover her bills and groceries. Despite the low expectations of employers assigning Daisy meager tasks, Dan never questioned her inability to hold a position. His avoidance of confrontation remained his preferred method of dealing with problems. Daisy accepted the role of daddy's little girl—it meant survival—but now her dependency ceased since her father refused to speak to her.

After a dozen employment dismissals in two years, Dan suggested she should pursue an activity she enjoyed which would also produce an income. With her love of art and pictures, he hinted that, perhaps, if he purchased a camera for her, she could operate a photography studio. Armed with a decent Kodak and a set of lenses, she eagerly taught herself the art of photography.

The hours she spent in the woods clicking snapshots of birds and wildlife calmed her. The solitude of practicing wide-angle shots and closeups convinced her she had discovered her natural talent. When the expense of buying and developing the film exceeded her budget, her father encouraged her to use her resources for income-producing photographs.

The weekly ad she had placed in the *Mason County Press* had rewarded her with modest success with the wedding shoots and numerous baby poses over the past year. Landing a client like Mrs. Wendworth would not only add legitimacy to her portfolio but would also propel her business to a self-sustaining level with referrals from someone so well known in the community. Daisy wished her father understood her ambition and not be so judgmental about her motives.

Monday was dusting day, and Daisy removed the books from the shelves. She meticulously wiped dust that had barely accumulated since Wednesday. She wiped the covers, the backs, and lastly the spines before returning the volumes to their rigid order. As she returned her cherished copy of *Charlotte's Web*, a photograph slipped beneath the back pages and sailed to the floor. When the Polaroid landed face down, her piqued curiosity caused her to reach for the photo.

The four of them—her mother, father, Lucy, and she—posed in front of their trailer. Either the image had blurred over time or the nature of the instant developing process had produced a murky appearance of the Campbells. Lucy stood a head taller than Daisy, her long brunette hair hanging in strings. Daisy noted that both were barefoot, wearing shorts and tops that seemed a few sizes too small, the gaps exposing their bellies. While both girls and Dan smiled, Doreen looked toward the right, with a cigarette balancing between her fingers. Since all four of them had posed for the photograph, Daisy wondered who had operated the camera. Maybe her father would know, but since he disowned her, she would not have that answer anytime soon. She placed the photo on her end table and returned the books to the shelf.

Just as she began sorting her mail, her doorbell rang. When she answered the door, she was surprised to see Jenny.

"I hope this isn't a bad time," Jenny said.

"No, just cleaning. Come in. Would you like some coffee?"

"Sure, if it's not any trouble, sweetheart."

Daisy prepared the coffee maker. "So, how's Dad?"

"That's what I came here to talk about."

Daisy set two mugs on the table. "I figured as much."

"You know he says things he doesn't really mean. He misses you, Daisy. He just won't admit it. You know he avoids things he doesn't want to deal with."

"Can you say I'm wrong for not knowing everything that happened when I was five? I mean, come on."

Daisy filled the two mugs and returned the carafe to the heating plate. She leaned against the counter with her arms crossed. Jenny recognized the look she secretly called "the Daisy pout."

"Well," Jenny responded. "Since it was such a traumatic time, we adults would rather not think about it. Since you were so young at the time, we thought it was best to shelter you from the pain. Mainly, our pain."

Daisy uncrossed her arms and waved them in manic motions. "I was five. Five! Didn't anyone think I hurt too? One day I'm playing with my sister like all the other days and the next a deputy takes her away and I never see her again. Did anyone *ever* think how that affected me? No. Everybody forgot about me. I should've stayed hidden under that table when the deputy and preacher told us that Lucy died."

Jenny blinked tears in tandem to the ones flowing down her stepdaughter's face. So many tears had been shed over the grief of losing Lucy.

"I'm sorry," Jenny whispered.

Daisy slumped in a chair. "Not your fault."

"Yes, it is. When I married your father, I promised him I would take good care of you. But he never spoke about Lucy and wouldn't allow me to either. We can't even celebrate Thanksgiving because . . . Well, that's why I never told you anything. He wouldn't let me."

Daisy leaned forward with her elbows resting on the table and cradled her head. "Doesn't matter. He stopped talking to me. Who do I have now? Nobody."

"That's not true. You have your father, and me too. Let me talk to him some more. He'll come around; he always does."

"Do you think it's wrong for me to take money from Mrs. Wendworth?" Daisy asked, leaning back in her chair and searching Jenny's face for an honest answer.

Jenny looked away. "That's not for me to say, honey."

Daisy walked to the end table and plunked the Polaroid in front of Jenny. "Do you know who took this?"

Jenny examined the image. That summer day . . .

Dan, Doreen, and the girls lived in the trailer then. Dan had confided to her the deteriorating state of his marriage between too many beers and a few stolen kisses. Jenny resisted becoming the wedge in their marital spats and told Dan to deal with his crumbling life on his own. Jenny had snapped that photo a few minutes later when the girls became fascinated with her camera producing instant snapshots.

"No, Daisy. I don't."

CHAPTER 9

Doreen pounded on the bathroom door. "I needed a shot, like, yesterday. Can you get your ass out here?"

Tasha swung open the door. "Getting ready for school."

Tasha wore tight jeans and a cotton shirt hanging loosely from her shoulders that exposed her cropped camisole. She brushed her hair while her mother impatiently stomped her foot.

"You wearing that hideous getup to school? Jesus Christ, you look like a whore. And do any of your clothes come in any color besides black?"

Tasha rushed past her mother in the narrow hallway, not caring when her shoulder butted her mother against the paneling.

"I'm getting your injection ready."

Doreen followed her to the kitchen. "You act like it's such a chore to help your sick mother."

Tasha retrieved the pen from the refrigerator and groaned. "I'm doing it, ain't I?"

"Don't get smart with me, little bitch. I might be old and sick, but I can still whip your ass. Hear me?"

Tasha swabbed her mother's shoulder with the alcohol pad. She jabbed the needle into Doreen's flesh, hoping the cold insulin stung just a bit.

Doreen repeated her question, and Tasha tossed the pen into the trashcan.

"I said, do you fucking hear me?"

"Heard you."

Doreen twisted Tasha's arm behind her back and ignored her daughter's moan.

"Then fucking answer me when I ask you a question."

Doreen released her grip.

Tasha washed her hands over a sink full of dishes that would wait for her return from school. The laundry she had ignored yesterday to focus on her homework now spilled over the hamper. The trailer stank of perspiration and rotted fruit. Doreen was content to live in the mess, but Tasha was not. Her only recourse was to clean it herself, which she had been doing since she had been old enough to hold a dishrag or maneuver a broom.

Doreen lit a Brandt. The smoke spiraled above her head and disappeared into the constant haze of nicotine clinging to the russet-stained ceiling.

"You coming straight home from school today?"

Tasha nodded while she rubbed her shoulder.

"Somebody needs to clean this shithole. Garbage piling up, starting to stink in here."

"Well, if you would open a window—"

Doreen interrupted. "And listen to those fucking loser darkies fight all goddamn day? I don't think so!"

"Mom, I really wish you wouldn't—"

Doreen lit a second cigarette with the butt of the first one before crushing it into a full ashtray.

"Don't give a shit what you wish for. It's the damn truth, whether you like it or not. Got that?"

Rather than risk another attack from her mother, Tasha shoved her notebook into her backpack. She fled outdoors and closed the door to seal off her mother's rant.

Jermaine leaned against her car waiting for her.

"Going to school today, Jer?"

He grinned and hopped into her car. "For most of the day."

"So, anything exciting happen last night when I was with my dad?" Tasha asked.

"Some of the guys and me waited 'til dark, and then we spied on that altar thing I showed you. Wanted to see who showed up and what the fuck they do there."

"And?"

Jermaine shrugged. "Nothing, nobody."

"Big surprise there. Can't believe you think some evil shit goes on down there."

Tasha rubbed her shoulder before shifting into Drive.

"Just because nothing happened last night doesn't mean it never does. I mean, it wasn't like it was a full moon or something."

"Well, I believe it's all bullshit. Somebody started a story, and now everyone's playing into it."

Jermaine shifted in the seat. "You calling me stupid?"

"No. It's just that I don't believe it's anything."

"Well, let's check it out tonight, then. Just you and me."

"Oh, *jeez* . . . "

"Well, if you're scared, stay home," Jermaine stated in a defiant tone. "Just don't call me stupid anymore."

"I'll go, if only to prove it's nothing."

Tasha parked her car in the school parking lot.

"I'll be at your front steps at ten tonight," Jermaine said before dashing off to meet his friends.

Tasha rubbed her shoulder again. There was no wickedness practiced in the woods. She knew where evil lurked. Trailer 12. Home sweet home.

CHAPTER 10

Dan returned from work and grabbed his customary Red's from the refrigerator. Working on cars all day at Gleason's had been especially tiring with the unrelenting restoration schedule of pounding out dents and painting. He often thought he would be more productive at work if Kevin allowed his employees to imbibe with a refreshing brew now and then, but Kevin's rebuttal included the reminder he could not afford OSHA to close his shop over one preventative mishap.

Dan had not bothered to unlace his work boots when he entered the kitchen. The coolness of the air conditioning failed to revive his fatigue. Jenny joined him in the kitchen as he cracked open his second beer. She noticed the clumps of mud that had dropped from his boots onto the clean floor and said nothing. She learned to choose her battles; the never-ending daily arguments exhausted her.

"What'd you do today?" Dan asked, not bothering to look up from the newspaper spread on the table.

The newsprint ink transferring onto his uniform's dirty elbows was hardly visible, unlike the black smudges smeared into Jenny's clean tablecloth

"Visited Daisy."

Dan jerked his head from the Want Ads. "Why?"

Jenny scoffed. "Why? Why not?"

Dan returned his eyes to his newspaper and slurped his beer in silence.

Jenny mulled over if she had enough energy for this con-

frontation and decided she did. "Because she's your daughter."
Her next sentence pierced Dan's heart. "You hurt her."

He slowly lifted his gaze from the words he was not reading.
He glared at his wife while he gulped the last drop of his beer. He
crushed the can in his palm before throwing it. The can denting
against the porcelain sink's edge was the last sound in the kitchen
for a full thirty seconds.

Dan wiped his mouth with the back of his hand.

"I hurt her, yeah."

His curled lips forming a smirk should have alarmed Jenny,
but it did not. Instead, she was surprised he had contributed to the
confrontation instead of avoiding her like he usually did. If Dan's
quarreling aptitude were comparable to an animal, he surely
would be an ostrich with his head hidden from conflict.

"She's trying so hard to make her studio work. She landed a
client, she was so proud," Jenny said before flaming Dan's temper
with her next utterance. "You just pissed on her parade."

"Oh, so that's what I did, did I? If it had been anyone—*anyone*—
but that damn Fletcher's sister, it would be different."

"Abigail Wendworth didn't harm Lucy. Christ, Dan, you were
in court when she testified against her sister."

"Yeah, that's right. I was there. You tellin' me that old bitch
couldn't have stopped them from druggin' Lucy? Fuckin'
really?"

"There's one thing you're forgetting, Dan. A big part of it."

"And what would that be?" Dan asked in a sarcastic tone.
"Please, tell me."

Jenny stared into her husband's eyes without a care whether
she remained married to him or not.

"Doreen was the cause of all the trouble in the first place."

Dan hung his head to avoid acknowledging the truth.

Jenny slammed a third beer on the newspaper. "Blame her, not
Daisy."

She stormed to the backyard. When she crossed her arms, the

sun glistened on her wedding band's small diamond and commanded her attention.

Good intentions. That was her motive when she wed Dan. Her love would heal him. Heal Daisy. Although she and Doreen had been friends, she had betrayed that bond. No amount of apologizing was acceptable to Doreen, and Jenny silently admitted she deserved the scorned woman's wrath. After nearly twenty years of attempting to salvage relationships and rectify past heartaches, she had accomplished nothing.

Endover had claimed another living fatality.

Dan showered. Cleansing away the sweat was easier than ridding himself from the guilt of shunning Daisy. Her personality had not changed much since she had been a child. Not really. Her round dimpled cheeks lent her the angelic appearance that mirrored her personality. Even during her teen years, when the sweetness of daughters morphed into defiance, Daisy maintained a happy-go-lucky disposition. She was the apple of his eye, and she knew it. Daisy was all he had after losing Lucy.

Lucy. His heart remained as broken as when it first shattered when he had received the news of her death. Everyone was wrong; time does not heal all wounds. His life was divided into two chapters: Before Lucy's Death and After Lucy's Death.

Before Lucy's Death: he had been married to Doreen and naively believed in the happily-ever-after scenarios his daughters created on their sketchpads. He chided himself for not paying attention to the lives his daughters led at the hands of Doreen. Although he would not admit it to Jenny, Doreen *was* the catalyst in the events that led to Lucy's death.

After Lucy's Death: he divorced Doreen and jumped immediately into marriage with Jenny. The marriage was an act of absolution on his part; the only way he could forgive himself for cheating. While he committed adultery in Jenny's bed, Lucy died alone in a stranger's bed. Jenny's personality contrasted with Doreen's when she offered nurturing to both him and Daisy. The union seemed to be the answer at the time, but he was not so sure of his hasty decision now.

He allowed the alcohol to push his regrets from his thoughts as he dried the dampness from his skin. He supposed he should ask Jenny what she and Daisy had discussed; although, he really did not want to know. Daisy needed to understand the consequences of tangling with those Bancor folks. He would not betray Lucy to coddle Daisy.

After he dressed, he approached Jenny in the kitchen as she swept the dirt from the floor. Jenny instinctively moved to the left, allowing him access to the refrigerator.

"So, tell me then," Dan said.

Jenny returned the broom and dustpan to the closet.

"Tell you what?"

Dan sat in a chair noting both his newspaper and the tablecloth had vanished. "Tell me what Daisy had to say."

Jenny washed her hands at the sink. "She's trying, Dan. Trying real hard to be on her own, to make something of herself." She dried her hands and added, "She wants you to be proud of her, that's all."

"I am proud, damn it."

"Then tell her."

Jenny proceeded to prepare a salad for dinner. The missing ring on her left hand went unnoticed by Dan as she set the table.

CHAPTER 11

The television blared with the game show audience's applause as the contestant won the grand prize. Doreen chuckled at the woman's ignorance; the taxes alone would cost a few thousand, so why gloat about winning a brand-new car? Doreen believed the show's producers rigged the outcomes by supplying the contestants with the answers before the cameras rolled. She was not convinced that the fat lady from Ohio knew the capital of Yugoslavia to win the car. Hell, how would anyone know that? She did not, and what's more, she did not care. Few things held her interest; living in Endover had stripped her of dreams years ago.

She did care that she had enough to eat. The ban from Kemp's proved problematic, since the nearest grocery store, Food Round Up, was located thirty miles away in Bancor. The grocery chain would accept her EBT card but getting there was the obstacle. She reminded herself to ask Tasha if the car had a full tank of gas. If not, she would force her daughter to badger Roy for cash.

She lit a Brandt and sipped her last Pfizz. She expected Tasha home in an hour, and then they would drive to Bancor. The arm-twisting this morning sent a good reminder to her smart-mouthed daughter that Doreen was the one in charge. If they could secure enough money from Roy, she would insist her daughter buy a pastel shirt to wear with her black jeans. All that black just reeked of death; it was time to put a stop to that trend too.

"Jesus, wearing black and running with blacks. Where did I go wrong with this one?" Doreen posed the question aloud to herself.

With no more Pfizzes stocked in the refrigerator, she rummaged through the kitchen cabinets.

"Damn it! Not one clean cup in the whole place."

She refused to dig under the heap of dirty dishes accumulating in the sink to find her favorite coffee mug. She held the sponge under the tap and squirted dish soap into a cup.

"Shouldn't have to wash a damn cup every time I need one," she grumbled and reminded herself to give Tasha a good tongue lashing about the girl's laziness since she started keeping company with that black kid.

She rinsed the cup and filled it with leftover coffee, since Tasha had not bothered to brew a fresh pot before leaving for school. After the microwave beeped, Doreen carried her cup to the couch to resume her television viewing. While the talk show host rambled about topics that did not interest her, Doreen sipped her stale coffee and lit a Brandt.

Outside the trailer, she heard laughter. She turned down the television volume and listened. Sharp pings pierced the trailer's siding.

"Hit it again, Ty."

What the hell? Doreen rose from the couch and peered from behind the protective cover of the curtain. She slowly cranked open the window. A young boy, the one she assumed was Ty since he aimed a pellet gun, shot a few more rounds at the trailer.

"I wanna do it now," the younger boy said.

Ty wrestled away the pellet gun from his cohort's reach. "No!"

Well, those little bastards!

Doreen seethed as she imaged craggy old man Jefferson, Westside Wheel Estates' owner, blaming her for the damages created by two juvenile punks. As she considered the best way to confront them, since they possessed a weapon, she heard the pair argue. When she peeked again, she spotted them walking in opposite directions, the boy carrying the gun heading to Trailer 5.

"That figures. The brat belongs to the junkie."

Doreen glanced at her stained bathrobe. If she had not bothered to dress yet, there was no way the juvenile delinquent's mother would be out of bed. If the whore had been awake, she would have known her son was absent from school.

The kitchen clock's hands pointed at 11:25. Doreen heated a second cup of coffee and fumed. Like a coiled rattlesnake, she would strike at the appropriate time. In the meantime, she smoked and planned her confrontation with the Porter woman.

Mornings were usually calm at Westside Wheel Estates with the children attending school, the retirees tending to their potted flowers, and the partygoers sleeping off hangovers. The police sirens responding to domestic disputes usually occurred at nightfall. Occasional crying from toddlers filtered from the playground as the mothers exchanged gossip and cigarettes while semi-supervising their unruly broods. The peacefulness allowed Doreen to nap during the day as she waited for Tasha to return from school.

Doreen created her perpetual nest on the couch with her blanket and slept away the afternoon. Her good dream about winning a new car on a game show ended when pings hammering the trailer siding resumed. She sat up, rubbed her eyes, and leapt from the couch with more energy than she had demonstrated in years.

"Oh, you little sonofabitch!"

She jerked open the door and surprised Ty, who dropped his pellet gun as Doreen charged toward him. The startled eight-year-old was no match for the angry woman who yanked his arm despite his struggle to run.

"Just what the fuck do you think you're doing? Huh? Wrecking my trailer?" She twisted his arm behind his back. "Get your ass moving!"

Ty winced at the pain shooting through his elbow. He continued to grapple away from the old neighbor lady whose grip tightened with each forced step toward his home.

Doreen held steady onto her young victim as she pounded

on the Porter's door. Since it was nearly four o'clock, the woman should be awake. Doreen hammered with her fist until a young girl answered the door.

"Ty?" Lakeisha questioned, the wild expression reflected in the angry woman's eyes frightened her. "What's going on?"

Ty pleaded to his sister. "Make her . . . Make her let me go!"

"Where's your whore mother?" Doreen demanded.

Lakeisha's eyes widened as she looked beyond Doreen's shoulder and saw Jermaine charging toward the steps. A rough shove pinned Doreen against the doorframe and forced her to release Ty.

Tasha shouted. "Jer!"

Doreen regained her balance and spun around to face Tasha's friend towering over her.

"Just what the fuck're you doing?" he shouted. His spit sprinkled Doreen's face like miniature raindrops.

Ty raced past his sister and into the safety of the trailer while Lakeisha leaned against the doorway, blowing pink bubblegum orbs between her giggles.

"That little shit—"

Jermaine stepped closer to Doreen. "That little shit is my brother, Ty. He's got a name, so use it. You ain't got no right yelling or smacking him, got that?"

Tasha tugged at Jermaine's arm. "Calm down. Everyone just calm down."

Doreen ignored her daughter's command. "That little brat shot holes into my trailer twice today, for your goddamn information, big brother. His ass should be in school, but your junkie-bitch mother ain't around to send him or watch him. If I have to pay, I'll be calling the fucking cops, hear me?"

"Listen, bitch," Jermaine answered. "If you ever lay a hand on him again, *I'll* be the one calling the cops. Do *you* hear *me*?"

"Just stop," Tash pleaded. "Stop." She gripped her mother's arm and dragged her toward their trailer.

Doreen yelled over her shoulder. "This ain't over, Blackie. Not by a long shot!"

Jermaine shoved Lakeisha into the trailer and slammed the door.

Once inside their home, Tasha scolded her mother. "Really, Mom. What's gotten into you? He's just a kid."

Doreen's hands trembled as she lit a Brandt. She exhaled her anger in a cloud of blue-gray smoke before she responded.

"That little bastard and his friend shot holes into the trailer with a BB gun. Who's going to pay for that? Not me. You think your little black boyfriend's mom has any money? If I get evicted over this shit, I'll whip that boy's ass, no matter who calls the cops."

"Just settle down, okay? He wasn't even holding a gun, so where's your proof?"

Doreen huffed. "He dropped it when I grabbed him, *duh*."

Tasha stepped outside and searched for the pellet gun. "Well, there's nothing here."

"Of course not, they're all thieves. Did you really think . . . "

Tasha retreated to her room and played loud music to silence her mother's endless droning. Jermaine's temper surprised Tasha, until she recalled his story about settling the score when his mother's boyfriend beat on his brother. Now, Doreen had committed the same offense.

Sometimes I do the balancing . . .

CHAPTER 12

Dan arrived home from work by six o'clock each night, and if he remembered to stock up on Red's—which he never forgot—he was drunk by eight. The alcohol's grip on him had occurred early in life. He attributed his addiction as an escape from Doreen's repulsive behavior; although, he would admit his father was more to blame that she ever was.

Dan pondered these thoughts as he sat in his lawn chair, staring at nothing in particular. His father, Al, who had raised him and his sister Stephanie after their mother's death, had no qualms about belittling and beating his children into submission. Dan vowed, after a childhood beating from Al's stinging strap, he would never abuse the children he would have someday in the same horrible manner, yet he had broken Daisy's spirit.

Daisy. Although she had become a woman, she would always remain his little girl. Dan took a swig of his Red's and smiled as he recalled her innocent manner of baby talk that she spoke long after the cuteness had lost its appeal to other adults. He did not care; she was simply being Daisy, and nobody could replace her. She sparkled while creating art, and no one could deny her gentleness toward all living creatures. Dan's heart ached at times with the overflowing love he possessed for her.

He kicked the dirt with his boot as he chided himself for not speaking to her. Now that he had reached the age of fifty-two, was he becoming the grouchy old man his father had been? Maybe Jenny was right. Despite Daisy's difficulty maintaining employment, she *had* followed his advice to improve her situation.

He tossed his empty beer can into the trash, along with his self-hatred behavior resembling his father's. He entered the house and dialed his daughter's number.

"Hello?"

"Hey, is this the girl with the new Nokia? How's it working?"

Daisy smiled. "Good to hear your voice, Dad. It really is."

"Well, tell you what. Been thinkin' maybe it's a good thing you got yourself that job."

Daisy hesitated to reply.

"You still there, honey? Can't hear you."

"I'm here."

"Just sayin' go ahead and take those pictures. I ain't gonna be mad about it, 'sall."

"You sure?"

"Sure I'm sure." Dan chuckled before adding, "I'm not the asshole everyone thinks I am."

"I never said—"

"I know you didn't. Well, come over when you can, okay?"

"I will, Dad. Thanks."

"For what?"

"For not being an asshole."

Daisy's laugh before she hung up convinced Dan his daughter accepted his apology. He opened the refrigerator and stared at an empty top shelf. He would need a case of Red's or more to patch the strife with Jenny.

CHAPTER 13

Tasha knocked harder the second time on the Porter's door. The loud rock music escaping the windows prevented any of the occupants from hearing much of anything else. When her rapping went unanswered, she turned the doorknob and entered.

"You ready?" she asked Jermaine as he dropped his grip on the interior doorknob.

"I was just about to answer the door. In a minute; come in."

While Jermaine disappeared down the narrow hallway, Tasha greeted the adults sitting on the couch. Adelle Porter, Jermaine's mother, ignored Tasha's weak *hello* to pass a joint to a bald man sporting a serpent tattoo coiled around his neck. With the music blasting to an ungodly level, Tasha wondered how they managed to hear the television. She stole a glance at the screen and immediately regretted it. She recoiled in embarrassment and horror as she witnessed the adults watching a porn flick while Ty constructed a structure from small building blocks on the coffee table.

"Grab Mom and Dick a beer," Adelle ordered Ty as she nudged him with her foot.

When Ty did not respond, the man kicked the structure with his dirty shoe. Small plastic bricks of red, yellow, and blue exploded into the air like confetti. Howling laughter from his mother and her latest lover ended Ty's protest.

"If you know what's good for you, you'll shut up and get that beer," Dick ordered.

Tasha was relieved when Jermaine returned to rescue her. She had secretly thought of Ty as a brat, but now she pitied him.

Jermaine's story of balancing was justified now that she had witnessed his mother's atrocious behavior.

Jermaine did not intervene as Ty served the beer while stifling his tears to resume playing with his plastic bricks. Jermaine motioned for Tasha to open the door, and they fled the madness of the trailer.

"Ready to check out the altar, *huh*?" Jermaine asked as he climbed into the car.

"Just to prove to you it's nothing."

"When we get there, you'll see. You'll be converted to a be-lee-ver!"

Tasha laughed at the way Jermaine pronounced *believer*, as if he were a television evangelist. The night air was warm, and it was a perfect evening to escape Doreen's demands and prove Jermaine's ridiculous claims were false.

As they neared the woods, Tasha maneuvered the ruts to reach the altar. Jermaine could barely contain his excitement as he instructed her to beam the headlights on the stone structure as he rushed to inspect it.

"Should have brought a flashlight," Tasha said as she joined him. "I don't see no babies sacrificed here. At least not today."

"Smart ass. I never said babies were being sacrificed, but some weird shit's been going on back here. Park the car closer to the trees and we'll watch."

Tasha backed the car toward the edge of the tree grove and parked.

"Let's watch from the back seat," Jermaine said.

"Why?"

"Because there's more room to duck, in case someone is lurking around. Just lock the doors and be quiet."

Tasha followed his instructions to appease him. She grew bored as they sat in silence for ten minutes. "Nothing's happening. Let's go."

Jermaine wrapped his arm around her and kissed her forehead.

"Well, *something* can happen." He raised her chin with his finger and kissed her. "Love you, babe."

Tasha's body responded to his gentle, wet kiss. She did not resist when Jermaine removed her blouse and unsecured her bra. Together they fumbled with the removal of their jeans and allowed their teenage hormones to take control. Afterward, Tasha rested her head on his chest and listened to the comfort of his heartbeat.

"You love me?" she asked.

"Sure."

She smiled. "Good."

She reached for her twisted clothing and got dressed.

"So, I'm kinda glad your devil worshippers didn't show up tonight. Got us some alone time."

"Well, it ain't all bad." Jermaine grinned and replaced his cap after pulling on his jeans. "We'll check it out another night to prove I ain't bullshitting you."

"You really wouldn't lie to me, would you?"

He kissed her forehead. "I'll stand by you. Always."

CHAPTER 14

Harold Jefferson took his daily stroll through the trailer-park grounds he had purchased fifteen years ago. If he had been wiser in his youth, he never would have fallen for the real estate agent's claim that owning a trailer park and collecting rent was "passive income." Operating the property required as much, if not more, stamina than the area farmers tending livestock or harvesting crops. Had he visited the town before responding to the ad, he never would have believed the second lie the agent had told him when he described Endover as a "sleepy, little Midwestern village." While the town's population had never exceeded four hundred residents, which Harold conceded *was* a small town, the rural area filled with degenerates was anything but "sleepy."

The premise of guaranteeing the protection of his investment by owning all twelve rentals plus his own trailer had sold Harold on the idea of his new career as property manager. By owning the trailers, they became permanent assets, which generated higher monthly lease income than other parks that only charged for lot rent.

His real estate agent, Bob Carney, had advised that by purchasing the property, Harold's "passive income" would increase steadily through rent increases each year until his retirement. At that point, he could sell the park and retire in luxury anywhere but in Endover. Harold put aside his doubts and signed the purchase agreement when he received the bank's approval for a business loan. Harold placed his confidence with the bank manager, Mr. George Warner. After all, Warner had reviewed the property's income and expense statement—he would not have approved the loan if it had not proven to be a solid investment.

Harold had changed the name from Carriage Homes to Westside Wheel Estates, hoping the name would attract better clientele. He had owned the park for exactly three days when the locals informed him that regardless of the name change, everybody referred to the park as Unlucky Thirteen. Two days later, he discovered that not only were Warner and Carney brother-in-laws, but the park's seller, Carriage Homes LLC, was a company owned by Carney.

Harold Jefferson had been conned with no recourse. He had no money for legal fees, and even if he could acquire the funds, the local attorney was likely related to half of the county. Harold resigned to existing in his nightmare in a sleepy, little village until some fool responded to his real estate ad and he could unload his investment.

Banging on the doors on the first of the month to collect rent was routine. So was banging on the doors on the second, third, and fourth days. Harold posted notices to the front doors of any tenant owing rent past the fifth day, until he realized no amount of shaming would convince the tenants to part with the portion of their welfare checks they felt entitled to keep.

Harold had not anticipated the constant maintenance, nor had he considered the cost of repairing damages. Since most of his tenants were poor or retired on fixed incomes, extracting reimbursements was the worst part of owning Westside Wheel Estates.

Today he stopped at the playground, which occupied a small corner of the property and consisted of two swings, a teeter-totter, and a sandbox. Harold had provided a picnic table in hopes the mothers would supervise their children, but it mainly functioned as a gathering place for teens to sneak sips of booze. He had ceased his attempts to snatch alcohol from the young kids and instead requested they use the trashcan to dispose of their cans and bottles.

He observed the pair of swings had been twisted around the top bar of the set's frame. Daily, he hauled out his ladder and untangled the chains. Harold emptied the trashcan and shooed a cat defecating in the sandbox.

Next, he strolled along the lane and inspected the trailers. The graffiti phrases of *Sue's a whore* and *Eat me* spray-painted on the side of Trailer 10 were new. Removing the graffiti had been a never-ending costly process. When the deputy—during his numerous responses to the park—confided in Harold that the graffiti made it easier to spot the troublemakers, Harold ceased painting over it and added a one-hundred-dollar credit to his monthly accounting ledger.

As he approached Trailer 12, the sunlight illuminated a random pattern of dents. Upon closer inspection, Harold recognized a BB or pellet gun had been the source of the damage. He knocked on the door.

A woman, whose features convinced him she must have been a stunning beauty in her youth, answered the door wearing a tattered robe with a cigarette dangling from the corner of her mouth.

"Yeah?" she asked.

"Hello. I'm Harold Jefferson and—"

"Write you a check every month, I know who you are. What do you want? I'm in the middle of something."

Harold looked past the woman. Dishes cluttered the sink and kitchen table. An odor of rotten eggs wafted from an overstuffed open garbage can. A large ashtray filled with butts rested on a stack of dog-eared, stained magazines on an end table near the couch. Whatever he was interrupting certainly was not housekeeping.

"I noticed damage to the siding. What do you know about that?"

Harold ducked when Doreen tossed her cigarette butt over his shoulder.

"I don't go out much. As you can see, I'm sick. Why don't you ask that little shit who shot the pellet gun why he did it?"

"So, you *do* know about it?"

"What I know is that you don't do your damn job around here. Fucking kids running wild all hours of the night, stealing and destroying shit, and you want me to do something about it? Come on, wake the fuck up, buddy."

Harold took a deep breath. Losing his temper never solved confrontations with the tenants. He responded in a calm, even tone. "I'm going to review my records. If you don't have a security deposit on file, I'll get an estimate and charge you for the damages."

Doreen leaned forward and pointed at him. "You do that. You just fucking go ahead. If I had any money, I wouldn't be renting a shit trailer from you, now would I?"

The door slammed in Harold's face before he had the chance to respond.

Two hours later, Doreen noticed a contractor's truck parked in front of her trailer. She sneered as she watched Harold Jefferson greet the man with a slap on his back, like two chums meeting at a high-school reunion. The men disappeared to the side of the trailer and returned to his parked truck ten minutes later. After a prolonged handshake, the contractor handed Jefferson a slip of paper and drove away.

Harold knocked on Doreen's door. When she refused to answer, he slipped the estimate under the door and returned to his office. He pounded his fist on his desk when his hunch proved correct; Trailer 12 had no security deposit on file. Since the tenant had been rude and refused to disclose which child had possessed the pellet gun, he decided he would make her pay.

Doreen's spying behind her curtain on the contractor and Jefferson ended when the slip of paper glided under her door. She ignored her backache and bent to retrieve the note.

"Eight hundred dollars? For fucking what?"

She scanned the proposal details printed in neat letters:

Replacement of two sheets of metal siding. $300 each, labor $200. Estimated repair time: one day.

In a sloppy cursive handwriting, she read:

Pay up in one month, or face eviction. Final! Harold Jefferson

"Oh, how fucking ridiculous! I ain't paying this. That fucking little brat's whore mother can give up her welfare check."

Doreen slipped out of her robe and into her tee-shirt and sweatpants. She lit a Brandt and paced. Her anger increased with each step. There was no way she would allow that brat to get away with this.

She slipped into her sandals and headed to the Porters'. Instead of knocking on the door, she yanked it open, startling Jermaine and Ty watching television.

"You little bastard! You're going to pay for this."

Jermaine leapt to his feet and guarded his brother from the raving neighbor.

"Hey, stop right there. You got no business busting into our house like that. Want me to call the cops?"

"You can ram that phone up your ass for all I care, Darkie."

Doreen shoved the estimate into Jermaine's chest, forcing him to grasp it and she pointed at Ty. "Your fun with that little pellet gun just cost your old lady her welfare check for the next two months, cause I ain't going to pay it. If I catch—no, if I *see* your little black ass even near my trailer, I'll beat the hell out of you right then and there. Got it? Got it, you little asshole?"

Jermaine shoved Doreen toward the door. "Get out!"

"Get your hands off me, you loser. And you stay the fuck away from my daughter too. You hear me?"

Jermaine slamming the door in Doreen's face ended her tirade.

He turned to his younger brother. "Stay away from that crazy bitch, you understand me?"

Ty hugged a pillow as a shield. He watched his brother shred the paper into confetti and sprinkle it in the trashcan.

"Jesus Christ, eight hundred dollars!" Doreen muttered on her way back home. She knew the Porter whore would never cough up the money even if she did have it, but it felt good to yell at that unsupervised delinquent and let him know she was watching him. Doreen would fix him for good if she faced eviction because of his destruction.

Tasha had left a note on the refrigerator stating she would arrive late from school since she was required to repeat some exams. Doreen used the opportunity to snoop in Tasha's room. Unlike the rest of the trailer, Tasha's room was orderly. She made her bed each morning as her father had taught her. Doreen had rummaged through Tasha's desk on previous occasions. Although she had discovered a diary a few years ago and was intrigued by the contents, the lock and hidden key always prevented her from reading it. The diary was not important.

Doreen lifted the diary to reach the cigar box underneath. She opened the lid and removed the envelope. Tasha had written the dates and amounts her father had given her on the front. The last entry had been just a few days ago when Tasha had dined with Roy.

So, she pocketed twenty bucks that day.

Doreen counted the tens and twenties. Tasha's calculations were accurate; she had saved nine hundred and twenty dollars. That total was enough to get old Jefferson off Doreen's case and prevent the eviction.

Doreen hurriedly shoved the cash in the envelope, replaced the diary, and closed the drawer when she heard Tasha enter the trailer.

"Home!"

Doreen walked down the hall to the living room. "Finally. I need a shot, like yesterday."

Tasha dropped her backpack to the floor. "Had to take that exam again. Chemistry is a lot harder than I thought it would be."

"Maybe if you quit running every night and opened a book, you'd be smart enough to pass on the first round."

"It's not that easy."

Tasha sunk the needle deep into Doreen's arm.

"Your ass is staying home tonight, that's all I can say."

"But . . . But I already promised Jer that—"

"Don't be promising that trash anything. Not after the mess his brother got us into. Damn degenerates. The whole damn bunch!"

"Not sure I know what you're talking about."

Doreen lit a Brandt and waved the match to extinguish the flame. "Just ask Darkie in school tomorrow, 'cause your ass is staying in tonight. Dishes to do, floors to sweep. Think of me for once."

Tasha cleaned the trailer while Doreen watched television. As soon as Doreen's snoring confirmed she was asleep, Tasha crept into the night and headed to Jermaine's.

"Hey, what's shaking?" Tasha asked as Jermaine stepped outside.

"Gotta get out of here. Let's go. I got a few bucks for gas."

After fueling the car, Jermaine suggested they investigate the altar. With no alternative plans to combat his suggestion, Tasha drove to the park.

"Pretty quiet out here," Tasha said after she shut off the engine.

Jermaine grunted. "Could use some quiet. Did your nutty old lady tell you about her fit at our house today?"

Tasha gasped. "She was at your house? Today?"

Jermaine nodded. "Oh hell yeah. Barges right in and starts screaming at Ty. Had some bill from Jefferson, thinking the kid's gotta pay."

"Pay for what?"

"Says he shot pellets into her trailer or something. Kid doesn't even own a gun. I should know."

Tasha puffed out her cheeks. "Man, sorry. She's always been like that."

Jermaine whirled his finger in a circular motion next to his temple. "Like, crazy?"

"Yeah."

"Well, crazy gets you balanced real quick. Nobody threatens my little brother. Not my mom, not your mom especially."

Tasha rubbed Jermaine's shoulder. "*Ah*, didn't you say the back seat has a better view?"

He smiled. "As long as the devil worshipers don't come around."

The pair removed their clothes and huddled under the blanket. Jermaine responded to Tasha's tender caress with a ravenous trail of aggressive kisses. Tasha closed her eyes and arched her back as her boyfriend entered her. She gripped his rocking hips until Jermaine's grunts concluded into a final groan.

"Love me?" she whispered.

He kissed her forehead. "Always."

Tasha reached for her black jeans rolled up on the floorboard. "Did you hear that?"

"Not funny, Tash."

"You're scared too. Let's get out of here."

Jermaine opened the car door and stepped into his jeans. "Nobody's around, but let's get out of here just the same."

Tasha dressed, and the pair hopped into the front seat. The ruts rocked the car, but she maintained her foot on the gas pedal and sped from the dark woods. When she safely entered the city street, she returned to the conversation about revenge.

"Jer, what about this 'balancing'? Don't you think it's better just to let things take care of themselves? You know, like karma?"

"You forget what I told you before. Sometimes I do the balancing to make sure justice is served. You just haven't been wronged enough yet to take matters into your own hands. When it happens to you, you'll do the balancing. I promise you that."

Tasha considered his words. Karma had not arrived at Doreen's doorstep.

Not yet.

CHAPTER 15

Jenny woke with a stiff neck. The couch was no replacement for a bed, but she had slept there since Dan threw his fit about not speaking to Daisy. Although the subjects of their arguments never changed—his unbridled spending, his fast driving, and his ban on celebrating Thanksgiving—the frequency of their disputes had increased. The disharmony in their marriage used to frighten Jenny, but now she accepted the disillusion of happiness. As her mother had explained about the stagnant condition of her marriage to Jenny's father, it just *was*. Like her mother, Jenny had settled.

She had known Dan since they had attended Greenville High. She had been thrilled when he invited her to their senior prom. Jenny had begged her mother to splurge on a flowing blue-satin gown that had cost one hundred dollars more than her mother had been willing to spend. When Dan had presented her with a white-carnation wrist corsage and told her how pretty she looked, Jenny winked at her mother. Dan had held her close during their first slow dance and happily abandoned the dance floor when the rock-and-roll music began, citing he needed to step outside for fresh air. Jenny had agreed to wait for him at the refreshment table.

While Jenny and her friends had been complimenting each other on their fashionable gowns, Doreen stood alone outside, leaning against the building and puffing a cigarette. The tight mini-dress she had borrowed hugged her curves and highlighted her cleavage. Ringlets flowed from her long brunette hair haphazardly secured in a loose ponytail. She had offered Dan a swig of vodka from the flask she produced from her purse. Fifteen minutes later, Jenny had discovered them in an embrace. Five minutes later,

Jenny's romance with Dan had ended with her mascara-streaked tears staining the corsage she threw at his feet while Doreen chuckled and adjusted her dress. Jenny forgave them with a smirk when their whirlwind romance had crumbled into a disastrous marriage. Now, her marriage to Dan had deteriorated as well.

Jenny rose when the coffee aroma was too tempting to resist. Dan sat at the table, sipping from his mug as he searched the Want Ads to buy things he did not need.

Jenny forced herself to mutter, "Good morning."

"Mornin'," Dan answered.

Acknowledging her after a fight was a positive sign, since he easily forced the silent treatment toward his wife for days.

Jenny offered an apology. "Sorry about butting in about Daisy."

Dan's eyes remained glued to his newspaper. "Nothin' to be sorry 'bout. We're talking again."

"Good. She really is trying."

Dan stood and filled his work thermos with coffee. "Yeah, she is. End of story." He bent and brushed Jenny's forehead with a kiss. "See ya later."

Jenny watched her husband square his cap onto his graying hair. His looks had not changed much from high school, not really. He was still handsome despite the deep wrinkles etched in his face. He was the prize she had confiscated from Doreen all those years ago.

His truck roared out of the driveway, and Jenny was left alone to collect her thoughts. She was relieved Dan had reconciled with Daisy. She did not ask how or when; she was just glad he had restored his relationship with his daughter. There was no way she would allow Daisy's dependency on Dan to transfer to her.

Dan dropped everything on a moment's notice to save Daisy from real or imaginary dilemmas ranging from killing a spider crawling in her bathtub to investigating strange sounds she claimed emitted from her walls. When Jenny complained about Daisy calling at two in the morning, suggesting a ghostly apparition floated above her bed, Dan cursed his wife's insensitivity and rushed to his daughter's side. Since Dan refused to place boundaries on his daughter's constant intrusions, Jenny dealt with her stepdaughter on her terms. If Daisy called and Dan was not home, Jenny interrupted Daisy's theatrics and instructed her to call later. Jenny noted, with a smugness, that all of Daisy's disrupted crises resolved on their own without her father's knowledge or intervention.

The warmth of the coffee mug temporarily soothed Jenny as she wrapped her hands around it. Dan still had not noticed the absence of her wedding band, while Jenny had grown used to not wearing it.

Daisy hummed as she drove to Mrs. Wendworth's to finalize the wedding shoot. Now that she had gained her father's approval, she happily anticipated her appointment. Her confidence soared, and she had not even needed to refer to the directions to reach the farm. Her life was improving, and she prided herself on the strides she had accomplished.

As she entered the long driveway, both dogs chased the tires in determination to guard their territory. Daisy parked and honked the horn to signal her arrival. Mrs. Wendworth appeared on the porch and scolded the dogs, who barked one last warning before scampering away.

"Daisy. So glad to see you again."

"Hi, Mrs. Wendworth. How are you?"

"Now, Missy, if we are to be friends, and I think we already are, I want you to call me Abby. All my friends do."

The void of baking aromas disappointed Daisy as she followed Abigail into the kitchen. The cozy atmosphere that had been created by the spices melding in the oven's heat had comforted her in the unfamiliar setting the first day.

"No baking today?"

"Why no. Not today, child. I baked six apple pies yesterday for the church fair. Thought my fingers would go numb peeling and slicing all those apples."

"I bet."

Abigail set two teacups with saucers on the table and filled them with piping hot coffee. "Do you bake, dear?"

"Afraid not, never learned how really."

"Oh my, you mean your mother—" Abigail stopped short. "I'm sorry, I didn't mean . . . "

Daisy offered a nervous smile. "No worries. You know my mother wasn't exactly the maternal type, still isn't. It's okay, really."

Abigail brushed her hands together as if she could erase the topic. "Yes, of course, on to better things then. You said you want to know about the lighting in the barn for your picture taking?"

"Yes. It's important the photos are shot in the best possible light. Is the wedding planned for the afternoon or evening? That makes a huge difference."

"*Ah* yes, I see your point. Two o'clock is the ceremony, reception following. After the wedding, some benches will be cleared from the barn and tables brought in for the dining."

Daisy sipped her coffee and jotted notes in her binder.

"Let's finish our coffee, and then I'll take you to the barn. It's empty now. Such a shame since it used to be a working barn when Charles was around to farm the land."

"Charles?"

"My late husband. God rest his soul. Was a working man. Rose early, worked hard, retired to bed early. Miss that man every day of my life. Lord willing, I'll join him someday."

Abigail hobbled to her center island and returned with a cookie jar. "Got some gingersnaps if you're hungry."

Daisy smiled. She felt at ease with Abigail and mourned the absence of a grandmother in her life. Doreen was estranged from her mother, Judy. Dan's mother, Olivia, had died in his youth.

Daisy basked in the elderly woman's attentiveness. When Abby's gnarled arthritic hands covered Daisy's, Daisy felt a calming sensation unlike any other.

Daisy refused the offer of the gingersnaps to maintain her daily caloric intake. She stood and informed Abigail she was ready to view the barn's interior. Abigail removed her cane from the back of her chair and motioned for the young woman to follow.

"Maybe you can open one of those doors, honey. I ain't got the strength I once had."

"Sure thing."

Daisy unsecured the door as Abigail shuffled behind her and switched on the light.

"See here—" Abigail pointed toward the ceiling "—the ceiling ain't got much for bulbs, so I'm guessing I'll need to call that rental place in Bancor. You jot down the kind of lights you need and I'll see if they carry them."

Daisy felt a brush against her leg. A gray cat circled seeking attention. *Gracie.*

Abigail stomped her cane. "Shoo, you darn cat!"

Daisy scooped up the kitten. "She looks like the one I used to have named Gracie. I miss her so much."

"You and your sister and those cats. Used to? What happened to it?"

My mother drowned both Gracie and Margie II. Taught us a lesson.

"Oh, I don't remember. It was a long time ago."

Beads of perspiration dampened Daisy's forehead. Hot. Why was the barn so stifling? The cat leapt from her tight grip, and she cupped her hands over her mouth to prevent screaming her secret. She blinked away the darkness. The barn's dimness enveloped her like her grandfather's shadowy garage. Behind the garage was the tank, and the tank was where her mother . . .

She rushed from the barn to the safety of the sunlight. She stooped forward and struggled to resume breathing. She was drowning on land, gulping dry air. She willed herself not to vomit.

"My dear, are you all right?" Abigail asked.

Daisy coped with the mechanism that soothed her as a child during her anxiety attacks; she silently recited a nursery rhyme.

One, two. Buckle my shoe . . .

Daisy lowered her hands and focused to steady her breathing. Now was not the time to panic.

"I just remembered . . . "

"You just remembered what, dear?"

Mrs. Wendworth waited expectantly for an answer from her silent guest. The girl's pallor indicated the memory she was recalling was not a pleasant one.

Daisy stuttered. "I'm . . . I'm . . . allergic. Cats make me wheeze."

"Well, it's a good thing I got rid of most of them. Let's go back into the house and finish our talk. Can I get you to close the door, please?"

Daisy squinted into the barn. Her eyes followed the cat as it crept across the loft. She thought she saw—no, it *couldn't* be— Lucy? She blinked. The image of a girl kneeling next to a box vanished. She cast off the odd moment. Her eyes played tricks on her when she was overwhelmed. And yet . . .

Three, four. Shut the door . . .

Daisy closed the door with a thud.

"Come on dear, I think a cold glass of lemonade is in order. The sun's awfully hot."

Daisy gulped the refreshing juice. Disregarding the calories, she eagerly accepted a second glass. She had calmed herself in time; Mrs. Wendworth politely dismissed her young guest's peculiar reaction to the kitten.

"Now, back to business. I did give you a deposit, didn't I?" Abigail asked.

"Yes, two hundred and fifty. Thank you."

"Yes, well, in my rush to reserve the date, I forgot to ask you for the total amount. Liz will be quizzing me soon about it, so I best have the answer."

Daisy fidgeted in her chair. Discussing money was not her strong point. She did not want to lose her golden opportunity by estimating too high, nor did she want to sound unprofessional by quoting a low bid. She was determined to prove to her father that she could operate a successful studio.

Daisy stared at the cotton tablecloth while she calculated a proper quote. She gulped the last of the lemonade, and after she centered her glass on a floral motif, she answered with a boldness that surprised herself.

"Depending on how many final photos you want, the total would be one thousand dollars."

The tapping of Abigail's crooked fingers on the table was the only sound in the room for the next few seconds. Daisy scolded herself for quoting a ridiculous sum and was prepared to lower her bid by several hundred dollars when Abigail spoke.

"Settled. Now when Liz calls I'll have the proper amount to tell her."

Daisy's eyes widened in astonishment when her client accepted the estimate without any dispute.

One thousand dollars? Just like that?

She averted a second panic attack by releasing her hand from the glass and concentrated on her breathing.

Five, six. Pick up sticks . . .

"Anything else, dear?"

"I don't think so."

"Good. Then I will do what every grandmother of the bride is instructed to do on the wedding day."

"What's that?" Daisy asked.

Abigail chuckled. "Wear beige and keep my mouth shut."

CHAPTER 16

Tasha removed the diary her father had presented to her on her thirteenth birthday from the desk drawer. Overlapping pink and white hearts of various sizes decorated the cover, but the most important item was the lock. The lock ensured her innermost thoughts remained private, especially from her mother's prying eyes. Tasha always kept the diary in the same place but hid the key in different locations each time she closed the book. She skimmed her fingers over the door trim for the key and unlocked the diary.

She amused herself reading her early entries.

> School is so dumb. I'm saving my money for a bike. Dad took me out to eat today.

The daily recollections of a typical kid filled the pages. When she reached her fourteenth year, her diary became a source of venting her frustrations.

> I hate math and the teacher is no help. Bobby Kingsley likes Sarah instead of me, who cares! Mom smacked me in the face with her fist today.

Tasha read the last entry a second time. The large loops forming her cursive writing indicated a carefree flair, but reviewing the sentence pained Tasha as much as Doreen's punch had hurt her. Since Doreen's fist had pounded her daughter numerous times, Tasha would have likely forgotten the details about that day if she had not recorded it.

Tasha recalled June 8, 1992.

Her friends planned to celebrate the first day of summer vacation by hanging out in the park all day. No teachers, no parents, no rules. Each girl promised to pack sodas, snacks, and swimsuits. The beginning of perfecting their tans could not begin soon enough. They had laughed yesterday when they christened their day as Freedom Fest.

Tasha managed to scrounge up a few coins laying around the trailer, but she had not collected enough to buy a soda. She peered in the refrigerator and spotted a six-pack of Pfizz. Surely, her mother would not miss one. She reached for it, and as she turned to smuggle it into her backpack, Doreen's glaring eyes pierced hers.

"What the fuck do you think you're doing stealing my Pfizz?"

"The girls are going to the park today and everyone's bringing a soda—"

Doreen snatched the can. "First of all, you ain't everyone. Second of all, that's my soda. And third of all—guess what?—you ain't going."

"But Mom . . . "

"Just because school's out don't mean you're going to run your ass all over day and night. You've got chores to do. Clean up this shithole for starters."

"My friends'll be here in a few minutes. Can't I go and clean when I come back?"

The impact of Doreen's fist knocked her daughter to the floor. Tasha instinctively covered her head as she struggled to kneel. When she drew herself to her knees, Doreen's sneaker sole soiled Tasha's white tee-shirt with repetitive kicks. Tasha lay defeated, dissolving in a puddle of tears.

Doreen snapped open the Pfizz and stepped over her daughter. "Next time, ask before you make plans to run all day. Now get your ass up and wash those dishes."

Tasha flipped the page. The next entry was dated two weeks after that incident.

Well, I don't get to watch anything I want on TV
or even eat a snack unless she says so. I hate her!
Hate her. This is a shitty summer. All my friends
are having fun and I'm a slave. Mom sits on the
couch all day yelling at me to do this and that. I
HATE HER!

"Wow, and I was only fourteen."

Had she simply adapted to her mother's horrible treatment? Daisy had always told Tasha she had no idea the suffering their mother had inflicted on Lucy and her when they had been children. Tasha's diary entries began at age thirteen, but she recalled her mother's abuse toward her much earlier.

Tasha turned pages without bothering to review them. The contents had one reoccurring theme: her frustration dealing with her mother. Tasha wrote an entry on a clean page.

Jermaine Porter is the best! He was my first and
will be my only true love.

Her mother's shouting interrupted Tasha's addition of a red heart followed by *xxxooo*.

"Get your ass out here, Tasha!"

Tasha locked her diary, preserving her loving thoughts of her boyfriend. After hiding the key under her mattress, she walked to the living room.

Doreen pointed to the kitchen counter.

"Need you to get my Brandts and that roll of DigestAids."

The trailer's small open floor plan of a combined kitchen and living room space allowed Doreen to rest on the couch while spotting her Brandts on the counter next to the sink.

Lazy bitch, Tasha thought.

"Wow!" Tasha remarked as she tossed the pack and roll to Doreen. "They were easy to find."

"Shut that sarcastic mouth. This damn heartburn feels like my chest's ripping apart. I'm sick, damn it. Don't know why I have to remind you every single day. It's getting old."

It sure is, Tasha thought. *It sure is.*

CHAPTER 17

The next afternoon, a boy set out to complete a mission. Ty collected rocks from the gravel entrance to Westside Wheel Estates. Since Bryant had stolen his pellet gun, he decided to test his new slingshot. He had mastered the mechanics by denting the playground trashcan. Now he intended to perfect his newfound talent against a bigger target.

His rear still stung from the beating Dick had delivered for sassing his mother. If his mother ever discovered the siding estimate Jermaine had destroyed, Ty could only imagine the whipping he would receive. His pent-up frustration and anger led him to the source of his problem: the nutty lady in Trailer 12.

He searched for the biggest rocks he could find and filled his pants pockets and turned-up shirt hem. Even at eight years old, he knew the rocks would not damage the siding like the gun's pellets, but the sound *would* annoy the woman and teach her a lesson for messing with him.

He hid behind a small maple tree. The first rock missed the trailer. His temper ignited, and he loaded a bigger rock into the sling. He stretched the band and imagined the crinkled siding was the old hag's face. *Pop!* He jumped in excitement when the rock smacked the wall. Encouraged with his aim, he loaded a massive rock and hurled it into the air. Instead of a *pop*, he heard a shatter.

Ty's chin jutted forward. An eternity passed in a second as he observed shards of glass exploding from the expanding spider-web-like cracks spreading across the window. He hurried to empty his pockets of the ammunition. The trailer door swung open; it was *her*.

"What the hell? You trying to kill me?"

Doreen grabbed the boy by the collar and pounded the top of his head while shouting obscenities at him. Residents from nearby trailers gathered to witness the free entertainment of the angry kook beating on the boy. The teens laughed and pointed while shouting, "Whoop his ass!" as the retired folks waved their hands in disgust and retreated inside their homes.

Tasha spotted a crowd heckling and cheering as she drove into Unlucky Thirteen and turned to Jermaine. "Now what's going on?"

"Stop. Stop the car now!" Jermaine shouted.

He leapt from the car before Tasha braked to a full stop. He sprinted toward Doreen and jerked Ty from her grip.

"Just what the hell's going on?"

Ty wiped snot and tears on his sleeve, not caring that the little kids witnessed his humiliation. He rubbed the knot on his head as he watched his brother, his hero, confront the wicked tormentor from Trailer 12.

"That little bastard broke my window, that's what the hell's going on. Don't know why you damn people can't watch your kids." She pointed at Ty. "That brat should be in locked up in a reform school."

Jermaine advanced toward Doreen causing her to step backward.

"You've got no right to lay a hand on my brother. Told you that once before, you too damn dumb to remember?"

"Jer!" Tasha interrupted. "That's enough. I'll take care of this."

"By *this* I hope you mean your crazy old lady?"

Chuckles from the crowd quieted at the sight of Harold Jefferson's truck approaching the circus-like exhibition of flamed tempers. Since the amusement had ended, nobody stayed around for Jefferson's interrogation. Although the residents often fought with each other on a continuous basis, they bonded in silence when the owner inquired about incidents. Everybody respected the creed: *Snitches end up in ditches.*

The manager's presence prompted Jermaine's instruction for Ty to run home. The young boy lowered his head and dashed away with his slingshot swaying from his back pocket. With his brother out of harm's way, Jermaine focused on Tasha.

"Later, Tash."

Tasha opened her mouth to respond, but fell silent when Jermaine stepped toward her mother.

Jermaine glared at Doreen. "This ain't over."

Sometimes I do my own balancing.

Doreen ignored Jermaine to focus on Jefferson approaching her with a disgusted expression.

Tasha escaped to her room and opened *Outre.* Chapter Six: Karma. What goes around, comes around. She no longer believed in an unseen force balancing goodness and evil. If that theory were true, her mother could not have hurt so many people while avoiding every repercussion. Tasha tossed the book. She believed Jermaine. Sometimes the power to right wrongs existed within you, *if* you had the guts to do your own balancing.

"What're you going to do about that brat now?" Doreen shouted to Jefferson. "Busted my damn living room window. Blew splinters all over my couch. Damn near killed me."

Jefferson rubbed the sweat from his brow with his damp handkerchief. He had risen early, before the temperature and humidity combined into a withering sauna to clear brush from the back of the property. He returned with intentions to take a cool shower and relax. Instead, he discovered a rowdy audience encouraging the wild antics from the tenant he referred to as Straightjacket Twelve.

"Calm down and tell me what happened."

"Well, look over there and look here," Doreen waved her hands in wild motions. Her right hand pointed to Trailer 5 while her left thumb jutted back to her trailer. "That damn kid—"

Jefferson returned his handkerchief to his back pocket. "I said, calm down. I can't make no sense of what you're saying with all that waving going on."

"Just fix my damn window, and don't you think for one minute I'm paying for it. Not with half of the trailer park witnessing that little hoodlum breaking it."

"You got two weeks to cough up the eight hundred." He sneered. "Don't worry, I'll replace the window." He tipped his cap. "Have a good day, lady."

Doreen shouted, "Fuck you!" with her hands cupped around her lips.

When Doreen stormed into her trailer, she nearly tripped over Tasha sweeping the glass splinters into a mound.

"Make sure that damn glass is off the couch cushions. Christ, don't need to be cut all over just laying on my own couch." She clicked her tongue. "Now, do you see that damn bunch is nothing but trouble? Do you?"

"He's just a kid, Mom. Maybe a stupid one, but still a kid."

"You can stick up for those no-good darkies all you want. I don't want nothing to do with them. Nothing! No wonder my gut hurts all the time with this kind of stress."

Tasha shook the blanket. Glistening slivers, like miniature blades, dropped to the floor.

"Watch out where you're walking with your bare feet, Mom." She swept the floor for the second time. "Cuts on your feet take a long time to heal with your diabetes."

"Well, now that you remembered I'm sick, where's my shot? It's getting late."

Tasha dumped the glass in the trash bin. She prepared the injection while Doreen inspected the couch before she prepared her lounging space with her blanket.

"At least we're getting a breeze now," Tasha commented while looking at the empty sill. Even the humid air was a welcome relief from the cigarette haze.

"Yeah, big enough for that goddamn brat to sneak in and steal shit. Maybe your boyfriend can manage to keep an eye on that poor innocent child."

"Never said he was innocent, Mom. But he is just a kid."

"And a fucked-up one at that. Keep hanging with that bunch, Tasha. Maybe you'll be blessed with a little fucked-up darkie too. Wouldn't that just be special?"

Tasha squinted and shook her head, discounting the vile words spouting from her mother's lips.

Doreen struck a match to her Brandt. "Grab me a Pfizz. It's hotter than hell in here now."

Tasha handed the soda to her mother. She paused at the gap that used to secure a window and observed the depressing scenery. Broken lawn chairs, dented coffee cans over flowing with cigarette butts, and crushed beer cans filled the spaces between the trailers. Beyond this trailer, beyond Endover and Mason County, a life waited for her. She counted down the days to graduation. Her personal Freedom Fest could not arrive soon enough.

"Damn it! There's still glass on this blanket." Doreen threw the blanket to the floor. "Go get me a different one."

Tasha removed the blanket from her bed and tossed it to her mother.

"Gonna take a lot of quarters to wash this," Tasha remarked as she folded Doreen's blanket.

"Well, call your piece-of-shit father and tell him Lil Dumplin' needs cash. I sure as hell ain't got any."

"Keep it," Tasha replied. "I don't need a blanket."

I only need a way out.

Tasha gripped her pillow to calm the waves of nausea. For the past three mornings, her stomach rolled in vicious pangs. Cupping her hands over her mouth, she rushed to the bathroom. She made it in time to purge into the porcelain bowl, unlike yesterday when the vomit splashed on her feet. Tasha rinsed her mouth and washed her hands before returning to bed.

The alarm clock would not buzz for another forty minutes, giving her time to recuperate before getting dressed for school. She had never been sick like this before; the nausea eased after she ate her breakfast toast, and by noon, it vanished.

Her favorite black jeans' waistband was snug, but she decided to wear them anyway. The loose-fitting black tee-shirt and combat boots completed her outfit. She added a touch of blush to her pale cheeks.

Before loading her books into her backpack, she removed two ten-dollar bills from her cigar box. She reasoned that would be enough to drive to the drugstore in Bancor, where nobody would recognize her. Ten for gas and ten for a KnowNow home pregnancy test.

Tasha's fears mounted. *What would Jer say? What would her dad say?* And most frightening of all, she *knew* what her mother would say.

Tasha earmarked her savings for college tuition, her ticket out of Endover. Her father encouraged her to achieve good grades in high school to increase her eligibility for college scholarships. If she were pregnant—the first time she visualized herself as a mother—it would ruin her future. She would become a failure like the other young girls trapped in a dead-end town with no education and babies propped on their hips.

She decided if she were indeed pregnant, she would keep it a secret and use her savings to pay for an abortion, as much as that thought distressed her. It would take a long time to recoup her savings, but that was the only sensible solution. Sacrifice a few years to delay college enrollment instead of losing her freedom for the next eighteen years raising a child she would resent. Tasha considered herself fortunate to have a solution to her dilemma.

Her last class of the day ended, and she was relieved Jermaine had skipped the entire day so she could drive alone to Bancor. She felt no sense alarming him with her secretive purchase.

Tasha had learned in biology class that stress was a factor in delayed periods. However, she knew her body's rhythms. Her periods arrived with the precision of a finely tuned clock, and she had never skipped one in five years. The absence of one would not have been a concern if not for the morning sickness.

Dayton's Hometown Drugs was a hub in Bancor. Besides the pharmacy, it housed a gift shop and an ice cream parlor. Tasha dreaded buying the KnowNow there, but she had no choice. She swallowed her nervousness and pulled open the heavy antiquated wooden door. She jumped when a jarring ring announced her arrival, since she had forgotten about the old-fashioned bell fastened to the door. Luckily, only a pair of elderly women oc-cupied the ice cream parlor. After a quick glance at her, they resumed their visit.

Tasha roamed the store. She entered the WOMEN'S PERSONAL CARE aisle and quickly exited when she spotted a woman comparing prices of sanitary pads. The ancient wood planks creaked under her combat boots as she hurried to the COSMETICS aisle and waited for the woman to determine which brand would save her fifty cents. When the coast was clear, she strode past boxes of sanitary pads, tampons, and cramp relief aids to the home pregnancy tests.

What?

Behind a locked glass cabinet, the KnowNow tests hung in neat rows. A sign instructed customers to ask the pharmacist for assistance.

No. No!

Her crimson cheeks reflected in the glass, negating the need for the blush she had applied that morning. Heat spread across her chest as she clutched her purse strap. She had heard plenty of conversations in the locker room about purchasing the test, but not one of her classmates had ever mentioned the locked cabinet securing the KnowNows. She had expected to hurriedly complete the transaction and exit the store; this initiation of requesting the test had not been part of the plan.

She browsed the store until she found the courage to approach the pharmacist.

Two customers waited in line at the counter. Tasha was grateful the on-duty pharmacist was a young woman. Although Tasha did not recognize her, she assumed the female clerk would be less judgmental than the elderly man who usually assisted customers. Tasha feigned interest in the bandage display until the customers departed.

"What can I help you with?" The pharmacist's nametag indicated her name was JOYCE.

Tasha glanced sideways and behind her. Assured she was alone at the counter, she made her request in a rushed whisper. "A KnowNow test, please. My sister needs—"

"I'll get the key, but let's ring it up first. Then, we'll just put the receipt in this bag in the aisle."

Joyce's smile calmed Tasha. *I'm not the first nervous teen she's waited on.*

Tasha agreed. "Okay."

"Ten dollars, no tax."

Tasha unfolded the bill and eagerly placed it on the counter. After Joyce rang the purchase, she enclosed the receipt in a small white bag stamped with the Dayton's logo.

"I'll be with you in a minute," she assured the woman who had finally settled on which brand of sanitary napkins offered the best value.

Tasha followed Joyce with her head bent, averting the gaze of anyone who may recognize her. Tasha wrung her hands while Joyce opened the cabinet. A simple turn of the key seemed to take forever.

Joyce paused to check the expiration date on the carton.

Just throw it in the bag and let me out of here!

Joyce slipped the carton into the box.

Tasha reached for it, interrupting the pharmacist's attempt to fold the top of the bag.

"I got it. Thanks," Tasha said.

"You're welcome." Joyce winked. "Best wishes to your sister."

Tasha rushed from the store to her car. She read the instructions and tossed the carton before concealing the test stick in her purse. When she arrived home, she hid the stick in the cigar box on top of her cash.

Tasha contemplated with absurdity that despite her achievement of obtaining stellar grades, mundane drops of urine would determine her future.

Tasha silenced the alarm clock twenty minutes early the next morning. The nausea had arrived late in the night and disturbed her slumber. Her bladder was full, and there was no reason to delay the testing. She pulled on her robe and concealed the KnowNow in her pocket.

Tasha said a quick prayer to the God she did not believe in and sat on the toilet. Warm urine dripped over her fingers. She stopped the stream, adjusted the stick's position, and assured herself her aim was correct and finished urinating. Tasha rested the stick on the counter while she washed her hands. She recalled the instructions advised positioning the test on a level surface.

Satisfied that her mother was not yet awake, Tasha dashed into her room and locked the door. She set the test stick on her desk. The clock read 6:43. The longest ten minutes of her life ticked by.

She lay in bed and worried as all sorts of frightening scenarios raced through her mind. What if she were pregnant, or "knocked up," as her mother would say; would she have an obligation to tell Jermaine? What if he insisted they keep it? Even get married?

A fake altar and wild teenage hormones would clinch the door of her personal prison.

Tasha glanced at the clock. 6:51. Two minutes to wait.

She would look.

No!

No.no.no.no.no.

A blue positive sign indicated the news she dreaded. She hid the test inside her cigar box and rushed for the bathroom. This time the purging expelled her hopes and dreams.

Jefferson pounded on Trailer 12's door at ten o'clock.

"Window repair!"

Doreen secured her robe and knotted the belt. "Like he can't do this shit in the afternoon," she grumbled.

She opened the door to discover Jefferson toting his toolbox and a heavy roll of plastic.

"Plastic? Where's my new window?"

"Had to order it. Custom size for this trailer. I'll have it in the next week or two." He wrinkled his nose at the rotting odor emitting from the unwashed dishes filling the sink, counter, and table. "Keeps the flies out at least until then."

Doreen sulked on the couch.

"Sorry, lady, but I'm going to have to move that couch to get to the window."

Doreen grunted. "Fucking inconvenience, you should discount my rent for it. You know it?"

Jefferson measured the window and removed a utility knife from his toolbox. He sliced a sheet from the roll and secured it to the paneled wall with duct tape. The sucking sounds from the toothpick between his lips reminded Doreen of Al Campbell. She despised both men.

"Still waiting on my eight hundred. Maybe the next tenant will appreciate the new window."

"I got your money, smart ass. Still think the welfare whore ought to pay for it, but I got it."

Harold waited while she disappeared down the hallway. Doreen entered Tasha's room, opened the desk drawer, and removed the diary from its usual position on the cigar box. She gasped when she opened the lid and saw the KnowNow test stick resting on the cash envelope. She quickly counted eight hundred dollars and returned to the living room.

"Window's done." Harold stood back and examined the opaque plastic sheet secured with crooked strips of gray duct tape. "Well, as good as it gets for now."

Doreen thrust the cash toward him. "Count it if you don't trust me. I want a receipt. Not paying this bullshit twice."

Jefferson thumbed through the bills. "Looks like it's all here. You'll get your receipt."

Doreen held open the door. "Good. If you're done, get out."

Jefferson tucked the cash roll in his shirt pocket and lifted his tool-box and sheeting. "Always a pleasure, ma'am. Always a pleasure."

Doreen slammed the door and returned to Tasha's bedroom. She examined the test in a better light. There was no doubting the result; the positive plus sign dominated the tiny screen. Although Doreen wondered when Tasha had tested and how her daughter planned to solve the problem, she had no doubt her daughter carried the black boy's baby.

She slid the cash envelope under her mattress and then planted the KnowNow test in a kitchen drawer where Tasha would discover it. Doreen grinned as she imagined the mortified expression from her daughter when Tasha realized her mother knew her shameful secret. Did her daughter really think she could hide anything from her?

Doreen hoped the intelligence her daughter excelled with at school extended to her street smarts to get rid of the thing. Doreen felt no empathy for Tasha's situation. Her daughter deserved the predicament she faced for ignoring her mother's advice.

Doreen lit a cigarette and grinned when she contemplated Roy's reaction. Daddy's Lil Dumplin' really did it this time. *Screwed up her life in every sense of the word.* She chuckled. *'Screwed' is right.*

Doreen plopped on the couch to watch television. Through the opaque plastic, she recognized Jefferson stroll by.

"Just keep on walking, lard ass," Doreen said aloud to herself.

Harold Jefferson returned to his office and dialed the contractor.

"Jay, got a window I need you to order and install."

"Let me grab my paper and pencil, just a sec."

After documenting the measurements, Jay requested the trailer number.

"Trailer Twelve."

"Your straightjacket nutjob?"

Harold chuckled. "Yeah, she's nuttier than either of us could imagine. Remember that eight-hundred-dollar siding estimate I asked for?"

"Yeah, kinda stretched that one," Jay said. "But, you requested that amount."

The justification in the contractor's voice amused Harold.

"Well, I figured when I gave it to her, she'd get pissed off and move out, or even better, wouldn't have the money and I could evict her. But no, guess what Nutjob does?"

"No telling. What'd she do?"

"The stupid bitch just handed me eight hundred dollars cash!"

Jay joined Harold in laughter. Harold cradled the receiver on his shoulder to rub his ribs. He had not laughed this hard in years. "She . . . She demanded a receipt."

"*Naw!*"

Harold wiped tears from his eyes. "Oh my God, how damn stupid . . . "

"So, bad news: you're stuck with her. Good news: you've got a wad of cash," Jay said.

"Well, if you think I feel guilty, I don't. She's a pain in the ass.

But I would feel guilty if I didn't at least cut you a share. So when the window arrives—"

"Harry, you don't have to—"

"Oh, I want to. We'll wait and see how long it takes Straight-jacket Twelve to realize her cash was spent on fifty cents worth of putty."

"Remind me to wear a bullet-proof vest when I install that window, Harry."

"Shit," Harold chuckled. "You and me both."

CHAPTER 18

Daisy felt more alive than she had in a long time. She had pocketed additional cash from her baby-portrait assignments derived from the weekly *Mason County Press* ad paid with her father's generosity. Although the babies and toddlers were adorable, they were nearly impossible to pose. The only challenge worse than controlling wiggling children was Daisy's dodging the mothers' criticism for not capturing the ideal smile that faded faster than her camera's shutter speed.

Criticism had plagued Daisy her entire life and she had never been able to disregard the negativity hurled toward her. She had learned to cower and internalize the remarks that pierced her self-esteem. She remembered her mother's cursing when Daisy had asked for assistance in learning to tie her sneakers when she had just turned four.

"Jesus, just twist two loops and pull. How goddamn hard can it be?"
"Show me."
Doreen stepped around her daughter who sat on the floor, holding her shoe.
"You stupid brat. Put the damn shoe on your foot first. Wouldn't that be the smart thing to do?"
Daisy struggled to ease her foot into the shoe she had outgrown last year.
"It won't fit!"
"Then go barefoot, if you're that damn stupid. I ain't wasting my time with a goofy kid who ain't even smart enough to put on a shoe, let alone tie it."

Daisy recalled she had not learned to tie her shoes until age six after her sister had died and was no longer there to help her.

Doreen had not been the only vile influence on Daisy's formative years. Her earliest memory centered on her grandfather, Al, and the shameless faultfinding actions he used to exploit his granddaughters. Daisy could never forget the memory that plagued her night terrors.

She was three years old and had found a small discarded washbasin near the spigot of his garage. She decided to give her doll a bath, but she did not have the strength to turn the faucet handle. She wandered into the garage, carrying her doll and dragging the basin.

The old mechanic sweated as he replaced a bicycle wheel.

She raised her doll toward him. "Ganpa, help."

"Busy here. You blind or what?"

Al ignored her while he tightened the wheel nut.

"Baby want a bath." She stomped her foot. "Baby want now!"

"Your doll has its clothes on. You have to take them off for a bath, little dummy."

Daisy frowned. She struggled to pull the dress over the doll's head. She offered the doll to her grandfather. "You do it."

"How can a kid be so stupid all of the time? Can't you see the buttons?"

Al grinned at his magazine, Naughty Nymphs, *laying on his workbench before hoisting his granddaughter next to it. He removed the doll's dress and flung it beside her.*

"Okay, little dummy, let's get you ready."

He untied the shoulder straps of her sundress and ran his hands over her soft skin as it dropped to her feet. He yanked down her panties.

"Me not taking bath." Daisy pointed to her doll. "Baby."

"Have to check something first, then your doll gets a bath."

He shoved his fingers between her legs.

"Owie."

"Just checking."

He pulled her panties to her waist and tied the dress straps. As he lowered her to floor, he scolded her. "You're a bad girl. Next time don't say owie. You hear me?"

Daisy understood. She was too frightened to say no or risk her grandfather's reproach. She did not say *owie* the next time or during the numerous molestations that followed.

Daisy recalled so many incidents over the years when adults ridiculed her abilities. Her frustrated teacher, Mrs. Breckel, insisted she *sound out* unfamiliar words in reading class. If the letters on the pages jumbled in unpredicted patterns like a secret code, how could she decipher their meanings? Her instructor scolded her for being lazy and restricted recess time instead of identifying the underlying problem as dyslexia.

She lagged behind her peers in gym class and accepted her role as being the last kid chosen for team sports. When she tripped and fell, causing her team to lose a relay race, Mr. Johnson spewed his disappointment by hurling a callous remark to her among her classmates. "If you weren't so chubby, you could run faster!" Her classmates pegged her with the nickname Chubby Campbell and made oinking noises whenever she walked by. Since that day in fifth grade, Daisy dieted religiously and shed pounds along with her self-esteem.

When the fashionable girls at Greenville High sported French braids, Daisy practiced the technique daily until she had mastered the hairdo. Although the popular crowd never extended a friendship to Daisy, she was relieved the braid camouflaged her awkwardness and lessened the bullying. When her father complimented her new style, she continued to braid her hair long after she had graduated from high school.

Her father's approval meant everything to her, as he was the only nurturing person in her life. Now that he had given his blessing for her to participate in Amanda Spark's wedding, Daisy lit a joint and allowed herself to daydream about her success.

She imagined Mrs. Wendworth—Abby's—barn decorated in glowing strings of miniature white lights. White tulle draped in sheets from the rafters descended into spirals wrapped around the support beams. Sprays of pink calla lilies accented with white roses and carnations attached to the walls wafted a hint of floral scent in the warm afternoon breeze. The unity candles positioned at the portable altar awaited the bride and groom as they exchanged vows before a captive audience.

Daisy's lighting stands perfectly positioned captured the glowing beauty of the bride's vintage wedding gown. Its classic design rivaled Daisy and Lucy's childhood sketches of princess dresses.

If anyone could produce a smile from the bride, Mrs. Wendworth had assured Daisy it would be her. Daisy imagined Abigail and Liz heaping praise on her when they examined the proofs and observed with happiness how Daisy had captured Amanda's genuine smile in each frame. At the end of the day, Amanda thanked Daisy for her outstanding talent and admitted privately that only Daisy's expertise in capturing the day had made the barn wedding bearable.

Daisy dreamed of collecting the check for seven hundred and fifty dollars and flaunting it to her father before cashing it. Referrals from guests shaking her hand after the ceremony and requesting her card boosted the success of DC Studios.

Daisy blew away her insecurities in a cloud of marijuana smoke.

Success was hers; it was all within reach, and all she had to do was embrace it.

CHAPTER 19

Tasha's combat boots pounded the weak floor as she stomped into the trailer. She threw her backpack in the corner, not caring when it landed on a sealed bag of trash Doreen had neglected to haul to the dumpster.

"Why so happy?" Doreen asked.

"I flunked that chemistry test again."

Huh, Doreen thought. *Flunked two tests in one day.*

"Well I told you. Told you to sit your ass down and study instead of running. I don't know shit, do I? Don't ask me to feel sorry for you."

Tasha slumped into a chair and rubbed her temples. "Not now, Mom. Please."

Doreen grinned. *'Not now,' sounds better than KnowNow. Should have told the boy that.* "Not now."

"What's one test out of a hundred you take?"

"You don't get it," Tasha whined. "I need good grades to get into college. Win a scholarship. I had a straight-A average until this one test. One!"

Doreen lit a cigarette. "Better join the Reality Club. You ain't no better than anyone else in Endover. Blame your dad for planting big dreams in your head, especially when he ain't got the money to send you."

Tasha shot back. "Well, he *had* the money."

"Just what the fuck's that supposed to mean? What bullshit has he filled your pretty Lil Dumplin' head with?"

"Nothing, I just know. That's all."

Doreen smirked and turned up the television volume. "You

think you know all about me? Well, won't you be surprised what I know about you too."

Tasha squinted in puzzlement.

Doreen pointed toward the sink. "Maybe get those hands soaking in some sudsy dishwater; that'll calm you down. Get my shot and then get the hell out of my sight."

Tasha administered the injection.

She washed the dishes.

She swept the floor.

She sulked in her room.

Every day was the same boring routine. She had to escape.

She opened her diary and wrote a new entry.

> *I have to get out of here. Have to. Have to.*
> *Have to.*

Jermaine hesitated but knocked on the Ferch's door anyway. He prepared to hop off the pallets if the old lady answered. He was not in the mood to deal with her madness. He sighed with relief when Tasha opened the door.

"You busy? Wanna talk to you."

From the couch, Doreen shouted, "If that's Jefferson, tell him I ain't in the mood for his bullshit."

Tasha faced her mother. "It's Jer. I'll be back in a bit." Tasha's closing the door prevented Doreen's predicted rant. "What's up?" Tasha asked Jermaine.

"Not here. Let's go to the park."

Relieved to escape her argumentative mother, Tasha agreed. They rode in silence until Tasha parked the car in the usual spot near the altar.

"I've had a rough day, so I hope this isn't about that altar," Tasha said.

"It's about your old lady. Getting real sick of her shit, you know it?"

Tasha rolled her eyes. "Well, join the club."

Jermaine sat up straight in the seat. "It's bad enough she calls me *Darkie,* but when she's cussing and beating on Ty, that's where I draw the line. I'm fed up with her shit, I'm telling you."

Tasha gripped the door handle and bolted from the car without bothering to close the door. Jermaine jumped from the seat to follow her.

"What's wrong?" Jermaine asked. "It's not like you don't hate her too."

Tasha wiped away the beginning of a tear. "I flunked my chemistry test."

Jermaine shrugged. "So, it's only one test."

"*Jeez,* Jer. As much as you hate Mom, you sound just like her right now."

"Oh really?" He smirked. "Thanks."

"You don't get it. It's our junior year. There are no do-overs. School's gonna be out soon. I've earned straight *A*s since my freshman year. I need those grades to win a scholarship, or I can't go." She shook her fists. "Can't go!"

Jermaine kicked a discarded beer can. "I got no use for college. Don't make you no better than anyone else."

"I want out of this dirty town. Maybe you haven't lived here long enough to hate it like I do. How else can I get out if I don't go away for college?"

"You got big dreams, girl."

"What do you have if you don't have dreams? I'm not going to live the rest of my life wasting away in a shitty little town." She crossed her arms. "I won't!"

"Guess you will unless you run away with the circus."

Jermaine's grin disappeared when Tasha spun away from him. Her shoulders shook as she sobbed.

"*Aw*, listen." Jermaine wrapped his arm around her. "That school shit ain't all it's cracked up to be. I'll probably get a job slopping hogs down at old man Sampson's place. I heard he pays pretty good. Can't be that hard throwing a bucket over a fence. That suits me a lot better than sitting in some classroom, learning shit I ain't ever gonna use. You like math; get a job doing books in an office in Greenville. Every business needs a bookkeeper. College ain't the answer to everything, you just think it is."

He lifted her chin with his finger.

"*Aw*, c'mon, baby. It ain't that bad."

Tasha glanced away.

Oh yes, it is.

CHAPTER 20

Jenny prepared to toss Dan's newspaper when the ad for Bancor's annual flea market captured her attention. The massive ad spanning a fourth of the page announced the event had expanded to over three hundred regional dealers. Jenny recalled fewer than two dozen booths displayed their wares when the flea market began ten years ago. While scanning the vendors' names, Jenny hurriedly dialed Lorraine's telephone number. She hung up on the second ring when guilt consumed her. Jenny had invited Daisy since she was a little girl; shopping for antique bargains was one of the few activities they enjoyed together. Jenny had smoothed things out with Dan, and she intended to keep the peace. She called Daisy, who answered on the first ring.

"Daisy, it's that time of year again!"

"Hi, Jen. Not sure what you mean."

"May, Daisy. Bancor's flea market."

Daisy glanced at her calendar. She had highlighted Saturday 27, as if the date's significance would slip her mind. "When? This weekend?"

"Yep. I'm looking at the ad now. They expanded it to a four-day event this year. Over three hundred vendors. Starts Friday."

Daisy mulled the invitation. "I have the Spark's wedding to shoot on Saturday, so let's go on Friday. I hope you don't mind, but I do have to stop at Mrs. Wendworth's to check if the rental lights have been delivered."

Jenny hesitated. "*Ah*, yes, I guess that would be okay since I have Friday off work. I'll pick you up at seven. I want to get an early start before the good stuff gets picked over."

131

"That works for me."

Jenny hung up. Dan would be pleased she invited Daisy. Perhaps her contrived interest in her stepdaughter would smooth some of the rocky bumps in her marriage. At the very least, Jenny had gained a shopping companion.

Two days later, Daisy woke energized. After an invigorating shower, she tamed her long hair into a braid. While she waited for Jenny's arrival, she sipped coffee and made a list of items to search for at the flea market. She had finished writing *plush yellow lion with brown mane* when Jenny appeared at her doorstep.

"Come in, Jen. Just have to grab my keys."

"Great, 'cause I want to get there as quickly as we can. That ad listed all kind of goodies."

Jenny's jaw tightened when Daisy strolled to the kitchen sink instead of retrieving her keys. Daisy ran the tap to wash her coffee mug. Although she rotated the sponge inside the cup more times than Jenny could count, Jenny was not surprised when Daisy inspected it twice before she rinsed it. Using a flour-sack towel, Daisy repetitively wiped the mug's interior before drying the exterior surface. Satisfied the cup was in pristine condition, Daisy hung it on a peg inside her cabinet. Jenny exhaled an audible sigh as Daisy precisely folded the towel into thirds. Once Daisy was satisfied the corner hems matched, she draped it over the stove handle.

Jenny brushed her hand against the brocade fabric of the living room curtains. "Are these new?"

Daisy grinned. "Yes, and so are the pillows on the couch and the lamp."

Jenny cleared her throat. "You must be doing good, honey, to afford all these new things."

"Well, I did keep Mrs. Wendworth's check, remember?" she said and then applied lotion to her hands. "I'll get my keys now so we can get going."

"But didn't you earmark that money to pay some bills?"

Daisy tucked her business card, shopping list, and keychain into her pocket. "Well, I paid my utility bill. Dad got the rest."

Jenny clenched her jaw for the second time.

"All set," Daisy said. "Let's go find some bargains. I need to decorate my bedroom next."

The women walked to the car. Jenny started the ignition while Daisy picked lint from the passenger's cloth seat.

"Are there crumbs on that seat? I keep telling your father not to eat in my car."

"No," Daisy answered. "I just don't like getting fuzz on my clothes."

Satisfied the seat's cleanliness met her standards, Daisy climbed in and fastened the seatbelt.

"Your bib overalls are cute, Daisy. Wish I was young enough to wear them."

"I like them 'cause they have so many pockets. I can carry my list and my money. I hate dragging my purse through the whole grounds. Gets heavy after a while."

"Sure does."

Daisy shivered. "And the germs . . . You can't be too careful."

Jenny gripped the steering wheel and concentrated on the road.

"Can't believe you've never been to Mrs. Wendworth's," Daisy said. "She says she's sold eggs to half of the county."

"I buy my eggs at Kemp's," Jenny replied. "Always so much fun to run into Doreen there, you know."

Daisy ignored the remark. "Well, despite what Dad says, Mrs. Wendworth really is a kind woman, like the perfect grandmother." Daisy gushed with enthusiasm. "Bakes something different every time I'm there. Cinnamon rolls, pies, cookies . . . "

Jenny stole a sideways glance at her passenger. "It's a wonder she hasn't fattened you up yet."

"I said she bakes it, didn't say I ate any of it."

"Sorry, I only meant—"

"I know, I know." Daisy shunned the unintended insult to resume her focus directing Jenny to the farm. Her manic mood increased as they left Bancor and approached their designation. "Anyway, I'm going to show you the way to Mrs. Wendworth's, and I want you to tell Dad I didn't send you on a wild goose chase or get lost. He always complains about my lack of directions, but I'm getting better."

Jenny observed her stepdaughter's wild hand motions. "Well, sure you are."

Daisy leaned forward and pointed. "Follow the blacktop to the curve that goes left. Yep, that's it. Keep going 'til you see a gravel road with a yellow house."

Jenny observed Daisy loosening the slack of her seatbelt to move forward to the edge of her seat. Daisy's head rocked side to side as she scanned the gravel road searching for her designation.

"Pretty soon, we'll see it. Keep going, keep going," Daisy said. She clapped her hands. "There it is! The yellow house."

"That house was white with a sagging roof a few weeks ago," Jenny said. "Guess the homeowners made out better than the farmers did with the hail damage claims."

Daisy giggled. "I'm glad it's yellow. Makes it easier to find, at least for me."

When Jenny approached the fork in the road, she turned right unto a gravel road without Daisy's prodding.

"Now, stay on this road for about five miles. The farmhouse is white," Daisy instructed. She pointed as they approached Mrs. Wendworth's farm. "Here we are. That's her house."

The two dogs barked their excitement, but their movements were restricted to the clothesline by chains attached to their collars. Three young women shared cigarettes on the porch, oblivious to the dogs announcing the vehicle parking in the driveway.

"Looks like Amanda Sparks is here. Finally get to meet her," Daisy said.

"I'll wait in the car, if you don't mind."

"No problem. I won't be long."

Daisy removed her business card from her pocket and approached the smokers.

"Hi. Is Mrs. Wendworth home?"

The blonde pushed her Christian Dior sunglasses to the top of her head. "She's busy. And you are?"

"Oh, I'm sorry," Daisy apologized and handed her business card to the woman. "I'm Daisy Campbell. Are you Amanda?"

"I'm Amanda. What does this cheap card have to do with me?"

Daisy swallowed hard and ignored the smirks from the woman's companions.

"*Ah*, I'm here to check on the lighting."

Amanda crossed her arms and tilted her head. "I'm afraid, Country Bumpkin, I don't understand bumfuck language. Can you enlighten me a bit? Now, I know that's a big word." She uncrossed her arms and created a slow, stretching motion with her fingertips as if she were pulling taffy until her hands were separated by a foot-long gap.

Daisy cringed as her card blurred into a white streak clutched between Amanda's blood-red manicured nails.

"Enlighten means, tell me what the fuck you're talking about."

The short woman standing next to Amanda laughed. "Mandy, you are too funny."

Daisy's face reddened to a shade darker than Amanda's nail polish.

One, two. Buckle my shoe . . .

"Your grandmother, Mrs. Wendworth . . . "

Amanda exaggerated a nod. "Yes, I know my grandmother's name."

The third woman joined the attack. "Amanda, are you *sure* that old lady in the house is your grandmother?"

Amanda threw back her head and laughed. "I guess I didn't realize that until the country bumpkin just told me. Nice bibs, by the way. Are they Guess?"

Three, four. Shut the door . . .

Daisy gulped. "She . . . She hired me to photograph your wedding."

Amanda glanced at the business card. "DC Studios. Take a look at this, Staci."

Staci accepted the card and torched the corner with her cigarette. She flung it to the ground when the flames engulfed the card. "Not wrecking my Manolo Blahnik's crushing out that fire."

"Staci," Amanda stated, "is the owner of Faces in Manhattan. Perhaps you've heard of her studio? The best in New York."

Five, six. Pick up sticks . . .

Daisy's business card burning on the ground prompted Jenny to approach the women. As she neared the porch, Mrs. Wendworth and a woman who was the older version of Amanda stepped outdoors.

"Jenny! So glad to see you," Mrs. Wendworth said. "Tell me, was the six dozen eggs enough for the Early Risers Club breakfast?"

Jenny shot a quick glance at Daisy but did not respond to Abigail.

"Mother, we have enough to do," Liz scolded. "Why are you selling eggs when we are preparing for the wedding?"

"Not selling anything, dear. This here is my church friend, Jenny. And I hired Daisy to photograph the wedding." She grinned at Daisy. "I see you've met Amanda. Now we're all set."

Liz slapped her forehead. "Oh, for Pete's sake, Mother. Another vendor to cancel? When will you learn to stop meddling?"

"It's okay, Mom," Amanda replied. "Miss Country Bumpkin here was just fired. One less fumbling idiot to worry about."

Abigail tapped her cane on the porch floor. "Amanda! Manners?"

Seven, eight. Lay them straight . . .

Daisy sprinted to the car. After offering Abigail a shrug, Jenny trailed her stepdaughter.

"I'm so sorry, honey—" Jenny said as she climbed behind the wheel.

"Go," Daisy whimpered and buried her face in her hands. "Just go."

Jenny shifted into Drive and returned an awkward wave to Abigail as they departed from the farm.

Nine, ten. A big fat hen . . .

A big fat failure.

Again.

"Dad? Come over please!" Daisy pleaded into the telephone receiver.

"*Aw*, honey, I just got home from work. Haven't even showered yet. Can't you drive over?"

"No. I have to talk to you without Jenny around."

Dan covered the receiver to stifle his groan. He exhaled his exasperation before resuming the conversation. "Then come over, she left with a friend to shop in Bancor. Her note here says she won't be home 'til seven or so."

"You sure?"

"Yes, I'm reading it right now. Drive carefully and come over."

Dan showered and cracked open a Red's as he waited for his daughter's arrival. He hoped her latest crisis was one he could solve in a few minutes. The long day of banging out vehicle dents at Gleason's had exhausted him, especially when Kevin insisted their heavily logged schedule validated working on a Saturday of a holiday weekend. Reading Jenny's note had guaranteed him a few hours of solitude, but Daisy's latest catastrophe interrupted his plans.

Before he could open the second beer, Daisy marched into the kitchen. Her red, puffy eyes indicated to Dan she had been sobbing for hours.

"Honey, whatever's wrong? Can I get you a drink or somethin'?"

Daisy shook her head and flung her purse on a chair. She pointed to the Bancor Annual Flea Market ad laying next to Jenny's note.

"This! This is what's wrong!"

Dan scoured the ad in puzzlement. "What's the hell's so bad 'bout a flea market? Thought you and Jen liked goin' to them."

"That's just it. We do. We were going to . . . but then, she . . . It was awful, Dad. Just awful!"

Daisy jutted her bottom lip, and her tears raining down her cheeks reminded Dan of her frequent childhood outbursts.

"What happened at the flea market?"

Daisy answered between sobs. "Nothing. We didn't go."

Dan sipped his beer and leaned forward. "Sorry, but you're losing me."

She wiped her nose with a napkin. "Me and Jenny were going to the flea market yesterday. But I said I had to stop at Mrs. Wendworth's to check on the lights, and Jenny was okay with that."

"Wait a minute. It's Saturday. Ain't you supposed to be takin' pictures at that wedding today?"

"Suppose to." Daisy thumped her fists on the table. "Suppose to, until Jenny wrecked it!"

Dan combed his fingers through his hair. Daisy's frenzied behavior contributed more gray strands as he struggled to understand his daughter's quandary.

"What do you mean? How could Jenny have anything to do with it?"

"She lied. Said she didn't know Mrs. Wendworth. Told me she's never been there before." Daisy pounded her temples with her fists. "But she lied! She lied!"

Dan gently wrapped his hands around his daughter's wrists and lowered her arms.

"Calm down, Daisy," he whispered.

"I . . . I told her to turn by the yellow house. And I didn't think much of it then, but Jenny . . . she said it was white not long ago before the insurance company paid for new siding. And then, then we get there, and Mrs. Wendworth asked her if she picked up enough eggs for the church breakfast."

Dan slapped his palms on the table. "What?"

Daisy jumped at her father's reaction. "The second time I went there to return the check, only I didn't, right? You know that time?"

"Yes, but—"

Daisy interrupted. Her words spilled from her mouth faster with each sentence. "Mrs. Wendworth had two business cards on her refrigerator, but I only gave her one. Honest. I didn't say anything because, well, they are thin, and sometimes they stick together. But they cost a lot so I'm careful. Careful. I know I only gave her one. Honest."

"So, you're saying?"

"Jenny wrecked it for me. And Dad, Amanda was awful. Just awful! Made fun of me and called me names in front of her friends while Jenny just sat in the car and watched."

"And you think Jenny put them up to this? On purpose?"

"She wrecked everything. Everything. I don't have a job because of her. I lost over seven hundred dollars. Seven hundred! I don't have the money to pay back the deposit. Jenny. Jenny did this to me!"

Dan held his sobbing daughter. "Daddy'll take care of it, honey. Both things. The money and Jenny. I promise you that."

Dan quenched his thirst and frustration by drinking his six-pack of Red's by the time Jenny breezed through the door, carrying two paper bags.

"Fun shopping today?" he asked.

"Oh, Bancor's flea market is always great. Lorraine and I found real bargains. Look at this antique coffee jar and these postcards. Could have filled a truckload of furniture, there was so much there to see."

Dan rubbed his chin. "Glad you had a fun time. Daisy says she never made it there with you yesterday."

Jenny rinsed the coffee jar in the sink. "Daisy was here?"

"Oh yeah. Seems she got cut out of a wedding job today. Don't suppose you know anythin' 'bout that?"

Jenny spun around and faced her husband. "I don't like your tone of voice or what you're implying, Dan. What crazy talk has she filled you full of this time?"

Dan slammed his fist on the table. "Don't ever . . . Don't you *ever* refer to my daughter as crazy. Got that?"

Jenny carefully set the coffee jar in the dish drainer, away from her husband's outburst. "Well, what do you consider her seventy-two hour visits at Melville to be about? It's not a resort."

"How 'bout you tell me about your cozyin' up to that old hag and settin' my daughter up?"

"Oh my God." Jenny smirked. "What nonsense bullshit am I getting blamed for now?"

"Honest truth, Jen. Did you set it up for Daisy to go to that old hag's house in the first place? Yes or no?"

"It wasn't like that."

"Yes or no?"

Jenny threw back her head and exhaled a deep breath. "Abigail mentioned at church that her granddaughter was getting married, and she had to hire a florist, caterer, and a photographer. I thought it would be a good opportunity for Daisy, and I gave Abigail her business card. Isn't that why Daisy gave us her cards? To hand them out?"

Dan crossed his arms. "Go on."

"Well, at the same time, Abigail said she would donate eggs for the Early Risers Club breakfast if I would stop and pick them up. So, I did. End of story."

"You sent Daisy there knowing I hate that damn family?"

"It was to help her. For Christ's sake, Dan, she can't hold a job. I was only trying to help her."

"Help her? *Huh.*"

Jenny wagged her finger inches from Dan's nose. "I get my ass out of bed every morning whether I feel like it or not to run the cash register at Delores's while hustling tables and working in the kitchen. I'm fifty-two and been doing it for years. Daisy couldn't even handle a register at Kemp's longer than two days. I'm tired of her bullshit. I work, and she can too, damn it!"

"You know she has problems . . . "

"Well, hell yes, I know. Most of my paycheck goes toward her bill at Melville. Her check-ins are so frequent, it's like a revolving door. All that money spent and for what? For what?"

"You sent Daisy to the house where Lucy was killed, knowin' I was set against it."

"She needs to stand on her own two feet, Dan." Jenny splayed her fingers on her right hand. "She's twenty-five, not five."

"She's *my* daughter."

"And it's my mistake thinking I could take care of the two of you. But you don't need *me*, Dan. No, you only need *your* daughter. And *your* daughter only needs *my* paycheck!"

Dan's hard slap stung his wife's cheek.

He locked eyes with her, both stunned by his action. As his wife rushed away, cradling her jaw, Dan slumped in a chair and covered his face in shame.

CHAPTER 21

Tasha rolled unto her back and stretched diagonally across her bed. The early morning nausea assaulted her stomach with repetitive pangs, as steady as ocean waves crashing against a rocky shore. She resisted the urge to stroke her belly to lessen the pain. Caressing her abdomen was too similar to a nurturing gesture. Tasha was not carrying a life; her body was concealing a problem.

She recalled the hushed whispers in the girls' locker room last year when Jackie Gardner disclosed that her problem-solving procedure had cost three hundred dollars. Although the monetary amount was astronomical for any teenager to raise, obtaining the funds was the first major hurdle. Boarding a bus and traveling two states away to the only certified hospital performing the operation was the second obstacle. Endover teens unable to overcome both barriers prepared for unwelcomed motherhood with or without a wedding band.

Tasha mentally calculated the costs. Her nine hundred dollars would cover the expense. She could explain her two-day absence and roundtrip bus fare by announcing her excitement to visit regional colleges. Although she was only seventeen, she was confident the fake ID she had purchased from the guy in Trailer 9 would pass at the hospital since it had always been effective at the area liquor stores. She realized she would need to act soon before her first trimester ended. She gained confidence making the preparations; she would dig herself out of this mess.

Tomorrow after school she would drive to Bancor and buy a bus ticket at the depot.

At least the first step will be easy.

She opened her desk drawer. She lay her diary on her desk top and opened the cigar box.

The box was empty.

Empty?

She remembered tucking the cash and the test inside the box, but perhaps in her haste, she had forgotten last time. Tasha removed the drawer from the desk, hoping the KnowNow and her money envelope had somehow fallen behind it.

Empty.

Her mother had predicted a burglary with the temporary window repair. Tasha dashed to inspect the window. She flipped on a light and saw no signs of tampering. The ugly gray duct tape remained in its original position pressed to the paneling.

Tasha sunk in a chair. She was not sure which stolen item she was more concerned about. Since Doreen never entertained and Tasha's shame prevented her from inviting friends into the trailer, Tasha knew without a doubt the thief's identity.

Mom.

Tasha drew her knees to her chest and wrapped her arms around her legs. The queasiness soured her stomach. She lowered her head and closed her eyes. The dizziness would pass, but this betrayal would not.

My money. My secret.

"Why in the fuck do you have the lights on so damn early? Woke me up."

Her mother's high-pitched voice pierced Tasha's eardrums like an ignited string of firecrackers.

"You sleeping or what?" *Pop pop pop pop!*

My money. My secret.

Tasha raised her head. "Not sleeping."

"Well, then why ain't you getting ready for school?" *Pop pop pop pop!* "Where's my coffee? *Pop pop pop pop !* "Jesus, you get up this damn early and don't put no coffee on?"

Tasha eyed her mother. In a tone barely louder than a whisper, she asked, "Where is it?"

Doreen lit a Brandt and waved the match to extinguish the flame. "Where's what?"

Tasha stood. "You know."

"Get some damn coffee brewing and quit talking nonsense."

My money. My secret.

"You took it. Why? Why?" Tasha shrieked. "I saved that money for years. Years!"

Doreen blew smoke from both nostrils. Tasha could not help but notice how much her mother resembled a gargoyle in the early morning light.

"I didn't take shit. I borrowed it to keep a roof over your head. Fucking Jefferson threatened to evict us over your darkie boyfriend's brother pulling bullshit."

"You stole it! You stole it, and I want it back!"

"Blame that little asshole with the pellet gun. Have his whore mother pay you."

"I want it back . . . I *need* it back."

Doreen opened a kitchen drawer. She tossed the KnowNow to Tasha. "Is this the reason you need it back? A little rye bun in the oven?"

Tasha's anger erupted into tears. She jabbed the test strip like a miniature sword toward her mother. "You. You!"

Doreen slapped the test from her daughter's hand.

"What's Daddy's Lil Dumplin' going to do about it? If it wasn't for that piece of shit losing the farm, you'd be living in that big ole ranch. I'm doing what I can to keep a goddamn roof over your head, and that's the thanks I get? Jesus fucking Christ!"

Tasha glared at Doreen. The instant hatred exploding in Tasha toward her mother frightened her; perhaps it had been simmering all along. Never had she felt such disgust toward another human being. She no longer recognized the woman sneering at her. Doreen Ferch resembled a creature in a horror movie, except this monster was real.

Tasha retreated from the argument by slamming her bedroom door. She ran her fingers over the cover of *Outre* as Jermaine's words replayed in her mind.

You just ain't been wronged enough yet to take matters into your own hands. When it happens to you, you'll do the balancing. I promise you that.

Tasha dressed in her black wardrobe and laced her combat boots. Usually her anger clouded her thoughts, but not this time. An affinity as clear as the miniature crystal ball resting on her desk spoke to her.

Her plans were not derailed, just altered. She would not allow this major setback to defeat her. Every soldier's training included identifying and eliminating the enemy.

Her enemy's name was *Mom*.

Jermaine believed in balancing, but Tasha believed in cleansing.

A flutter in her belly, as subtle as a butterfly expanding its wings, reminded Tasha there was no time to waste.

The purification ritual involved planning, and she would convince Jermaine to assist her.

Tasha grinned.

She imagined a life with no mother.

It was easy.

CHAPTER 22

Unlike most people, Daisy looked forward to Mondays. Her cleaning routine provided serenity and relieved her anxiety in a manner the marijuana never did.

The dusting ritual always started with her bookcase. She removed the books from the highest shelf. After spraying furniture polish—always lemon scented—onto her cloth, she wiped the shelf in six circular motions before tackling the corners. The difficulty of cleaning the corners infuriated her. No matter how many times she pushed the cloth deep into the crevices, she never achieved her desired level of cleanliness. She rarely entertained visitors, but she knew the filth caused them to project bad thoughts about her, even if her guests did not voice their disappointment.

She continued dusting until she had completed the second and third shelves. The next task was to return the books in their specific order: the highest shelf contained the blue books; the middle shelf held the green volumes; and lastly, the bottom shelf displayed the red covers. Satisfied with the fixed arrangement, she had focused her energy on dusting the coffee table when the doorbell buzzed. Since she was not expecting company, she prepared to tell the door-to-door salesman she was not interested in whatever product he was selling.

She opened the door.

"Jenny?"

Her stepmother stood with her arms crossed. Daisy recognized the angry look Jenny reserved for arguments with her father.

One, two. Buckle my shoe . . .

"Mind if I come in?" Jenny asked as she stepped past Daisy.

Daisy closed the door.

"*Huh,* noticed you aren't asking me why I'm here. Because you know, don't you?"

Daisy raised her shoulders with upturned palms. The wild look in Jenny's eyes frightened her.

Three, four. Shut the door . . .

"Did you really think your dad wouldn't tell me about your blaming me because you didn't take the wedding photos? *Huh,* really? What did I have to do with it? You liar."

Daisy struggled to breath. Her chest heaved as her panting grew louder. She paced in a circle while rapidly rubbing her palms. Her knees weakened, and she slumped into her chair to prevent collapsing on the floor. She leaned forward and rocked.

"Stop the crazy act! It only works on your dad, not me. I'm sick of paying for your little field trips to Melville. If I had my way, I'd send your ass there for good."

Five, six. Pick up sticks . . .

Jenny jabbed her finger toward Daisy. "If you ever, and I mean *ever,* fill your dad's head full of bullshit lies about me again, I swear I'll reserve you a permanent bed at Melville. Got that? And get a real job, join the adult world, and quit freeloading off your dad and me."

Seven, eight. Lay them straight . . .

"So, you're just going to cower and not say a damn thing? Fine. I'm done here, and I'm done with you."

Nine, ten. A big fat hen . . .

Jenny slammed the door.

Daisy rushed to her bookcase and hurriedly yanked the books from the top shelf. She wiped the space in six circular motions and cleaned the corner crevices twice before replacing the blue volumes.

Jenny had seen the dirty corners. That's why she was so angry.

Daisy vowed to do better next time.

CHAPTER 23

"Sorry, Dad, but I already made plans for tonight. How about tomorrow?"

"Well, I was looking forward to tonight, but let me check my social calendar," Roy joked. "Looks like tomorrow's going to work. Pick you up about five?"

"Sure," Tasha answered. "Thanks for understanding, Dad."

"You might not believe this, Dumplin', but I was young once too. I know what it's like. At least I think I remember."

"Oh Dad, you're not that old. Yeah. Five works. See you tomorrow."

Tasha hung up and immediately dialed Jermaine.

"We still on tonight?"

"As far as I know," Jermaine said. "I cancelled my other date. So, yeah."

"Funny, asshole. I have some serious shit going on. I'll pick you up in a half hour. Be ready."

"Aye, aye, captain."

Tasha pulled her tight, black tee-shirt over her head and flung it into the hamper. She chose to wear her loose-fitting blouse instead. She did not need Jermaine to notice her recent modest weight gain. She had not yet decided if she would tell him her secret; it all depended on his willingness to help her.

"Heading to Delores's or the park?" Jermaine asked when he jumped into the car.

"The park, or rather the woods behind it. Need privacy. Not going to get that at the diner, with farmers and their wives lingering over fish and fries."

"Well, that combo does sound good, you know it?"

Tasha uttered a *tsk*. "Get serious, Jer."

Jermaine raised his palms. "My, my. What's making you so crabby?"

Tasha parked the car near the altar before answering. "My mom."

Jermaine chuckled. "How's that news?"

"She did something I can never, ever forgive her for."

Jermaine arched his left eyebrow. "Like calling me *Darkie* and pounding on my brother ain't enough. What'd she do to piss you off?"

Tasha turned to face Jermaine. "Stole my money."

"Wow!"

"Yep. Nine hundred dollars."

"Holy shit, Tash. Where'd you get that kind of money?"

"Been saving it for years. My dad gives me money for birthdays and Christmas and sometimes in between. Some of it was my babysitting money." She slapped her thighs and continued, "Doesn't matter now 'cause she stole all of it."

Jermaine rubbed his hand over his lips. "So, did she say anything about it? She knows you know, right?"

"She knows." Tasha formed quotation marks with her fingers. "Borrowed it."

"Let's get out of the car. I need some air."

Tasha followed Jermaine to the altar. He rubbed his hand across the bricks. "Don't look like anyone's been back here."

"Don't care about that. What am I gonna do?"

"Well, shit. If my old lady stole that kind of money from me, I know what I'd do. Balance her ass right on the spot."

"But you'd get caught. Then you'd be punished instead of her."

"Told you once before, Tash. People only get caught 'cause they can't keep their trap shut. Best to handle your own shit; you don't get caught that way."

"But what if you needed help?"

"If you're going to do real damage, like take someone out, it's best to do it alone. Just talking about it makes you a conspirator. That guy gets as much of a sentence as the guy who committed the crime. Who's gonna take that risk?"

Tasha hooked her fingers through Jermaine's belt loops and pulled him close. "Someone who cares about someone else."

She leaned forward and kissed him.

Jermaine squeezed her tight before releasing his embrace. "You know I'd do anything for you. But you know my rule: keep your mouth shut."

Tasha's memory of Doreen's sneer infuriated her, and she walked a few steps away from Jermaine. "She has to pay for what she's done. Damn bitch. I'm pretty much used to her yelling and slapping, but stealing from me? She didn't even have the guilt to lie about it. Somehow, I would've respected her for lying about it, if that makes any sense, but she just gloated about it." Tasha cocked her head and raised her voice an octave. "Like no big deal."

"You wanna make it a big deal?"

Tasha nodded.

"Then keep your mouth shut. It's the only way I'll help you."

Jermaine wrapped his arms around her as she promised, "My lips are sealed."

He smiled. "Well, maybe don't seal them so tight I can't kiss them. You still got that blanket in the back seat?"

"*Uh-huh.*"

They held hands as they walked to the car. When Jermaine returned Tasha's initial soft pecks with ravenous kisses, she seized the advantage of his sexual craving. Tasha sealed the deal by pleasuring Jermaine, who burst into ecstasy as he gladly lost control. They lingered in a silent embrace for a few minutes as she stroked his chest.

Her whisper broke the silence. "You'll help me?"

"Keep cool. We'll think of something."

Tasha grinned. "I know we will."

Roy honked his usual signal announcing his presence at Trailer 12. As he promised his daughter, he arrived on time for their dinner date.

"Dad's here!"

"Too bad his ass can't come to the door like a real gentleman," Doreen said.

Tasha retrieved her handbag from the closet. "Don't know why I'm bothering to take my purse," she sneered. "Not like there's any money in it."

Doreen exhaled cigarette smoke. "I'm sure Daddy No Bucks will treat his little girl just fine. Might want to mention your flunking two tests on the same day."

Tasha refused to dignify her mother's insult with a reply. She exited Doreen's sarcasm to greet her father.

"Hi, Dad."

"Howdy. Let's drive up to Bancor for a real treat. What'll you say?"

"Sure."

Roy reversed his truck while looking at his rearview mirror. He guided his steering wheel to the left to avoid striking a mangy black dog content to rest in the lane's center. As his truck lunged forward, he watched a girl scold the dog. The girl's kick thwarted the mutt's feeble attempt to hobble away. Roy observed the dog's unnatural gait was due to the stray's missing rear leg. He did not speculate how the mutilation had occurred; any horror was possible at Unlucky Thirteen.

Roy concentrated on entering the highway, leaving the poor dog behind to suffer the girl's maltreatment.

"How's summer vacation? Looking forward to your senior year?"

Tasha gazed from the window at rows of crops swaying in the breeze as they accelerated down the highway. Cornfields alternated with soybean fields in a landscape filled with a green redundancy that farmers called *income*. She referred to it as *boring* and wondered if she would ever experience skyscrapers illuminating the metropolitan landscape and welcoming her to a bright future.

"Haven't been doing much. Mom keeps me busy cleaning and driving her around. Mostly just hanging with my friends."

"You finish the year with straight *A*'s again?"

She resumed staring at the fields. They mocked her with their permanence. Many family farms spanned generations. Plain folks content to live off the land and never stray more than a hundred miles from their homesteads during their lifetimes. She could imagine no bleaker existence.

"Well, no."

Roy could not disguise the surprise in his voice. "No?"

"I flunked chemistry."

Roy squeezed her knee. "It happens, Dumplin'. Don't get all down about it. Hell, I know I ain't smart enough to pass half of the classes kids have nowadays."

"But I want to go to college. Get away from here. There's no future in slopping hogs or milking cows."

Roy winced.

"Sorry, Dad, but you know what I mean."

The cycle of the corn crop sustaining the cows that produced milk sold to dairies held generations captive to their land like a criminal pointing a gun to their heads. Mason County was void of art museums, symphonies, or any sign of culture found in the urban populations. Life stagnated as the old were too tired to leave and the young were too naïve to venture beyond the barbed-wire fences to discover excitement. Tasha believed a better life existed, and she was determined to find it.

"I know what you mean. I wish I could have provided better for you. But I was a fool, a fool in love. There's a lesson for you right there. Don't be fooled by love."

Tasha rubbed her belly. "Don't worry, I'm not that disillusioned."

"Let's hope not, at least not yet."

Roy parked his truck in the rear parking lot of Sebastian's to avoid the valet.

When they rounded the corner to the entrance, Tasha exclaimed, "Wow, Dad. This is a fancy place. I should have worn better clothes."

"Nonsense. You're fine. You'd just wear your other black outfit." Roy playfully stuck out his tongue and opened the restaurant door while motioning for his daughter to enter.

The hostess' greeting silenced Tasha's retort. "Table for two?"

Roy removed his cap. "Yes, please."

The pair followed the hostess to a small table.

As she placed the menus on the table, she said, "Your waiter, James, will greet you in a minute."

Tasha surveyed the restaurant's ambiance of heavy wooden tables situated around a fireplace constructed of multi-colored stones. Diamond-patterned woven valances framed the multitude of windows. Endless white faux candles lighted the brass chandelier. Tasha grinned when she noticed the wall sconces were miniature replicas of the huge chandelier. As she admired the wallpaper on the far wall, the hostess seated a couple at a nearby table.

Joyce the Pharmacist! Tasha turned her head and gulped water from the crystal goblet. *What if Joyce said hello? How would she explain meeting the woman to her father?*

"Where are the restrooms?" Tasha asked.

Roy glanced from the menu. "Towards the back, follow that aisle."

Tasha wasted no time rushing from the table. Inside the safety of the restroom, she splashed cold water on her face. Tasha's reflection grew pale when she reached for a paper towel and saw

Joyce approach the long vanity. Tasha remained silent when Joyce paused to apply lipstick.

"Hi," Joyce said in the casual manner strangers use to greet one another. She disappeared in a stall not waiting for a reply.

She doesn't remember me.

Tasha dried her face and rushed back to the table.

"You hungry?" her father asked.

"I am now."

James appeared and refilled the water goblets. After reciting the special, he jotted their orders on a small pad. With the menus tucked under his arm, he assured his guests their meals would arrive shortly, and he strolled away.

"You must be doing good at the hardware store, Dad, to afford a place like this."

"Oh, I've been saving up. It's important to save your money. Then you can get the things you really want, the things that matter. You're still saving for college, right?"

My money. My secret.

"Yeah, Dad. I'm always saving."

"Well, then I've done my job as a father to instill that value in you. Never let anyone balance your accounts or handle anything you can do yourself. Trust me. I learned that the hard way."

Balance your accounts.

"I know. Too bad Mom stole your money like that."

"Maybe *squandered* is a better word, but yeah, water over the dam. Can't live in the past."

James returned with two salads and a breadbasket. "Your entrees will arrive shortly. Enjoy."

He balanced the huge tray on his palm and approached Joyce's table to serve her and her guest.

"Dad, what would you do if someone hurt you real bad?"

Roy buttered a breadstick. "Why would you ask such a thing?"

Tasha shrugged. "Just wondering. What would you do—forgive them or get even?"

"Well, it depends on the severity of their actions. I'd like to say forgive them, but that's not always easy. Get even? I've never been the revengeful type either. Best to just let things be, I guess."

Tasha twirled her fork. "Don't you think some people deserve to be punished?"

"That's for the courts to decide, Dumplin'. Not you or me. Why all these questions?"

Keep your mouth shut.

"Just a movie I saw. That's all."

"Maybe you best be watching something else, like my westerns. Seems the marshal always settles things in them."

"Westerns? Oh, please."

Roy ladled dressing on his salad. "You want some of this?"

"No, I'm fine."

"Well, eat up. You sure as hell don't get this kind of food at home."

Tasha grinned. "Neither do you."

Roy chuckled. "You got me there."

Tasha regretted her father's late discovery of her mother's financial mismanagement of the family dairy farm. Her mother's pilfering had caused them both life-alternating hardships, but their approach to retribution differed. While Roy passively filed for bankruptcy and watched the county assessor auction his property, Tasha decided not to be a victim.

All she had to do was wait.

Wait and keep her mouth shut.

Doreen sat on the pallet steps, waiting for Tasha's arrival. The plastic covering the window heated the trailer to an ungodly temperature. With no air conditioning, she was suffocating in the tin can she called home.

As Doreen smoked, Ty and Bryant rode by on their bikes. When she glared in their direction, Ty flipped his middle finger at her.

"Come back here and do it again, I dare you!"

Much to Doreen's disappointment, neither boy paused their peddling to confront her.

Her back ached, and she stood to stretch. She lit a Brandt and puffed away her frustration. She grinned when Roy's truck neared the trailer.

"Oh shit. What's she doing outside?" Roy asked.

"Who knows?" Tasha replied. "Even vampires need fresh air sometimes."

Roy parked his truck and hurriedly kissed Tasha's forehead before she hopped from the seat. He quickly scanned the area for children or animals before shifting the gear into Reverse. Doreen's hurling insults toward him was as predictable as the trailer-park children throwing rocks at vehicles—only the stones inflicted less damage.

Doreen pointed to Roy's truck. "Hey, everybody! There's the loser with no sense to milk a couple of cows. Get a good look at the big dummy right there. Driving a piece-of-shit truck that ain't paid for."

Seated at a picnic table nearby, a recent parolee and his girlfriend halted their poker game to discover the source of the ruckus. When they observed it was the next-door weirdo yelling at the top of her lungs, they ignored her and resumed shuffling cards.

"Yep, that's him." Doreen pointed. "Big ole dairy farmer until he lost his ass. Lost it big time!"

Roy shuddered and pressed the accelerator. The three-legged dog attempted to chase the rear tires as Roy sped around a discarded bicycle in his mad dash to escape his ex-wife's tirade.

The parolee shouted to Doreen. "Nobody gives a flying fuck but you, so shut up!"

"Yeah, well, you're a loser too. Probably know all the words to those prison chain-gang songs. I bet your mama's proud."

When the man stood to intimidate Doreen, she locked gazes with him. When he broke the stare, she tossed her cigarette butt in triumph and entered her trailer.

"You could have stayed out there," Doreen said to Tasha. "I was saying goodbye to your piece-of-shit father."

"Heard you." Tasha replied and groaned. "The whole place did."

"So, did you tell Daddy No Bucks he's about to become a grandfather?"

"None of your business."

"The things that go on in this house *are* my business. Suppose you're too damn ashamed to tell him or anyone else you've got a licorice jellybean growing inside you. I don't think there'll be enough in my check to buy maternity clothes, so you better tell him. Those jeans you're wearing now look pretty tight in the waist."

Tasha stepped toward Doreen. "I said: it's none of your business."

"Since when?"

"Since you stole my money!"

Doreen slapped Tasha's face. "Never stole it!"

Tasha returned the slap. "You're a thief and a liar, and I'm not going to take your shit anymore. Not anymore!"

Doreen rubbed her jaw. "Why you little bitch."

"Get used to it, Door-reen. You're not my mother. Mothers don't do half the shit you do. Your fucking day is coming."

"Oh, so now that you're knocked up, you think you know everything? Well, little girl, guess what?" Doreen jabbed her finger into Tasha's collarbone. "You don't *know* shit. You *are* shit. And that darkie baby of yours will be the *color* of shit!"

Tasha doubled her fists. "I could . . . I could just—"

"If you don't want your secret out, I'd suggest you adjust your attitude," Doreen gloated. "I've got nothing to lose by flapping my lips."

"I hate you!" Tasha shouted. "Everybody does."

Doreen lit a Brandt and casually tossed the match into the ashtray. "Never gave a shit about what anyone thinks of me. Never have, never will."

Tasha fled from the trailer. She ran down the lane to Trailer 5 and found Jermaine and Ty sitting on lawn chairs, reading comic books.

"Tonight," Tasha said between breaths. "We have to plan it tonight."

Jermaine stood and brushed back her hair. The palm print on Tasha's cheek explained the urgency in her voice. He tilted his head toward Ty. "Don't say anything more. Pick me up after dark."

Tasha agreed and walked slowly back home.

As soon as she opened the door, Doreen yelled from the couch. "Get me a Pfizz."

"Get it yourself," Tasha shouted and slammed her bedroom door.

As Roy traversed the highway, he considered the conversation with Tasha about revenge and wondered if her questions were a thinly disguised discussion about Doreen. He had said the proper thing about forgiveness and allowing the law to handle matters, but he hid his true feelings. Like the Wild West depicted in his western movies, he admired the cowboys whom ignored the law and practiced vigilante justice.

If he had not truly known Doreen after eleven years of marriage, how well did he know his daughter he only visited on weekends? Roy hoped Tasha was truthful when she said she was only discussing a movie. Roy dismissed his paranoia. Tasha was a sweet kid despite Doreen's influence.

He drove to Greenville for a whiskey at Jake's Keg. Seeing Doreen for the first time in months had rattled him. An aura of evil surrounded her, and he never understood how it blinded him when he fell in love with her. Her crystal-blue eyes that had lured him to love her now cast an icy stare that frightened him to his core. Seeing her today had jolted him like the time he had accidentally touched an electric fence and the volts surged frenzied energy through him. A few shots of Phillips always soothed his nerves, but the liquor could not erase the wrenching memories or the belittlement from her ongoing vile confrontations.

Roy's answers, like Dan's, were never found floating in alcohol. The secret both men had learned was to drink until the numbness swirled their heads and blocked Doreen from their consciousness. Some nights it took longer to achieve the effect, and most mornings they paid dearly for over imbibing, but both men admitted it was always worthwhile to forget about the wench, if only for a few hours.

Nightfall could not arrive soon enough for Tasha. She blasted music in her bedroom while writing a new diary entry. When her mother's shouting pilfered through the locked door warning her to decrease the volume *or else*, Tasha snuggled her headset over her ears and drowned out her mother's bellowing.

After darkness surrounded the trailer, Tasha hid her diary key inside a sock in her drawer. She tiptoed past Doreen lightly snoring on the couch, oblivious to an infomercial promising to vanish wrinkles with a new-age skin cream. Tasha imagined bored viewers parting with their cash by dialing the toll-free telephone number flashing on the screen.

Tasha creeped to the hallway closet to retrieve a lightweight jacket. She carelessly forgot about the loose hinge, whose alarming squeak woke her mother.

Doreen raised up on one elbow. Her flattened hair plastered to one side of her head highlighted her disheveled appearance.

Tasha was grateful only the light from the television screen illuminated her mother's ghastly image.

"Where in the fuck do you think you're going at this time of night?"

"Out."

Doreen flipped on the lamp and reached for her Brandts. She crumpled the empty package and tossed it to the floor. "Hand me my cigarettes."

"Get off your ass and do it yourself. I'm not your slave, not anymore."

Doreen sat up. "You listen here . . . "

Tasha pulled on her coat and slammed the door.

"Well, fuck me, ain't this a new kettle of fish to fry? Those pregnancy hormones must be making the girl goofy in the head," Doreen said.

She rose from the couch to retrieve her Brandts and a fresh can of Pfizz. She puffed and tuned the channel to a late-night movie. She grinned. The classic movie channel aired the Bette Davis movie *What Ever Happened to Baby Jane?* and Doreen loved watching a villain. She snuggled under her blanket and watched for the next two hours as Davis's character, Jane, tortured her sister, Blanche. Doreen forgave Tasha for waking her; she would have missed one of her favorite movies if she had remained asleep.

Tasha hesitated to honk this late at night, since Jermaine was expecting her. After her previous visit inside the Porter's trailer, she decided waiting a few minutes in her car was a better alternative than witnessing Adelle and her weird boyfriend getting high. She listened to the radio, and when the third song ended, she realized she had waited nearly ten minutes. When a pair of men she did not recognize lingered too close to her car, she fled to the Porter's and knocked on the door.

"Yeah?" Lakeisha asked.

Tasha watched as the two men disappeared into the playground's shadows.

"Jermaine. Is he home?"

Without bothering to step away from the door, Lakeisha yelled, "Jermaine!"

The girl's shout exploded Tasha's eardrums.

"Jermaine! Jermaine!"

Tasha lowered her hands from her ears. "Can't you just go get him?"

"Don't tell me what to do, bitch."

Lakeisha returned to the couch and resumed watching television with her three friends.

Ty appeared as Tasha turned the doorknob to leave.

"Jermaine's getting dressed. He took a shower. You're supposed to wait."

"Okay, thanks," Tasha answered.

Lakeisha sneered at the intruder imposing on her gathering. "Wait outside; you ain't no guest to my party."

Lakeisha's friend, Chrissy, sporting her new hairstyle in a shocking red shade with blonde highlights, chuckled. "Nobody would invite that butt-ugly ass to anything."

Lakeisha high-fived Chrissy and passed the shared wine bottle to her.

Tasha dodged the insults from the four twelve-year-olds by hurling one of her own. She pointed to the glue strip, peeling from the ceiling from the weight of the dead flies. "I'll leave the door open, Lakeisha. I'm sure you'll want to add more flies to your collection. Guess a frog like you couldn't manage to catch them all with that long tongue of yours."

Tasha exited the trailer with a smirk. She did not witness Lakeisha amuse her friends by sticking out her tongue while simultaneously flipping both middle fingers.

Jermaine pulled a shirt over his head as he neared the living room. "Where's Tasha?"

"She had to go lay down beside her dish," Lakeisha answered. "Woof, woof, Jer."

Jermaine snubbed his obnoxious sister and joined Tasha in the car. "Sorry. I was running late."

"Your sister's got some kind of mouth on her."

"Yeah, I know. Just ignore her like I do. Stop at the liquor store. I've got money for a six-pack if you've got your ID."

Tasha started the ignition. "My ID is about all I have in my purse."

Jermaine waited in the car while Tasha purchased the beer at Grover's. The annoyed cashier hadn't asked for any identification. He rang the sale that interrupted his television show without bothering to provide a bag or a receipt. Tasha grabbed the change, relieved not to exchange banter with the old man.

Tasha drove to the park woods and successfully maneuvered the ruts, preventing Jermaine's beer from spilling on his shirt. When she parked the car, he handed a can to her.

"So, you're finally fed up enough to carry out a plan?"

Tasha sipped her beer and cleared her mind from worrying about the alcohol's effect on her unborn baby. Tonight was not about the baby; it was about her mother.

"After yesterday? Hell yeah."

"First of all, you've got to be smart about it. One mistake, you get caught, and you're done for."

Tasha pursed her lips. "I know."

"No, you don't know. Do you want to spend the rest of your life in prison rotting away in some cell?"

"No."

Jermaine shook his finger like a schoolteacher scolding a student. "Then you better take this seriously. Not even sure I should be giving you advice, but I'm only helping you 'cause I hate your old lady as much as you do. Maybe more."

Tasha turned to face Jermaine. "I'm serious."

"Well, you can't do anything out of the ordinary. Cops hone in on that shit faster than anything else. You have to make the jigsaw puzzle fit. One piece out of place draws attention to the rest."

Jermaine finished his beer in three gulps.

"Start here," he said. "What does your mom do every day? Her routine. Start with that."

Tasha balked. "Well, that's easy. She lays on the couch, watches TV, smokes, and drinks Pfizz."

Jermaine digested the information. "Well, the cigarettes will kill her, but not fast enough for you. Maybe put something in her Pfizz?"

"Like what?"

"The guys in Chicago said that anti-freeze will kill a person. It works 'cause you can't taste it."

"But, it can be detected in toxicology reports. I flunked chemistry, but I know that much."

"*Huh.* Yeah, if they did a autopsy." Jermaine opened his second beer. "Does she do drugs? Or use prescription drugs?"

"No." Tasha raised her beer and then jerked it from her lips. "Wait. Yeah, insulin."

"How does she take it?"

"I usually use a pen. It's real quick, no messing around with a syringe or vials."

Jermaine rubbed his chin. "What happens if she don't take it?"

"Then her blood sugar drops, and she can sink into a coma."

"Really? Damn. Well, you don't want her in no coma. You want her gone."

"Right. But let's say she gets too much. An overdose could kill a person."

"You know that for a fact?"

"Well, when she first got diagnosed, a nurse gave me a training lesson—when to give it, how much, what to do if her blood sugar level gets too low, things like that. So . . . I think so, yeah."

"Does your mom ever give herself shots?"

"Sometimes, if I'm not home, but mainly I do it."

"Well, if it's a pen, you just jab it into her, right?"

"*Uh-huh.*"

Jermaine considered a scenario for a few moments. "Couldn't you just give her a regular shot and then sneak up on her and load her up some more? I mean, if you're only jabbing a needle, you could do it quick before she had a chance to do anything about it, right?"

"I suppose, but . . . then what? I don't want to watch . . . well, you know."

Jermaine pitched his two empty cans from the window and opened a third beer. "Hell no, you don't wanna be around for that. Do you have a friend to hang out with overnight?"

"Kristi. You know her."

"Well, make plans to spend the night at her place the day you do it. Then you ain't around for suspicion. Plus, when you come home, make sure she's a witness. Then act surprised; make sure you cry and all that shit, then call nine-one-one."

Tasha tossed her empty can. "It all sounds so simple."

"Because it is. But you can't tell nobody. Nobody. Like I said, I ain't sitting in no filthy cell avoiding Bubba who thinks I owe him a favor, if you know what I mean."

Tasha accepted the beer Jermaine offered. "God, I hate her. What's anyone going to say at her funeral? There's not one damn good thing anyone can say about her."

"Focus. Just call Kristi and arrange that sleepover. Tell her you're out of gas so she has to pick you up. That way you know for sure she's with you when you come home."

Tasha considered his words. "Well, that would work."

"Another thing, don't go checking out any information, like going to the library and looking up shit on diabetics or asking questions. Don't write nothing down. If you got—What are those books girls write in?"

"Diaries."

He snapped his fingers. "That's it. If you got one, burn it. Tonight. That's the kind of shit the cops look for right away."

"Got it."

"And one more thing, I can't be associated with none of this. Wait a week after the funeral before you contact me."

Tasha swallowed hard. "But, I'm not sure I can pull this off without you. I need you, Jer."

"The sooner you do it, the sooner we'll be together. Get your ass moving and call Kristi."

"I'll miss you, Jer. Just wish—"

"Wishing is for fools. Let's finish our beer in an early celebration."

Tasha hugged and kissed Jermaine.

"I'll stand by you," he whispered. "Promise."

CHAPTER 24

"Been a long time, Lorraine. How you've been?"

Lorraine regretted answering the phone as soon as she recognized Doreen's high-pitched voice.

"My hip's been acting up ever since I walked the fairgrounds at the flea market with Jenny. Sucks getting old."

"Well, I'm sure she enjoys spending Dan's money. She's got a habit taking what ain't hers."

Lorraine frowned and was grateful Doreen could not see her disgusted expression.

"Been over twenty years, Dori, when you getting over it? You married someone else too."

"Well, that's why I'm calling, in a way. Do you suppose I could hitch a ride to Greenville with you? I have to cash a check at Farmer's Bank. Since Roy wrote it, I want to cash it quick before it bounces."

Lorraine searched for an excuse not to drive Doreen to town. "Ain't your daughter old enough to drive?"

"She usually does, but she can't today. What'll you say? I'll give you gas money."

Lorraine conceded. "What time?"

"I can be ready in an hour. Really, Lorraine, I owe you."

"What's your address?"

"Unlucky Thirteen. I'm number twelve. It has a big-ass sheet of plastic covering the window, you can't miss it. And thanks."

"See you in a bit, Dori."

Lorraine hung up the phone. "Great, just the way I want to

spend my afternoon by hauling her bony ass to Greenville and back."

She looked across the highway at the Campbell's and remembered the dumpy trailer Dan and Doreen had lived in before Dan inherited his father's house. Even twenty years ago, Doreen had been a taker and never a giver. She had hounded Lorraine for cigarettes daily, but Lorraine drew the line at offering her rides. That duty fell on Jenny, Doreen's only friend.

Doreen's request for a ride surprised Lorraine, but she figured Doreen had burned so many bridges; she had depleted a list of people willing to help her.

When her phone rang a second time, Lorraine eagerly picked up the receiver hoping the caller was Doreen cancelling her request.

"Hey, Lorraine. I'm headed to the Thrifty New To You. Wanna go bargain hunting today?"

"No, afraid not, Jenny."

"Your hip still giving you trouble? Sorry about making you walk so much last week."

Lorraine groaned. "I've got trouble, but it's not my hip. It's worse."

"What could be worse that having pain like that?"

"A pain in my ass."

Jenny further questioned Lorraine. "What?"

Jenny heard a loud sigh before her neighbor's explanation began. "Dori just called and talked me into giving her a ride to the bank. *That's* the pain in my ass."

"Whoa! Well, I hope she doesn't see anyone she holds a grudge against. You do know about the public scenes she makes, right?"

"Jenny, I ain't talked to her for over two years. Calls me up like we're best buddies. I can't even believe I got roped into this."

"Don't pick her up. You don't owe her anything."

"Well, if I don't, I'll be on her shit list." Lorraine resigned to her unfortunate stroke of bad luck. "It's okay. I'll run her to the bank quick and back home."

"Well, call me and let me know how it goes."

"Believe me, I will."

Lorraine drove to the south side of Endover, the area of town any sane person avoided if they did not have a justified reason to enter Unlucky Thirteen. She had not visited the trailer court for maybe five years or more, since the church feared for their volunteers' safety and terminated the practice of delivering holiday food baskets. Judging from the horror stories Doreen had shared about growing up there before the county shuffled her to foster homes, Lorraine could not believe Doreen returned to settle in the armpit of Endover.

Lorraine honked to attract the attention of two children who sat in the center of the lane, blocking her entry. The blast did not break their concentration, as they remained fixated on something they jabbed with sticks. She hesitated before she cut the engine. Fearing for her own well-being, she apprehensively approached the girls who appeared to be between the ages of six and eight.

"Girls, could you please move to the side of the road so I can pass?"

Her weak smile and emphasis on *please* did not falter the older girl who glanced at Lorraine briefly before resuming her instruction to her partner.

"Get it! Get it, Tammy."

Lorraine leaned over the shoulder of the girl called Tammy. She cupped her hand over her mouth to stifle a scream. The coffee she had enjoyed that morning churned into brown bile as it inched up her throat.

A wounded rabbit, not much bigger than a squirrel, lay on its side with a broken twig jutting from a cavity where its eyeball should have been. The girls, in tandem, stabbed the animal's belly with sticks until the gash ripped away the fur and revealed its pink innards. The last deliberate jab snapped the weapon in Tammy's fist and stifled the rabbit's quivering.

Lorraine rushed to the safety of her vehicle, locked the doors, and blasted three long alarms. She turned the ignition key and waited. Surely, an adult would arrive to investigate the commotion.

The eldest girl kicked the rabbit with her sneaker, testing the creature's probability of viable life. When their rock throwing failed to revive the rabbit, the girls lost interest in their torturous game. The oldest girl flung the rabbit into the weeds before escaping inside a trailer with her cohort.

"My God!"

With her pulse racing, Lorraine drove the short distance to Trailer 12 and honked again.

Doreen hobbled from the pallet steps with her cigarette dangling from the corner of her lips.

Same ole Dori. She never changes.

"Didn't have to blast your horn; I was ready."

"Well, there were some kids and—"

Doreen rolled down the window. "Don't have to tell me about the damn brats running around here like freaks."

The open window compromised Lorraine's safety, but she guessed not too many attackers would confront Doreen's mouth or survive their attempt. She drove to the highway entrance and waited until the traffic cleared before accelerating onto the blacktop.

"You might want to buckle up, Dori."

Doreen flicked her ash toward the ashtray and missed.

Lorraine winced as Doreen's sneaker ground the residue into the floorboard carpeting.

"*Naw*, nothing ever happens. That belt just wrinkles your clothes all up."

Lorraine doubted Doreen had ever owned an iron or even possessed the ability to use one. The wrinkled cotton blouse she wore with faded sweat pants testified to that fact.

"Farmer's Bank, then?" Lorraine asked.

"Yeah, then I need to stop at Food Round Up."

Lorraine clenched her jaw.

"Probably should stop at the thrift store, but I ain't got that much money today."

Thank God, Lorraine thought.

The fifteen-mile drive consisted of Doreen smoking and prying gossip from Lorraine. Lorraine's answers were curt, since she did not want Doreen confusing a one-time favor as a friendship revival. With no lingering concern about her security, Lorraine drove with an open window to alleviate the thick cigarette haze clinging to her hair and clothing. Although Lorraine enjoyed a satisfying nicotine break, she wondered how Doreen could chain smoke for so many years and not have developed lung cancer.

"Here we are. Drive-up lane, or are you going in?"

"Have to go in. They make me show my ID every single time. You'd think they'd take the time to know their customers, but hell no; they take one look at my address and start quizzing the hell out of me."

"Yeah, banks are fussy like that. I'll wait for you out here."

Doreen entered the foyer. Through the glass door, she recognized a familiar face leaving the teller's counter. She stepped back and waited like a cougar hiding in the tall grass stalking its prey.

"Daisy? Is that you?"

Daisy shuddered and gripped her purse.

"Don't be scared. It's Mom."

One, two. Buckle my shoe . . .

Doreen grinned. "I keep telling Tasha to invite you over, but she never does. She says you don't have any friends, that nobody likes you. Is that right?"

Three, four. Shut the door . . .

"You were such a pretty little girl with chubby cheeks. Now look at you; you're nothing but skin and bones. *Tsk. Tsk.* I guess starving yourself is just part of you being crazy."

Five, six. Pick up sticks . . .

Wallace Harvey, the bank manager, focused on the women's interaction while he monitored the security cameras. The older woman spoke mere inches from the young customer's face. He recognized the young woman who had just cashed a check, noting her politeness was rare among her peer group. Now he observed her gripping the wall with splayed fingers and her purse dangling from one extended arm. She concentrated on the floor tiles like a prisoner searching the marble squares for a secret escape code. When the older woman stepped closer to the frightened customer and wagged her finger while uttering words Mr. Harvey could not decipher, he rose from his desk to investigate.

"Ladies, is everything okay out here?"

Doreen stepped back and smiled. "Of course. Just saying hello to Daisy Campbell, here. I've known her since the day she was born. Isn't that right, dear?"

Mr. Harvey waited for a response. He noticed goosebumps covered the young woman's arms as she lowered her hands to her sides. He reminded himself to adjust the air-conditioning temperature. It was foolish to waste money if his customers were uncomfortable. She clutched her purse as if she were the victim of an intended robbery.

He repeated his question. "Miss, are you all right?"

Daisy's sandals clicked on the tile as she dashed in circles searching for the exit. Doreen flung open the door, and Daisy rushed from the building like a caged bird set free. Both Mr. Harvey and Doreen watched Daisy rush to her vehicle. In her haste to escape, Daisy nearly sideswiped a parked station wagon before screeching away in her white Nissan.

Doreen rotated her finger in a circular motion against her temple and whispered, "She ain't all there, you know."

Mr. Harvey buttoned his suit and returned to his desk while scrutinizing the woman as she approached the teller window.

The teller, Debbie, smiled nervously at Doreen while noting Mr. Harvey's observance. "Good afternoon. How may I help you?"

Doreen dug in her purse. "Got a check to cash, if I can find the damn thing." Doreen tossed cigarettes, sunglasses, and tissues from her purse onto the ledge before retrieving her wallet. "Here it is."

She slapped the folded check on the counter.

"Please endorse it, and I'll need to see your ID."

As Doreen continued to rummage through her purse's contents, Debbie interrupted the accumulation of articles amassing on the counter by providing a pen. Doreen jotted her signature and waited as Debbie examined the check.

"Your ID, please?"

"I come in this bank all the time. All the time! Why can't you folks take the time to know your customers?"

Debbie glanced across the room to Mr. Harvey. "I'm just following procedure, ma'am."

Doreen yanked old receipts from her wallet as she searched for her identification. After accumulating a pile of crinkled paper atop her jumble of belongings, she flung the card toward Debbie. "This good enough? Show it to you every goddamn time I'm in here."

Debbie reviewed the ID before counting the cash. She offered Doreen an envelope.

"Don't need no fancy bank envelope. Do you really think I don't need to spend this money right away? I ain't got the pleasure to store it away like some people do."

Doreen snatched the cash from Debbie's outstretched hand. She dropped the coins onto the heap of possessions before scooping the contents into her purse. Doreen departed before Debbie had the chance to utter the customary *thank you*.

As soon as she vacated the bank, Mr. Harvey gathered the customer's name and account number from Debbie. When he noted Doreen Ferch's address, he nodded. Her brash behavior was common from the folks residing at Endover's trailer park. Some days he wished he did not have to obey federal guidelines and allow anyone who chose to cash their checks to conduct business in his bank.

Doreen climbed into the SUV.

"That didn't take long," Lorraine remarked. "I swore I saw Daisy leave the bank."

"Really? Didn't notice. Was busy pulling my ID out of my purse for the hundredth damn time. Ready to run to Food Round Up?"

"That's in Bancor, Dori. Why not shop at Kemp's? It's just a few blocks away."

Doreen lit a cigarette. "Because Bill Kemp's an asshole. He makes sure everyone waiting in line behind me knows I'm paying with my food-stamp card. I hate the prick."

Lorraine cleared her throat. "You do know he's my cousin, right?"

"What the fuck does that matter? If you don't want to drive to Bancor, just say so."

Her passenger's ungraciousness did not faze Lorraine, but she intended to end the shopping spree as quickly as she could. "If you only need a few items, I'll stop at Freedom Oil. They carry most things."

Doreen lit a Brandt. "Ain't got much choice since you're driving." She flung the match from the window. "Yeah, stop there and I'll grab some bread and milk, Pfizz and cigs."

Lorraine exited the bank's parking lot and drove the eight blocks to Freedom Oil. "Looks crowded today; guess I'll have to park in the back. My hip can't take much more today. I'll wait in the car."

"Suit yourself," Doreen replied and slammed the door. "Could have dropped me off in front, but I'll manage."

Lorraine watched her churlish passenger disappear around the corner of the building and swore she would never offer Doreen as much as a *hello* once she ridded herself of the parasite.

"You're blocking the damn aisle!" Doreen shouted to a three-year-old who was happily rearranging a potato chip display.

The girl frowned before glancing in all directions, seeking her mother to rescue her from the gray-haired lady whose shopping basket smacked her head when the tormentor passed her.

Doreen forged toward the dairy aisle. "Whole milk, two-percent, one-percent, skim . . . Whatever happened to just *milk*?" she grumbled.

When she opened the dairy case door, she caught a reflection in the glass and spun around. "Well, hello Daisy!"

Daisy halted her reach for an apple from the mountain of fruit displayed in a pyramid-shaped mound. She resumed her erect posture and glanced sideways in the direction of the voice without moving her head.

"No wonder you're so damn skinny. That's all you're buying—an apple and a banana?"

Daisy tightened her grip on her shopping basket.

"You'd think your dad or those people from the loony bin could teach you how to shop. I mean, don't they do things like that, or do they just tie you up and let you bang your head against the wall all goddamn day and night?"

Doreen's high-pitched laughter mimicking the cackle of a witch attracted the attention of nearby shoppers. A mother snuggled her baby closer to her chest. Daisy shielded her eyes in mortification; the mother was Candace Bremer, president of the PTA. Daisy's contract with the after-school programs surely would be cancelled once Mrs. Bremer called an emergency meeting alerting all parents to avoid the deranged photographer.

Ten-year-old Sarah pointed to Daisy and looked at her mother. "That girl is crazy?"

"*Shh!* Mind your own business and your manners," Sarah's mother scolded.

She tugged her curious child from the scene. The laughing woman's hysterics echoed down the aisle and silenced the clacking of Sarah's sandals and her protest to scrutinize the first insane person she had encountered.

A male shopper standing near Daisy studied her reddened face.

Daisy dropped her shopping basket and nearly tripped over the three-year-old child Doreen had chastised earlier. Daisy uttered a quick apology to the little girl before dashing toward the exit.

Doreen smirked. "Look at her go! Running back to Melville!"

"Melville?" the male shopper asked Doreen.

"It's the damn nuthouse up north. Stay away from that girl. She's goofy in the head."

An elderly couple comparing lightbulb prices hindered Daisy's path to escape. In her effort to slow her steps and choose the next aisle, Daisy could not prevent hearing Doreen's insulting conversation with the man.

Doreen grinned in satisfaction knowing her daughter heard her vindictive revelation about Daisy's private life to the man and all the nearby customers.

Daisy fled for the second time in less than a half hour to escape the demon she once had called *Mom*.

Doreen forged ahead with her purchases, not trusting Lorraine. Doreen was positive her driver would desert her if she lingered too long in the store. She purchased the milk, bread, and Pfizz. She debated whether she should splurge on some chocolate bars she knew were Tasha's favorites. She reasoned she could hide them in her room to sample without Tasha's knowledge and tossed four in her basket. Doreen sighed loud enough to garner attention from other shoppers when she assumed her place in an extraordinary long line at the checkout counter.

A teenage cashier, whose severe acne spoiled her good looks, rang up purchases as quickly as she could while offering genteel small talk to the customers.

Doreen's arms ached from the weight of her basket, and she dropped it to the floor.

"Can this line move any slower? My milk's getting warm!"

A man with silver hair blended with stark white streaks waited behind Doreen. He patiently held a can of motor oil and commented, "She's new, give her time. Give her time."

Doreen spun around. "You're so damn old, wouldn't think you'd have that much time left to waste."

The man raised his palm in surrender.

Doreen counted six people ahead of her and shouted at the cashier a second time. "Hey, Pizza Face, don't you have anyone else to open that other cash register? Jesus Christ, I ain't got all day."

A dark shade of crimson camouflaged the cashier's pimples as embarrassment swept over her face. She quickly completed her current transaction before knocking on a door to the left of the counter.

A well-groomed man wearing a white shirt and tie magically appeared as if on cue.

"I can help someone over here, please?" he announced.

Doreen pushed her way toward the second register. "Well, about goddamn time!"

A teenage boy extended his arm, preventing Doreen's rush to the head of the line. "No cutting in line."

"Go fuck yourself!"

Doreen's insult drew a collective gasp from the crowd. The white-haired customer cupped his hand over his heart and stepped backward.

"Ma'am!" The elder cashier reprimanded the unruly customer. "Clean up your language or leave."

Doreen examined the items in her basket. She was not leaving Greenville without her purchases and she yet had to request the Brandts from behind the counter. She remained silent and glared at the people ahead of her as they exited the store.

She broke her silence when it was her turn to approach the counter. "Not my fault you ain't got enough help in your store. I should turn your ass in to the manager."

"I *am* the manager."

"Then you should know better. Give me two packs of Brandts—regulars, not menthol."

She tossed her EBT card beside her food purchases and slapped cash on the counter for the cigarettes. The manager bagged her items and returned her change.

"Have a good day, ma'am."

Doreen scowled and snatched her bag. "I will now that I'm leaving."

"Me too," said the white-haired man and exchanged a sly grin with the manager.

Doreen ignored the fools and exited Freedom Oil. She noted that Lorraine had taken her advice and parked in the front lot.

"Glad I didn't have to walk all around to the back."

"Well, most of the cars left the front lot by the time you got done. Ready to head back, Dori?"

Doreen struck a match to a Brandt.

Lorraine counted eleven additional cigarette butts that Doreen had deposited beside her single one since their trip began.

"I guess so. Accomplished what I set out to do."

Doreen alternated her smoking with eating a chocolate bar during the fifteen-mile drive to Endover.

Lorraine tuned the radio to a local country western station to lessen the noise from Doreen's lips smacking.

"You're just like Dan and Jenny. Can never drive without a radio blasting."

Lorraine clicked off the radio, and the pair rode in silence until they reached Unlucky Thirteen. The trailer park was eerily quiet with nobody in sight. Lorraine instinctively raised her window and locked the door.

"Where . . . Where is everybody?" she asked.

"This time of day the old people are napping, and the drunks are sleeping off hangovers. If I'm lucky, the brats are lost in the woods, or better yet, playing tag with knives in the center of the highway."

Lorraine winced at Doreen's callous remark toward the children. She whispered to herself, "Wow." She faced Doreen and said, "Okay . . . then . . . see you, Dori."

Doreen tossed her candy bar wrapper on the floorboard and grabbed her bag. "Don't be a stranger, Lorraine."

Lorraine rolled up the passenger's side window and locked the door. She willed herself not to dwell on the memory of the girls killing the rabbit, since she did not want nightmares plaguing her. Driving into Unlucky Thirteen was a venture she would not repeat any time soon. There were worse things than being on the wrong side of Doreen's temper; the drive into the trailer park confirmed that.

Jenny sighted Lorraine's SUV returning to her driveway and wasted no time dialing her neighbor's phone number. Lorraine answered on the first ring.

"How'd it go?" Jenny asked. "Any big scenes?"

"Nope, not at all. She refused to shop at Kemp's and I refused to drive all the way to Bancor to Food Round Up, so we settled on Freedom Oil. Other than soothing that over, the trip was uneventful."

"*Huh!* Imagine that."

CHAPTER 25

Daisy's tires screeched to a sudden stop as she parked in her driveway. Luckily, her arrival home had not included a speeding ticket, which she would have admitted she deserved if a cruiser's flashing lights had detained her. She sat in her locked car for a moment while she separated her apartment key from the rest on her keyring. When she did not spot any pedestrians on the sidewalk, she sprinted inside her apartment and locked the door.

It was *her*.

Daisy had not seen the woman since . . .

She recollected the memory about the incident.

Not since . . .

Think. She tried to think. She had moved from Endover to her apartment in Greenville three years ago. She had returned home from Melville, and the counselors suggested to her dad and Jenny that she would thrive in a larger city with opportunities. Daisy's isolation hindered her progress, and the suggested cure—*the plan*—was to encourage her to meet new people by attending community events. Endover's tiny population stifled her emotional growth.

The favorable option was for Daisy to move to Bancor, but she rejected that choice. Bancor's large population was overwhelming with its confusing street patterns—and in Daisy's opinion—too far from her father's home. Thirty miles was a long distance for him to reach her during a crisis. They compromised, and her father leased the Greenville apartment for her.

She hated losing the security of her father's home, but Endover's population of less than four hundred did not qualify as a town or even a village. The county gave it the appropriate tag: Unincorporated—which, in reality, meant nobody was in charge.

Enter at your own risk. Daisy had no intention to adhere to *the plan* by meeting new people or engaging in community activities. She agreed to move to Greenville for a more personal reason: to avoid chance encounters with her mother.

She moved right after . . .

Tasha was fourteen and called Daisy, begging her to come to the trailer and rescue her. Daisy thought it odd that her sister would use the word "rescue" and assumed it was the latest teen jargon that Daisy was no longer privy to, since her high school years were behind her.

"Come quick, please. Get me out of here," Tasha pleaded.

"What's wrong?"

Daisy heard their mother yell in the background. "Get off that phone, you're grounded!"

"Please. Please, just come get—"

The connection ended. Daisy stared at the telephone, wondering what to do. She lacked decision-making skills during times of stress. Her father and Jenny were at work. Roy was too. She pounded her head with her knuckles. Decisions, decisions . . . Decisions overwhelmed her. Tasha was in trouble, yet going there would mean a confrontation with Doreen. Daisy's defenses were weak against her mother. She pushed her inadequacies aside and focused on her sister. What if her mother had hurt Tasha? Really hurt her bad? She heard Doreen yell about Tasha's grounding, which meant she violated some sort of rule. Daisy knew the types of punishments her mother enforced. Daisy resisted responding to her sister until she envisioned Tasha's needless suffering because of her own selfishness.

Daisy hopped in her car and drove to Westside Wheel Estates, fretting during the short two-mile commute, as she feared the scene she would encounter. Had Doreen gone too far this time? She rapped on the door repeatedly. Her concern deepened when she received no response. She held a deep breath, mustering the courage to open the door. She gripped the knob, hoping she had not arrived too late—too late for whatever hell her mother had inflicted on Tasha.

Daisy summoned her courage. She could do this. She had to.

She pressed her weight against the door.

"Get out!" Doreen screamed from the couch.

Daisy's eyes darted around the room. Was she already too late?

"Tasha. Where is she?"

"None of your goddamn business. Get out before I call the cops."

Daisy had ridden in squad cars during some of the transports to Melville, but never for an arrest. She shuddered. Maybe she should just leave. The hatred in her mother's eyes penetrated her. How could a mother despise her own child so much?

"Daisy."

Daisy turned her head in the direction of the faint voice calling her name. Only when the hand reached out from beneath the kitchen table did she discover her sister's hiding place. Blood and dirty sole prints desecrated the whiteness of Tasha's tee-shirt. Her chin-length hair was snarled in knots caused by Doreen's hair-jerking tugs familiar to Daisy.

"Tasha?"

"I said, get out," Doreen repeated.

Daisy focused on her sister's injuries. "What did she do to you?"

Daisy brushed away her tears and wiped her runny nose with the back of her hand. A rage exploded within Daisy as she examined her sister's weakened condition.

No. Not again. First Lucy and now Tasha.

She turned to Doreen. "What did you do? What did you do to her!"

Without waiting for a response, Daisy ignored the filthy floor and crawled forward. She reached out to embrace her sister and that's when . . .

Daisy trembled. She hugged herself and sobbed. So many times in therapy, she had refused to surrender to the pain that consumed her. She could not admit to herself, let alone to a room full of strangers that her mother—her *own* mother—hated her. What did they expect her to say? *Hi, I'm Daisy Campbell and I'm here because my mother hates me.* Daisy's low self-esteem taunted her with vile names: the Lowest Denominator, Pity Princess, or the most apt fitting, Queen of The Crazies. She could not admit to herself that her mother hated her, no matter how many psychiatrists during her numerous stays at Melville encouraged her to conquer her demons.

That's when . . .

Daisy stared into her sister's piteous eyes. A gigantic welt protruded from Tasha's eye socket, and a trace of blood dripped from her lips. Daisy reached to embrace her sister.

Then . . .

A quick jab.

The stinging knife tip seared Daisy's shoulder blade. She instinctively arched her back and flinched. Rip, rip, tear. The wetness soaking her blouse was blood. Blood! Daisy scrambled to her feet.

A sadistic sneer spread across her mother's face as she rotated the paring knife. Doreen rose from her knees and jabbed the sharp point toward her daughter's chest.

"Get out! Not saying it again!"

The blade glistened as Doreen twirled it.

Daisy glanced quickly at her sister collapsed on the floor. She feverishly rubbed her palms. She had to get away. She had to get help. When Doreen lunged toward her, Daisy rushed outdoors to safety.

When she returned home, she locked the door and tossed her ripped blouse in the trashcan. She called First Stop Hardware and instructed the woman who answered the phone to inform Roy there was an emergency at his ex-wife's home involving his daughter. She hung up when the woman asked for her name.

Daisy had never shared the harrowing experience with her father, Jenny, or the counselors at Melville. Daisy never knew the incident's outcome or if Tasha had been aware of Daisy's intervention, since they had never discussed it. In her private thoughts, Daisy mulled over the harsh treatment her mother inflicted on her over the years. Since Daisy had avoided contact with her, the memories of her mother's abuse blended in a vagueness she was able to push away.

Until today.

Her mother's recent taunting changed Daisy's perspective. The resurrection of the blade-welding monster embroiled a rage that replaced the years of fear. Why had this beast's approval— love—mattered to her?

Daisy's determination to settle an old score revived her.

She would slay the dragon.

One, two. She could make it come true . . .

CHAPTER 26

Doreen thumped her breastbone with her fist. The indigestion had returned, and she cursed herself for not buying a roll of antacids at Freedom Oil during her trip with Lorraine. The distraction of meeting Daisy twice in one day and the laziness of the pimple-faced cashier caused her to forget her purchase of DigestAids.

The dull pain crept upward from her chest, compressing her airway like a twisted vine tightly clinging to a fence post. Doreen lay down until the sensation eased. Although the pangs lasted mere seconds, the episodes had increased in frequency during the past month. Her medical assistance coverage would pay for a checkup, but Doreen's stubbornness prevented her from making an appointment.

During her last appointment, Dr. Haggard had drilled her about her diabetes maintenance. His arrogant attitude toward her maintaining a healthy lifestyle infuriated her. His first scolding always centered on her smoking. Doreen grinned at her memory of setting him straight.

"So, Mrs. Ferch," Doctor Haggard said as he scanned the health questionnaire Doreen had completed, "you noted that you continue to smoke."

Doreen shivered beneath the worn cotton gown the nurse had insisted she wear.

"First of all, I ain't Mrs. Ferch. I'm Doreen. And second of all, I'm freezing."

The doctor handed her a lightweight cotton blanket from a cabinet. "How many packs a day do you smoke, Mrs. . . . ah, Doreen?"

"*Maybe two or three. What difference does it make? Been smoking since I was fourteen. That don't have shit to do with diabetes or heartburn.*"

"*Healthy habits are important in managing your diabetes. All factors contribute to your health. Do you drink plenty of water?*"

"*I drink Pfizz.*"

"*Pfizz? I assume that's a soda?*"

"*Well, no shit.*"

"*Sugar-laced beverages are not the healthiest choices. I recommend diabetic patients keep orange juice on hand if a sudden blood sugar drop should occur, but other than that . . .*"

The doctor shaking his head while lifting the next page of the questionnaire reminded Doreen of all the teachers, social workers, and know-everythings she had ever encountered in her life shaming her. And what was this prick's problem? She hadn't asked to get diabetes.

"*I came here for my indigestion. Maybe you could concentrate on that?*"

"*Describe your symptoms, please.*"

"*Really? You don't know from all those medical books on your shelf? It starts like a burn in my chest and goes up to my throat. Doesn't last long but happens a lot. All I want is some medicine. Can I get that and then get my clothes back on? Christ, I'm freezing in here.*"

The doctor tapped his finger against his lips as he cradled his chin.

"*I would recommend some further tests. Your symptoms may seem like indigestion, but they could be related to more serious matters, like your heart for instance.*"

Doreen stood. "*All I want is something stronger than DigestAids. Don't need you milking my medical assistance card to pad your retirement. You got a prescription or not? That's all I'm needing.*"

Dr. Haggard turned away from the distressed patient. He scrawled on a prescription pad and handed the slip to her.

"*This may help, but I need to impress upon you that, considering your medical history, I strongly recommend further tests.*"

Doreen snatched the paper. "*I recommend you leave so I can get dressed and get the hell out of here.*"

That incident six months ago had ended her appointments with Dr. Haggard. The medical assistance program did not cover the prescription he had written, and Doreen was not willing to spend the fifty dollars buying what she assumed was nothing more than DigestAid in a fancy bottle.

Her heartburn episodes had increased since then, but she chose to endure the pain rather than tolerate the scolding of Dr. Haggard or any of the other geniuses at Greenville Family Medical Clinic.

After all, she reasoned, she had survived much more than heartburn in her lifetime. This too would pass.

CHAPTER 27

Tasha studied the calendar in her room. Kristi's birthday: June 17. Tasha had reminded Kristi that her golden birthday—becoming seventeen on the seventeenth, occurring on a Saturday—was a bonus reason to party. She accepted Jermaine's advice and called Kristi to make plans to spend the night. Tasha resisted the urge to circle the date, also heeding his advice not to leave any crumbs for eager detectives to find.

Tasha was in a celebratory mood; her mother would be dead in two weeks.

"Get out here, Tasha!"

Pop.Pop.Pop.

Tasha increased the volume of her CD to silence her mother's explosive shout. She stood before her opened closet, choosing an outfit to wear to the party. Classmates from Greenville, who always snubbed the Endover crowd, would occupy themselves by whispering gossip and hurling insults toward less fortunate girls like Tasha. Kristi had disclosed that she had invited Nancy, a classmate Tasha detested and openly referred to her as Narcissistic Nancy.

Doreen pounded her fists against the bedroom door.

"Goddamn it, girl! Open that door."

"What now?" Tasha faced her mother. "Can't walk three feet to the counter for your cigarettes?"

Doreen grabbed Tasha's tee-shirt collar. "Don't get smart with me. You hear me?" She released her daughter with a slight shove.

Tasha smoothed the puckered cotton.

"What? What!" Tasha demanded.

"My fucking heartburn is acting up again. Drive into Greenville and get me some DigestAids and some more Brandts."

"Now?"

"What the hell else you got to do?"

"I don't have any money. You got money?" Tasha asked.

"I got a twenty. That'll cover it, and I want my change. All of it."

Tasha shut off the CD player and smirked. "You want your change. Unbelievable."

Doreen closed her eyes and waited for the latest pang to pass.

"Shut your smart mouth and get me my medicine right now. Christ, I could die, and you wouldn't care."

Tasha grabbed her car keys from her desk. "You're right."

"About what?"

"Twenty should cover it."

Tasha jammed Doreen's twenty into her purse. As she headed toward her car, Jermaine strolled by.

"Hey, I've got to run to Greenville for my mom. Wanna ride along?"

Jermaine accepted the offer. "Don't see why not."

As Tasha entered the highway, Jermaine tuned the radio to a rock music station.

"You call Kristi yet?" he asked.

"Yep. All set."

"When's this party you're going to?"

Tasha answered with a new confidence. "June seventeenth. Her birthday. Already made plans to stay overnight and everything."

Jermaine nodded. "Good. You remembered to ask her to pick you up and bring you home, right?"

"Well, yeah. I mean, I haven't exactly asked her for the ride yet . . . "

"No offense, Tash, but you're not tending to the details. You sure you can pull this off? 'Cause if you can't, it's cool." He raised his palms. "It's cool."

Tasha passed a slow-moving van before replying. "Just makes me nervous. I mean, what if it doesn't work?"

"Then your old lady survives and throws your ass in jail." He spit from the window. "And if you do kill her but fuck it up by leaving any evidence or worse—crack under pressure and confess—your ass still goes to jail. That's why I keep warning you. This is serious shit."

"I just hate her. Hate her so much! She makes my life a living hell."

"So does my old lady, but hating and killing are two different things. Just sayin'."

A disguised plea replaced the confidence in her voice. "Are you trying to talk me out of it, Jer?"

"Told you before: I ain't saying to do it or not to do it. I'm just saying I ain't involved."

Tasha pouted. "Well, that's a lot of help."

"Exactly," Jermaine said. "That's all the help I'm offering."

They rode in silence for the remaining eight miles while Jermaine fiddled with the radio dial, searching for his favorite tunes. Tasha drummed her fingers on the steering wheel lost in her deliberations. Did she have the courage to accomplish her plan?

"I'm thirsty," she said as she parked the car at Freedom Oil. "Let's grab some soda."

She placed two rolls of DigestAids and soda on the counter and requested three packs of Brandts from the manager.

"You old enough to smoke?" he quizzed as he smoothed his tie against his shirt.

"Sure am," Tasha answered as she tossed the twenty and her fake ID on the counter.

The manager glanced at the card before he totaled the items and counted her change.

As she turned the ignition key, Tasha sighed. "Guess it's time to head back. At least the drive was a break from the witch."

Jermaine gulped his lemon-flavored soda as they passed miles of green fields surrounding both sides of the highway.

"Those corn fields are supposed to be, what? Knee-high by the Fourth of July? Ain't that what the farmers say?" he asked.

Tasha snapped open her soda can. "Guess so."

"Well, they sure as hell going to need some rain or something. I mean, I ain't no farmer, but—"

Tasha interrupted him with laughter. "You can say that again."

"What? What's so funny?"

"Well, Chicago Inner-City Boy, cornfields *should* be knee-high by the Fourth of July."

"That's what I said. So, why're you laughing?"

"Because," Tasha answered. "You're looking at soybeans."

Jermaine shifted his eyes from her and resumed looking at the fields. "Well, don't expect me to know this country shit."

"I just hope you know what you're saying about getting rid of Mom."

Her doubt slashed his ego, and he defended his stance. "I just hope, Tash, that you got the guts to do it. Those southside Chicago bitches would have done it and danced on her grave by now. Not a coward in the bunch."

She accepted Jermaine's challenge with defiance. "Well, maybe I'll head to Chicago afterward. And, hell yeah, I'll do it. I don't have any choice."

"We'll see. Just be smart about it, that's all. Just be smart."

Doreen peeked from the curtain, checking on Tasha's arrival. The burning sensation in her chest had worsened since she had sent her daughter to Greenville. She spied from the door and watched the boy kiss Tasha before exiting the car.

She pounced on Tasha as soon as she entered the kitchen.

"About time you got back. Why'd you take Darkie with you?"

Doreen counted the change Tasha deposited next to the bag on the table. "How come you've only got ten dollars in change?"

"Three packs of Brandts are almost six dollars alone, then your medicine, and I bought two sodas. Didn't think two cans of Glacier Ice would break the bank."

Doreen grumbled. "My money don't go to treating losers."

"Stop!" Tasha shouted. "Two cans of soda. A whole dollar and twenty cents. *Jeez*, you ought to be grateful I even went."

Doreen ripped open the bag. "Yeah, I'm grateful all right. Suffering from damn heartburn almost round the clock. Wish you could suffer half of what I do, maybe you'd see things a little differently." She pushed aside the DigestAids for her cigarettes. She tapped the pack against her palm, ripped off the cellophane, and tossed it to the floor. After she lit her cigarette, she added, "Before you go brooding in your room, get my shot ready."

Tasha waited for Doreen to step away from the refrigerator to retrieve the pen. She gripped her mother's arm with a tight squeeze.

"Christ, take it easy!" Doreen said.

Tasha sunk the needle into her mother's flesh and envisioned stabbing the needle repetitively until she silenced her mother for good.

"There," Tasha sneered. "Anything else?"

Doreen wrestled her arm away. Her daughter's raised eyebrow quizzing her unnerved Doreen in a way she could not rationalize.

Tasha's voice commanded Doreen's attention. "Anything else before I go to my room?"

Doreen silently crawled under the blanket on the couch.

"Good," Tasha said.

She entered her room, retrieved the key from her sock, and unlocked her diary. She penned a rushed entry.

Chicago bitches, just watch me.

She grabbed a red marker from her desk drawer and circled June 17.

Freedom Fest.

CHAPTER 28

Daisy heard the noise. Again.

She tiptoed from the living room to her bedroom. She paused to listen.

Clawing.

But from where?

She cautiously opened the closet door. Nothing. Her clothes hung in their specific categories above her shoes lined in perfect rows on the floor.

She listened again. Clawing.

She raised the window blind. She smiled at the gray cat pawing the screen.

"Oh, you came back 'cause you're hungry." Daisy rushed outdoors and scooped the cat into her arms. "I'll just bring you in and fatten you up."

Daisy removed the cat food from the refrigerator, discarded the lid, and set the container on the floor. The stray hesitated, but after sniffing the bowl's contents, he gobbled the meal.

"You must be starving. Where do you go between visits? Do you have a home?"

Daisy watched the cat groom his face after he finished eating. She carried him to her rocking chair and stroked his shorthaired coat. The rocking motion soothed the stray, who purred his contentment.

With the cat snuggled against her, Daisy closed her eyes. The rhythmic motion caused her mind to drift into a meditated state. Her thoughts, as always, floated to her childhood memories. She continued to stroke the stray as she remembered the cat she loved years long ago.

Her father had kept his promise and presented a kitten to her and Lucy. Daisy had abandoned her stiff plastic doll for a live baby to love. Gracie had belonged to her, and Daisy had handled the responsibility as seriously as any five-year-old could manage. She had fed Gracie, cuddled her in blankets, and groomed her fur, even when the cat resisted.

One day, Gracie was gone. Vanished. Daisy had scoured everywhere for her baby. Lucy did too, since both kittens had disappeared.

Daisy's rocking stopped abruptly.

At age ten, she had discovered the horrific truth behind the kittens' disappearance. That was when the unbearable night terrors began. Most nights, Daisy shivered while drenched in sweat, trapped in a hellish dream cycle replaying the last moments of Gracie's life.

Daisy remembered. How could she ever forget?

"Mommy, do you remember my kitty, Gracie? The one Daddy gave me when I was five?" Daisy asked during her weekend visitation.

"Shit," he brought home cats a couple of times, even when I told him not to. Never listened."

"Gracie was gray. And Lucy had Margie, a calico. Remember?"

"I remember cats shitting on the porch and pissing on the carpet whenever they got the chance. Hated cats then and I hate them now, so I can't say I paid any attention to what names you gave them."

Daisy smiled. "Me and Lucy dressed them in doll clothes and carried them in blankets like real babies. We had so much fun." She sighed. "Too bad they crawled into Grandpa's tank and drowned." Daisy comforted herself with a hug. "Lucy cried the most; I remember that."

"Really?" Doreen laughed. "Now that you mention it, I do remember those two scaggy cats. They drowned all right . . . with a little help."

"What do you mean, Mommy?"

"Jesus, Daisy, are you that dense? That tank was at least three feet deep. How in the hell could two tiny kittens crawl into it?"

"But they were in there. We found them and the Kahler girls took them out with a bucket."

"I didn't say they weren't in there, did I? People who don't want cats drown them. Happens all the time."

Daisy squinted in confusion. "But we wanted them."

"Well, I sure as hell didn't."

Daisy sucked her bottom lip as she digested her mother's comment. Horror replaced her puzzlement when her gaze met her mother's grin.

"So, figure it out yet, dumbass? I got rid of those stupid-ass animals and made sure your damn fool of a father never brought home more."

Daisy buried her head in her hands and sobbed.

"Quit your crying. It was only a cat."

"Only a cat . . . " Daisy murmured and kissed the stray's head.

Her thoughts shifted to the frightening encounter with her mother at Farmer's Bank. When her mother had pinned her against the cold marble wall, Daisy's chill resembled Gracie's plunge into the icy water. And like the cat, Daisy had clawed at the wall in her attempt to escape the darkness shadowing her mother's eyes. Daisy had frozen in place, too frightened to respond to her mother's accusations.

Daisy tightened her embrace on her cat, but it leapt from her arms.

"I guess your visit's over, *huh*? Time for you to go."

She carried the stray outdoors and set him free.

"Stay away from your mama," Daisy called out. "Stay safe."

Daisy darted inside her apartment, secured the lock, and closed the blinds.

She was safe.

For now.

"Strange not to hear from Daisy for a few days," Dan said to Jenny as they cleaned the garage.

"Maybe she's been busy."

"Busy doing what?"

"I don't know," Jenny said. "Whatever people who don't work do all day."

Dan tossed empty oilcans into a bin. "This again? Your harpin' is gettin' old."

"Not harping. You asked my opinion. I offered it," Jenny said and replaced the scattered tools to their proper brackets on the wall.

"I know you think she's an adult. Well, she *is*, but not really. I can't help worryin' about her. What if that wedding business got her all shook up and she tries to . . . tries to hurt herself again?"

"There comes a time, Dan, when she has to learn to stand on her own two feet. If you want my honest opinion, without getting angry about it, I'll give it to you."

"Go on, I'm sure I've heard it all."

"Promise not to get mad?"

He waved away his reluctance. "Just say it."

Jenny hung a handsaw next to the pliers. "I think she fakes it."

"That ain't what the doctors up at Melville say."

Jenny planted her hands on her hips. "Then why don't they keep her? Think about it. If she really was cra— *ahh* . . . as unstable as they claim, why do they always send her home after three days?"

"'Cause my insurance don't cover more time."

"She could be covered under medical assistance or qualify for social security disability benefits. Those programs help mentally ill people. But she's not covered under anything, and they just drain our pockets with her short stays."

Dan dismissed his wife's advice. "She has to be diagnosed as . . . as . . . Well, I ain't allowing that." He rubbed the dust from his pants in a determined fashion as if the gesture would wipe away the stigma of his daughter's condition.

"So, if you don't want her diagnosed and the doctors play along to drain us, what makes you think she ain't faking it?"

"Because I know my daughter. *Jeez*, even with Lucy, that teacher kept pushin' to get her 'help.' Lot of good that did. I'm not lettin' the same thing happen to Daisy. She has problems and can't handle pressure, I know that. But she's not gonna be locked away in some loony bin with real disturbed people."

Jenny faced the wall so her husband would not flare at her disgusted expression. "Then keep an eye on her, Dan. Make sure she takes her meds. I guess that's the best you can do."

"Been doing that for twenty-five years now. Ain't gonna stop now."

"Of course not."

Jenny gripped a hammer. She hung it on a peg but secretly wished she could use it to knock some sense into her husband.

Poor mixed-up Daisy. Smart enough to fool her father, dumb enough to mess with me.

The next day, Daisy's serious demeanor alleviated Dan's worries about her when he stopped at her apartment and discovered her sorting bills at her kitchen table.

"Have you figured out the amount you need, honey? I can write out a check while I'm here."

Daisy tallied the columns of expenses on her tablet for the sixth time.

"You done yet?" Dan asked.

"Please stop drumming your fingers! You get me all mixed up and I have to start all over again."

Dan scraped the chair away from the table and crossed his arms. He sat motionless as he watched his daughter total the sum for the final time.

Daisy rubbed her temples while staring at the paper. "I thought Mrs. Wendroth's check would cover all of this, but now . . . "

"Don't worry 'bout all that. I just need an amount to write out a check. You'll have enough to pay all your bills, and please, buy some groceries this time. How much you needing?"

She added a checkmark after each entry. "Rent, car payment, insurance and some minor stuff. Looks like it comes to about four-hundred fifty dollars."

"You got your medicine covered?"

Daisy grumbled. "Yes."

"I'll write it out for an even five-hundred, but you have to promise me you'll buy food."

Daisy approached her cabinet and opened it. "I have food."

Dan raised an eyebrow. "Honey, you have . . . how many boxes of macaroni and cheese?"

Daisy grinned. "Twenty-four, Dad. I always keep twenty-four. When I eat one, I buy one to replace it. See how they all fit perfectly in a row?"

"Nice that you have a system. Mind if I peek in your refrigerator?"

She chuckled. "Go ahead. You won't find any Red's in there, if that's why you want to snoop."

Unsure of the surprises he would discover, Dan slowly opened the refrigerator door. The top shelf contained a hoard of glass jars in a variety of sizes filled with water. Dan quit counting after twenty.

"You keep a lot of water on hand, I see."

"It's good for you and has no calories unless you add a lemon slice, which I never do."

"You have a dozen eggs, that's good. What's in this container?"

"Cat food."

Dan's hand recoiled from the plastic bowl. *No, she wouldn't . . .*

"So, tell me, what do you do with the cat food?"

Daisy rolled her eyes. "Feed the cat, silly."

Dan shut the refrigerator door and scanned the small apartment. He supposed a cat could be sleeping on her bed, but he had not noticed one when he had arrived. "Where's the cat? I didn't know you had one."

"Remember Gracie? The cat I had when I was little?"

"I think so. A gray one, if I remember right."

Daisy nodded. "Yep, she was gray. Lucy's Margie was a calico. Well, both of them, actually. Lucy had two cats."

Dan glanced to his left and then to his right before addressing his daughter. "Is Gracie here?"

Jenny will pitch a fit if I have to call Melville.

"Oh, Dad, you're so funny. How could a cat I had when I was five be here now?"

She cupped her hands over her mouth to stifle her hysterical laughter.

"Well, you said . . . "

Daisy exhaled a deep breath to speak. "There's a stray cat that's gray that I feed whenever I see him." She resumed her laughter as if she had revealed the punch line to the world's funniest joke.

Dan could not tolerate his daughter's hysterics. He had witnessed too many irrational behavioral episodes caused by skipping her medication.

"And you don't see the cat now, right?"

"Of course not. Do you?"

Dan fetched the checkbook from his rear pocket. "Here's the money, sweetheart. Pay your bills and maybe buy some fruits and vegetables when you buy groceries."

"Thanks, Dad. I will. Promise."

"Good."

Daisy wiped a tear from her eye as her giggling erupted for the second time. "So, you really thought . . . "

Dan kissed her forehead. "Goodbye, Daisy."

Dan reflected on Daisy's behavior as he drove home. Jenny had accused Daisy of faking her illness. What had he just witnessed in her apartment? Had she purposely mentioned the cat in such a way to convince him she was talking about the present while describing the past? Could she be that cunning? He doubted that when he pondered her genuine pride of her ability to fit two dozen boxes of macaroni and cheese onto one shelf. Was that rational thinking? Why did she store water in jars when it was readily available from the tap? Maybe he should have insisted on checking her medications to ensure she was on track.

Dan had no answers for his daughter's intermittent bizarre behavior. He decided to heed Jenny's guidance and keep an eye on his daughter. He had followed his own advice when he kept his visit and the five-hundred-dollar-handout a secret from Jenny.

CHAPTER 29

"Tomorrow's the day," Tasha whispered to Jermaine.

"And you're sure?"

Tasha lowered her gaze.

He lifted her chin with one finger. "Then why the tears?"

She swallowed hard.

"Is this about more than her stealing your money? 'Cause, if it is, tell me. I want to know."

Tasha dropped her arms to her sides when she realized she was rubbing her belly.

"No," she answered.

"Be smart. Remember, no more contact until a week after the funeral."

Tasha wiped her tears with the back of her hand and headed toward Trailer 12. She paused halfway and turned around.

Jermaine gave her a thumbs-up signal before disappearing into his home.

Tasha resolved to shake her somber mood by focusing on the stolen money, her bleak future, and the baby she would relinquish. Her pulse raced, and exhilaration rejuvenated her spirit. She would do it. She would.

"Tomorrow's the day."

CHAPTER 30

Doreen pounded on the bathroom door for the third time. "Are you going to get your ass out here for my shot?"

Tasha stood sideways in front of the full-length mirror that hung crooked on the door. She studied her reflection and wished she could blame her distorted image on a funhouse mirror. Her belly swelled with a modest bump, but a bulge nonetheless. Before too long, Jermaine—or worse, her father—would notice. She could not predict her boyfriend's reaction, but she imagined her mild-mannered father offering her advice to remain in Endover and *work it out*. Tasha had only one plan: to get out.

"In a minute!" Tasha answered.

She sucked in her stomach to snap her jeans. As much as she abhorred her mother's advice, she would need to buy jeans in a bigger size soon.

The pounding escalated. "I'm waiting, damn it!"

Tasha pushed open the door, clipping Doreen's leg. "Can't I even get dressed first?"

"Don't smart mouth me," Doreen said with her lips twisted around a Brandt. She leaned to examine the scuff on her calf. "You know I need that damn shot."

Tasha marched past her mother to retrieve the pen from the refrigerator. "You know how to do this; don't know why you think it's my job."

Doreen crushed her Brandt with unnecessary force into the heaping ashtray. "I'm sick, damn it. Is it too much for you to help your sick mother? You forget about shit that don't pertain to you."

Tasha jabbed the needle into her mother's arm while Doreen continued her rant.

"Christ, I got fucking heartburn every day, a bad back, and diabetes. Not that anybody around here gives a shit."

Tasha tossed the pen into the trashcan. "Spending the night at Kristi's. Gonna have a pizza party for her birthday."

Doreen lowered her shirtsleeve. "Might as well stay out all night, you're already knocked up, what difference does it make? Not like you can get knocked up *more*." Doreen carried her Brandts and lighter to the couch.

Tasha curled her lip in a sneer. "That must really bug you."

Doreen blew smoke from the corner of her mouth. "What? That my daughter's a whore? At least I was married before I had kids. Both times."

Tasha's simmering rage burst into a rapid boil. Her mother's insults fueled her determination to silence her wagging tongue permanently. Today.

Tasha removed the second injection hidden beneath a kitchen towel. "Like that made you Mother of the Year or something."

Doreen inhaled a long drag. Blue-gray smoke escaped from her lips and nostrils when she spoke. "Makes me better than you. Ever notice that *my* kids are white? That ain't no accident. God, how embarrassing to have a little darkie growing inside you." She exaggerated a fake shiver. "It's sickening, really, when you think of it. Having something that . . . that grotesque wiggling around in your belly. Might even be born with two heads or three arms."

Doreen paid no attention to her daughter approaching the couch and continued hurling insults. "Oh God, I wish I could call Roy right now and give him the worst fucking news of his life. Hey, Roy! Lil Dumplin's got a big surprise for you. Did you know there are other dumpling grains besides bleached-white flour? Did you know that, Roy boy?" Doreen closed her eyes and howled in laughter.

Tasha stared at the contorted face of the demon heckling her. For the first time, she noticed her mother's short spiked-gray hair was one shade darker than her ashen skin. Tasha inhaled the perpetual cigarette haze that surrounded her mother's head like a vile halo. She noted the hatred etched in each wrinkle of her mother's face and the scent of stale coffee emitting from her breath. During the last few moments of her mother's guffawing, Tasha focused on every detail of her enemy in her mission to destroy her.

Tasha lunged with the pen.

Doreen jerked her head as she opened her eyes to locate the source of the sting penetrating her shoulder. "What the fuck're you doing? You already gave me my shot, dumbass!"

Doreen rubbed the injection site as if the action could rid the dosage from her system.

"Oh yeah," Tasha replied in a sleepy tone. "Guess I forget shit that don't pertain to me."

Doreen blinked. The television images blurred as she cradled her head to ease the lightheadedness. "Get me a Pfizz, quick! My blood sugar's all fucked up."

Tasha pressed her palms against her cheeks, tilted her head, and answered in a sarcastic tone. "Sorry, can't do that. You're supposed to quit drinking soda. Doctor's orders. Right, Mommy?"

"Get it!"

Tasha returned from the kitchen with a half-filled soda can. She held it mere inches from Doreen's reach.

"Go ahead. Grab it," Tasha said.

She allowed her mother's trembling hand to touch the aluminum before jerking it away.

"Whoops! It spilled," Tasha said and poured the liquid on the floor. "All gone. Just like my money."

"You bitch!"

Doreen struggled to stand. Her grip on the couch arm was futile; her fingers slid from the vinyl like frosting on an ice cube. Her knees weakened, and she slumped on the cushions.

"Get my . . . "

Doreen massaged her forehead to ease the dizziness. Perspiration beads dripped from her hairline and funneled down her clammy cheeks. Repetitive blinking did not halt the room's spinning. She raised her head and saw two images of Tasha standing before her, and she swatted at the nearest one.

Tasha dodged her mother's feeble attempts to strike her. A mixture of anxiety, fear, and curiosity gripped her as she observed her mother's struggle. *How long would this take?* She glanced at the clock. Kristi would arrive in one hour. Tasha monitored her mother's condition as she strolled toward the kitchen.

"You getting my . . . You getting . . . my . . . "

Tasha called over her shoulder. "Yeah, I'm getting it. Now, where could it be?"

After what seemed like an eternity in Doreen's altered state, Tasha returned to her mother's side. Doreen's blurred vision made it difficult to discern the object in her daughter's fist. Whatever it was, it was not a Pfizz.

Tasha stabbed two more injections into her mother. "Die! Die!"

"Damn . . . Damn you . . . Help me . . . get . . . "

Doreen collapsed deep into the couch cushions. When cradling her head did little to ease the dizziness, she reclined in a prone position. The stained ceiling tiles in her vision morphed into one large brown blot. Air. She needed air. Doreen widened her jaws and smacked her lips like a beached fish fighting to survive on shore.

When the gurgling noise vibrating from Doreen's throat warbled in tandem with her eyelids opening and closing, Tasha could no longer bear looking at her mother's bulging eyes. She escaped to her room for her backpack she had prepared the previous night.

When she returned to the living room, Tasha paused to observe her mother. Except for the spit foaming at the corner of her mouth, Doreen's appearance resembled her usual position of sleeping on the couch. Tasha reached for her mother's wrist to check her pulse. The jarring ring of the telephone cause her to recoil, and she abandoned the idea. She debated whether to answer the phone. She reasoned it could be Kristi calling with a change of plans, but she dared not answer it. She heeded Jermaine's advice to leave behind no clues. She observed her mother's paleness and determined if her mother were not already dead, she soon would be. Tasha concluded that her mother dying peacefully in her sleep seemed unjustified compared to the suffering Doreen had inflicted on others.

"Gotta get out of here!"

Tasha threw a blanket over Doreen. The gesture was an effort to hide her body rather than provide comfort. She certainly did not want to *see* her upon her return tomorrow morning. She checked her wristwatch. Kristi would arrive in twenty minutes if she were not late, which Tasha prayed would not be the case.

As Tasha waited on the pallet steps, Ty approached her.

"What're you doing?" he asked pointing to her backpack. "There's no school."

"Waiting on a friend," she answered. "Go play."

Ty crinkled his nose. He motioned for Bryant who was leaving the playground to join him. When Bryant met his friend, Tasha became alarmed at the handful of matchbooks the boy carried. Bryant dropped the loot into Ty's hands before producing a lighter from his pocket.

"Hey!" Tasha called after them. "No playing near my trailer today, okay?"

Neither boy responded as they sprinted toward the woods edging the property.

Tasha composed herself with a deep breath. *That's the last thing I need, the trailer on fire.* She had not planned the details with Jermaine only to have his brother ruin everything by the summoning of fire engines.

The telephone rang in repeated shrills. Tasha entered the trailer to ensure Doreen remained in her present state, which prevented her from crawling to the telephone. Since her mother—or, *the body*—lay hidden beneath the blanket, Tasha was confident her plan's outcome was successful.

Tasha fled this time without bothering to lock the door. She fought a gagging reflex when she thought of her mother's existence now as a dead body. Tasha leaned against the door to calm herself and to *act normal*, as Jermaine had instructed her. She cringed at the plastic window repair. If Kristi and her friends saw it, she would never survive the bullying at the party. She decided it was best to meet her friends closer to the highway and not risk having them enter Unlucky Thirteen.

Traffic was brisk along US Highway 81 as people fled Endover by heading north to Greenville while semi-trailer trucks breezed through Endover, hauling cargo to southern designations. Tasha prepared to flag Kristi's car by walking on the road's shoulder.

The black three-legged dog raced along the ditch a few paces ahead of her. Each time the dog attempted to cross the highway in a zigzag pattern, the rushing traffic forced him to return to the side of the road. Tasha gasped when she watched the mutt dart across the blacktop between a white Nissan cruising southbound and a semi-trailer truck heading northbound. The dog leapt in the air and completed the last stretch of his heroic journey by landing safely in the tall weeds of the ditch.

"Stupid hound!" Tasha yelled.

Kristi's Chevy pulled onto the opposite shoulder.

"Hey!" she called to Tasha.

Tasha glanced both ways and raced across the highway in the same reckless manner the cursed dog had run. She hopped into the front seat of her friend's car.

"What are you doing walking on the highway like that?" Kristi chastised.

"Just anxious to get going, I guess."

"Got to be careful. Tash. You and that stupid dog both could have been killed."

Kristi drove a quarter mile and turned around in a driveway. "Got your ID? Plan to stop at Grover's on the way to my house."

"Got it, but not much money," Tasha confessed. "Actually, none. That's why I needed a ride; no gas. Sorry I couldn't get you a present."

"No sweat, we need to pick up Nancy when we get back to Greenville."

Tasha groaned. "Narcissist Nancy?"

After slaying one dragon, Tasha had little strength to battle another one. She hoped the liquor store clerk would accept her ID and she could drink to gain a buzz without becoming heavily intoxicated. She needed to safeguard her secrets—all of them.

The ringing phone jarred Doreen, and she pulled off the blanket. Hot. Sweat drenched her shirt, and she fanned it away from her skin. She rubbed her eyes with her fists as she sat up, but her vision remained cloudy. How long had she been out? Minutes? Hours?

The familiar heartburn pangs stabbed her chest as she gripped the couch to steady herself to stand. She rubbed her hand over her left breast and shuffled to the refrigerator in slow, deliberate steps. She gripped the door to stabilize her balance and reached for an opened can of Pfizz. The cold soda quenched her thirst, but the carbonation aggravated the heartburn. She was surprised her daughter had not emptied every can during her assault.

"That bitch tried to kill me," Doreen slurred; the utterance sounded like *tha ba tried ta quill me.*

Doreen pawed at her shirt. Clammy skin replaced the sweat, and the fabric stuck to her like glue. The heartburn's usual path rising from her chest and erupting in her throat now stalled behind her breastbone. She winced as she set the Pfizz on the counter and dragged her feet toward the couch.

"Damn!"

A thunderclap exploded in her chest, resounding in arrhythmic heartbeats. Doreen held her side and winced as sharp blades crisscrossed and pierced her lungs with each labored breath. She lay down and pulled the blanket to her chin. As she waited for her blood sugar and heart rate to stabilize, the nausea overcame her, and she vomited.

As Doreen raised her head slightly to determine where a *snip-snip* noise originated, she saw her daughter standing over her.

"Help me," she croaked.

She cringed when a second sharp pain stabbed her chest. Her ribs ached when she inhaled too deeply. She raised her head to locate her equilibrium by focusing on the stained ceiling tiles and planting one foot firmly on the floor. Her action paused the dizziness, but she now feared she had lost her sight.

She could not blink away the thin white film obscuring her vision. A strange veil of heat clung to her nose and lips, offering her brief reprieve when her exhalations formed pockets of air away from her face. When she gulped for oxygen, the pall hugged her face like a molded mask. Weakness in her arms prevented her from lifting the fog. Doreen accepted the cloud as the sign of impeding death; the white light everyone witnessed before they left this mortal coil.

Doreen's tense fists relaxed when her breathing stopped.

CHAPTER 31

"Harry, that window for Trailer Twelve was delivered today, right on schedule. When do you want it installed?" Jay asked.

Harold cradled the phone on his shoulder, and he shuffled papers on his desk. "Bring it over around noon. That work for you?"

"Sure. See you then."

Two hours later, Jay parked his truck in front of Trailer 12. When a swarm of bored children gathered, he shooed them away. During his last trip to Westside Wheel Estates, someone had stolen his brand-new Craftsman socket set from his truck bed while he worked a mere ten feet away. He stepped on the pallets to knock on the door and wondered why Harold was too cheap to install decent steps.

Jay knocked a second time and checked his wristwatch—12:17 p.m. Harry had scheduled the repair for noon; surely, the old bat would be awake by now. He pounded on the door and jumped from the pallets, expecting the woman to hurl a string of cuss words at him. With no response, he locked his toolbox in his truck cab and walked to Harold's office.

"Need you to wake up number twelve, Harry. She ain't answering," Jay said as he entered Jefferson's office.

Harold grunted and lay his sandwich on a paper plate. "Shit, just sat down for lunch. Let me grab the passkey."

As the two men strolled, Jay asked, "You mean you can just unlock her door like that? Don't need the crazy bitch calling the cops."

"No problem. I figured the window would arrive today, so I

slid a twenty-four-hour notice under her door yesterday. Serves as a legal notice of entry."

Jay stood behind Harold as the landlord knocked.

"Knocking for good measure," Harold explained. "Sure as hell don't need to barge in and see that scarecrow naked."

Jay chuckled. "See? No answer. Maybe she ain't home."

Harold pointed. "*Naw,* the car's here. She don't go nowhere without her kid hauling her ass." Harold inserted the key and turned the knob. "*Huh.* It wasn't locked after all."

Except for a tuft of gray hair, a blanket concealed the woman as she lay on her side facing the back of the couch.

"She's sleeping," Jay whispered.

"Well," Harold replied. "We have to move the couch to get at that window." He directed his attention to the tenant. "Hey! Window repair!"

Jay stepped back. "Man, she's out. She ain't moving."

With no response and his patience wearing thin, Harold yanked the blanket from her face.

"Whoa! Oh shit!"

Before Jay could ask what was wrong, Harold bolted past him to rush outdoors. Harold leaned, gripped his knees, and purged chunks of bologna and white bread. Jay took a cautious step forward. When a fly crawled from Doreen's gaping mouth to join the hoard feasting in the vomit pool, Jay covered his mouth with both hands and fled from the trailer.

"Jesus, Harry. Call nine-one-one!"

Both men trotted to Harold's office.

After he had replaced the receiver, Harold reached into his desk drawer and withdrew a pint of vodka. "Snort?"

"Ain't ever seen anything like that," Jay repeated for the third time. He tilted his head and swallowed the alcohol. The image of the flies, not the vodka burning his throat, caused him to flinch. "Never."

Harold tossed the remainder of his sandwich into the trashcan and squinted when he burped. "Fuck. Hope to hell to never see that kind of shit again."

The ambulance and squad cars' sirens alerted the residents who poured outside in droves to witness the latest incident. Some spectators, disappointed the event was merely a medical emergency and not an arrest, disappeared into their homes.

"Oh, they're going in Trailer Twelve!" Shirley said to her neighbor.

The man, known as Tie-Dye Bill for wearing tie-dyed shirts to accent his unfashionable bald head-and-ponytail combo, replied, "Good. Let's hope she don't make it."

Shirley tugged at her collar. "That's a horrible thing to say."

Tie-Dye Bill spat on the ground. "One less piece of trash living here is how I see it."

The paramedics transported an empty gurney into the ambulance. The vehicle left the scene without the sirens blasting or with the urgency in which it had arrived. When the hearse entered the property, Tie-Dye Bill took that as a good sign and wandered back to his trailer.

A pair of deputies remained on site and secured the trailer with yellow caution tape with **POLICE LINE DO NOT CROSS** printed in repetitive phrases.

Jay whispered to Harold. "Ain't gonna be no window replacement today."

Harold shuddered. "Let's just hope the bitch don't haunt the place."

Since he could remember, Roy loathed Sundays. When he was a child, his parents forced him to attend Greenville Baptist Church. He would not have minded the Sunday sessions if they were like summer vacation Bible School, where the children created art projects and played games in the park. Each Sunday, he fought boredom perched on a hard pew between his parents while the preacher droned on about the wages of sin and asked the congregation to accept Jesus as their personal Lord and Savior.

The only two activities that had filled a Sunday in his teen years were recovering from a hangover or watching football, and sometimes doing both simultaneously. Those carefree days ended when he inherited the dairy farm and milked cows daily, regardless if he suffered from over imbibing. Today Roy was bored, and although it was not his designated visitation weekend, he decided to drive to Endover and treat his daughter to lunch.

The trailer park was unusually calm as he parked his truck. He had not called before arriving, since he wanted to surprise Tasha. Her car parked next to the trailer assured him she was home. He blasted his usual horn greeting and waited. When a repeat of the signal failed to rouse his daughter, Roy reluctantly approached the trailer.

He knocked and stepped back.

Tie-Dye Bill shouted from his deck. "Ain't nobody gonna answer that."

Roy walked to the opposite side of the lane. "Did somebody pick them up? I came to see my daughter, Tasha, if you know her."

Tie-Dye Bill chuckled and fingered his goatee. "Guess you could say that. At least they hauled the old bitch out of here today." He waved his hand. "Good riddance."

Tie-Dye Bill's amusement puzzled Roy.

"You don't mean . . . Were the cops here? Did Doreen get arrested?"

Tie-Dye Bill spat a puddle of brown tobacco juice. "I don't know the old lady's name, but yeah, the cops were here. But they didn't take her out of here, the hearse did."

"Oh my God!" Roy exclaimed. "Where's . . . Where's Tasha? Is she all right?"

Tie-Dye Bill spewed his spent tobacco wad on the gravel. "Don't know your girl's name, but both girls were gone when they hauled the old lady out on a stretcher." He flattened his palm in a horizontal motion. "Stiff as a board."

"If you see my daughter, tell her to call me. Call me right away. I'll leave a note on the door, but if you see her, tell her, won't you? She's only a kid. She doesn't need to . . . Oh my God!"

"If I see her . . . " Tie-Dye Bill answered and strolled into his trailer.

Roy jotted two notes. He secured one in the doorframe and the second message under the windshield wiper blade of Tasha's car. Since he was in Endover, he drove to the Campbells'.

Jenny was surprised when she answered the door and discovered Roy Ferch on her doorstep. His distraught expression indicated this was no friendly Sunday afternoon visit.

"Roy. Come in. What's wrong?"

"Dan home?"

Dan paused at the kitchen entry. "Sure am." He yawned and stretched with his arms high above his head. "What else would I be doin' on a Sunday, goin' to church?"

Jenny interrupted Dan's laughter. "Dan, something's wrong. What is it, Roy?"

Roy removed his cap and wrung it.

"Oh, shit. Sorry," Dan apologized. He pulled down his tee-shirt to cover his exposed belly. "What's going on?"

Roy looked at the floor. "Doreen."

Jenny and Dan exchanged baffled expressions.

"Doreen? What's she done now?" Dan asked. "Better not have hurt one of our kids."

"No," Roy said. "Well, I don't think so. I don't know where Tasha is."

Jenny pulled a chair from the table. "Sit, Roy. Please, tell us. What's going on?"

"Doreen."

"Doreen, what?" Jenny asked.

"Doreen. She's dead."

CHAPTER 32

"Man, I didn't think your old lady could yell so much," Nancy said. "Slow down, Kristi, my house is right there."

Kristi parked the car. "Her bitching sure doesn't help my hangover any."

"Well, good luck with that." Nancy hopped from the backseat and trotted to her doorstep.

"Did she need to slam that door?" Kristi lamented to Tasha. "Like my head ain't already pounding."

Tasha offered a weak smile. Nancy was the least of her problems facing her arrival home.

"You're so quiet, Tash. You're not going to puke in my car, are you?"

Tasha shook her head *no*.

"Still can't believe my mom came downstairs and busted us with the vodka," Kristi said. "Lucky us, I hid the second bottle."

Tasha leaned against the coolness of the window and wondered what scene awaited her and Kristi. Would her mother still be lying on the couch? Maybe she rolled to the floor? Was that even possible? What would she look like—like the zombies that stumbled in horror movies? What if . . . What if she had managed to get to the phone?

"Right, Tash?"

"*Huh?*"

Kristi huffed her annoyance. "Are you so hungover you haven't heard a word I said?"

Tasha stretched in her seat. "Sorry. Thinking about my mom. Hope she's okay."

"Why wouldn't she be?"

"*Ah . . . Ah*, she was kinda sick when I left."

Kristi entered Westside Wheel Estates after honking at some children playing catch to move out of the lane.

"That little shit just flipped me off!"

"That's why they call this Unlucky Thirteen. I'm unlucky twelve."

Kristi drove until she reached the Ferch's trailer. "Jesus, what happened to your window?"

Tasha shielded her shame behind a cupped hand against her forehead. "Just another little shit causing trouble. Long story. Wanna come in for a minute?"

Kristi shook her head. "You heard my mom. I'm supposed to drop off you guys off and get my ass back home. Pronto."

"You sure?" Tasha pleaded. "Just for a minute."

"I'm not listening to her bitch all day. So, no," Kristi answered.

Tasha sunk into the comfort of the car seat and stared at the trailer door.

"Well, you getting out or what?"

"Are you sure—"

"Damn it!" Kristi yelled. "That snot-nosed brat just threw a rock at my car. C'mon, Tash, I gotta get out of here."

"Sorry." Tasha hugged her friend. "Thanks. Thanks for everything," she said as she willed herself to exit the car.

Kristi gunned the engine toward the exit, spraying a gravel shower in her path. She glanced in the rear-view mirror and chuckled at the brats choking in the dust cloud. The kids abandoned the rock throwing and instead covered their mouths to stifle coughing fits.

Tasha ignored the children and stared at the door. After a few moments filled with dread, she summoned the courage to open it.

She paused when she discovered a folded white paper wedged in the doorframe. *Jer?*

Tasha tugged the paper free and unfolded it.

Tasha–call me <u>right away</u>. Dad

He knows.

She opened the door.

She regretted taking a deep breath as soon as the pungent odor of sour, curdled milk assaulted her nostrils. She flipped on a light. Her eyes automatically focused on the couch. For the first times in years, her mother was not perched in place, puffing a cigarette.

Tasha covered her nose. *That smell.*

She inched closer to the couch and realized the putrid odor's source originated from the olive-and-tan patches of dried vomit crusted to the cushions. She gagged and raced to the phone. She practiced shallow breathing as she dialed.

Pick up. Pick up. Pick up.

"Dad? Dad, I'm home—"

"Stay put, Tasha. I'll be right there to get you."

"Where's . . . Mom's not here."

"I'll explain when I get there. Just wait for me, okay?"

"Okay."

After hanging up, Tasha took a quick inventory of the trailer; nothing *appeared* out of place, at first. She noticed her mother's blanket was missing. Who would steal that? She rushed into her bedroom. She nearly tripped over the empty desk drawers thrown haphazardly in a stack near the door. Her drawer contents cluttered her desk top sans her diary and key. A faded rectangle masked the wall where the calendar had hung.

My diary!

Jermaine had warned her to burn it, but destroying it meant erasing four years of her life. She had left behind crumbs. She imagined her father raising her baby while she rotted away in some nasty prison cell. Maybe her mother had not died; maybe she was playing a sadistic game to teach Tasha a lesson. Maybe . . .

Roy turned the key in his old truck's ignition and sped to the highway.

"Damn Sunday afternoon sight-seers!" he yelled as he passed a Cadillac driven by an old timer.

Roy had watched the four gray heads bob for the past six miles in his attempt to avoid on-coming traffic and pass the vehicle, maintaining a steady forty mile-per-hour speed on the highway. Roy embarrassed himself by sneering at the driver as he passed, but he just as quickly forgave himself. He reasoned his reaching his destination and comforting his distraught daughter was more important that offending senior citizens gawking at cornfields.

His temper flared again when he attempted to enter Westside Wheel Estates and a beat-up, rusty car parked sideways blocked the lane just past the entrance.

"Fuck this!"

He blasted his horn repeatedly until a woman inched her obese frame from her trailer and stood on the steps. "Got a problem, asshole? My babies were sleeping 'til you woke 'em up."

Roy leaned from his window. "*My* problem? Is that your car blocking me?"

The woman crossed her flabby arms. "So what if it is?"

"Move it. I'm in a hurry."

"It's out of gas, so fuck you."

The woman eased all three hundred pounds of her chunky frame sideways into the trailer's narrow door.

Roy shifted into Reverse and wondered if the three-legged dog still lingered at the property. After parking to the side of another trailer, he locked his truck and noticed the fat woman watching him from behind the protective, ripped screen of her front window. He fought the urge to curse her as he approached Trailer 12.

While Tasha waited, she remembered Jermaine's advice and

plucked a few nose hairs to induce crying. Her eyes watered with fake tears as she raced toward her father.

"Dad!"

She rushed to his outstretched arms. His tight embrace nearly squeezed the breath from her.

"Dumplin', c'mon to the truck. I'm taking you back home with me. You got that trailer locked?"

"Where's Mom? What happened? Is she in the hospital or what?"

Roy wiped his hand across this chin. "She's . . . She's not at the hospital."

"Well, where then?"

Tie-Dye Bill yelled across the lane to Roy. "That one your daughter?"

Roy nodded. "Yes, thanks." He turned to Tasha. "Not here. I'll tell you in the truck, c'mon."

Tasha walked with her father. As they approached the truck, the obese woman emerged sideways from her trailer, shaking her fist. "Better never, ever, wake up my damn babies again!"

Roy ignored the woman's threat.

"Get in the truck, Tasha. Now."

Tasha obeyed as she quizzed her father. "Dad, would you just tell me? What's going on?"

Roy shifted into gear. "Sorry, Dumplin', don't know how to tell you this 'cept to just say it. Your mother passed away yesterday."

Tasha widened her eyes and gasped the way she had practiced the reaction in the mirror for the past week.

Roy waited for the traffic to clear before entering the highway. He squeezed his daughter's knee. "It'll be all right, honey. Promise."

"But how? How did she . . . "

"Don't know how. Guess that's for the coroner to determine. I only know the trailer park manager found her, called nine-one-one, and the ambulance and cops came."

Tasha squirmed in her seat. "Why would the cops come?"

"Any time there's a medical emergency, all rescue crews are dispatched. Your neighbor—that guy that talked to me just now—told me yesterday that they roped off the area for a bit while the sheriff and deputies searched the trailer."

"For what?"

Crumbs.

"I guess they get involved if a death looks suspicious."

Sheriff department? Suspicious death? Tasha's real tears replaced the fake ones. Had she forgotten something? Messed up somehow? The police search explained the missing blanket, calendar, and diary. She shivered imagining the *clank* of a jail cell door locking behind her.

"But you're not saying they think someone—"

"Don't worry your pretty head about it. It's just a routine they do. We'll likely find out Doreen died from a medical condition or something. Happens all the time to people. Unfortunately, it happened to her this time."

"I can't believe it," Tasha whispered. "She's really gone."

"Death's always a shock. No matter how old you get or how many times you hear the news of a loved one's passing, it never gets easier."

"Maybe I should have stayed home last night. She was all alone. I could have—"

Roy interrupted his daughter. "There's nothing you could have done. Don't blame yourself. These things just happen."

These things just happen. Would the sheriff department reach the same conclusion?

Roy continued with his explanation. "It's the cycle of life. Someone dies; someone is born. It comes full circle."

Mom's dead. Baby's coming. Karma. What goes around, comes around.

"Don't worry. I'll take good care of you, honey. No matter what."

Tasha nodded. "I know, Dad. I know."

The only thing that traveled faster than the wind-blown litter tumbling along the ditches in Endover was gossip. News of Doreen Ferch's death breezed up US Highway 81 and touched down in Greenville. The first stop was Jake's Keg, where the sober and not-so-quite sober patrons rivaled to share the story to newcomers entering the bar.

Although her cause of death had not been officially released—she had only been deceased one day—that fact did not prevent the rumor mongers from adding to the previous versions of the scenario they had heard from the unnamed source who had *been there*.

"Lots of crime at Unlucky Thirteen," Jed Nelson declared to the engaging crowd. Even the perpetual sports broad-cast airing on the television above the bar took a backseat to the amateur detectives' theories.

Bob Knutson nodded. "There's that seedy bunch from Chicago that lives there. Seem's like Harold allows just about anybody to move in anymore."

"You mean that big black dude with arms like this?" Jed demonstrated by forming a circle with his hands, as if he were grasping a telephone pole.

"I wouldn't fuck with him," Ted Andrews added. "Wonder why Dori thought that was a good idea?"

Jake spat his disgust into the trashcan along with the sunflower shells tucked into his cheek. Doreen Ferch had not been his favorite former employee, but he respected her death. Jake wiped the counter with broad strokes, as if his white bar rag could purify the macabre talk.

"Looks like the Hornets are behind, guys. Maybe watch the game, *huh*? It's the only reason I opened on a Sunday afternoon," Jake said.

"Only going to say one last thing, Jake. Something we all agree on," Bud said. "That woman had the sweetest lookin' rear end in Mason County."

Jake whipped his bar rag down on the counter in contrast to the hands lifting mugs and bottles and shouting, "Here, here!"

Down the road at Kathy's Kut 'N Kurl, clients' tongues spun faster than the ceiling fan blades in the reception area as women arrived for their Monday morning appointments. The offensive, ammonia, permanent-wave fumes mingling with Aqua Net hairspray created a less toxic atmosphere than the gossip filtering between hair dryers.

"So, they found her alone, or was someone with her?" Anne Baxter asked her stylist.

Joanne wrapped a lock of hair around a curler and secured it with a pin. "Heard she was all alone. What a sad way to die."

"Well, she didn't exactly have any friends. I mean, really, who could put up with her mouth?"

Lisa giggled from the next chair. "Mouth like a sailor. Glad I never got on her bad side."

Anne smoothed the vinyl apron draped over her lap. "She got kicked out of Kemp's a few weeks ago. Raising hell in front of a nun, of all people. That's what I heard."

Lisa resumed her giggling. "Raising hell in front of a nun . . . "

"Wonder if the girl's gonna live with Roy now?" Anne asked the group.

Joanne secured a second curler in Anne's hair. "That poor girl. Hate seeing any kid lose their mother, but since it was Doreen, might be for the best."

The women nodded in unison and returned to their *Good Housekeeping* and *People* magazines. None of them gave Doreen Ferch a second thought after they tipped the stylists and returned to their homes, except Lisa, who giggled each time she thought of Doreen's curse words shocking the poor nun.

Bill Kemp had been one of the last to hear the news. Customers clamored to him in their excitement to be the first to disclose

Doreen's demise. By the end of the morning, Bill Kemp had responded, "I heard," twenty-seven times. He surrendered to his office for the remainder of the day. The pork loins he had intended to slice to fill the meat case would wait until tomorrow; gossip was the only juicy tidbit his customers were buying today.

Lorraine drove home from Kemp's and hastily put away her groceries before dialing Jenny.

"Jen, is it true?"

"Hi, Lorraine. You mean about Doreen? Yeah, Roy told us."

"*Daaaaaaamn.*" Lorraine dragged out the word for three seconds.

"Quite a shock, *huh*?" Jenny asked.

"Well, *how*? I mean everyone's talking about it, but nobody said how she died."

"Not sure," Jenny answered. "Dan's home. I gotta go."

"If you hear any—"

Lorraine stared at the receiver after the *click* resounded in her ear. *Dori's dead and still causing trouble.*

"How was work today, hun?" Jenny asked as Dan hung his cap on a peg. He slid a twelve-pack of Red's in the refrigerator after removing a can."

"Well, you can guess what the hot topic was today, and it sure wasn't the Hornets' loss."

"I can only imagine. Glad I had the day off. I'm sure Delores served plenty of coffee with side orders of gossip ala mode. By the way, Roy called."

"He did? About what?"

"He said social services agreed to pay for the . . . body preparation, I guess you call it that, and a basic casket. Greenville Baptist Church has offered to conduct the funeral, and since she was a Campbell, they've agreed to bury her at no charge in the family plot your grandfather established."

"Reverend Joe was my great-grandfather," Dan said.

"Oh." Jenny paused for a minute. She considered Dan's

lineage and remembered that Dan's grandfather had been Leroy Campbell. "Anyway, it's all set for Thursday, one o'clock."

Dan sipped his beer. "If it wasn't for Daisy, I wouldn't bother goin', but who knows how she's goin' to react. Did you call her today?"

"Tried a few times," Jenny lied. "Her phone was busy or she didn't answer."

Dan rubbed his chin. He quenched his thirst by finishing his Red's before picking up the receiver. He wrapped the cord coils between his fingers and squeezed them.

"Fuck! No answer. Just what I need after a long day. I better go check on her."

He slammed the beer can into the trash and put on his cap.

"Should I wait on supper, then?" Jenny asked.

Dan scooped his keys from the table. "How in the hell should I know?"

Dan approached Daisy's apartment and noted her Nissan parked in the driveway. He knocked three times. With no response, he stared at the door, as if he possessed a superhuman power to open it by using his vision. He could have—probably should have—called Daisy yesterday when he received the news, but he needed time to digest Doreen's death and did not want to deliver devastating news over the phone. Besides, Jenny had said that Daisy had not answered her phone all day.

"Please don't be home," Dan mumbled.

She could be away with friends, except she did not have any, at least none that she ever mentioned. He pushed aside the harrowing thought of Daisy hurting herself if she had heard about Doreen's death from the local gossips. Dan consoled himself with the fact that a year had passed since Daisy last attempted to harm herself. He selected her key from among his, exhaled a long breath, and slid the key into the lock.

Silence.

Her apartment was in its meticulous condition. Her phone lay centered on her coffee table.

"Daisy?"

He searched her bedroom. The tautness of the coverlet on her bed would have passed a military inspection. *Wow, hospital corners and everything.* Dan wondered how he even knew that term and contributed his knowledge to his visits to Mercy Hospital where his mother had died. He shook off the creepiness causing the fine hairs on his neck to itch. He had been forced to deal with death too often during his fifty-two years.

He felt foolish, but he did it anyway. He knelt and peeked under the bed. There was no way of predicting Daisy's behavior when she skipped her medication. He discovered a small cardboard box instead of his daughter playing an irrational game of hide-and-seek.

Dan walked down the hallway to the bathroom. He knocked on the closed door.

"Daisy. You in there?"

Christ, don't let me find . . .

He turned the knob.

The shower curtain concealed the tub. Dan closed his eyes and jerked the vinyl to the left. He peeked. Empty.

Where in the hell could she be?

As he returned to the kitchen, Daisy entered the apartment. "Dad?"

"Been lookin' for you. You didn't answer your phone. Jenny said she tried to reach you all day. Where've you been?"

Daisy stepped back and gripped the doorknob. "Don't yell at me. Why are you yelling at me?"

"Christ, Daisy." Dan ran his hand through his silver-speckled hair. "I thought . . . thought you . . . never mind. Where were you?"

She released her grip. "I put the cat outside. He's a stray, I think. If he comes back again, I'm going to keep him."

"*Huh.* So, you haven't talked to nobody?"

Daisy shook her head. "No, the cat keeps me company." Her eyes darted toward her bookshelf. "What did Jenny want?"

"Daisy," Dan sighed. "Somethin' bad happened."

Daisy's eyes remained focused on the bookshelf. "Jenny told you about the dirty corners, didn't she? She was so mad, but I cleaned them. I did. Right after she left. I'll show you."

Daisy removed a book from the shelf. She stacked two more on the table and reached for the fourth when Dan grabbed her arm.

"What're you doing?"

"The corners. They're clean. Jenny got so mad, so I cleaned them again. Twice. Honest."

Dan rubbed his chin to relieve the ache in his clenched jaw. The pounding in his head began like it always did when his daughter's speech rattled into unrelated tangents. Circles. She always spoke in maddening circles.

"When was Jenny here?" Dan asked.

"On Monday, dusting day. I always dust on Mondays and Wednesdays, but she was here on—"

Dan interrupted with a raised palm. "What did she want?"

Daisy planted her hands on her hips. "I told you. She was mad." Daisy returned the books to the shelf, ensuring their spines lined up with the others.

Hoping to redirect his daughter's focus and stop the eternal spiral of her replies, Dan questioned his daughter like an attorney cross-examining a witness.

"Jenny was here last Monday, and she was mad, right?"

"Yes."

"Did she call you today?"

"No."

Dan rubbed his chin. "Are you sure? Except for a few minutes ago, you had your phone with you all day, right?"

"Yes. Why don't you believe me?"

"Honey, I think it's Jenny that I don't believe, not you. Can you sit, please? I have to tell you somethin'. It's gonna be upsettin' so just listen, okay?"

Satisfied her books were in the proper order, Daisy sat on the couch next to her father.

"Don't know how to say this . . . "

Daisy crossed her arms and prepared for another scolding.

"Your mother—"

Daisy jutted her bottom lip in a childish pout. "I already know."

Dan tilted his head. "You already know? Who told you?"

"I know Mom's mad too, because she yelled at me at the bank."

Dan huffed. Circles. Topics always looping, yet never connecting. He returned to his prosecutor's tone. "When did Doreen yell at you at the bank?"

"When I cashed your check. She was mean, really nasty. The man made her stop."

"Sorry 'bout that, honey. But somethin's happened, Daisy. Doreen . . . died."

"Did the man—"

"No, Daisy, the man didn't have nothin' to do with it. She died at home—was sick or somethin'."

Daisy rubbed her palms in a feverish motion. Dan watched in awe and thought if his daughter held a stick between her hands, she could ignite a campfire.

"I did it."

"You did what, Daisy?"

She increased the friction motion between her palms. "I didn't mean to. She yelled at me. I wished she was dead and now she is. She is!"

Dan drew his daughter into his arms and whispered, "You didn't do nothin'. Don't go blamin' yourself, all right?"

Daisy pulled away from his embrace. "But I wished—"

"That don't matter. Wishin' don't really work none."

Daisy frowned in confusion. "But you always said . . . "

Dan cradled his child. In these confusing, heart wrenching moments, she was just that. A child.

"Only good wishes come true, honey." He stroked her hair. "Only the good ones."

Dan's mouth was dry, and he craved a Red's.

Circles. Always circles.

"So, was she all right, Dan?" Jenny asked not bothering to look up from her magazine.

He reached for a Red's. "You tell me."

"What's that supposed to mean?"

"Seems like you were there last Monday, screaming at her?"

Jenny threw her magazine on the coffee table. "What? What reason would I have to scream at her?"

"Because her bookshelf was dirty."

Jenny laughed. When a snort erupted, she howled even harder.

"You find that funny?"

"Oh my God, Dan. Do you really think I would drive to her place in Greenville on my day off just to yell about her housekeeping? Christ, you and I both know we could eat off her floors."

Jenny wiped tears from her eyes and resumed reading.

"Well, she said—"

"Yeah, Dan she *said*. She also said fairies live in her flowerpots and chlorine adds calories to water. Should I go on?"

Dan tilted his Red's and sucked down the last drop. He tossed the can into the trash bin and immediately wrapped his hand around a second one. "So, you weren't there. *Huh*. She said she thinks she's killed Doreen 'cause she wished her dead after Doreen yelled at her at the bank."

"Are you sure *that* even happened? I know for a fact Lorraine hauled Doreen to the bank, and she never mentioned anything about Doreen seeing Daisy or even talking to her."

"Don't know what to believe anymore, to tell you the truth. Maybe Daisy shouldn't go to the funeral."

He switched on the television. The oval track the cars raced on mirrored one more circle in Dan's life. Like the last driver in the pack, Dan was far from reaching the finish line. Instead of waving a checkered flag of his life's accomplishments, he resorted to flapping the white flag of surrender.

"If she's going to cause a scene, maybe not," Jenny replied. "Not exactly looking forward to going myself."

Dan conceded to his wife's advice. "Well, it's still a few days away. I'll check on Daisy again before then."

Jenny handed a third beer to her husband. "Going outside to pull weeds from the flowerbed."

Dan accepted the Red's. Nine more beers and he could forget Doreen was dead and still messing up his life. Nine more.

Jenny walked past her perfectly manicured flowerbed and crossed the highway to Lorraine's. She knocked on her neighbor's door. "Lorraine, you home?"

Lorraine answered the door sporting a ponytail and her clothes speckled with a hue of aquamarine paint.

"Jen, come in. Glad you have time to talk. I've been wondering what's been going on."

"You sure this is a good time? Looks like you're in the middle of something."

Lorraine motioned her friend inside. "Can you tell? Painting my bedroom, but it's time for a coffee break. I hate painting. Where's a man when you need one?"

Jenny kicked off her shoes. "Mine's home sulking in front of a TV. Living with one is not all that it's cracked up to be."

Jenny followed Lorraine into the kitchen and sat while Lorraine scooped instant-coffee crystals into two mugs and set the teakettle to boil.

"Yeah, what's up with Dan? You'd think he'd be glad Dori's gone . . . I mean . . . well, you know what I mean," Lorraine said.

"It's not so much about her as it is about his precious daughter. He has to guard her fragile feelings, even when she lies about shit. Gets old real fast, I'm telling you."

"Lies about what?"

Jenny crossed her arms and bobbed her head. "Okay, for example, remember the day you took Doreen to the bank?"

"Yeah, kinda feel guilty now for being pissed at her. You know, if I had known only a week or so later—"

"That's not it. Daisy claims Doreen blew up at her at the bank. But I told Dan you were with her, and Doreen didn't pull her usual shit that day."

The teakettle's whistling prompted Lorraine to shut off the burner. "Well, you know, I *thought* I saw Daisy leave the bank that day, but Doreen said she hadn't noticed because the bank was hassling her about her ID."

Lorraine poured steamy water into the cups and offered Jenny a spoon.

"Doesn't matter," Jenny replied, stirring her coffee. "Daisy lies so much, you can't believe anything that comes out of her mouth." She stirred her coffee and added, "Must have inherited that from her mother."

"So, tell me, how *did* Dori die?"

Jenny sipped her coffee before replying. "Don't know."

Lorraine set down her mug after nearly spewing coffee from her lips. "Don't know?"

"Doubt we'll ever be told. Daisy's the next-of-kin, and they ain't exactly going to notify a mental case."

"Well, my guess is all those cigarettes caused a heart attack. How in the hell could anyone smoke three or four packs a day for forty years and not have it kill them? I'm still airing out my SUV from our trip."

"Her funeral's Thursday at one o'clock. You going?"

"Where's it at?"

"Greenville Baptist Church."

Lorraine snickered. "Probably the first time Dori's been in a church her entire life."

"Right," Jenny said. "You know she hated Pearson's Funeral Home, so probably a good thing it's not going to be held there. Remember Al Campbell's funeral? She practically laughed through the whole thing. Never saw anything so disrespectful in my life."

"Yeah, I remember. Then at Lucy's funeral, she acted bored. Like she couldn't wait for it to be over with." Lorraine hummed recalling the memory. "That poor little girl."

"Well, the church is burying Doreen next to Lucy in the family plot. That's another reason Dan is so keyed up. Can you imagine?"

Lorraine refilled her mug. "In a perfect world, yes. A mother should be laid to rest next to her child. But in this case, it's sacrilegious, in my opinion."

"Just promise me, Lorraine, that you'll be there. Please. Dan will be hovering over Daisy. I need someone to lean on."

Lorraine raised the teakettle above Jenny's mug. "More coffee?"

"No, I better head home. You've got to finish painting and wash those blue specks out of your hair. You'll be there?"

"Wouldn't miss it for the world."

CHAPTER 33

Roy ushered his daughter into his one-bedroom apartment. After living in his cousin's den for a year, the apartment size seemed ample for his needs, but it shrunk as he prepared it for two.

"Make yourself at home. You hungry? We can head to Delores's Diner in a bit, if you want," Roy said to his daughter.

Tasha dropped her purse and backpack on the floor. Her father's basement apartment, with its dark brown paneling and burnt-orange carpeting, always reminded her of a dungeon. The scant windows and slight mildew odor contributed to the claustrophobic cave-like atmosphere.

She snuggled in his La-Z-Boy. "Not now."

"Just let me know. Go ahead and watch some TV if you want. I'm going to strip the bed and get it ready for you. You can have my room."

Tasha frowned. "No, Dad. The couch is fine. You don't have to give up your bed."

"You sure?"

"Sure I'm sure," she said with a grin. "The TV's out here."

Roy did not return his daughter's smile. He lowered his voice to gain her attention.

"Tasha, you haven't told me where you were when . . . Were you out all night? I mean, it's okay if you were, I just want to know."

"I stayed overnight at Kristi's for her birthday. Mom said it was okay."

You're already knocked up, what difference does it make?

"And what time did you leave?"

"About five; around there sometime."

Roy considered his daughter's answers and pressed on. "Your mother seemed fine when you left?"

"Yeah, except for yelling like she always does . . . did."

My daughter's a whore. A whore. At least I was married . . .

Her father's questioning made Tasha uneasy. Did he suspect anything?

Tasha added, "She was smoking and watching TV like always. Why?"

Roy spread his fingers over his mustache and rubbed his chin. "Just wondering what could have happened, that's all. Nobody else was there, right?"

"Who would I invite into that messy trailer? You haven't seen the inside of it, but it's embarrassing."

God, how embarrassing to have a little darkie growing inside of you.

"I don't want to worry you, Dumplin', but there's some unsavory characters in and out of that trailer park. Did she have any recent run-ins with anybody? Anybody you know who would want to harm her?"

Wish I could call Roy right now and give him the worst fucking news of his life.

"No, Dad, I don't." Tasha stood. "I'm feeling kinda hungry now, if we can still go out to eat."

"Sure thing, honey."

Roy escorted his daughter through the double glass doors of Delores's Diner. The evening crowd had dispersed, as none of the locals would consent to consuming their supper later than seven o'clock and miss their favorite television series. A few truck drivers hunched over their plates at the counter, devouring the home-style meals Delores was famous for serving.

Roy and Tasha slid into a rear booth.

Delores, being the only employee on staff besides the cook, rushed to greet them. "Howdy, Roy. Menus?"

"Hello, Delores," Roy said and set his cap on the booth seat. "Depends. What's the daily special?"

"Beef tips and gravy on mashed potatoes."

Roy winked at his daughter. "Sounds good to me. How about you, Tasha?"

"Sure. Can I get a cola, please?"

"Coffee for you, Roy?"

"Yes, please. Thanks, Delores."

"Two beef platters coming right up," Delores said and sped to the kitchen for a few moments before returning with the beverages. She served the drinks and then headed to the counter to ring up a truck driver's tab.

"She's got really good food here. I probably eat here more often than I should," Roy confessed. "Never had much talent for cooking."

"Neither did Mom."

Roy watched Delores approach their booth. "Yeah, I remember."

Delores placed the large tray on a nearby table. She set Tasha's entrée in front of her, before reaching for Roy's. "Coleslaw on the side and dinner roll. Silverware and napkins in the caddy there. Holler if you need anything more. All set? Enjoy."

Delores returned the empty tray to the counter and watched with curiosity as Roy dined with his daughter. After all the talk the past two days of his ex-wife's death, the eagerness in which the girl shoveled food into her mouth surprised Delores. She disguised her attentiveness on the pair by filling saltshakers, but she noted Roy's daughter devoured the meal faster than any hungry trucker ever did.

Ten minutes later, Delores approached the booth. "Clean plate for the missy. I like to see that. Dessert?"

Roy pushed his plate toward the table's edge and tossed his crumpled napkin on top of his half-eaten meal. "None for me. It's really good, Delores, but it's so filling."

Delores smiled. "And what about the lady? Apple pie? Baked fresh this morning."

"Apple pie with a cheese slice and vanilla ice cream," Tasha requested. She turned to her father. "Is that okay?"

"Whatever you want, honey."

"Let me clear these plates, and then I'll fetch that pie," Delores said. She returned with a saucer containing a pie slice hidden under scoops of ice cream. "So sorry to hear about your mother, dear. That's gotta be hard."

Tasha pierced the pie with her fork and scooped a dollop of ice cream before popping the sweet mixture into her mouth.

Roy lightly kicked his daughter. "Tasha?"

"Thank you," she mumbled while chewing.

"Supper's on the house, Roy. You've enough on your mind. Take care, and God bless."

Roy accepted his host's generosity. "Mighty kind of you, Delores. Thank you."

Delores offered a smile and reminded herself to tell Jenny about the girl's ferocious appetite. She waved goodbye to the pair as they exited the diner.

"Something just don't set right," Delores said to the empty diner. "Folks, especially the youngsters, grieve for their family. Guessing that girl hasn't shed one single tear. Not one."

Tasha changed into the tee-shirt and sweat pants she had worn at Kristi's and settled on the couch with the blanket and pillow her father supplied.

"The TV's not too loud?" she asked her father.

"No, don't really matter. Doubt I'll be getting much sleep tonight." He leaned and kissed Tasha's forehead. "Night, Dumplin'."

"Night, Dad."

The television noise was the distraction Tasha craved as she mulled the consequences of her involvement in her mother's death.

She wished now she had asked Jermaine more questions about the sheriff's investigation. Would a detective question her about her diary entries? She cringed knowing law enforcement officers were privy to her private thoughts. She spent years hiding the key from her mother in creative spots, but now a bunch of strangers scoured the pages, searching for clues. Tasha rationalized all teenage girls wrote about arguing with their mothers, and since she had not actually divulged her desire to kill her, she felt confident her diary yielded no importance to the men who violated her privacy by confiscating it. She also disregarded the date circled on the calendar since it was Kristi's birthday. One telephone call to her friend's parents would confirm the date. She reasoned the only other evidence the detectives could possibly have gathered was fingerprints and hair samples, but since she inhabited the trailer those were moot points too. Tasha's anxiety diminished when she realized that the *A* grade she had achieved in the science forensic class provided her with the necessary knowledge to avoid an arrest.

A commercial featuring a baby giggling while his mother secured a disposable diaper around his chunky thighs reminded Tasha of her other problem. Her belly's roundness soon would disclose her secret. How could she approach her father with the news? He had been friendly to Jermaine when he met him, but that was different than accepting the boy as the father of his teenage daughter's illegitimate child.

Jermaine. What was he doing at this moment? Was he thinking of her? She wished she could call him just to hear his reassuring voice. The waiting to contact him was dreadful. Tasha was lonely.

She clicked off the remote. The full supper at Delores's Diner had induced drowsiness. She punched her pillow and dozed into a fitful sleep. For the first time in months, she dreamt.

A black sedan with tinted windows appeared at her father's apartment, and a man wearing sunglasses and a felt fedora ordered her

father to surrender his daughter. When Roy refused, the man arrested
him. He called a colleague to detain Roy while he forced Tasha into the
vehicle to deliver her to police headquarters.

Tasha sat alone in a windowless room. The warm air was stagnant,
yet she felt a chill penetrate her bones. She sat on a hard, steel chair
and waited for her captor to return. After an eternity, the door opened.
Jermaine entered with the man wearing the fedora.

The man raising his palm prevented Tasha from rushing toward
Jermaine.

"Is she the one?" the man asked.

Jermaine stared into Tasha's pleading eyes. "Yes, sir. She's the one
who killed her mother."

"Jermaine. Jermaine, how could you—"

"Silence!" The man commanded. "You are pronounced guilty and
condemned to die. Condemned to die! Condemned to die!"

Tasha bolted awake. She kicked the tangled blanket to the
floor. She squinted in the darkness until her head cleared. Tasha
remembered she was at her father's apartment, not imprisoned in
a cell. She was at her father's; her mother was dead . . . and she
had killed her.

The nightmare had shattered her earlier confidence about the
sheriff's investigation. Jermaine had advised her to leave behind
no crumbs, but she realized now he was the link. He was the only
person who knew about the stolen money and could provide the
motive the detectives sought to solve the murder.

If Jermaine testified against her, he would unwittingly put his
child's mother behind bars.

Tasha rushed to the bathroom. She sank to her knees and
gripped the toilet. She purged the meal she had enjoyed just hours
ago and wondered if she would ever enjoy anything again. She
ignored a slight flutter in her abdomen.

Tasha had not solved her dilemma.

She had boxed herself into a corner.

Roy decided to rise and start his day instead of tossing in bed and anticipating the sleep he knew would not arrive. Too many unanswered questions remained surrounding Doreen's death. Had she died of natural causes or had something sinister happened? He cringed thinking about the inhabitants of Unlucky Thirteen. Some were vagrants, most were criminals, and sadly, the children were the unintended victims subjected to poverty and violence. The only reassurance about the trailer park Roy accepted was his daughter would not live there anymore.

Since he was on bereavement leave and the funeral was not scheduled until tomorrow, Roy decided to be productive and contact the sheriff's department. The past four days of speculating the circumstance of Doreen's death had been worrisome, and he reasoned any update concerning Doreen's death would put his mind at ease. If an enemy had targeted Doreen, he wanted law enforcement's assurance that his daughter would be protected from the thugs.

He stepped past his sleeping daughter and headed to the kitchen to brew his morning coffee. He conducted every movement as quietly as he could, but he grimaced when the spoon he dropped echoed a *clank* against the tin canister's lid. He set his coffee pot to brew and grabbed the phone.

After identifying himself and disclosing the nature of his inquiry, Roy's call was transferred to Detective Hershel Monroe. When the detective inquired if Roy was able and willing to speak to him and grant permission to interview his daughter, Roy agreed to a one o'clock meeting at the Mason County Sheriff's Department.

Tasha rose weary-eyed from the couch when she heard her father's voice. "Who were you talking to? You were on the phone, right?"

Roy poured coffee into two cups. "Sit."

Tasha brushed the hair from her eyes and sat across from her father.

"I was talking to a detective about your mother."

Tasha sat up taller in her chair. "Why?"

"Because I wanted an update on the . . . the situation. I made an appointment for us to talk to him at one o'clock today. He'll tell us more then."

Tasha drummed her fingers on the table. "Well . . . I don't . . . well . . . What's he gonna tell us? Wouldn't he tell us if he already knew something?"

"Not waiting to find out. If there's someone out there who hurt your mother, you'd want them to arrest that person, wouldn't you?"

Tasha swallowed hard. "What are we going to tell him? We don't know anything."

"Just relax, Dumplin'. He'll do all the talking. We just have to listen. I'm making eggs for breakfast. You want some?"

Tasha shook her head. She doubted she would ever gain an appetite or enjoy anything ever again.

"I need some fresh clothes, Dad. Been wearing these since I came home from Kristi's. They're all I had in my backpack. I need to go home."

"You *are* home."

"But all my stuff is back at the trailer."

Roy cracked two eggs against the pan's edge. "Tell you what. Get ready, and we'll head up to Bancor early. I'll buy you a new outfit— two, if you want. It's not safe to return to that trailer now."

"You're worrying about nothing, you know."

Roy snapped his head to the right and faced his daughter. "And how do you know that?"

Tasha mumbled. "Nothing."

When she returned to the couch and snuggled under the blanket, she cursed. Roy glanced around the corner at his daughter and imagined if she had a cigarette dangling from her mouth, she would have been the spitting image of her mother.

Roy prodded his daughter. "Might want to get ready while I finish my breakfast."

With a sour pout, Tasha headed to the shower.

He finished his eggs in welcomed solitude. He swallowed two extra-strength Aspirin with the last of his coffee. The dirty dishes could wait. He turned off the light.

"Time to go," he shouted toward the bathroom.

Tasha emerged with damp hair, wearing the black outfit she had worn for the fifth consecutive day.

"Can't wait to get out of these clothes!" she complained.

Roy snatched his keys from the wall hook and squared his cap. "Soon enough."

Roy parked at the mall in Bancor. He handed Tasha eighty dollars after admitting he would happily wait in the truck while she shopped. Listening to his radio was preferable to following a teenage girl through the maze of clothing stores. He was not surprised when she emerged from the building wearing black jeans and a flowing blouse, with her old clothes secured in a bag.

"That didn't take long."

"Well, when you shop for black, it simplifies everything. I even have eleven dollars left."

Roy looked at the clock on his dash. "Good. It's just noon now. We have time for lunch."

Tasha looked down at the floorboard. "I'm not very hungry."

"Well, if you're worried—"

"Not worried. Why should I be worried?"

"I'm just saying . . . just saying it's a stressful time, that's all." Roy pointed toward the east side of the parking lot and smiled. "My goodness, I haven't seen one of those for ages. A hot dog cart. Let's drive over and get a foot long."

"Whatever you say."

Tasha sat in silence while Roy chowed his hot dog and washed it down with a soda. After wiping mustard from his mustache, he drove to the sheriff's department. Once inside, they approached a receptionist typing behind an acrylic wall.

"May I help you?"

"Yes, thank you." Roy cleared his throat. "We have an appointment to see Detective Monroe."

The woman held up one finger while she placed a telephone call. "Have a seat. He'll be right down."

Tasha crinkled her nose as she sat next to her father. An odor of pine-scented cleanser meant to conceal the grime embedded in the cracked asphalt floor tiles permeated the musty air. Tasha guessed the tattered magazines piled haphazardly on a corner table were older than she was, judging by their dog-eared and missing pages. A sign affixed on the wall notifying visitors that a surveillance camera was in use was hardly necessary unless one could not see the camera perched high in the corner. Tasha sat with her legs crossed, bouncing her foot with nervous energy while waiting for the detective.

The shuffling of footsteps grew louder from the hallway. A tall man wearing a blue suit opened the door and approached Roy, who stood at attention as if he were a trained soldier.

The man introduced himself. "Detective Monroe. And you are Roy, Roy Ferch?"

Roy extended his hand. "That's me. This here's Tasha, my daughter."

Detective Monroe shook Roy's hand and instructed the pair to follow him.

Tasha trailed her father and the detective down a long hallway. She expected he would escort them into a windowless interrogation room like the one in her dream. Instead, she was surprised when the detective's office resembled her high school counselor's office. Detective Monroe motioned them to sit in comfortable leather chairs in front of his desk.

After exchanging pleasantries, Detective Monroe focused on the interview. "With your permission, Mr. Ferch, I would like to ask you both questions, but separately."

"Well, sure, but . . . Do you have any information about . . . what happened?"

Detective Monroe's grin unsettled Tasha. Clearly, he had an agenda he had not fully disclosed to her naïve father.

"We'll get to that. If I could, I'll ask you to wait in the next room while I interview your daughter. She lived at Westside Wheel Estates with her mother, am I correct?"

"Yeah, but . . . Maybe this is a mistake. I thought you were going to tell us what happened. How can we tell you? Neither of us were there," Roy protested.

"Let me explain," Detective Monroe leaned forward and clasped his hands. "An investigation relies on the people closest to the victim. Now—"

"Oh my God . . . Victim?" Roy asked. He shot a nervous look at Tasha.

"Let's just say we're investigating a suspicious death. Toxicology results likely won't be available for weeks. In the meantime, it's best for everyone to share information. The most mundane thing can break a case wide open, but unless we interview people, we can't begin to discover what may or may not have happened. Does that make sense?"

Roy stroked his thin mustache. "I guess so. I want to get to the bottom of this. So, yeah, you have my permission."

"Good. I'll have you wait right outside my door while I interview . . . Tasha? Then I'll ask you the same questions, and you'll be on your way. Please sign this form acknowledging your consent."

Roy complied and signed the form without bothering to read it. "I'll be right outside, Dumplin'."

Tasha stared at the closed door, diverting her gaze from the detective. She slowed her breathing and remembered Jermaine's instructions not to divulge too much, just answer the questions with the fewest words possible.

Detective Monroe situated a tape recorder on the edge of his desk. He explained to Tasha that the audio interview was the most accurate documentation method for transcription purposes before he hit Record.

After he had read her the Miranda Rights off a small index card he had produced from his breast pocket—and stating he advised everyone of their rights for their own protection after seeing Tasha's face grow in panic—he began with the first official question. "State your full name, please."

"Tasha Alice Ferch."

After recording her date of birth and address, Detective Monroe delved into questioning her about the day Doreen died. "Tell me about June seventeenth. Where were you?"

"Home and then went to my friend Kristi's house for a sleep-over."

"What time did you leave for her house?"

"About five?" She cocked her head. "Yeah, about then."

Tasha complied with the detective's request and furnished Kristi's full name, her parents' names, and address.

"You were there all night? Were others there?"

"*Un-huh.*"

"Miss Ferch, please answer yes or no."

Perspiration beaded on her forehead. "Okay. I mean, yes."

"Where was your mother, Doreen Ferch, when you left?"

"On the couch."

"Did she say anything when you left?"

"Have fun?"

"Did your mother travel? Take trips? Buy souvenirs?"

Tasha squinted in puzzlement.

"Yes or no?" Detective Monroe asked.

"No, why?"

"Just a no is sufficient, Miss Ferch."

"What about her hair style? Did she have a recent haircut, or trim it herself?"

"No. She wanted to, but didn't have enough money, she said."

"Did your mother have any enemies that you're aware of?"

"Well, she argued with a lot of people. That's hard to say."

"To your knowledge, did she argue with anyone on June seventeenth?"

"No."

"Did your mother use drugs? Prescription or illicit ones?"

Tasha shook her head. *They know about the insulin.*

He pointed to the tape recorder. "Again, Miss Ferch, please respond with a yes or no."

"No."

"Did you see anything suspicious? Anything the day or night before?"

"No."

Detective Monroe stopped the tape recorder. "Good job, Miss Ferch. Could I ask you to send your father in now?"

Tasha exited the room and rushed into her father's arms. He ended the embrace when Detective Monroe summoned him into his office. Tasha mentally reviewed the session and was confident she did not incriminate herself.

After Roy endured a similar line of questioning, Detective Monroe asked if he had any questions.

"Yes," Roy said. "So, you say 'suspicious death'. That means you don't have any leads, right? That's all I'm wanting to know. I have to protect my daughter."

Detective Monroe folded his hands. "A possible homicide investigation is not solved in an hour like the television dramas, and I wouldn't insult your intelligence by suggesting we are even close to drawing any conclusions. It can take weeks, months, and sometimes years to solve a case. Sometimes, we never discover the answers we seek. It's just the way it is."

Roy leaned forward in his chair. "But, this still could be a death by natural causes?"

"Of course, I can't disclose to you the confidential information in the case file. But I can tell you we've sent evidence and toxicology reports to the state lab. Depending on their backlog, like I said, it can take a long time to obtain the results, and it may not even be what we expected. I can only ask for your patience, and thank you for your time in allowing the interviews today."

Roy nodded as he digested the information. "I don't want to sound ungrateful. I know you're doing all you can." Roy stood and firmly shook the detective's hand. As he was about to exit the office, the detective's next sentence caused Roy to pause.

"I do have one suggestion for you, Mr. Ferch."

"That is?"

"Keep your ears open. Criminals themselves are most likely to be their own worst enemies. Some brag, some confess to people they trust. Listen and report if you want to help the investigation."

Roy shook the detective's hand a second time before leaving the office. He guided Tasha out of the building with his hand placed on the small of her back. Tasha was relieved to climb into the truck and head toward her father's apartment, her new home.

"Wasn't so bad, *huh*?" Roy asked as he started the truck's engine.

"Did he tell you anything?"

Roy shifted into Drive. "Not really, Dumplin'. Guess we just have to wait. Wait and see."

"For how long?"

"Now that seems to be a question the detective couldn't answer. Don't matter, there's no statute of limitations on murder."

"Statute of limitations?"

"Well, yeah. A person can be arrested for murder any time. Today, tomorrow, or thirty years from now if they suspect you."

Tasha turned toward the window, lowered her head, and rubbed her temples.

Any time.

CHAPTER 34

With the exception of the alcove addition built twenty years ago, Greenville Baptist Church had not changed since Reverend Joseph Campbell—Dan's great-grandfather—had founded the church in 1881. Although he had hired contractors to build the structure, Reverend Joe, as he insisted everyone call him, practically laid each brick himself. Reverend Campbell was a hands-on preacher, from visiting the sick to sweeping the floors after the Sunday sermon.

Dan approached the church, dabbing sweat with the white linen handkerchief from his suit pocket. The polyester suit Jenny had miraculously discovered in the back of his closet was as hot and itchy as he remembered from the last time he had worn it. Even in death, Doreen caused him misery. He stopped walking when he noticed Daisy was no longer in step with him and Jenny.

"Daisy?"

Dan watched his daughter dodge imaginary blockades on the sidewalk as she mumbled a childhood rhyme. "Step on a crack, break your mother's back. Step on a crack . . . "

"Honey, didn't I explain that thing about wishing?"

She stopped leaping in her imaginary hopscotch game and began rubbing her palms in a fire-starting motion Dan recognized as her tension release technique.

"Only good wishes, right?" Daisy answered. "Only the good ones."

"Yes, honey," Dan answered and tugged on her elbow to stop the hand rubbing. "We have to go in the church now."

Daisy bent her head, her long braid trailing down her back. "Don't want to. I can't."

"I gave you the chance to stay home. We're here now. We have to go in," Dan said with a sterner voice than he intended. He scratched his wrist to relieve the itch from the polyester chafing his skin.

"Of course, we have to go in," Jenny said. "What's the matter?"

Daisy stuttered. "Do . . . Do we . . . Do . . . have to *look* at her?"

Dan comforted his daughter by wrapping his arm around her. "Well, we can sit in the back, honey."

Jenny corrected her husband. "Dan, relatives always sit in the front pew."

She shot a what-are-you-thinking expression to her husband before distancing herself from the scene she predicted would happen. She had exhausted all her words last night arguing with Dan about Daisy's attendance at the funeral. She spotted Lorraine approaching the church and abandoned Dan to deal with Daisy's breakdown.

Lorraine tilted her head toward Dan and Daisy and whispered to Jenny, "How's *that* going?"

"How do you think? Twenty-five years old and she's scared she'll see Doreen laid out."

Lorraine glanced at Dan's repeated attempts to prevent Daisy from rubbing her palms. "Well, she does have problems."

Jenny huffed. "You're telling me?"

Reverend Collins greeted the women as they entered the chapel's foyer. After exchanging pleasantries with a few acquaintances, Lorraine and Jenny stepped into the sanctuary.

"Closed casket," Lorraine observed. "Should we go out and tell Dan?"

"*Naw*. He can deal with it."

"Well, I must admit, those are beautiful white roses on the casket. Does that ribbon say *Mom*?"

"Oh yeah, round two of the big argument last night. The floral spray was Roy's idea, but of course, he's broke. That bouquet cost over a hundred and fifty dollars. They're supposed to split the cost. Dan told Roy not to worry about it and repay him when he can."

"Well, that was nice of Dan, considering—"

"Considering I wrote the check from *my* checking account, it was real nice," Jenny snapped. "Then Dan thinks he's going to spend another two hundred on a new suit. For what? To wear for a couple hours? I got even with him. Told him to wear the one in the back of his closet, the one that itches like hell."

Lorraine glanced back to the foyer. "There's Dan and Daisy now. Suppose I best find a place to sit, since you'll be escorted with the family members."

Jenny remained and faced the casket. She expelled her frustration through tight lips. "Doreen."

Jenny spun abruptly and bumped into a woman she did not recognize. The woman's flaxen-gray hair hung in strands and framed the deep wrinkles carved into her face. Tufts of animal fur and lint clung to her matching ebony blouse and slacks, which contrasted against her white, scuffed canvas shoes. Jenny detected an odor of stale liquor emitting from the woman as she apologized for colliding with the stranger.

"Oh, I'm so sorry," Jenny said. "I didn't see you there."

The visitor pointed her crooked finger toward the casket. In a monotone voice accompanying her stoic expression, she said, "Paying my last respects to my daughter today."

"Judy?" Jenny asked. She mentally calculated the years since she had last seen Doreen's mother. Doreen had been an eight-year-old when the county had shuffled her to the first foster home. Judy left town shortly after she had lost custody of both of her children. Forty-four years . . .

The woman squinted suspiciously. "Who're you?"

"Jenny Campbell. Well, you would remember me as Jenny Abbott. Doreen and I were friends in school."

Judy's gaze focused on the pine box.

"Don't know," Judy said. "Lost all contact with folks here. If I didn't pay for the local press to be mailed to my house, I wouldn't even knowed she died." She whispered, "She died."

"Oh, I'm so, so sorry. Where do you live now?"

"Michigan City. Moved closer to the prison to visit Timmy. At least one of my kids still wanted to talk to me."

Judy hoisted her cracked vinyl purse strap over her shoulder and approached the casket. After inhaling the roses' scent, she briefly patted the casket. With a crumpled tissue she pulled from her pocket, she dabbed her eyes and wiped her nose. She said nothing as she passed Jenny to exit the church.

Curiosity overcame Jenny, and she trailed Judy down the church steps. Judy disappeared into a waiting car that spun away from the curb as if the driver's patience had worn thin during his short wait.

"Wow, drove for three hours to spend five minutes saying goodbye and didn't even stay for the funeral," Jenny said to herself. She took a deep breath and muttered, "Doreen."

Jenny walked to Dan's side as Reverend Collins greeted Dan. "How're you kind folks holding up?"

Dan shook the minister's hand. "Fine, thanks."

"I'll ask all family members to meet me downstairs in my office in a few minutes. I'd like to offer a prayer and my personal condolences before the service. Would that be all right?"

"Sure. I see Roy now. I'll tell him," Dan answered.

Dan gathered his family with Roy and Tasha and directed the group to the office. Daisy, still clinging onto Dan, sat next to him in the leather chairs, forcing Jenny to sit with Tasha behind them on folding chairs, while Roy leaned against the wall.

"Everyone here?" Reverend Collins asked before he sat behind his desk. He acknowledged the group's nods and continued. "Please accept my personal condolences. Doreen Ferch was a fine woman." He smiled. "She raised the two beautiful daughters

I see here today. She enriched every life she touched. We never know the reason God calls home those close to us; it's not for us to question His ways. Seek comfort in the love you feel—the love Doreen left behind. Please join me in prayer."

Tasha cupped her hand over her mouth to prevent snickering when the pastor asked God to deliver her mother's soul to Heaven.

Reverend Collins continued speaking to the group after he uttered *amen*. "When we return upstairs, you'll be escorted to the reserved pews in the front. Once the service has concluded, there'll be a short gravesite service. Fellowship will follow with refreshments in the community hall."

When the reverend motioned for the group to exit, Daisy's tight grip on her father's arm thwarted Jenny's attempt to join Dan's side in the stairway. Jenny's effort to attract Dan's attention proved futile as he walked with his head down and scratched his neck as the sandpaper-textured polyester irritated his skin.

The organ chords wafting familiar tunes Roy once knew the lyrics to summoned the mourners to the pews. Reverend Collins nodded for the ushers to escort the family members to the reserved pews as he stepped behind the altar and opened his Bible.

Tasha regretted plunging onto the hard, wooden pew and guessed that regular church members grew thick callouses on their rears from years of sitting on the unpadded benches.

She whispered to her father, "Why does that ribbon say *Mom*?"

"Because those flowers are from you and Daisy."

Flowers from me? I doubt that was Daisy's idea.

Tasha glanced behind her shoulder and silently counted an attendance of twenty-three mourners. She was surprised that many people even *knew* her mother. The only people she recognized were Lorraine Simon and Jake Hensley, who owned the bar. Most likely, some of the people attended the funeral to gawk or to collect first-hand accounts to feed the rumor mill.

"Shall we bow our heads in prayer?" Reverend Collins asked the parishioners.

Another prayer? Tasha thought. *Probably going to take a lot of them to get Mom into Heaven.*

After a few mumbled *amens*—one coming from her father's lips—the minister read from the pages of his worn, leather-bound Bible.

"In Genesis chapter three, verse nineteen, we read, 'In the sweat of thy face shalt thou eat bread, till thou return unto the ground; for out of it wast thou taken: for dust thou art, and unto dust shalt thou return.' We are here today to pay our last respects to Doreen Farnsworth Campbell Ferch. Doreen was a lifelong member of the Endover community. She is survived by her mother, Judy Farnsworth; brother, Timothy Farnsworth; and daughters, Daisy Campbell and Tasha Ferch. Her daughter, Lucy Campbell, preceded her in death."

It's Ta-sha, not Tash-a.

Tasha picked at her cuticles while the pastor droned on about dust, ashes, and other biblical nonsense that peeved her. The moisture forming in her father's eyes did little to impress the somberness of the occasion to her; she was bored and wanted to leave.

She focused on a statue of Jesus in the corner and contemplated the meaning of forgiveness. She doubted if any of the people attending the funeral forgave her mother for her transgressions, and why should they? Doreen Ferch, the real one—not the false persona the reverend praised—was nothing but a mean-spirited woman. Tasha suspected if people were honest, they would admit they did not miss her mother. She surely did not.

Tasha pressed against her belly to lessen the pressure of a cramp. Earlier in the morning, she had felt a few spasms but not as strong as the sharp pain that now attacked her side. For a moment, she considered her mother's spirit sought revenge for Tasha's opposing attitude during the funeral, but she did not believe in ghosts any more than she believed in the Jesus statue. She took a deep breath, and the pang vanished as quickly as it had occurred.

After the congregation responded with the final *amen*, Reverend Collins stepped from the altar and traversed the aisle with his head bowed. Pall bearers—volunteers from the church—wheeled the casket behind him as ushers magically appeared from the side wings and gestured to the parishioners to follow the family members to the Campbell cemetery plot.

Daisy's hand remained gripped on her father's arm as they exited the aisle. Jenny finally assumed her place beside Dan once they walked outdoors. She shot Dan a concerned glance as they approached the open gate leading to the cemetery.

Dan strolled past Reverend Joe's prominent monument. Erosion had depleted layers of the limestone, making the name and date barely visible. A small rounded stone simply inscribed, DELLA CAMPBELL, WIFE, referenced a footnote in Joe's life. The graves of Leroy and Mary Campbell rested next to Dan's parents, Alvin and Olivia. The six graves compromised the final resting place of three generations of the aged couples, interned side by side in pairs.

Dan paused.

He shook his elbow free from his daughter's grasp to reach for his handkerchief. He cried, unashamed as he read the inscription on a tiny, flat marble slab.

LUCY M. CAMPBELL 1968-1975

Confused by her father's sobbing, Daisy sought Jenny for an answer. Without a word, Jenny pointed to the stone bearing Lucy's name. Daisy trembled and reached for her father's sleeve, but Jenny's headshaking discouraged Daisy.

"Let him alone," Jenny whispered.

The pallbearers positioned Doreen's casket next to Lucy's burial spot as the handful of mourners gathered in a semi-circle with careful steps in their collective avoidance to intrude on the nearby graves.

"Shall we pray?" Reverend Collin's question was a directive.

Again? Tasha wondered. She stared off to a large oak tree as the crowd bowed their heads.

Lorraine inched forward and placed her hand on Jenny's shoulder. Jenny reached back and patted her friend's hand as Dan continued his unabashed sobbing. Jenny bit her trembling lower lip to prevent a deluge of tears from falling and combining with those of her husband's renewed grief.

Reverend Collins concluded the prayer and added, "The family respectfully requests your presence in the church hall for refreshments and fellowship." The reverend patted Dan's shoulder as he walked from the casket, through the gate, and headed inside the church with the handful of mourners following him.

All except Dan, Jenny, and Daisy.

"Never noticed before . . . Never noticed how small her marker is . . . How tiny compared to the rest," Dan choked out the words between drying his eyes with the damp handkerchief. "She . . . just . . . It seems . . . she's all alone."

Jenny rubbed her husband's back.

Dan pointed. "Look. Just look at the others. All adults. All buried with their spouses. She's alone with nobody . . . *Nobody!* Didn't even get a chance to get married. Didn't get even get the chance to . . . grow up!" He pressed his fingers against his temples. His eyes remained glued to Lucy's marker.

Jenny consoled Dan. "It's not fair, I know."

"She's with Mom now," Daisy whispered.

Dan raised his head and glared at the floral spray adorning Doreen's casket with the ribbon spelling MOM.

"Mom. Mom? That's *all* she gets?"

Jenny placed her arm around Dan. "Honey, you're upset. It'll be—"

"Okay? Is that what you're gonna say? How in the hell is it *okay*? That bitch waitin' to be buried is the very *reason* my daughter is laying alone in the dark ground. My baby. *My* Lucy!"

Daisy rubbed her palms in rough circular motions. "I want to go now."

Lorraine appeared at the gate. "Is everything fine, Jen?"

"Come on, Dan," Jenny coaxed. "Daisy's right. Let's go home."

Dan yanked the ribbon from the floral arrangement and stomped on it. "*Now* everything is *okay*. Let's get out of here."

He resisted Jenny's hug and marched past Lorraine waiting at the gate. Jenny shook her head in frustration at her friend who motioned for Jenny to look behind her. Daisy remained in place, rubbing her palms.

"Daisy. Daisy! We're going," Jenny called.

Daisy approached Jenny in slow, shuffling steps. Jenny gently shoved her through the gate before closing it.

Lorraine offered Jenny a hug as Jenny muttered into her friend's ear, "Damn Doreen."

CHAPTER 35

After shaking Reverend Collin's hand and thanking him for presiding over the funeral, Roy scanned the fellowship hall. Since Dan and Jenny had not bothered to appear and he did not know any of the few people enjoying the cake the volunteers served, he decided there was no point in lingering.

"I guess I'm ready to leave, if you are," Roy said to Tasha. "Unless you want some of that cake."

"Nope. Ready to go."

During the drive home, Roy could not help noticing his daughter wincing and pressing against her belly.

"You feeling all right?"

Tasha leaned against the coolness of the window. She sucked in a deep breath to ease the throbbing ache pulsating in her belly. "Not really, Dad. Think I'll lie down when we get home."

"Well, it's been a pretty emotional day, probably a good idea. I'll likely take a nap too."

Tasha stifled a moan as the cramps increased in frequency and intensity. She folded her arms across her stomach and pressed hard, waiting for the pang to pass.

Something's wrong, very wrong.

She crossed her legs when dampness accompanied the cramps.

Relieved when her father finally crossed town and parked his truck, Tasha scrambled to the door. She was thankful her black pants hid the stain from her father.

"Hold up! I have to unlock that door," Roy said.

Tasha stood to the side and grunted. As soon as her father

opened the door, she bolted past him and darted into the bathroom. Red. Dried and fresh blood stained her underwear.

"Dad. Dad!"

Roy rushed to the bathroom door and was shocked when his daughter limped from the room hunched over and clutching a towel. She braced herself against the wall with her palm.

"Honey?" Roy asked.

She lifted the towel from her crotch, revealing blood seeping through her jeans. "I need . . . a doctor. I'm sorry."

Roy grabbed a second towel and guided his daughter back to the truck. He helped her onto the seat and slammed the door before racing to the driver's side.

Tasha whimpered. "Sorry."

Roy started the engine. "Nothing to be sorry for, Dumplin'. Let's just get you some help."

Tasha did not attempt to conceal her pain now that her body divulged her secret. She groaned and pressed her palms against her stomach. The long ride to Mercy Hospital in Bancor would take some time. She wished she had swallowed some Aspirin before leaving home to block the agonizing pain.

"Sorry," she repeated. "I . . . Well . . . Jer and me . . . "

Roy patted her head. "Just relax. None of that matters now."

Her father's implied acceptance and reassurance did not calm Tasha. She sobbed from the pain, from her father's disappointment, for the unborn baby she had not wanted until now. Everything was all wrong—all twisted like the blades slicing into her gut.

Roy escorted Tasha into the medical emergency center. Once he had explained his daughter's condition, the nurse led Tasha into an examination room. Roy provided insurance information to the admissions clerk before walking to the adjacent waiting area.

Roy paced. He smiled weakly in acknowledgement as the nurse returned to the waiting room. Since he was the only person there, she confirmed his daughter had suffered a miscarriage, and a dilation and curettage procedure was necessary to empty her uterus and prevent possible infection. After granting his parental consent, the nurse assured him his daughter would be resting in her own bed in a few hours.

Roy strolled down the hallway, seeking a beverage vending machine. He inserted coins into the slot and wondered if the dispensed cup would land upright. As he predicted, thick brown mud disguised as coffee filled a paper cup. He tossed the cup in the trashcan without tasting the nasty brew and returned to the dreary waiting room. He chose to ignore the magazines and the canned laughter of a sitcom airing on the television. He drummed his fingers on the chair arm as the longest day of his life droned on.

After what seemed like an eternity, the nurse appeared, pushing Tasha in a wheelchair. "Mr. Ferch, it's a good idea to pull your vehicle up to the admittance doors. Your daughter here may still be a little woozy from the anesthesia."

"Is she all right?" Roy asked the nurse. He leaned toward Tasha. "Honey, you okay?"

Tasha returned a groggy smile.

"Here are the discharge instructions, including a mild pain reliever. She sailed through, just fine," the nurse answered. "Any questions or concerns, please call. That's what we're here for."

Roy drove home slower than normal, avoiding jarring potholes that his old truck's shocks would not absorb to lessen his daughter's discomfort. Her head bobbed from the window to her chest and back against the window again indicating the medication lingered in her system. When they returned home, he carried her to his bed. He observed her slight wakefulness as he pulled the blanket to her chin.

"How're you feeling, Dumplin'?"

"I know. I know why it happened."

Roy sat on the bed's edge. "Maybe because you're too young?"

Tasha shook her head. "No, because of karma."

"You've been through a lot today. Just rest for now."

Roy returned the blanket to her chin.

"It's karma. If you do bad things, bad things happen to you," Tasha muttered. "Bad things."

Roy brushed the hair from her face. "You made a mistake. You're not the first teenager—"

"I did something bad. I did. I killed, so my baby died. Karma."

Roy raised an eyebrow. "Who did you kill?"

Tasha closed her eyes.

Before drifting into sleep, she mumbled, "Mom."

CHAPTER 36

Roy rose from the couch after spending a sleepless night pondering the conversation with Tasha. He discounted his daughter's confession, alluding it to the influence of heavy medication and experiencing an overly emotionally charged day. After he finished his breakfast, he decided to assess her condition before he left home.

He gently knocked on the door. "You awake?"

"Yeah, come in."

"Hope you're feeling better. Thought I best check on you before I leave for work today."

Tasha yawned. "Still a little groggy. Hardly remember going to sleep. Was wondering why I was here in your bed. Was I that out of it?"

Relief washed over Roy's face. His hunch was correct; the medication had caused her disoriented comments.

Roy smiled. "Just a little. Listen, I have to return to work today, but I'll be home at five, and I'll bring home some dinner. Probably a good idea for you to take it easy today, okay?"

"Well, there's my stuff I need from the trailer. My clothes, shoes. Plus, my car is still there. I was thinking I could call Kristi for a ride today."

Roy shook his head. "That's not a good idea. I don't—"

"Dad!" Tasha protested. "I need clean underwear, for starters."

Roy conceded. "Pick up your things and drive your car home. But don't linger in that trailer park. You got that?"

"Got it. Can you leave a few dollars? I need some . . . Well, I'm going to need to buy some pads."

Roy's blushing expression matched his crimson shirt as he pulled a ten-dollar bill from his wallet. "Come straight home."

After Kristi agreed to drive Tasha to Westside Wheel Estates, Tasha wasted no time filling the back seat and trunk of her car with clothes and personal items. Although the trailer park was noisy and full of unscrupulous people, it had been her home and she missed it. The empty couch looked barren as she imagined her mother reclining while watching television. Doreen once bet Tasha she could blow the perfect smoke ring, and after five attempts, she had. Tasha allowed herself to smile at the memory of one of the rare, fun moments she had shared with her mother. If Tasha were honest with herself, she would admit she missed Doreen.

She gathered her CD collection and remembered two discs belonged to Jermaine. Her arms ached to hold him. She had agreed not to contact him right away, but surely returning the CDs had nothing to do with incriminating him. She had to see him.

Tasha approached Trailer 5. She was surprised the mismatched lawn chairs Lakeisha and her friends usually occupied were gone. A chorus of barking dogs reacted when she knocked on the door. Dogs? Jermaine said Adelle hated dogs. Tasha envisioned tiny breeds her mother always referred to as *yipper-yappers* guarding the trailer with ineffective barks. A voice from inside the trailer—growling louder than the dogs—shouted for the dogs to *shut up*.

A woman in her sixties with charcoal-black hair spiking like a fountain from a tight rubber band perched on her head answered the door. A barking Chihuahua cradled in her arms partially hid the faded image of Ozzy Osbourne on her Black Sabbath tee-shirt.

"Yeah?"

"I'm looking—"

The woman shook the snarling dog. "Rocket, shut up!" She returned her attention to the teenage girl holding two CDs. "Looking for who?"

"Jermaine."

Tasha peeked into the trailer. Posters of heavy metal bands

plastered to the walls stunned her. The Porters had never displayed anything except a flyswatter next to the stove.

The woman focused on the second dog's attempt to escape from the door. "All right, damn dog. You get back." She kicked the dog, sailing it unto its back.

The dog whimpered and scuttled from his attacker.

"Don't know nobody by that name."

Tasha fought a gagging reflex when she noticed the woman had not bothered to insert her top denture. Tasha diverted her gaze from the pink-gray fleshy gum that reminded her of the erasers she had used in elementary school.

"I'm his friend. He lives here. He loaned me these CDs."

The woman snorted and swallowed. "Only ones living here is me and my old man. Moved in yesterday."

"But . . . " Tasha stammered. "The Porters, where did they go?"

The dog struggled from the woman's grip. She knelt and tossed him to the floor. "Scoot now."

"The Porters. Adelle, Jermaine, his sister, and brother. Where'd they go?" Tasha repeated.

"I told ya. I moved in here yesterday. I don't know no Porters. The only thing I know about who lived here before is they left the place a mess. I still ain't got it all cleaned up." She glanced behind her at the tiny dogs ripping a pillow in a game of tug-o-war. "Damn dogs are tearing up. Gotta go."

The door closed with a heavy *thump*.

Tasha remained on the steps, staring at the numeral five on the door, as if her action could miraculously make the Porters appear.

He promised to stand by me.

She walked to the manager's office and knocked on the door.

"Can I help you?" Harold Jefferson asked.

"*Aw,* just wondering if you can tell me where the Porters moved to?"

Harold pushed aside the calculator on his desk. "Well, when tenants owe three months' worth of rent and move out in the middle of the night, I'm generally the last person they say goodbye to."

Tasha hung her head. She willed herself not to cry in front of Jefferson.

"Say, ain't you the Ferch girl from Trailer Twelve?"

Tasha nodded. "Yep."

Harold eyed the eight-hundred-dollar entry in his ledger. "Sorry to hear about your mother's passing."

"Thanks."

"I hate to bring this up to you, since you're just a kid and all, but what are the plans with that trailer? I got a waiting list of people wanting to rent, and if you're not going to be living there anymore, I really need to know."

"Don't know. I'll have my dad call you."

"Well, you do that, sweetheart. I'd appreciate that."

Tasha ran to her car. She sobbed as she inserted the key to unlock the door. Why hadn't Jermaine bothered to say good-bye?

From his window, Tie-Dye Bill watched the girl from Trailer 12 enter her car.

"She's finally picking up her car," he said to his wife, Mary.

"Can't hear you, come in here," she bellowed.

Tie-Dye Bill dropped the curtain into place before trotting to the back bedroom. Mary, his six-hundred-thirty-two-pound invalid bride of nineteen years, lay sprawled against the headboard of her bed.

"The girl from Trailer Twelve. She's finally getting her car."

"Nobody's vandalized it, I hope," Mary said.

"Nope, but that narc in the black sedan was back yesterday asking a lot of people a whole bunch of questions."

"Hand me my water, Bill." Mary pointed to a small plastic bottle on her dresser. "What'd you tell him?"

"Not much. Don't need him notifying my parole officer of shit. Told him what I told you. The girl left before the ambulance came. That's all he needs to know."

Mary struggled to reach the bottle from her husband's outstretched hand.

"You tell him about the other girl? The one you said had a braid half-way down her back?"

Tie-Dye Bill grunted. "I saw nothing. That's what I told him."

Tasha wiped her tears on her shirt hem and started the engine. Jermaine was gone. He said he loved her and would stand by her. She rubbed her belly as she drove. Maybe she had made a mistake by not telling him she was pregnant. If he had known, he might have convinced Adelle to remain in Endover. Tasha should have told him. Her tears flowed again when she realized none of it mattered, since she had lost the baby.

Tasha drove to Greenville, but she did not want to return to her father's empty apartment. She decided to lean on her big sister and headed to Daisy's apartment.

The knock on the door startled Daisy. She had been anxious since her mother's funeral.

"Who is it?" she called through the locked door.

"It's me. Tasha."

When Daisy opened the door, Tasha was shocked to see her sister's disheveled appearance. Daisy wore faded pajamas, and her hair hung loose around her shoulders.

"Is this a bad time?" Tasha asked. "I should have called."

"No, I'm fine. Glad to have someone to talk to. Have a seat. Want a soda or something?"

"A soda would be great, thanks."

Daisy returned with two cans of diet soda. "What's wrong? You've been crying."

Tasha sniffled. "Everything. Everything's wrong."

Daisy cocked her head to the side and waited for her sister to continue.

"Just now I went back home to the trailer to get my stuff. Stopped to see Jermaine and he wasn't there."

"Maybe he had to run an errand or something?"

"I wish. No, nothing like that. I hadn't talked to him since Mom died. So I went there today, and this weird-ass lady answered their door and said they moved."

Daisy gasped. "Moved? Where?"

"That's what I asked, but she didn't know. I asked the owner, and he didn't know either. How could Jer just leave like that? How?"

"Maybe he didn't have a choice. Maybe he was in trouble."

"He didn't have any trouble," Tasha protested and pointed to her chest. "I did it. He said not to talk to him for a week, so nobody would put two and two together."

Daisy squinted in puzzlement. "You did what?"

"*Jeez*, first I flunk chemistry and blow my chance out of here. Then Mom stole my money—"

Daisy's held up her palm. "Whoa. Back up. Mom stole money from you?"

Tasha folded her arms. "Oh yeah. About nine hundred to keep us from getting evicted. She didn't even ask. Just took it!"

"Did you tell your dad?"

Tasha shook her head.

"He could have gotten it back." Daisy pursed her lips and blew a whistling breath. "Nine hundred? I don't even make much that in a year."

"I didn't tell him because he would just ask why I needed it so bad. He just knew I flunked chemistry and lost my scholarship chance."

"It sucks she took it, but you said you *needed* it. Needed it for what?"

Tasha pouted. "Doesn't matter now. She stole it. I lost my scholarship chance. Mom died, and Jermaine's gone. Everything just sucks right now."

"I've got something that'll make you feel better. Hold on," Daisy said.

Tasha heard a few notes of mechanical music float from her sister's bedroom. Daisy returned with her marijuana stash sealed in a small plastic bag. Tasha watched spellbound as Daisy rolled two fat joints with a few rotations of her fingers.

"Herbal therapy, the best kind," Daisy said and handed a joint to Tasha.

"Mega-therapy, from the size of them," Tasha said.

Daisy struck a lighter to the end of her marijuana cigarette. "Smoke 'em if you've got 'em."

The sisters leaned back, closed their eyes, and smoked in silence. After they extinguished the roaches, Daisy asked, "Feel better?"

Tasha grinned. "Feel dreamy."

"I like feeling dreamy," Daisy said. "Keeps the doctors and demons away."

Tasha giggled. "Demons, gargoyles, witches, Doreen."

Daisy playfully slapped her sister's arm. "Say that again."

"Demons, gargoyles, witches, Doreen."

Both girls howled in laughter.

"Again," Daisy said. "Only say it real fast three times."

Tasha accepted the challenge. "Demons, gargoyles, witches, Doreen. Demons, Doreen. No. Witches, demons. Oh, I messed up!"

Daisy hugged her ribs and wailed. "You said it wrong. You said it all wrong."

Tasha sat erect and cleared her throat. "Demons, Doreen. Well, she's a demon, all right."

Daisy's snickering halted. A serious expression replaced her grin. "*Shh*! Get down!"

"Wha—"

Daisy shoved Tasha to the floor and whispered, "Demon Doreen." She pointed to the corner of the room. "She's standing over there."

"Daisy, you're stoned. We both are. Mom's not here."

"*Shh*. She's coming to kill us. She killed the cats and now us, Lucy. Hide. Hide!"

Tasha burst out laughing. "Jesus, Daisy. Get a grip. Haven't you ever been high before?"

Tasha stretched out her arms from her sides and teetered. "Fly, Daisy. Don't touch down."

"Will you stop it?" Daisy scolded. "She's gonna see us."

"Nobody's there. Nobody's there. Knock, knock," Tasha called out. "Who's there?"

"Hide!" Daisy cowered to the floor with her hands over her head as if she were practicing for an air raid drill. "She gonna kill us. Kill us, Lucy."

Tasha giggled. "She ain't gonna kill us."

"*Uh-huh*. She's watching us."

"No," Tasha said. "She ain't watching us, Daisy. Mom's dead."

Daisy leaned and cautiously inspected the corner. Demon Doreen had vanished.

"Mom's dead? Really?"

"Yep. I killed her."

Tasha maintained a stone-faced expression for three seconds before both girls exploded in laughter.

"You killed her. That's funny," Daisy said.

CHAPTER 37

Jenny inspected the messy condition of her house and was grateful to have the day alone to clean. With all the commotion dealing with Doreen's funeral and the aftermath of watching Dan drink himself into a stupor, a full day of housekeeping would deplete her nervous energy. She laughed to herself. When was the last time she craved mopping floors and washing laundry?

"God, I must be getting old."

After sweeping the floors, she replaced the broom and dustpan in the hallway closet. As she closed the door, she was surprised to hear the doorbell. She cringed. Wearing her oversized sweatshirt and raggedy jeans was not a respectful appearance to greet company, even if the guest were only her neighbor, Lorraine. She did not want to be an ungracious host, especially since Lorraine had been her rock during the last week, but if Jenny rested now, she would never get the floors mopped before Dan's arrival home.

She mentally prepared her excuse to deny Lorraine coffee as she approached the front door. When she opened it, she was startled to see a man sporting an impeccable haircut and clad in a tailored pinstriped suit.

"Jennifer Campbell?"

"Yes, that's me. What can I—"

"Detective Hershel Monroe." He offered his business card to her. "I'd like to have a few words with you, if you don't mind."

Jenny swallowed hard. *Detective?* The black sedan in her driveway made sense now.

"Well, sure . . . I guess. What's this about?"

"May we speak inside, Mrs. Campbell?"

Jenny absent-mindedly smoothed her hair in place. Her shabby clothes no longer felt comfortable.

"Sorry, come in. I was cleaning. You know, I don't always look like this. Don't trip over that mop and bucket." She led him to the kitchen. "Please, sit. Coffee?"

"If it's no trouble, thank you."

Jenny poured two cups. She tightened her grip on the cup handles to steady her shaky hands. She offered the detective a weak smile as she joined him at the table.

"Thank you," Detective Monroe said and sipped the coffee. He skipped the unnecessary pleasantries—commenting on the coffee's taste or the current agreeable weather—and commenced his purpose for the meeting. "You're likely aware that I'm interviewing people who were acquainted with Doreen Ferch."

The detective making his rounds had been the latest gossip topic at the diner. The farmers and the business owners had compared notes as to whom the detective had approached and the type of questions he had posed. Many customers had asked Jenny if she had been interviewed. Her righteous reply had always been *no.*

Jenny shook her head. "No, I hadn't heard that."

"Surprising that you hadn't. Seems most folks in Endover and Greenville know each other, or in most cases, I'm discovering, are related to one another." He grinned. "Small towns, you know."

"What is it you need to know? I'm not really sure what I can help you with."

"I just have some basic questions. Every answer, no matter how insignificant, helps the investigation. Do you mind if I record our session?"

Jenny leaned forward and inspected the small recorder the detective withdrew from his breast pocket. "Well, I'm not sure. I don't know how these things work."

"Trust me. I just need to gather some preliminary information, that's all."

Jenny crossed her legs and hugged herself. She was unable to discern if the detective flashed a grin to relax or to intimidate her. "Okay, I guess."

After he read her rights from his small index card, she stated her full name, date of birth, address, and occupation, and he began the interview.

"Jennifer Campbell, are you related to Doreen Ferch?"

"No. She's my husband's ex. Well . . . *was*."

"Did you have a relationship with Doreen Ferch?"

Jenny paused. She searched for the words to explain the complexity of her history with Doreen.

"Well, years ago we were friends. Then her and Dan divorced, and we got married—Dan and me."

Detective Monroe nodded. "So, how would you describe your relationship with Doreen Ferch?"

"She hated me."

"And how did you feel toward her?"

Jenny refreshed her dry mouth with a quick sip of coffee. She silently scolded herself for bluntly answering the question and putting herself on the detective's radar. She took a second sip before retracting her statement.

"Well, when I said she hated me, I don't mean she *hated* me. I mean, maybe that is too strong of a word. I mean she wasn't happy when I married Dan, but that was years ago. We didn't run in the same social circles or anything. I really didn't have anything to do with her."

"You didn't answer my question. How did *you* feel toward *her*?"

"Nothing. Like I said, we really didn't see each other."

"Until a few weeks ago at Kemp's Grocery. Can you tell me about that?"

Man, he has *been talking to people. Wonder who told him about that?*

"Doreen pitched a fit every time she saw me. Didn't matter where it was," Jenny answered.

"But you just said you rarely saw each other."

Jenny fidgeted in her chair and drummed her fingers on the table. "I mean, socially. Ask anyone. If you were on her shi—I mean, on her bad side, she caused trouble." Jenny justified her position by adding, "She was that way towards everyone. The woman enjoyed causing trouble. Ask anyone."

Detective Monroe tapped his finger against his lips. His stoic expression revealed none of his thoughts to Jenny. She had no idea if her answers built a good defense or if she had offered indiscretions for the detective's consideration.

"So, you weren't the only one annoyed by her? Do you know of anyone who may have wanted to harm her?"

"No."

"Do you travel, Mrs. Campbell?"

Jenny rubbed her right temple as an initial throb signaled the beginning of a headache.

"Rarely. About three months ago Dan and I took a trip for a few days."

"Where did you go?"

"Nashville. Dan loves country music. We needed to get away, so we went."

"Did you buy any souvenirs?"

"Well, sure. It was a mini-vacation, like I said. Dan bought a cap and a couple of tee-shirts." Jenny paused. "What does our trip have to do with Doreen?"

"Did you have any reason—any reason at all—to give Doreen Ferch souvenirs from that trip?"

"No. Why would we?"

"What was the name of the store or stores you shopped in?"

Jenny drummed her fingers on the table as if the action cleared her thoughts. "There were a few. One I remember was called Nashville Guitars or something like that. I really don't remember."

"Perhaps, Guitar Go?"

Detective Monroe leaned forward waiting for a response.

Guitar Go. The store Dan had insisted they enter because of the cardboard cutout of his favorite singer—Renee Lynne—displayed in the window. Bought an overpriced sweatshirt and wore it out of the store like an idiot tourist.

"I don't remember," Jenny answered. A sickening heat crept up her neck. "Why is where we shopped so important?"

"What would you say if I told you a white plastic bag with a Guitar Go logo was found near the body? Could you explain how Doreen Campbell would have acquired it?"

Jenny offered a quick response. "Maybe she got it from the Thrifty New To You shop. They put purchases in used bags and ask for more all the time."

"Is Guitar Go the store you shopped in?"

"Yes, but that doesn't mean it's the same bag. Lots of people travel."

Detective Monroe leaned back in his chair, sipped his coffee, and studied the woman's demeanor. The icy gaze he cast toward Jenny induced an alarming chill. She rubbed her arms and hoped the interrogator had not noticed her prickling skin. The detective's silence frightened her.

Just as she readied herself to offer him a justification about her vacation purchases, the detective spoke. "The Charge-It receipt recovered from the bag contains your name and signature."

Jenny leaned backward. Her gaze darted around the room as she remembered.

That damn sweatshirt! Dan insisted on buying it, but didn't have the sixty-five dollars in cash, so I charged it to my credit card.

"I think you need to come back when my husband's home."

"And you're currently married, correct?"

Jenny huffed. "Of course I am!"

"I noticed you aren't wearing a wedding ring."

Jenny glanced at her bare finger. "Well, I *am* married."

"When would be the best time to reach your husband?" Detective Monroe asked.

Jenny mumbled. "Later."

Jenny peered from the living room curtain and watched the black sedan slowly reverse in her driveway. The detective appeared to be surveying the property before he entered the highway.

She paced. Dan would arrive home in another three hours. She did not trust the detective with the steely blue eyes. Suppose he was driving directly to Gleason's to interview Dan? Maybe she should warn him with a phone call. She had not mentioned her husband's employment, but she had no doubt the deputy knew more about the Endover residents than they knew about themselves.

She glanced at her mop and decided to continue her household chores.

At least my house will be clean when he returns to arrest me.

"What a long day! So glad to be home," Dan said as he unloaded his Red's into the refrigerator. He stepped back onto the rug near the door and removed his work boots. The lingering pine scent indicated Jenny had mopped the vinyl floor. Removing his boots at the door eliminated one argument.

Jenny rounded the corner. "You're glad to be home? Well, so am I."

Dan raised an eyebrow. "*Jeez*, Jenny. Can't you wait until tonight?"

His snickering offended her.

"Well, you won't think you're so funny when I tell you about the day I've had."

Dan's grin vanished. "Let me grab a beer. I'm guessin' I'm gonna need one, right?"

"Yeah, you will. But don't drink too many. You'll want to be sober when he comes back."

Dan opened his Red's. "Who's he?"

Jenny leaned against the counter. "That dumbass detective that's been making the rounds. Paid me a visit today."

"You've got to be kiddin'. Why you?"

"Well, remember our getaway trip to Nashville?"

Dan popped open his can and sat at the table. "There's a law against going on vacation?"

"No, idiot. Remember the Renee Lynne sweatshirt you bought? The one you just *had* to have?"

Dan set down his can. "Not sure why a detective's interested in what clothes I buy on vacation. What's he investigatin', a clothing-theft ring?"

"Doreen's death."

"Oh, c'mon. He thinks I killed her with my sweatshirt?" Dan smirked. "If it was that easy to get rid of her, I would of done it when I bought it."

Jenny burst into tears. "Jesus, Dan. Can you fucking be serious for a minute?"

"Sorry, Jen, but none of this is makin' sense."

Jenny wiped her tears as her face reddened in anger. "Let me spell it out for you. Back in April, Daisy was admitted to Melville, remember? We decided to get away, to go to Nashville and concentrate on us for a few days. You bought that damn sweatshirt and other stuff."

"Okay, I remember all that, but how does—"

"The cops found the shopping bag next to Doreen's body!"

"Like it was the only one made," Dan scoffed. "How do they know it was our shopping bag?"

"Because my credit card receipt was in it."

Dan pounded his fist on the table. "Damn!"

Jenny was both frightened and pleased as Dan's flippant

attitude turned serious. Now that she captured his attention, they could prepare for the detective's return.

"Yeah, damn is right."

"How in the hell did Doreen get it?"

"Well, after the detective left and I could finally think straight, I asked myself that same question. There's only two people who handled that bag after it left our house."

"What do you mean?"

"Think back to the barbeque. Remember I gave Daisy that box with her childhood drawings in it? It was dusty, and she insisted to cover it with a bag. You know—her germ phobia and what not. Anyway, none of the grocery bags were big enough, so I gave her that bag from Nashville."

"Yeah, so?"

"Well, only her and Tasha had access to it once it left our house."

"Did you tell the detective that?"

"Hell no. I was so shocked when he told me they found it at Doreen's I'd forgotten about it, and now he's coming back to interview you."

Dan's grip tightened around the beer can. "Well, I'm not telling him that shit."

"You aren't?"

"No, why would I get Tasha in trouble?"

"What makes you think it was her?"

"Well, *duh*, she lived in that trailer with Doreen. Daisy didn't. Daisy would rather die than even come within a mile of Doreen. As far as I know, she hasn't seen her since we moved her up to Greenville."

"You think Tasha . . . ?"

"Well," Dan said. "If you fuckin' had to live with Doreen, wouldn't you want to kill her?"

Jenny ran her fingers through her tousled hair. "You didn't see the look on that detective's face, like this shit-eating grin that he knows the answers before you tell him anything. And he's coming back. He's coming back—"

"Let him," Dan answered. "If he knew so much, he wouldn't still be poking his nose around in people's business. I got nothin' to hide or nothin' to tell him, either."

"I need to get out of these old clothes. I'm going to soak in a hot tub. Been a helluva long day," Jenny said.

As the water and bubbles filled the tub, she opened the vanity drawer. There it was. She slipped on her wedding ring. The stone glistened and cast a bluish hue from the facets—the identical cool shade as the detective's glowering eyes.

CHAPTER 38

Since the stray pawed at Daisy's window daily, she decided to claim the cat as her own and protect him within the walls of her apartment. The arrangement satisfied the pair; the cat received food and shelter while Daisy welcomed the companionship.

After feeding the cat, she decided to name him. She studied his characteristics for inspiration. While most of his body consisted of gray fur with subtle stripes, his chest, paws, and tip of his tail were white. She searched for a regal name, but none suited him. She picked up the cat and noticed he had gained weight since she began feeding him a few weeks ago.

"Well, you're just a big ole Toby, aren't you?" She giggled. "Yep, that's your name. Toby. I like it."

She carefully set Toby on her bed. The cat groomed his fur with determined strokes of his tongue. Toby's conscientious hygiene habits pleased Daisy.

"Your cleaning reminds me. It's Wednesday, and that means dusting day."

She began the ritual of removing the books from her shelf. Once she had stacked them in neat, even piles, she retrieved her dusting cloth and spray. Daisy had just completed the third circulator motion with the rag when her doorbell rang. She did not welcome the intrusion, unless it was Tasha returning for another visit.

Daisy stood behind the locked door. "Who is it?"

"Detective Hershel Monroe. May I speak with you?"

Daisy swallowed hard. Was he here to impound Toby? She hadn't stolen him. Nobody had responded to the lost pet flyers she had posted. She cautiously opened the door a crack.

A young woman with childlike facial features greeted the detective. Her enormous blue eyes that filled her gaunt face silently quizzed his presence at her doorstep. Her bangs curled forward while the rest of her hair twisted in an elaborate ponytail.

"Who are you looking for?" she asked in a hush barely above a whisper.

"Are you Daisy Campbell?"

She nodded.

"May I step inside and have a few words with you?"

She glanced at her feet. Her palms merged, and she resisted rubbing them.

"Why? I didn't do anything wrong."

The man smiled at her when she managed to face him.

"No, I didn't say you did anything wrong. I just have a few questions, that's all. It'll just take a few minutes."

He offered his business card. After examining it, she conceded. "Well . . . okay."

She opened the door and gestured for him to enter. She hurriedly closed her bedroom door to hide Toby.

The detective waited until she returned to ask if they could sit. When Daisy pointed toward the couch, he sat across from Daisy as she settled in her rocking chair.

Detective Monroe observed her living room. "You like books."

"They're all mine. None of them belong to the library. I don't have overdue books. You can check. I'll open all of them. You'll see."

"I'm not here to talk about overdue library books, I assure you."

Daisy focused on the dirty corners. He would notice them soon enough and get angry like Jenny.

"I'm cleaning the shelves now. Mondays and Wednesdays are dusting days. I'm not done, so if you see any—"

Detective Monroe held his finger against his lips to silence the young woman. When she quieted, he spoke. "Miss Campbell. I'm not here about the condition of your apartment; although I must say, you do a really good job at keeping it looking nice."

Daisy disregarded his compliment and continued her defiant stance. "I didn't do anything wrong. You can't arrest me or take me away."

"Please calm down, Miss Campbell. I'm not here to arrest you, just to ask some questions, and then I'll leave. Is that okay?"

Daisy sat motionless in the rocker. "Toby's mine. Mine! Nobody else fed him. So, I'm keeping him."

"Who's Toby?"

"My cat. You can't take him away. He's mine!"

"I'm not here about a cat. I'm here to talk about Doreen Ferch."

"I didn't do it. My dad said so."

The detective's ears perked. "You didn't do what?"

"I didn't kill her. Dad says bad wishing doesn't work. I didn't do it. I didn't!"

"You wished her dead?"

Daisy scowled and hung her head. "She was mean."

"She was mean, and you wanted to get even? Did you hurt Doreen Ferch?"

"You can't take me to jail or Melville. I'll call my Dad."

Detective Monroe leaned forward. "Melville." He paused and asked, "Why would I take you there?"

"Because . . . "

"Because you've been there before?"

Daisy slapped her palms together. The rapid motion produced heat that dried her sweaty hands. Her tongue darted from her mouth as she panted. Her chest rose and fell in rapid successions as she struggled to breathe. She blurted her explanation to the detective between gasps.

"I don't . . . do bad things. The corners are dirty. I know . . . I *know* that." She gulped and continued, "I was dusting . . . I *was* . . . and then you came, and I had to stop. Had to . . . honest."

She studied the floor's wood grain pattern as the man stood.

"Relax. Take some deep breaths. I'm going to leave now. Will you be all right?"

Daisy slowed the friction. Her hands burned.

"I'll let myself out. Thank you, Miss Campbell."

Daisy jumped from her chair as soon as she heard the doorlatch snap shut. She raced to lock the door. She leaned against the frame to regain her composure. Her mouth was dry, and she headed to the kitchen. She removed a water jar from the refrigerator and drank steadily. After she refilled it and returned it to its exact place, she rushed to the bedroom to ensure Toby was safe.

She climbed onto the bed. Her hug woke the cat from his slumber. Daisy released her grip, and Toby stretched in an arch from his tightly woven position.

"That man," she said. "He wanted to take me away. Take me from you. Who would care for you, then? *Huh?*"

Daisy knew by the way the man's icy sapphire eyes examined her bookshelf that he was disappointed like Jenny had been. Daisy was a good person. She maintained a rigid cleaning schedule, she captured precious smiles from her clients' children, and she had rescued Toby. She did not understand why people always wanted to hurt her and make her feel bad. The man said he wanted to talk about her mother. She was the one who had hurt Daisy most of all.

She did not lie to the man; she *had* wished her mother dead. If Daisy tallied all the incidents of abuse and ridicule that her mother had inflicted on her, she guessed the number would be infinite, like the solutions to impossible algebra formulas.

Stroking the cat calmed Daisy, and her breathing returned to a natural rhythm, unlike the last breaths her mother inhaled. Daisy placed the blame on Doreen; she should have answered the telephone when Daisy called using her Nokia while driving down the highway.

The terror that her mother—the monster—had inflicted at the bank and the convenience store unleashed a tempestuous rage that erupted from the deepest core of Daisy's spirit. Her mother's mockery burned in her memory.

You'd think your dad or those people from the loony bin could teach you how to shop. I mean, don't they do things like that, or do they just tie you up and let you bang your head against the wall all goddamn day and night? The monster ridiculed Daisy in a boisterous tone while pointing at her, alerting nearby shoppers to pause and observe the crazy girl while she publicly shamed her daughter. The monster intended to embarrass her, discredit her achievements, and to encourage the shoppers to laugh at her. She was not Daisy Campbell, proprietor of DC Studios; she was the nutcase held captive behind the walls of Melville.

Daisy recalled startled Mrs. Bremer, president of the PTA, hugging her infant—the sweet baby Daisy had photographed a month ago. Who would trust their children's safety with the insane woman who secretly banged her head against the wall while tied in restraints? News, especially dirty laundry, spread swiftly throughout Greenville. Daisy was positive the PTA had already scheduled an emergency meeting. The church congregation would be alerted next by the gossips at Kathy's Kut 'N Kurl, whose tongues would ignite their husbands' reprehensible discussions at Jake's Keg. The monster's antics guaranteed the announcement of Daisy Campbell's unbalanced mental state would supply fodder for the locals to dissect her every movement.

Daisy had wished her mother dead and had hatched her revenge plan during the drive home. Daisy's intent was to humiliate her tormentor, and she gathered the necessary tools to implement her plan: scissors to hack Doreen's hair, the lighter to singe her remaining locks, and the permanent marker to inscribe hurtful words across her face, disfiguring the last of her beauty. Daisy purchased twine at First Stop Hardware—*she* would be the one to restrain the crazy one. To prevent her victim from crying for help, Daisy conjured the idea of balling a dusting rag into Doreen's mouth. She savored the irony of the lazy wench choking on a dirty cloth. When Daisy discovered she did not have a bag to secure the items, she remembered the souvenir bag under her bed.

Satisfied she was armed, she dialed the phone. As she listened to the repetitive rings, Daisy was pleased her first wish was granted. Lazy Doreen could not be bothered to answer the phone. Since Tasha did not respond either, Daisy deduced her sister had already left for the sleepover she had previously bragged about without sparing Daisy's feelings of having no friends of her own.

Daisy dialed three more times during the drive and grew confident each time the six repetitive rings produced no results. This was the reason her father had gifted her the Nokia—his motive became clear to her now; he wanted her to succeed. She glanced at her DC Studios card pinned to her windshield visor. She was somebody; she *was*.

Daisy nearly cancelled her plan when she spotted Tasha walking along the highway, but with her pent-up fury exploding, she accelerated the gas pedal. After nearly hitting the stupid three-legged dog, she arrived at Trailer 12 just moments later. She surveyed the trailer park when she locked her car and saw a funky old man in a multi-colored shirt watering plants. She turned the doorknob. The door opened easily, as if it invited her inside.

Daisy peeked inside before entering. Doreen moaned from the couch, and Daisy approached in soft footsteps then she stood behind her. She observed her mother's weakened condition as she lay in a stupor, which both shocked and pleased Daisy. She would not need to restrain the beast. Daisy walked to the couch edge and leaned forward to monitor her mother's shallow breathing. The scent of the fresh vomit was hardly noticeable amongst the other rancid odors polluting the trailer's interior. Daisy pressed her forearm against her nose to evade the wicked smells, which reminded her of her grandfather's house.

She emptied the contents from the bag and reached for her scissors. She snipped a lock of hair from the center of her mother's bangs. She paid no attention to where the hair fell as she cut two more large chunks from the side of her mother's head. She reached for her lighter to singe a few spots but stopped when Doreen's eyes opened.

When the monster muttered a feeble plea for help, Daisy got scared. That was not part of the plan. She could not risk her mother calling Melville and telling them Daisy was bad. She raised Doreen's neck a few inches and slipped the bag over her head. Her mother could not see her now.

Doreen convulsed.

Daisy freed the bag with a quick jerk from Doreen's face. She was startled when her mother's head lolled onto her chest. Daisy had not intended for her mother to die; she had only planned to humiliate her. She panicked and covered Doreen with the blanket, gathered her weapons, and fled the trailer. The bag lay discarded on the floor.

Daisy rushed to her apartment and tossed the weapons into the dumpster. She contemplated the impact of her wishing. She wanted her mother dead, and now she was. Her father said only good wishes come true, but it *was* a good wish.

She would not allow that man to force her to Melville. It was *only* a wish.

Toby needed her.

CHAPTER 39

"Shit, he's back," Jenny shouted from the kitchen.

Dan grunted as he rose from his easy chair in the living room. Jenny had served a delicious dinner, and he planned to spend the evening watching television. Jenny's alert had interrupted his viewing of the regional car racing finals he had looked forward to all day.

Dan glanced out the window above the kitchen sink. A man wearing a tailored suit parked his car and approached the door. Dan would have bet his last paycheck this guy's suit was not hot and itchy like the cheap one Dan owned.

"Let him in," Dan instructed.

Jenny opened the door before Detective Monroe had a chance to knock. She greeted him but did not force a smile. "Come in."

"Mr. Campbell, I'm Detective Hershel Monroe. I'm interviewing folks acquainted with Doreen Ferch."

"Have a chair. Don't know what I can tell you," Dan said.

The two men sat at the table while Jenny served coffee before joining them.

"I usually record my interviews; it's easier than taking notes. Do you mind?"

Dan snorted and cleared his throat. "Suit yourself."

Detective Monroe removed the recorder from his pocket and centered it on the table. After reading Miranda to Dan and requesting the preliminary information of Dan's full name, date of birth, and occupation, the detective dove into the questioning.

"Doreen Ferch was your ex-wife, correct?"

"Yep."

"How long were you married?"

"Too long."

"Okay, let me rephrase the question. What year did you get married, and when did you get divorced?"

Dan squinted as he recalled the dates. "*Um,* divorced in seventy-six and got married right after graduation in sixty-one."

"What was your relationship like after your divorce?"

"Didn't have no relationship with her. Ain't that what *divorce* means?"

Detective Monroe sipped his coffee while Dan assessed his opponent.

"Do you know anyone who would want to hurt her?" Monroe asked.

Dan held out his hand and counted on his fingers. "Let's see. She pissed off Bill Kemp at the grocery store; she pissed off Harold Jefferson, who owns the trailer court; she pissed off half the county workers at social services; she pissed off my old man more than once, but he's dead so he don't count; she pissed off—"

Detective Monroe interrupted. "I get the picture."

"Good, then we're done." Dan stood and slid the chair under the table. "Anything else? I'm missing my TV show." He leaned in the doorway, glimpsing at the television in the next room.

"Your daughter seems to think she 'wished her dead.'"

Dan snapped his focus back to the detective. "What? When did you talk to Daisy?"

"This afternoon. She stated—"

Dan ground his fist into his palm. "And who in the hell gave you permission to speak to my daughter?"

Dan glared his silent accusation at Jenny.

Jenny raised her palms in defense. "Dan, it's the first I've heard of this, really."

"She's of age, certainly if she lives in her own apartment," Monroe answered.

Dan pointed at his chest. "I'm her power of attorney. You had no business botherin' her without consultin' me. None!"

"She mentioned Melville."

Jenny covered her mouth and stared at the floor.

"Yeah," Dan sneered. "Maybe that was your *first* clue you shouldn't have been talkin' to her, *huh*? I'm her goddamn guardian, buddy. I don't give a shit that you drive a brand-new Infiniti or your damn suit costs five hundred dollars, you've got no right— *no right*—talkin' to her without my permission."

Detective Monroe watched the reels rotate in his cassette player. He tipped the cup and swallowed the last of his coffee.

"One last question for you, Mr. Campbell. How did your ex-wife gain possession of your shopping bag? Any idea?"

Dan smirked. "You're the big-shot detective runnin' around, badgerin' people with all your questions, and for how long— about a week now? You can't solve a crime committed in a town with less than five hundred people in it? You tell me."

Jenny tugged at her husband's sleeve. "Dan."

Detective Monroe stood. "Thank you for your time."

"And unless you have a warrant, stay the hell away from my family. My daughter especially, damnit," Dan said.

Jenny escorted the deputy outdoors. "Sorry, he's sensitive about . . . well, all that Melville stuff. I'm sure you can understand."

"I understand a lot more than people give me credit for."

Jenny shook his hand and covered their clasp with her left hand, alluding to the appearance of her wedding band.

"You have a good evening, Mrs. Campbell." He paused. "Pretty ring."

Dan watched the exchange from the window although he could not hear the conversation. As soon as the car exited toward the highway, he dialed Daisy's telephone number.

"You all right, honey?"

"Sure, Dad. Why wouldn't I be?"

"Well, I just want to make sure that man didn't upset you with his visit today. I told him not to bother you anymore."

Daisy glanced at her bookshelf.

"I told him I own my books. So, I don't know why the library sent the cop to check."

Dan shut his eyes tightly and rubbed his forehead. "That's okay. He won't be back."

"He's not taking Toby away. I won't let him."

The throb of an impending headache attacked Dan's temples. "Who's Toby?"

"My cat."

Dan forced his next question and braced himself for the answer. "And he's real, right?"

"He's on my lap right now. Aren't you, Toby boy?"

"Daisy!" Dan gritted his teeth. "Is the cat a real one? Just tell me 'cause I gotta go."

Dan heard her huff her annoyance.

"Are you still there?" Dan asked.

Damn it! I don't have time for these games. Dan thought.

"Daisy!"

"What?"

"Is Toby there with you?"

"Yes. He's on my lap."

"That's good, honey. Well, I gotta go. Good night now."

Dan reached into the refrigerator for a Red's and joined his wife in the living room. She was watching the Movie of the Week.

"Fuck! I missed the whole fuckin' race!"

"No, you didn't, honey." Jenny smiled. "I taped it on VHS."

"Thanks. It's about time somethin' good happened around here. About fuckin' time."

CHAPTER 40

Hershel Monroe checked his wristwatch as he traveled the highway. Seven o'clock and he had not eaten dinner. He left Endover and headed to Greenville to dine at the restaurant located on Main Street he had passed earlier in the day. Home-style cooked meals served in greasy diners made it bearable to work in the field, but they seemed to be the only advantage.

As he drove, he reviewed some of the unsavory characters he had interviewed in the past week. Starting with the trailer park, there was William Jay Holdenfeld, convicted felon of burglaries. Although Bill had not disclosed his background, it had not been necessary. Monroe had already acquired his lengthy criminal record. Monroe snickered. Living in the decrepit trailer surrounded by meager possessions, he deduced Bill had not been successful in his life of crime. Bill's true sentence was tending to his wife's every need—imprisonment without bars. Monroe knew that unless homeowners surprised burglars during their invasions, they rarely committed murder. He crossed Holdenfeld off the list of suspects.

Harold Jefferson and Jay Wiley had discovered the body, but their alibis checked out. Monroe had no reason to suspect either of the knuckleheads who had inquired when the police tape would be removed so they could install a window. Obviously, their only concern about Doreen Ferch's death was the delay in their renovation plans. Monroe secretly thought Jefferson would be money ahead to torch the entire place, but suggesting a property owner should commit arson for an insurance claim was illegal.

Monroe ran the license plate of a beat-up 1977 Chevy Silverado belonging to Richard Curtis. When he returned to Trailer 5 to interview the man and his girlfriend, Adelle Porter, they had vacated the trailer with no known forwarding address. Despite the rumors Monroe gathered from the locals about "the Chicago gang member," neither the man nor the woman had an arrest record.

Monroe turned his attention to the relatives next. Roy Ferch impressed him as a man who could not lie even if he possessed the desire. He was the only person who had contacted law enforcement and arranged an interview. His young daughter impressed Monroe as a typical teen—aloof, until the questioning began, then was overwhelmed with nervousness. He concluded she possessed no information about the bag or the raggedy haircut, since she had not responded with any interest when he had posed the questions.

The Campbells were an interesting bunch. Monroe had enjoyed toying with them. Dan Campbell reminded him of a banty rooster—all posed to attack with ruffled feathers. Dan's abrasive answers concerning his ex-wife and his empty threats about interviewing his daughter provided Monroe valuable insight about the man. Hot air filled Dan Campbell's puffed up chest, and the man's antics quickly bored Monroe. If not for the delicious coffee his wife served, the trip would have been worthless.

His wife . . .

Jennifer Campbell played him for a fool, insisting she had not heard of his investigation. Monroe was not an idiot. He was aware small-town locals gathered their gossip and tidbits at one place—the local diner—coincidently, her place of employment. She defended her marital status yet had not bothered to wear her ring until his second visit when she practically thrust it in his face. She had seemed genuinely shocked he had known about the bag and furnished a knee-jerk explanation as to how it could have been found at the Ferch residence. Liars wanting to cover their tracks always delivered the instant response to solidify their story. Monroe recited the facts of the case in relation to Jennifer Campbell.

The bag belonged to her.

The receipt included her signature.

Witnesses testified she had argued in public with Doreen Ferch shortly before the victim's death.

Jennifer Campbell was a liar.

But was she also a killer?

CHAPTER 41

Detective Monroe parked in front of the well-lit diner. Through the large glass windowpanes, he observed two men hunched at the counter and a pair of teenagers sitting in a booth enjoying malts. He checked his watch as he entered. Monroe noted that the Greenville crowd had digested all the gossip and daily specials by 7:18 p.m. and deserted the restaurant for their couches and television sets.

As he entered the restaurant, fried-chicken aroma hung heavy in the air and reminded him he was famished. The only sound in the building was the hum of the over-worked air conditioning system that battled to overcome the lingering heat from the ovens and grill.

He sat on a red vinyl stool at the far end of the counter, giving the other two men plenty of elbowroom to shovel their chow. Detective Monroe's observation skills were not required to see that the pair were blue-collar workers refueling after a hard day of manual labor. Their muddied boots and stained work shirts reminded Hershel that his office job was a blessing. As he studied the daily special scrawled on a blackboard, the kitchen doors swung open. A portly woman wiping her hands on a used-to-be-white apron greeted him.

"Hi. How are you? What can I get you?" Her eyes seemed to disappear when she flashed an oversized grin.

"Coffee and the daily special, please,"

Despite him being the only customer waiting for service, she raced for the coffee pot and reached behind the counter for a heavy porcelain cup.

"Black? Sugar or cream?"

"Black, please."

The way the waitress poured coffee amused Monroe. She aimed the coffee stream high above the cup with the flair of an orchestra bandleader before lowering the carafe close to the cup's rim. Her expertise of serving coffee over the years was evident as she raised and lowered the carafe in a yoyo motion until she filled the cup.

Monroe's quizzing nature never lay idle.

"May I ask? Are you Delores?"

"Sure am. Delores Mayfield."

Her second grin did not conceal her eyes, and Monroe noted they were a rare shade of emerald.

"Owned this diner for . . . oh, I don't know for how many years." She pointed with her thumb to the doors behind her. "Some days it feels like I was born in that kitchen."

He extended his hand. "Nice to meet you. I'm Hershel Monroe."

"Don't mind me asking, but are you that detective?"

Monroe chuckled. *"That* detective? Has my reputation preceded me?"

"Well, I didn't mean it that way, really I didn't. Let me get your plate fixed, and we can talk. My goodness, after all, you did come in here to eat."

Delores disappeared behind the swinging doors and returned with a platter of chicken, mashed potatoes smothered with gravy, and fresh green beans. She darted back into the kitchen and returned with a buttered dinner roll.

"Looks delicious," Monroe said.

"Let me heat up that coffee. What I meant was folks have been talking about this big-shot detective all week long. I was wondering if you'd stop in here. Honestly, I was curious as to what you look liked." She chuckled. "Heard you wore pretty expensive suits."

Monroe bit into the chicken. The taste and texture were a close second to his grandmother's recipe. He took another satisfying bite before wiping his hands on a paper napkin.

"Well, the suits aren't that expensive." He smiled. "I'm guessing you know just about everyone in Greenville and Endover, serving up food this delicious."

Delores accepted the bait of his compliment. She rambled as Monroe had hoped she would. He enjoyed his meal while she spoke.

"Well, I know you're asking questions about Doreen. I can't tell you much about her, since she never frequented the diner, but her ex—Dan—used to stop in from time to time for takeout orders. Seems she wasn't much of a cook. They had those cute little girls back then, and I'd always throw in a miniature toy for them as something special."

Monroe nodded and continued chewing.

"Don't like to speak ill of the dead, you know, respect and all that, but most people didn't care for Doreen. Didn't like her filthy language or her brash attitude. It's no wonder they got divorced after the one girl passed on."

"Their daughter died?"

Delores nodded. She fetched the coffee carafe and filled his cup. "Ethel Fletcher killed her with an overdose of sleeping pills. Why, that was years and years ago. Most folks never forgot it; although, they don't talk about it out of respect, you know."

"Was this Daisy Campbell's sister?"

Delores nodded. "Daisy's a whole 'nother story. Don't get me started."

Monroe finished his meal and pushed the plate aside. "That bad, huh?"

"I only know what Jenny tells me. Jenny's her stepmother; she works for me. Not a day goes by that she ain't complaining about that girl."

"Step families don't always blend too well," Monroe said.

"Blend? You'd think after twenty years they would. But Jenny says the girl is lazy, crazy, and everything in between—her words, not mine." Delores scanned the diner as if she had to guard their conversation. "She's not all there, that girl. Probably because of Doreen, so I can't say as I blame the poor thing." Delores paused with a smile. "Daisy was so cute when she was little."

She turned her gaze toward the men at the counter when they waved for her attention. "Be right there, fellas." Delores rang the tabs and counted their change. She handed each man a complimentary mint. "Thank you, boys. Don't be strangers, now. Pete, tell your ma *hi* from me."

The teens ambled to the register, saving Delores a trip to ask if they had finished. She accepted their cash for the two malts, dispersed mints, and invited them to come back another time. When the diner was empty, she dashed back to the detective.

"I got one slice of peach pie left. Compliments of the house, if you have room."

"Not going to turn down pie, thank you," Monroe answered. He was not about to leave now that the topic focused on Jenny Campbell.

Delores returned from the kitchen with a dessert plate and a clean fork. "Added fresh whipping cream. Hope you like it."

Monroe dug into the flaky crust and for the second time that night, thought of his grandmother's cooking. He missed his family and decided to finish his interviews by the next day to leave Endover and Greenville behind.

"So, Jennifer Campbell. What's your take on her?" Monroe asked.

"She's a hard worker, that much I'll say. Customers like her. Her personal life is something else though. Already told you about Daisy. When she ain't driving Jenny nuts, Jenny deals with a husband who drinks too much. Hard to believe her and Doreen used to run together when they were younger."

"I take it Jennifer cut ties with Doreen?"

Delores sighed. "Probably shouldn't say this, and I'll deny if you put me under oath, but . . . "

Monroe raised an eyebrow. "But?"

Delores leaned on the counter, and for a moment, Monroe thought she was going to whisper into his ear.

"Doreen found out Jenny slept with Dan. She's the one who ended that friendship, not the other way around."

Monroe covered his mouth to prevent spewing his bite of pie. He knew everyone concealed secrets, but Delores's disclosure was as juicy as the pie she served.

"More coffee?" Delores asked.

"No, I think I've had enough."

Hershel left the diner, and contemplated whether he had the stamina to drive the lengthy commute to reach his home in Madison, located east of Bancor. Another twelve-hour day of investigating had depleted his energy, and the generous serving of chicken dinner with the mouth-watering peach pie induced a pleasant drowsiness. When he spotted a nearby motel, he decided to spend the night. He had prepared for the long days of travel by storing an overnight bag in his trunk.

After checking in at the front desk and securing a key, he headed to his room. He decided to forgo the local newscast and go to bed early. He stripped from his suit, tie, and slacks. As he showered, he considered Delores's words about Jenny Campbell. Like the other people Monroe had interviewed, he formed his impression about the second Mrs. Campbell.

Jennifer Campbell possessed the trait of selfishness with a dash of narcissism. She seemed to care little about how her actions affected those around her. She considered her troubled stepdaughter a nuisance and tolerated an alcoholic husband. Monroe was not surprised she was "good with customers," as the mask she wore generated an income and tips. Hearing the disclosure from Delores that Jennifer Campbell had betrayed Doreen Ferch by sleeping with Dan fueled Monroe with enough suspicion to keep Jennifer Campbell on his radar.

He finished his shower, turned off the lights, and slid beneath the blanket. He reminded himself to contact the state forensic lab for any updates on the evidence. The sooner he could close this case, the better.

He slept peacefully until his dream shifted into a nightmare.

He sat on the red stool at Delores's counter, eagerly waiting for his dessert. Jennifer Campbell, wearing a blue waitress uniform served him a slice of peach pie. He bit into the warm crust smothered in whipping cream and savored the first bite. His enjoyment ended abruptly when Hershel threw down his fork and spit into his napkin to dislodge a peach pit fragment that threatened to crack his molars. Jenny Campbell wailed in uncontrollable laughter and rallied the customers to enjoy the spectacle of the big-shot detective choking on his pie. Hershel unfolded the napkin fearing the discovery of his broken bridgework aside the pit. What he discovered what more horrific than a damaged dental crown.

"I believe that's mine!" Jenny Campbell said. She plucked her diamond wedding band from his napkin. She faced Hershel with a demented stare. "Might want to keep your nose out of other people's business!"

Hershel jolted upright in bed.

He confirmed his revolver lay on the nightstand.

He tested the door lock.

He set the alarm for seven o'clock and then changed it to six.

Hershel Monroe vowed to leave Greenville and never return.

CHAPTER 42

Tasha curled on the couch like a hibernating bear in a dark cave for the third consecutive day. The restrictive boundaries of her father's tiny apartment induced a cabin fever seclusion that contributed to her gloom. The narrow street-level windows hindered light from entering the basement quarters. She had no idea if the sun shined, nor did she care. Depression and isolation were her only companions.

Jermaine. She missed him. She had been a fool not to tell him about the baby—their baby. Her misguided assumption that he would anchor her in place was her selfish justification for not confiding in him. Because she had foolishly focused on the scholarship as her only escape, she had not realized Jermaine was her ticket out of town. The Fosters had never settled in one place for very long; they had no reason to grow roots in Endover. Now he had moved on without her. She punched her pillow and sobbed knowing she would never embrace her first love again.

When her crying for Jermaine ended, fresh tears appeared as she pondered her disappointing future. She flung the empty tissue box across the room. Nothing mattered. No opportunities awaited her. She had sacrificed parties and friendships to study in solitude to earn straight A's on her report card, and she had gained nothing from her diligent effort. Her college dream, along with her funds, had been stolen.

Tasha rose from the couch and entered the bathroom. A quick glance in the mirror revealed dark under-eye circles and unwashed hair. For a split second, she saw her mother's image transposed over her face. She hated to admit she resembled her mother when people complimented her good looks and compared her beauty to Doreen's. She blew her nose with toilet tissue and returned to the refuge of the couch.

The void of her mother's high-pitched voice constantly yelling unsettled Tasha in an unexpected way. She had dreaded the daily confrontations, and yet, she missed her mother. The permanence of Doreen's death affected Tasha in a way she had not been prepared to handle. Jermaine had been right: hating and killing were two different things. Tasha mulled over the implications of killing her mother. Not only was Doreen gone, but the sheriff's investigation hung over Tasha's head. She considered that her life would be less complicated if she confessed and faced the consequences, since she had no future. She acknowledged the irony that her one chance out of Endover hinged on her arrest.

She glanced at the clock above the kitchen stove. Her father would arrive home in a few hours. His patience and understanding would likely wear thin if he returned home to discover she was still moping in bed. She had promised him this morning she would *do something*. Tasha decided to shower and visit Daisy, hoping her sister's herbal therapy would alleviate her despair.

After filling her gas tank with the money her father had left on the kitchen table, Tasha purchased two Glacier Ices. She disregarded the memory of her mother complaining about the two sodas she had purchased with Jermaine. Doreen's barking seemed like it had occurred a lifetime ago, instead of mere days.

Tasha grinned when she sighted Daisy's vehicle in the driveway indicating she was home. Daisy always possessed the magic to perk up Tasha's moods. Tasha balanced the two sodas in her left hand while she knocked.

Daisy called through the locked door. "Who is it?"

"Me. Tasha."

Daisy lay her dusting cloth on the coffee table and opened the door.

Tasha handed Daisy a soda. "Hope you aren't busy. I had to get out of my dad's apartment. It's depressing as hell."

"No, it's okay." Daisy noted the soda was not the diet variety. "Wednesday's dusting day."

As Daisy slid the Glacier Ice into the refrigerator next to her water jar collection, Tasha inspected the immaculate condition of the apartment. "You have designated days for chores?"

"How else would you keep a place clean?" Daisy asked. She glanced at the bare shelves and her books piled on the coffee table. In a matter of minutes, Tasha would inspect the bookcase and become angry like Jenny and the detective. Why did people visit on Mondays and Wednesdays?

"Don't ask me. I just tried to clean up whenever I had to. Not like Mom ever cared or helped." Tasha sat on the couch and opened her soda. "Can I ask you something?"

"What?"

"Well," Tasha said. "Do you . . . Do you miss her?"

Daisy slumped in her rocking chair and stared at the floor.

"Do you?" Tasha repeated.

Daisy slowly pressed her palms together. The sliding motion that chafed her dry hands elicited a sandpaper-like sound. "Not going to say anything bad. Bad things happen when you do."

"You mean like karma, Daisy? Do you believe in it? I do."

"Mom was mean. I wished she wasn't around. Then she wasn't."

"Well, I told you she stole my money, right? But I didn't tell you why I needed it."

Daisy stopped her palm-rubbing routine to listen. "Why?"

"You can't tell anyone. Promise?"

Daisy nodded.

"Okay." Tasha inhaled a deep breath. "I needed it for . . . well, I was pregnant and didn't want the baby."

Daisy turned her head and faced the window. "Was?"

"Mom stole my money and I couldn't afford to get rid of the baby. But it didn't matter 'cause I lost it, right after the funeral."

Daisy thought of Toby sleeping on her bed. No one would ever harm her precious cat, *her* baby.

"Mom killed your baby," Daisy uttered.

"No, not exactly. It wasn't like she did it."

"Mom killed our cats," Daisy said in a hypnotic tone.

"She wasn't a good person, for sure."

"Only good people go to Heaven. That's what Lucy told me when Grandpa died."

Tasha scoffed. "Well, I doubt Mom went to Heaven. I'm not afraid to say I hated her, Daisy. At first, I was glad she was gone, but now I kinda miss her. How weird is that?"

"I don't miss her," Daisy admitted. Her empty palms clashed together.

"Do you know how she died, Daisy?" With no answer from her sister, Tasha continued. "I'll tell you, but you have to promise you won't tell."

"Promise."

"I mean it, Daisy. If you ever tell anyone, I can go to prison for life. Life."

Her sister's harsh tone frightened Daisy. "Promise."

"You laughed last time I said it, but it's true. I killed her. She wrecked everything for me! So, I got mad and made a plan. Then I just did it." Tasha paused. "I just did it."

Daisy shook her head.

Tasha pointed at her sister. "You can't tell nobody. Nobody."

Tasha stepped into the kitchen to toss her empty soda can in the trash bin. An empty prescription bottle with its cap removed lay sideways on the counter, abandoned and seemingly out of place in the meticulously organized kitchen. Tasha returned to the living room, noticing Daisy's knuckles wrapped tightly around her dusting cloth.

Daisy glanced at the dirty corners of the bookshelf. If her sister had noticed the filth, she had not mentioned it. Tasha did not get mad at her like the others did. Daisy would return the kindness and keep Tasha's secret.

"I won't," Daisy said. "I won't tell anybody."

Tasha's bottom lip trembled, and she burst into tears.

"I said I won't!" Daisy repeated.

Tasha ran her fingers through the short locks of her hair. "Everything's shit right now, Daisy. Everything. Jer's gone, I lost my scholarship. My money. My baby. The cops are asking questions. What if I get caught? What if?"

Daisy sat next to her sister and patted her shoulder. "I'll help you."

"How? How can you help me?"

"If the man comes back, I'll tell him."

Tasha turned and faced Daisy. "What man?"

"The man who said I had overdue library books. Dad told him not to come back, but if he does, I'll tell him."

"The detective?" Tasha quizzed.

Daisy tossed the rag on the coffee table and retrieved a card from her kitchen drawer. She handed it to Tasha. "This man."

Tasha gulped. "You'll tell this man . . . What?"

"I'll tell him the truth."

"I just told you, Daisy. You can't tell anyone. Especially a detective! Are you cra—"

Daisy scowled. "I said, the truth."

Tasha jumped up and squared her hands on Daisy's shoulders. She maintained direct eye contact with her sister. "What truth? What would you tell him?"

"I did it," Daisy confessed.

"You did what?" Tasha's voice climbed an octave. "What?"

Daisy dropped her gaze. "The bag. I was only going to scare her. Honest. But then she couldn't breathe, and I got scared. It was her fault. I called first, lots of times. Why didn't she answer the phone? Why?"

A wild look of terror and disbelief filled Tasha's eyes. "Daisy. Start at the beginning. Tell me everything. Everything."

Daisy pouted. "You know."

"I know what?"

Daisy leaned to grab the dusting cloth, but her sister's grip prevented her movement.

"You're getting mad like Jenny and the man. You saw the corners, but I wasn't finished dusting."

Tasha sunk her nails into Daisy. "This is no bullshit, Daisy. Don't you get it? Knock the crap off. What bag?"

"The one Jenny gave me. You were there. I put the box in it."

Tasha recollected the barbeque. "That bag Jenny gave you?"

Daisy nodded. "Dad and Jenny went to Nashville when I was in—"

"You were in . . . Where?"

"You have to go now," Daisy whispered.

"Not until you tell me what you did with that bag. Tell me."

Daisy wrestled from her sister's grip. "I scared Mom with it. I put it over her head. I didn't mean to—"

Tasha's loud voice boomed into Daisy's skull. "Then what?"

"She . . . She just shook all over and I pulled the bag off and ran. I was scared."

"Did anyone see you?"

"Only Mom was home."

"I mean, did anyone see you go in or out of the trailer?"

Daisy had worked so hard to blot out the memory her sister forced her to recall. She paced in a circle, slapping her ears to stop the interrogation.

"I don't know. I don't know!"

"Did Mom say anything to you?"

"She said something like 'help.'"

"Stop pacing, Daisy! Sit down."

Daisy cowered in her rocking chair.

"Okay, listen. Can you listen for a minute?" Tasha paused to gain her sister's attention. "We can't tell anyone what happened. You don't tell anyone what I said, and I don't tell anyone what you said. If we do, we'll be in big trouble. Big trouble."

"Will they take Toby, my cat, away?"

"They will take *you* away. Do you hear me? Don't tell nobody! Got it?"

The threat of returning to Melville frightened Daisy. Nobody would feed Toby in her absence.

"I have to finish dusting now. You have to go."

Tasha hugged her sister. "Daisy, are you okay? I don't want to leave if you're not."

"I will be after I put the books back. I have to put the books back."

Tasha kissed her sister's cheek. "I'll call you later."

Daisy nodded.

"I love you," Tasha said.

Without a response, Daisy sprayed the shelf with lemon-scented polish and began her dusting ritual. Wednesdays exhausted her.

"What the hell just happened?" Tasha said aloud as she drove away.

She had never witnessed Daisy behave in such a disoriented manner when she clearly had been sober. The pacing, vigorous hand motions, and childlike responses were mannerisms so unlike the older sister who threw caution to the wind and unwound with a few tokes of marijuana. Daisy had always been Tasha's rock, but today her sister instantly crumbled when Tasha brought up the subject of their mother's death.

Tasha recalled the events of the day Doreen died to make sense of Daisy's disclosure. She had ignored the telephone ringing, assuming it was Kristi, but Daisy had confessed she was the caller. If Tasha had answered the telephone like she always did when she was home, Daisy would have been aware that Doreen was not alone. She remembered the stupid three-legged dog darting between the semi-truck and the little white car. Had Daisy whizzed by so quickly that Tasha had not noticed her Nissan?

So, she was there, but why?

Daisy's peculiar actions puzzled Tasha, and she realized now she had not asked Daisy the reason she intended to scare Doreen. As far as Tasha knew, the two women had not seen each other since Daisy had moved to Greenville. Tasha was at a loss, imagining what traumatic event had triggered Daisy's obsession to frighten their mother. Daisy mentioned being *sent away* when her father and Jenny had vacationed in Nashville. Even Dan and Jenny had acknowledged this place, but where was it, and why was it a secret?

Nothing about Daisy's behavior made sense to Tasha. If Daisy could be believed, it meant their mother had survived Tasha's attack. *Maybe I didn't do it . . .*

She recalled the empty prescription bottle on the kitchen counter. Was Daisy's bizarre conduct related to medication? Had she run out of pills, or worse, had she taken too large of a dose?

Tasha's uncertainty led her to Delores's Diner.

There was only one thing to do.

She had to contact Jenny.

CHAPTER 43

The noon crowd slowly dispersed from the diner with bellies filled with Delores's daily special. A few members of the Ladies Floral Club lingered over their coffee, discussing their fall agenda. A pair of gentlemen checked the time and headed to Jake's Keg, trading their caffeine buzz for the much-preferred alcohol lull.

Delores recognized Roy's daughter when she entered even though she could not recall the girl's name. The teen wore a tight black tee-shirt with matching trousers and combat boots. The multiple necklaces of crosses screamed blasphemy when worn in that manner according to Delores's strict moral code. She wondered where today's young people gained their fashion sense as the girl approached the counter.

"Jenny here?"

Delores believed every conversation started with introductory pleasantries. Manners, it seemed, fell by the wayside along with the dress code of this young generation.

"How are you?" Delores asked.

"Hi," Tasha said. "Jenny. Is she here?"

"You're Roy's daughter, right?"

Tasha looked beyond Delores toward the kitchen. "Yeah."

"I'm sorry. I don't recall your name."

"Tasha. Can you get Jenny? I have to talk to her right away."

The girl drumming her ragged nails coated with black fingernail polish indicated to Delores that patience was not this teen's virtue.

"Tell you what, Tasha. Have a seat on that stool, and I'll fetch her."

Tasha remained standing while Delores trotted into the kitchen. Jenny appeared with Delores at her side.

"Tasha, what a surprise. What can I get you?" Jenny asked.

Tasha ignored Delores's hovering.

"Didn't stop by to eat. What time do you get done?"

"Not until two-thirty. Is something wrong?"

Tasha glanced at Delores and back to Jenny. "Maybe . . . I don't know. Can I talk to you in private for just a minute?"

"I'm going to rinse the plates, Jenny. Why don't you take a break and help Tasha out?" Delores said.

Jenny tossed the towel she held over her shoulder. "Let's sit in a booth, Tasha. I've got five minutes."

Delores's watchful eye followed the pair to the booth. Once they sat, she returned to the kitchen to tackle the heap of dishes. The girl could request all the privacy she wanted; Delores knew Jenny would disclose the entire conversation in a play-by-play manner to her as soon as the girl exited the diner.

"What's going on?" Jenny asked as she slid in the booth.

"It's Daisy."

Jenny sighed. "What now?"

"I just left there. She's acting really weird."

"Weird? Like how?"

Tasha fumbled with her necklaces. "I don't want to get her in trouble, really I don't. It's not like when she smokes pot; I mean, I know the difference."

Jenny huffed her annoyance. "What did she say?"

"She doesn't want to go back to that place."

"Melville?" Jenny asked. "She told you about Melville?"

Tasha cocked her head in puzzlement. "Isn't that a—"

Jenny nodded. "Yes, Daisy's no stranger there, trust me."

"I don't want to get her in trouble, but I saw an empty prescription bottle on her counter. So, I think maybe she's not taking what she's supposed to, or maybe she took too much."

Jenny pulled the towel from her shoulder. "If she's talking

nonsense, she's out of meds. Thanks for letting me know. I'll call Dan."

Jenny stood to return to work.

"Jenny?"

"Yes, Tasha?"

"Well, it's none of my business, but is Daisy . . . well, you know."

Jenny slumped back into the booth. "Well, now you know her little secret. Yeah, she's not right in the head. Acts perfectly normal on meds, a basket case when she skips them. You just haven't seen her off meds. Don't pay any attention to what she says; she lies all the time."

"Okay."

Tasha left the diner with conflicted feelings. Even if Daisy disclosed what Tasha had told her about attacking their mother, nobody would believe her. But, if Daisy had told the truth about being inside the trailer, Tasha had to guard her sister's secret.

There were worse places to rot away than Melville.

CHAPTER 44

Detective Monroe had showered and packed before the alarm clock blasted an annoying series of beeps. He returned his keys to the motel's front desk while the clerk debited his credit card. He drove down Main Street for the final time. He drove past Delores's Diner and did not rescind his decision to skip breakfast. The disturbing dream of choking on the peach pie had absolved his appetite.

Monroe tuned the automobile's radio to classical music as a distraction, but his thoughts centered on his investigation as he traveled to Bancor to return to his office. He had investigated metropolitan crime for many years, and the anonymity of both the victims and criminals had hardened him. Investigating crime in small rural towns paralyzed his brain. Every citizen concealed a veiled agenda and hid a discrete persona from their families and friends. Monroe trusted no one and observed everyone, whether he spoke to them or not.

The cheerful receptionist greeted him as he entered the sheriff's department. He stopped in the hallway alcove and poured a cupful of coffee on his way to his office. He placed his briefcase at his feet while he unlocked his office door. Before he had the chance to sit, his assistant appeared with an armload of files.

"Good morning," Connie said.

The pile of manila folders slid from her arms like a small avalanche to the center of his desk.

"All this doesn't add up to a good morning. But, thanks."

He wasted no time sorting the files for Doreen Ferch's autopsy report.

"Are the medical examiner's findings in here somewhere? For

319

Ferch?" Monroe asked while stacking the folders in a somewhat orderly manner.

"Yep, it arrived late yesterday. Suppose to tell you from Dr. Islee that your badgering him didn't produce the quick results. The backlog finally diminished, giving him time to expedite the file, in case you're apt to bothering him again."

Detective Monroe chuckled. "Sounds like Bob."

Connie searched through the mammoth pile. "Here it is." She handed the report to her boss. "Anything else?"

"Not at the moment, thanks."

"Okay then," Connie said with a grin. "See you next Thursday when you dig yourself out from under that stack."

Monroe sighed in response as Connie closed the door behind her. He eagerly flipped open the medical examiner's report. He sipped his coffee and read the notes. He jerked back his head in surprise and brought the file closer to his face to ensure he was reading the report correctly.

Manner of death: Natural / Cause of death: Sudden cardiac arrest

Monroe continued reading the medical examiner's notes alluding that the deceased's history of diabetes, heart failure, and nicotine usage as contributors to the cause of death. Toxicology tests yielded negative results.

"Incredible," he said.

He placed a call to Roy Ferch's home. When he received no answer, he called First Stop Hardware. The manager answered and asked Monroe to wait while he summoned Roy.

"Roy Ferch here."

"Hello, Mr. Ferch. Detective Monroe. Do you have a few minutes to spare? Is this a good time?"

"As good of a time as any I guess. What's up? Did you arrest someone?"

"No, in fact, that's why I'm calling. You'll be relieved to know that there'll be no arrest. I received the medical examiner's report. Doreen Ferch died from sudden cardiac arrest."

"A heart attack?"

"Well, not exactly classified as a heart attack in the medical definition. Heart attacks are caused by a blockage to the arteries of the heart. A sudden cardiac arrest involves the electrical system to the heart and causes the heart to beat dangerously fast."

Roy sighed. "I don't much care how it's labeled as long as I know there ain't nobody lurking out there to hurt my daughter."

"Of course, I understand. You'll want to obtain some certified death certificates. You'll need them for your daughter for insurance, schooling, benefits—things like that. They should be available at the courthouse in a few days."

"All right, thanks."

"My condolences to you and your daughter, Mr. Ferch."

"Appreciate it. Goodbye."

The conclusion to the Ferch file meant Detective Monroe would not be required to return to Endover or Greenville. If only closing the file could diminish the lingering fragments of his nightmare. He was glad to return home to the security of his family. No matter how much he enjoyed his grandmother's baking, he vowed never to consume another piece of pie.

CHAPTER 45

"Well," Delores asked. "What's all the secrecy about?"

Jenny washed her hands at the sink before joining Delores to clean the kitchen after the noon rush.

"Same old thing. Daisy acting goofy again. Only this time she did it in front of her sister."

Tasha's disclosure about Daisy's marijuana habit infuriated Jenny, but she chose not to divulge the information to Delores. Jenny planned to save that tidbit for ammunition against Dan during their next predicted argument about supporting Daisy.

"Can't say I blame the girl for being concerned."

Jenny stacked clean plates on a shelf. "Concerned is right. Well, if Tasha expects me to run directly to Dan about another spacey episode, she's got another think coming."

Delores loaded the dishwasher for the second time. "Might be a good idea, Jenny, to take some time for yourself. Do something you enjoy."

"Good idea, Delores. I had already planned to stop at Berman's Nursery after work to browse for some new ornamental plants for my garden."

The whirl of the ancient dishwasher drowned out the chance of the pair to continue their conversation. Delores smiled her approval before heading to the front counter to greet newly arrived customers.

Jenny remained in the kitchen. She wiped crumbs and spills from the stainless-steel surfaces, scrubbing vengefully until her reflection revealed her scowl. Delores was right; Jenny needed time for herself. She dismissed Daisy's dilemma and concentrated on the plants she planned to purchase. She had read that the lavender scent promised a small degree of tranquility, exactly the aromatherapy cure she sought.

When her shift finished, Jenny counted her tips before hanging up her apron. With a quick goodbye to Delores, she enjoyed a quiet drive to the outskirts of Greenville to arrive at Berman's Nursery. She smiled when she approached the front lot and spotted a sale sign. Her tips would cover the cost of two lavender plants.

Jenny relished the soothing scent during the drive home. She had no pressing worries and no reason to interrupt her current good mood by conversing with Dan about Daisy.

Today was *her* time.

CHAPTER 46

"Dad, it's that guy from the trailer park for you," Tasha yelled while cradling the telephone receiver.

"Be right there," Roy answered.

He buttoned his shirt after changing from his work uniform. Nobody ever telephoned him, and this was the second call today. The first message had delivered good news. Roy hoped he was on a winning streak.

"Roy, here."

"Hi. Harold Jefferson from Westside Wheel Estates, *again*. The rent's due on Trailer Twelve in five days. I need to know if you plan on keeping it. If you are, I need the rent paid. If you're not, I need you to clean it, so I can rent it out."

"Sorry about not getting back to you. Things have been hectic, as you can imagine."

Harold snorted, and Roy winced when he heard Jefferson swallow.

"That's fine and dandy, but I'm running a business here."

Roy brushed his hand through his hair. He wondered how he managed to have any strands left after dealing with Doreen's final affairs.

"Yeah, I get it. I get it. Tell you what, I'll stop over tonight and load up as much as I can and finish tomorrow. Is there a deposit on that trailer?"

"Deposit? No, so that brings up another thing. I need that trailer clean. Clean enough for the next ones to move in, or there'll be a cleaning charge."

"I'll be there tonight. It'll be empty and cleaned. I got five days?"

"Five."

The clank resounded in Roy's ear.

"What was that all about?" Tasha asked.

"Well, after supper tonight, we're gonna have to clean that trailer. Move out the furniture, get the dishes packed, and stuff like that. He needs to rent it out."

Tasha groaned. "Tonight?"

Ray set a frying pan on the stove and retrieved pork chops from the refrigerator. "Yes, tonight. What else you got going on that's so important?"

"I thought I would check on Daisy."

"Didn't you say you were there today?"

"Yes, but—"

"No *but*. This needs to get done now. Don't need Jefferson hounding me any longer."

The pair dined in silence. Roy decided he could only handle one drama at a time from his teenage daughter. He chose not to discuss Doreen's cause of death with her today. The news could wait—wait until he had more patience to deal with it.

After Tasha finished washing the dishes, she followed Roy to his truck, and they began the trip to Endover. Roy spoke to fill the void of silence between him and his pouting daughter.

"Wonder if that cursed three-legged dog is still hanging 'round here?" Roy asked as they neared Unlucky Thirteen's entrance.

Tasha sat straighter in the seat and leaned forward to peer down the lane. The maimed dog was not in sight. She curled her lip when the woman from Trailer 5 attached her two Chihuahuas to short leads.

"Those are cute little pups," Roy said. "Your ma always called them—"

Tasha interrupted. "Yipper yappers."

Roy's chuckle relaxed his daughter's scowl.

"Oh yeah, she hated those little buggers," Roy said. "Oh well, we're here. Let's get busy."

Roy unlocked the door. The torpid hot air absorbing the multitude of sour odors stung his nose. He rushed to open every window while he instructed Tasha to leave the door open.

Tasha leaned from the door toward the fresh outdoor air. "God, it stinks in here!"

Roy surveyed the encrusted dishes in the sink covered with green-white slimy mold. Several stains on the countertop and stove surface concealed dried puddles of food substances. He hesitated to ask Tasha to avoid embarrassing her since he already knew the answer, but how had she and Doreen lived in such filth? If the kitchen was in such disarray, he certainly did not want to venture into the bathroom.

"Honey, can you get those boxes out of the truck? There's no use trying to clean up this mess. I'm just going to chuck it all in the dumpster. The sooner, the better."

Tasha obediently carried the boxes to her father and stood while he filled them with the contents of the sink and cabinets.

"I know they stink, but can you grab that one and show me where the dumpster is?" Roy asked.

Tasha held her breath and grabbed the box. She motioned for her father to follow her to the end of the lane. After they hurled the boxes, they returned to the trailer to find Tie-Dye Bill waiting for them.

"Hey, anything you don't want, let me know," Tie-Dye Bill said. "I mean, any good stuff that you don't want to haul away."

"I doubt it, but I'll let you know," Roy answered.

Tie-Dye Bill perched in his lawn chair to scrutinize the items Roy removed from the trailer.

"Dumplin', gather anything you want to keep, like pictures and stuff, and load them in the back of the truck while I sort through this mail."

Tasha entered her former bedroom. The desk drawers heaped

by the door unsettled her although she had previously observed the stack. She scoured her room and filled a corner of the truck bed with her possessions under Tie-Dye Bill's supervision.

Returning to her room, she balled the bedsheets and proceeded to her mother's room. Doreen's twin-sized mattress was easier to maneuver, and Tasha pulled off the sheets in two tugs. She raised the mattress to remove the dust ruffle from the box spring and uncovered a surprise. Her cash envelope. She counted the bills and recovered seventy-two dollars of the money her mother had stolen. She tucked her money into her pocket.

"Doreen never was good at opening mail," Roy said aloud to himself.

He blocked the memories of her sabotaging his dairy farm as he ripped open envelope after envelope. The incredible mound of paper slowly shrunk from the shelf as he pitched junk mail, overdue notices, and rent receipts into a plastic bag. He uncovered a yellow envelope. Unlike the others, this parcel was addressed to Tasha A. Ferch with a return address from Greenville High School.

"Tasha, come in here," Roy called. "I think this is something for you."

Tasha appeared with an armload of books. "Be right back," she said as she headed to the truck.

When she returned, Roy handed her the sealed envelope.

"What's this?" Tasha asked. "A letter from school?"

"Seems that way."

Tasha ripped open the envelope and tossed it to the floor. Roy watched his daughter's eager eyes glow as she skimmed the letter's contents. He smiled in response to her grin.

"It's about the Scholastic Merit Program!"

"That's great, Dumplin'."

Tasha continued reading.

"Wow! I'm a semifinalist. All I have to do is fill out this application and write an essay about myself and I'm entered in the competition to win a scholarship."

Tasha jumped excitedly while holding the letter and application in each hand. "I'm in, I'm in!"

Roy picked up the ripped envelope from the sticky floor. As he prepared to pitch it into the bag, the postmark attracted his attention. He cautiously asked to view his daughter's notice.

Tasha handed the letter to him. "Sure, read it. Read my great, wonderful, fantastic news!"

Roy's eyes remained fixated on the letter as he ignored Tasha's enthusiasm. His daughter did not detect a seriousness to his tone when he had addressed her.

"Tasha, it says here that the application must be received within six months of notification of your status."

"Don't worry, Dad. I'll mail it tonight. I'm not going to risk losing my chance. No way."

Roy cleared his throat. "Dumplin' . . . "

"What Dad?"

"*Ah*, well, it's dated November fifteenth."

Tasha counted on her fingers. "November, December, January, February, March, April . . . "

Roy watched helplessly as the realization of missing the deadline struck Tasha with a force that felled her to her knees.

"Fuck, fuck, fuck!" she screamed and pounded the floor with her fists.

Although Roy had never heard his daughter use vile curse words, he understood her despair and consoled her. "It's not the end of the world, Dumplin'"

Shock replaced Roy's empathy at his daughter's second utterance.

"Now I *am* glad Daisy killed her. Fucking glad!"

CHAPTER 47

Dan punched the time clock and waved goodbye to Kevin.

"Enjoy your week off, you lucky bastard!" his boss yelled.

Dan grinned. "Damn right I will. Try to run the place without me."

Kevin raised his wrench in the air and smirked. "We'll try."

Dan rushed from the shop and hopped into his truck. He celebrated his freedom by stopping at Grover's for a case of Red's before heading home. Although he had no formal vacation plans, he looked forward to fishing at the nearby lake. After a brief conversation with a customer, Dan had obtained a name and telephone number of a retiree selling a fishing boat. He patted his shirt pocket to confirm his contact information was secure. During the drive home, he considered his best strategy to persuade Jenny to consent to the boat purchase. Maybe she would settle for a fine dining experience at Sebastian's if he offered the invitation as a romantic gesture. The phrase *just the two of us* had always worked in the past; there was no reason the scheme would not be successful tonight. Dan chuckled—he may even get laid if he played his cards right.

He parked the truck and swung the case of beer under his arm as he entered the house. The baking aroma of chocolate and vanilla swirling from the oven offered hope his wife was in a cheerful mindset. He set his beer on the counter. He approached his wife from behind, wrapped his arms around Jenny's waist, and nuzzled her neck with eager kisses.

"Chocolate chip cookies, my favorite," Dan said. "Baking means you're in a good mood."

Jenny wrestled from his embrace. "You act like I'm always bitching or something."

Dan bit into a warm cookie. "Well, I didn't mean—"

"I know what you meant," Jenny said and softened her tone. "Hey, I was thinking, since you have a week off, let's get some chores done around the house and maybe spend a few days away. That new bed-and-breakfast opened in Hadenville. I heard it's gorgeous."

The image of the fishing boat popped into Dan's head, and he dismissed her proposal. If he treated his wife to one of those cottage places she always begged to visit, he would not have the funds to buy the boat.

"I'm not sure we can afford that about now. It's almost the first of the month, with our mortgage and Daisy's rent—"

Jenny's mood soured. "Daisy's rent would cover a weekend away."

"Well, yeah, but . . . "

Jennie pulled a cookie sheet from the oven. "When's the last time you talked to Daisy?"

"Last week or so. Maybe longer. Why?"

"Maybe you can take some cookies over to her. I heard potheads always crave munchies after a good smoke."

Dan popped open a beer. "What?"

"Oh yeah. You're spending our vacation money to pay her rent, and she's wasting money buying pot. Another reason I believe she's faking shit. Go ahead and ask her if you don't believe me."

"Oh, for Christ sakes, Jenny."

Jenny twisted the oven dial to Off. "Fuck you, Dan!" She stormed from the kitchen to sulk in her garden.

Dan finished his beer in three gulps and opened the second can. He dialed Daisy's number and received no answer.

Daisy smoking pot. What other shit did Jenny hear at the diner?

He sunk in his recliner and nursed his beer. After the third can, he decided he had no choice but to return to Greenville and confront Daisy about Jenny's allegation, to settle matters in his household. He wanted to inspect the boat the day after tomorrow. Dan deduced two days was sufficient time to pacify Jenny. He conceded that sleeping in an antique bed with a lace-trimmed bedspread at some stupid hostel was the required sacrifice to purchase the boat. However, the sentence of lingering around a large wooden table, sipping flavored coffee and munching bran muffins with strangers seemed unjust.

He was a simple man; he just wanted to fish.

Daisy sought refuge from the voices by huddling in the corner of her living room. Her flimsy flannel pajama pants wore thin as they absorbed the blood from her raw kneecaps. Time elapsed from moments to minutes to hours as she rocked on the hardwood floor. Fleeting images swirled and collided within her head. Tasha. Doreen. Tasha. Doreen. Dead. Tasha's voice murmuring, *Don't tell don't tell don't tell,* amplified from whispers to shouts. Daisy cupped her ears to silence her sister. When Tasha's yelling continued, Daisy slapped her ears until the stinging diminished the racket. Daisy's rapid panting exhausted her.

One, two. Buckle my shoe . . .

Tasha's voice faded as Jenny's took command. *"Melville, Daisy! Do you want to be locked up in Melville? Oh yes you do. It'll be good for you, honey. Real good. Make you feel lots better. Like the last time . . . "*

Lucy chimed in: *"Tasha won't tell because they'll put you away. You better not tell on her either."*

Don't tell don't tell don't tell don't tell

"Tasha's my sister," Daisy said. "I won't tell on my sister."

"Don't tell don't tell don't tell don't tell," Tasha's voice pleaded.

"I'm your sister, Daisy. You told on me all the time. Liar, Liar Lucy! I'm telling. Don't we all have the same mother? I didn't kill our mother. You and Tasha did. Tasha. Tasha. Tasha. And Tasha's not sorry."

"Shut up, Lucy!"

Three, four. Shut the door . . .

Lucy giggled. *"The only door shutting is the one at Melville. The one they lock so they can watch you like a bug in a jar. Bug in a jar."*

Daisy willed herself to a standing position. Her muscles tingled when the blood restored circulation to her legs. Thirsty. The panting parched her throat. She limped to the kitchen. Her balance was unstable, and she gripped the countertop to steady herself. She did not notice when the empty prescription bottle tumbled to the floor. She reached for a glass in the cabinet until a moment of clarity reminded her the safe drinking water was stored in the refrigerator. Daisy opened the door and selected a large jar. She drank the refreshing cool liquid until the massive container slipped from her shaky grip and shattered on the vinyl floor. Daisy did not speculate how the jug disappeared into thin air as she inspected her empty palms. She winced as something bit her feet. The wet, glistening shards sliced into her soles as she stepped away from the refrigerator without bothering to close the door.

With her feet burning and bleeding, Daisy resorted to crawling into her bedroom. She spied the art box under her bed. Whenever she and Lucy had become overwhelmed as youngsters, they drew princess pictures to decorate their bedroom walls. Daisy sought that relief. She opened the lid, removed the pages, and taped them to the walls.

"They look good, Daisy." Lucy said.

Daisy admired the pages covering her bedroom wall.

"Thanks, Lucy. Do you want to color? I'll share with you."

Daisy lay on her stomach. She divided the six crayons between her and her sister. After filling the pages with princess images, she ripped away the sheets from the sketchpad and secured them to the second wall. Satisfied with the arrangement, she decorated the remaining two walls. She pouted when she ran out of paper, fearing Lucy would become angry again. She rummaged in her desk drawer and removed a lined notebook. The drawing frenzy continued as she sketched more princesses, unicorns, and rainbows. She tore the pages from the metal spiral binder and secured all eighty pages to her living room walls.

The search for more paper was futile, so she considered Lucy's suggestion and ripped pages from her books.

"The corners are clean, so quit looking!"

Lucy shouted. *"Wasn't looking, so there!"*

"Wasn't talking to you, was I? Talking to Jenny, she always gets so mad, so mad." Daisy answered.

Don't tell don't tell don't tell

Daisy sat in the center of the living room, tearing page after page from her cherished books, not caring that the growing heap of damaged spines formed a jumble of hues in no specific order. The afternoon sun transformed long shadows into the onset of dusk. She closed the curtains, switched on a lamp, and continued the art binge with her sister. Daisy's passion whirled into a haunting obsession as the days morphed into nights and the evenings warped into mornings. Her bedside alarm clock's hands dutifully displayed 10:21 a.m.—the exact time it had stopped ticking five days ago, the day of Tasha's visit. When she exhausted the pages of her books and lost the tape, Daisy scribbled directly on the walls. Her multiple days without medication concluded with childish doodling scrawled on every inch of the apartment walls.

Daisy felt a pang of hunger but translated the feeling to her cat. She did not comprehend the growl from her stomach as a signal for being famished. She had not eaten in nearly four days.

"Toby?" she called.

The cat's meowing confirmed his hunger, and she followed him to the kitchen. She stood in front of the opened refrigerator, searching for the tuna can. She flung tablespoons of pate directly to the floor atop the glass shards.

She angrily stomped her foot on the glass splinters as she observed the nineteen previous piles of tuna she had tossed to the floor each time Toby indicated his hunger. Like all the other times, Daisy became frustrated at the cat's refusal to eat.

"Bad kitty! You meow, but don't eat. Go to your room. Now!"

Toby refused to move so Daisy tucked him under her arm and set him on her bed. She grinned when she discovered a blank piece of paper partially obscured by a blanket on the floor.

Five, six. Pick up sticks . . .

She jumped and clapped her hands. Blood seeping from between her toes stained the beige carpet.

"Hip, hip hooray! Look what I found Lucy." She turned her focus to Toby. Shaking her finger at him, she shouted, "You stay on that bed. Do you hear me? Do you? Do you hear me?"

Doreen's voice echoed Daisy's. *Do you hear me? Look at me when I—*

Daisy stuck out her tongue. "I'm the boss."

Seven, eight. Lay them straight . . .

Scolding Toby prevented her from hearing the first three knocks on her door. The rapping increased to pounding.

Dan called out. "Daisy. Daisy?"

With no answer, he unlocked the door and stepped inside. He gagged when the sour odor of rotted fish wafted from the kitchen. The living room was oddly dark except for a small desk lamp abandoned sideways on the floor and the glow from the refrigerator's opened door. A shimmer of sunlight peeked through the living room curtains' gap. Dan flung open the panels and spun around. He gasped and covered his mouth. His brain sped to comprehend what his eyes observed. A moment of disbelief passed quickly. There was no doubt. Dan stared at multiples of scribbled pages fastened to the walls like shingles overlapping on a roof.

What the fuck?

He cautiously called out for his daughter. "Daisy?"

Daisy's voice alerted him she was in her bedroom. Dan followed a trail of blood down the hallway, fearful for her safety. His anxiety transformed into confusion when he discovered his daughter laying on her stomach with a yellow crayon gripped in her fist. Oblivious to her father's presence, Daisy scribbled a circle with determined strokes.

Dan knelt beside her. "Honey, what're you doing?"

Daisy's tongue hung from the corner of her mouth as she increased the diameter of the yellow circle.

Dan observed his daughter's disheveled condition. He cringed at the strong urine odor released from the dried and damp stains from her pajama bottoms. The multitude of blood-oozing slices mutilating her dirty soles alarmed him. Her long hair had unraveled from a tidy braid into snarled locks cascading down her shoulders.

Dan brushed back her bangs. "What're you doing?"

Daisy huffed and swatted away her father's hand. "Coloring with Lucy."

Don't tell don't tell don't tell

Dan recoiled from Daisy's touch. His shivering triggered goosebumps.

He whispered into his cupped hand, "Lucy?"

Keeping a watch on Daisy to avoid startling her, he reached over a plush toy animal on the bed and picked up her Nokia. The blank screen indicated no charge.

"Damnit!" He tossed the telephone next to the toy.

The movement on the bed attracted Daisy's attention. "Be good, Toby. You stay on that bed," Daisy ordered.

"You be good too, Daisy," Dan said. "I'll be right back."

Ignoring her father's instruction, Daisy returned to sketching.

Dan trotted around the heap of abandoned book covers and crusted-tuna mounds littering the floor. He opened the door and hesitated. He struggled with the decision to abandon Daisy while he got help but decided he must leave. Listening to Daisy converse with her dead sister warranted his urgency in obtaining help for his daughter.

He started his engine, pressed the clutch of his Ford, and shifted quickly into gear. He ignored the speed limit as he drove the two miles to Freedom Oil. When he arrived at a red light, he looked both ways, and accelerated. He disregarded the need for laws during an emergency. After screeching to a halt in the parking lot, he dropped a quarter in the pay phone slot and dialed his home telephone number.

"Jenny!"

"Why are you so out of breath?"

"Listen." He gulped hard. "I was just at Daisy's and she's . . . well, she's really in bad shape. She's got paper scraps on the walls . . . ripped books all over . . . Looks like she ain't ate or slept for a week. She just told me she's talking to Lucy." He stifled his tears. "Oh my God, Jenny."

"Calm down. I'll call Melville and tell them you're coming. You're taking her there, right?"

Dan coiled the cord around his fist. The tautness was comparable to the compression squeezing his chest.

"I'm . . . I'm gonna have to," he stuttered. "She's just . . . so out of it. She's really gone this time."

"Drive safely. I'll call them and I'll see you when you come back, okay?"

"Jen."

"What?"

"I love you."

"Love you too. Take care of your—*our*—daughter."

Dan raced to Daisy's apartment with focused determination. The single traffic light was green this time, and he throttled through it. On his way, he considered how he could coax Daisy into the vehicle, since the cajoling was always difficult during one of her episodes. He hated the lying—promising his daughter he was taking her to a recreational attraction—but there had been no other way. He removed his toolbox from the cab and secured it in the truck box. Previous transports had taught him to secure loose items from his daughter's reach. Her unpredictable behavior could turn violent without notice.

Dan stood on her doorstep, closed his eyes, and exhaled a deep breath. His rapid pulse assured him he had summoned enough courage to rescue his daughter from her chaotic breakdown. He rapped gently on the unlocked door and entered. For the second time, the putrefied fish stench assaulted his nostrils as he stepped around the miniature mounds of dried cat food and glass.

Daisy rummaged through her kitchen drawers, throwing towels and utensils behind her.

"Where's the tape? Tape."

Dan examined the empty prescription bottle he picked up from the floor. According to the date, Daisy had depleted the dosage nearly ten days ago. *My God, she's never missed more than three days of pills.*

Plastic serving spoons flew from Daisy's hands as her frenzy continued. "Tape, tape. Tape!"

Dan approached his daughter. "I don't think you need tape right now."

Daisy ignored her father until he asked her a question.

"Daisy, how 'bout I take you to . . . *ah* . . . Candy . . . Candy Mountain. Would you like that?"

Daisy wrung a potholder. She squinted in confusion. "What's that?"

Dan snuggled her close. "It's an amusement park. Lots of carnival rides and cotton candy. It's real fun."

Daisy's expression lit up like an excited five-year-old. "Can Lucy go?"

Dan winced.

"And Toby?"

"Sure, honey."

Daisy applauded as she jumped from his embrace. "Hip, hip hooray!"

Dan sighed.

"I'll go get them. Wait. Wait here, okay?" Daisy asked.

"*Ah*, sure baby. Everybody gets to go."

Daisy sprinted to the bedroom and returned with the plush toy under her arm. "Toby was bad, but he's sorry now. So he can go. Me and Lucy are ready."

"Good. Do you know where your shoes are, honey?"

Daisy pointed next to her. "Lucy's barefoot!"

Dan's shoulders hunched in an uncontrollable shiver. He ran his hand over the back of his neck to settle the chill each time Daisy referred to Lucy.

"That's okay, Daisy. You can go barefoot too."

Dan worried about abandoning the cat. With his strenuous work schedule, he could not commit to return to the apartment daily to care for Daisy's pet. Despite Jenny's allergies, he decided to tote the cat to their home.

Dan scoured the apartment. "Where's Toby?"

Daisy uttered a *tsk*. "I'm holding him, *duh!*"

A sick feeling punched his gut. This trip to Melville would not be a short stay. Dan had never wished more in his entire lifetime to quench his throat's dryness with a Red's. An entire case would taste even better.

He escorted Daisy and Toby to the truck. After Daisy sat, he fastened his daughter's seatbelt. He flinched when the *click* reminded him of the hospital's restraints. He pushed down the lock before closing the door. She was secure for the two-hundred-mile ride to the hospital.

Dan climbed in behind the wheel.

"It *is* too my turn to sit by the window, Lucy! Daddy, tell her," Daisy pleaded and shoved her imaginary sibling.

Dan rested his chin on his chest and slowly shook his head. He had failed his daughter. He cupped his rugged hands over his eyes and bawled. His shoulders trembled as he swallowed tears. Tears of regret, tears of defeat.

His father Al's voice penetrated his skull, affirming Dan's stance as a disappointment. *Can't do anything right, boy, can ya? Ya fuck up everything you touch. Everything.*

Dan had failed both daughters—one lost in a bittersweet childhood, the other trapped in a cerebral abyss.

Both gone.

Gone.

In his despair, Dan recalled Al reciting the story of his father, Leroy, slamming his vehicle into a utility pole killing himself and Reverend Joe. "Problem solved," Al concluded, noting the accident was an appropriate conclusion to his drunkard father's loathsome life. At the time, Dan thought his father's words stung with an unnecessary callousness. Now he understood.

Dan examined his lifetime of fifty-two years in a flash of eight seconds. The copious amounts of liquor he guzzled *consumed* him. He had lost his willpower to quit drinking years ago—if he had ever possessed it at all. His two marriages had been fiascos. He contributed nothing to society except banging dents from autos, and Kevin would replace him in a heartbeat if anything happened to him. Dan reconsidered his father's comment. If Dan were honest, was his hollow existence any better than his grandfather's?

Ya fuck up everything.

"Daddy, I wanna go now."

Dan wiped his tears on his shirt hem and started the ignition. He shifted into Drive and headed north on US Highway 81. He focused on the power poles lining both sides of the highway.

He passed pole after pole after pole. He could choose which one . . .

It would be so easy.

Daisy giggled and clapped her hands. "We get cotton candy and be happy. We want to be happy. Right, Daddy?"

Dan shifted his trance from the poles to his daughter's cherub-like smile.

"Yes, Daisy. Happy."

He returned his gaze to the deserted ribbon of highway. The poles blurred into a lengthy brown streak, and the distance between them shortened as Dan accelerated to ninety miles per hour. He imagined slamming into one pole and causing the others behind it to fall like dominoes into a mass of spilled toothpicks. Nobody would blame him. Nobody would know. Dan contemplated the repercussions; there were none. A reunion with Lucy would end his and Daisy's suffering.

Daisy fidgeting with the window crank snapped Dan from his morbid fog.

"Honey, leave the window alone."

"*Uh-oh*. Toby jumped out!" Daisy cried as the toy tumbled from her grasp. "Stop, you gotta get Toby. He's hurt."

Dan grunted and slowed the truck to a reasonable speed. After a mile of listening to Daisy's protests, he spotted a farm field inlet and reversed his direction toward the spot where the gray plush animal landed on the highway shoulder. He parked and observed no oncoming traffic.

"Stay here. I'll get him."

Dan scooped up the toy. He handed it to Daisy who inspected her cat for injuries. Dan reached inside the open window and unlocked the door. He cranked the window closed before securing the door lock. He hopped in the cab and started the engine.

"He didn't die like Margie. Cats get killed by the road," Daisy said.

Margie died.

Lucy died.

She offered her pinkie. "I won't get killed by the road, promise Daddy?"

Dan swallowed the lump in his throat. Such innocence shined in his daughter's blue eyes. Wasn't a father supposed to protect his child? And he had been thinking it was better just to . . .

Dan wrapped his finger around hers. "I'll keep you safe. Promise."

He drove the remainder of the trip focusing on his daughter's laughter and ignored the hypnotic poles. Dan switched on the radio to drown out his father's cursed voice. He tapped his fingers against the steering wheel, keeping rhythm to Renee Lynne crooning a country song about celebrating life.

Dan achieved one thing in his lifetime.

He honored his promise.

Daisy returned home from Melville a week later embracing new medications . . . and Toby.

THE END

ABOUT THE AUTHOR

Unraveled Ties is the second novel written by Dawn Taylor. Her debut novel is *Something's Not Right with Lucy.*

Dawn has also written short stories and flash fiction pieces published by Scout Media in the *Of Words* anthology series. *The Double Nickel Tour* appears in A Journey of Words, while *Pepe* appears in A Haunting of Words. Her flash fiction piece *For the Want of a Name* appears in A Flash of Words.

Seakay's Guide to Storytelling published her short story, *The Price of Admission.* Her first flash fiction piece, *Dirty Gypsy Girl,* was published in Fiction Writer's Group anthology, Hallowe'en Drabbles.

Dawn paid homage to her hometown by co-writing a nonfiction book of the town's history, *Chauncey's Place: 1854-2014 A Pictorial History of Austin, Minnesota.*

Dawn resides in her hometown. She has enjoyed reading and writing since childhood. When not at the keyboard drinking copious amounts of coffee while creating a new adventure for readers, she teaches her Parson Russell terrier new tricks and cuddles with her cats. Red is her favorite color. She's a self-proclaimed introvert enjoying her solitude during the long Minnesota winters.

Thank you for reading *Unraveled Ties*. This story is the sequel to *Something's Right Not with Lucy*. Both stories are stand-alone novels.

If you enjoyed my book, please leave a review at the retailer site or book club of your choice. Reviews are helpful for readers to discover authors and enjoy their collection of stories.

Please visit my website dawnmtaylor.com and sign up for my newsletter. You'll receive announcements and exclusive excerpts on my new releases.

CPSIA information can be obtained
at www.ICGtesting.com
Printed in the USA
FFHW021827141118
49394557-53720FF